The Rhythm of the Road

The Rhythm of the Road

ALBYN LEAH HALL

THOMAS DUNNE BOOKS
ST. MARTIN'S PRESS ☙ NEW YORK

This is a work of fiction. All of the characters, organizations, and events portrayed in this novel are either products of the author's imagination or are used fictitiously.

THOMAS DUNNE BOOKS.
An imprint of St. Martin's Press.

www.thomasdunnebooks.com
www.stmartins.com

Lyrics from "Let Me Touch You for a While" written and composed by Robert Lee Castleman copyright © 1989 Farm Use Only Music BMI. Used by permission of Farm Use Only, the owner of all rights to sell and publish the same.

Design by Sarah Maya Gubkin

ISBN-13: 978-0-312-35944-7
ISBN-10: 0-312-35944-6

First Edition: January 2007

10 9 8 7 6 5 4 3 2 1

To my mother and father

Acknowledgments

Alistair at Edwin Shirley, Hamish Brown, MBE (retired Detective Inspector, New Scotland Yard), Melody Burke, Nicola Chalton, the Del McCoury Band, Carol Deppen, Michael Cendejas, Club Z and Brunners Motel, Detective Jeff Dunn, Sergeant Ronan Farrelly, Paddy Glackin, Becky Harris, Danielle Harvey, Simon Hellyer, Brett Kahr, Rabbi Daniel Karobkin, Rebbetzin Karen Karobkin, and their family, Rabbi Jim Kauffman, Andrew W. Keehnen, Bill Mayblin, Dr. Edward Petch, Detective Sergeant Mike Thomson, Rick Ferrari and lorryspotters.com, Harriett Goldenberg, Ed Goodall, Larry Grogan and Velia Ramirez, John Lowit, Carmen Miranda, Tracey Morgan, Irish Ned, Criminal Investigator Irma Z. Partida, Supervising Investigator Wayne Maxey, Steve Prentice, Dr. Reid Meloy Criminal Investigator Reyes Franco, Jayne Pell (the real queen of the road!), Sean P. Suber, Dr. Jack Shale, Simon Waspe, Lewis Smith, Tropic II, and Katherine Wootton.

And a very personal thank you to:

Robert Lee Castelman (who wrote the song that made it all happen), Ivan Coleman, Alison Fell, Arthur Golden, David Jacobs, John Pleshette, Lynn Pleshette, Andrea Levy, Valerie Martin, my beloved Friday Master Class: Jude Bloomfield, Harriet Grace, Lynn Kramer, Nicolette Hardee, Wendy Maier, Jo Pestel, Bev Thomas, and Aruna Wittman. And finally, to my editor, John Parsley, and my agent, Mary Ann Naples, for their unstinting dedication and belief in my work.

Part I

I NEVER THOUGHT I'D SEE
YOU IN THESE PARTS

CHAPTER I

1 9 9 8

I was twelve years old when Cosima first rode with us.

I hadn't heard of her then. Nobody had. She was just another girl, a hitch-hiker with a name you might not remember.

A few things were different about her. She was American, but it wasn't just that. On the road, we met just about everybody: Welsh people and Irish people and Scots, German people and Spanish people and Americans and, of course, people from every part of England. The American hitchhikers were mostly the natural-looking kind, all denim and well-brushed hair, who could have been English apart from flat, unfunny voices and a dislike of our food, like beans on toast or Marmite. More than one of them tried to tell me that pretzels were better than Twiglets and that the Little Chef wasn't like a real American coffee shop. I told them it wasn't trying to be.

Cosima was a cowgirl, at least to look at. She wore a cowboy hat and a belt with a brass buckle. She wore a suede jacket, its fringe damp and tangled from being sat on in so many cars and lorries (or trucks, because they didn't say *lorry* in the U.S.A.). Her accent wasn't broad, but her voice had gaps in it wide enough to park a lorry in. I'd ask her a question and she wouldn't say anything and I'd think she hadn't heard me. Just when I was about to ask it again, she would answer. Cosima always kept you waiting, even when she was right there next to you.

The second thing was her fiddle. The road had its musicians—it was full of them in summer—but they were mostly boys with guitars or the occasional girl with a guitar. Bobby used to play the guitar once, and he liked to ask what kind of guitar he or she was carrying and maybe have a look at it if we stopped for a cup of tea. We'd met boys with fiddles, but not many girls.

It was six years ago, but I remember everything about that day. We had eaten our lunch. We were seventeen miles north of Birmingham. We were listening to Charlene Sweeney, our favorite country singer. The cars were like slugs all around us, creeping along in the warm, grimy rain. I had that feeling I had in my stomach that I got when we weren't moving. It was a stuck and heavy feeling, as if I'd eaten bricks.

She stood with her thumb out, a slim, neat, cowgirl-looking girl, sandy hair to her shoulders. I turned down the volume on Charlene Sweeney.

"Stop, Bobby."

He stopped. I shifted over to the flat area between the seats. A boy sat on the grass behind her, or a kind of a boy. He had bleached hair and he wore eye makeup. Sometimes girls pretended to hitch alone, when really there was a boy just behind them. But this boy didn't seem interested in us. He got up to read our registration plates and he wrote something on a piece of paper.

She climbed up beside me. She had green eyes, wide lips, and a flat nose—a little too flat, which is what kept her from being an absolute beauty. She was about twenty-four years old, maybe twenty-five.

Bobby leaned across our laps to open her door again and shut it properly because there was a knack to it that nobody got except for him and sometimes me. He loosened her seat belt to give it more slack. She watched his hand as he did this. She sucked her stomach in so that it didn't touch his hand.

"I'm Cosima Stewart," she said. "Thanks for the lift. My friend's got your license-plate number in case anything happens."

It was a funny way to say hello. What did she think would happen? There were bad men on the road, but they didn't have kids with them. Bobby was in no way dodgy, and he was the safest driver she would ever meet.

"Right enough." Bobby wove us into the middle lane. "It's nice to meet a girl who takes care of herself. Not like that poor wee thing in July."

Cosima Stewart looked confused.

"He's talking about a girl who was found in a bag in a ditch in Oxfordshire," I explained. "We knew that girl, or we knew her when she was alive. We gave her a lift once."

"Did you." She clutched her handbag to her lap.

There wasn't much talking after that. The rush hour cleared and we were quiet with just the motorway sounds. Her jacket smelled nice, like trees after rain. I wanted to ask her about the boy with the eye makeup, if he was her boyfriend. He didn't look like a boyfriend to me.

But it was she who asked me a question first.

"Do you go to school?"

I was disappointed. This was the one they all asked.

"Sometimes."

"And yourself, Cosima?" asked Bobby. "What do you do?"

"I'm a singer-songwriter. I'm in a country-and-western band."

He took his eye off the road just long enough to look at her. "Aye?"

"Listen." I turned Charlene up just as our favorite song came on, "I Ain't Makin' No Hay."

"Charlene!" said Cosima. "She's the best! I love that harmonica intro."

Though we had listened to "I Ain't Makin' No Hay" more times than I could count, I'd never thought, *Oh, I love that harmonica intro*. But now that she'd said it, I could see that it was very much a thing to be loved, wailing happy and sad through the drums in a happy wail. Cosima strummed her fingers on the dashboard and Bobby drummed his fingers on the steering wheel. We sang along, the three of us:

> *I ain't the kind of girl*
> *To sit around all day*
> *Waiting for a boy to pick me up*
> *In some old Chevrolet . . .*
> *I got wheels of my own and I'm never at home*
> *And I live my life on the road.*
> *So if you wanna fuel my desire*
> *Don't change my tire*
> *You just gotta love my highway . . .*
> *'Cos unless you got power*
> *A hundred miles an hour*
> *I ain't makin' no hay!*

I thought of Cosima before she met us, driving on the wrong side of the road like they did over there, playing the song over and over until she had all the words. I thought of us doing the same thing, here on the M1 or M6, maybe even on the same day.

"Do you like Alison Krauss?" I asked her.

She seemed to shake her head, as though she was about to say no. "Alison's the best."

"What's your favorite album of hers?"

"That's hard."

"I like *Too Late to Cry* the best."

"Jo," said Bobby, "you told me that *So Long, So Wrong* was your favorite at the minute."

"I did not."

"You did."

We passed a sign: MANCHESTER, 36 MILES.

"I'll get off at Manchester," said Cosima.

I started going through all the CDs, as if I could make her stay by finding the other good ones.

Usually, when we picked up girls, I enjoyed them for a while. I liked sitting next to someone different for an hour or two. One thing I particularly liked was being near to the hair of other girls. I had hair like my dad's—brown, gloppy hair that just sat there, neither short nor long—and I was always interested in how older girls wore their hair, even when the girls themselves weren't so pretty. Most girls had more definite hair than mine: straight or curly, long or short, a pure color like black or ginger or yellow, even if it was dyed to make it that way.

And yet we usually ran out of things to say pretty quickly. Most of them didn't like country music, which made me feel funny when Bobby put it on. My bum would begin to hurt from sitting on the hard seat. By the time we dropped them off, I was ready to see them go.

Every now and again they stayed the night. There was one who rode all the way to Inverness with us. We didn't sleep in the lorry that night, or even in the truck stop. We slept in the Trusthouse Forte Hotel, which was too expensive really, and I didn't notice her paying anything toward the bill. I had my own room and Dad shared a room with her. In the morning she had breakfast with us. I didn't talk at all then, not out of shyness but because I didn't want to. The morning made her look whiter and fatter. She dipped her toast in her tea and dribbled her eggs with tomato catsup. She kept staring at Bobby and I felt sick looking at her.

After that we'd see her sometimes, at the same junction we'd picked her up at, near Wakefield. She was there so much I wondered why we'd stopped for her when so many drivers didn't. Each time we'd swing round the roundabout, she'd be looking my way, but it wasn't me she was looking for. She was standing up tall, trying to look at Bobby.

"Poor thing," he said. "Every time we see her, she's holding a different sign."

"Why?"

"Going nowhere, I suppose."

Cosima was definitely going somewhere. She had gigs and places to go to, and another country waiting for her to come on home.

Twelve miles south of Manchester, Bobby's hand was tight on the wheel. His knuckles were white, and I could hear him breathe. He wanted a cigarette, but he never smoked with girls in the cab, unless they were smoking as well. When Bobby wanted to smoke and couldn't, he asked more questions.

"From the states, Cosima, aye?"

"Texas . . . I live in London, though."

"What is it that brings you here? The band, is it?"

"Yes, and my boyfriend's English—we're in the band together."

"Fancy that, eh? Coming to England to play country music!"

"We're kind of 'alternative' country. People like that sort of thing in Europe. I couldn't get arrested in Texas."

"What do you mean, 'get arrested'?" I asked.

"She means they couldn't get a gig," said Bobby.

"What does that have to do with being arrested?"

Cosima looked at me. "You're cute," she said.

"She's not a bad wee thing," said Bobby.

We came up to a roundabout. Bobby let three cars go before him. When a driver finally let him go, Bobby raised his hand to thank him. I looked at Cosima to see if she'd noticed. "Sure, it only takes an extra two seconds to show a little courtesy," he'd say sometimes, though he didn't say it now.

"Do you have any of your music with you?" I asked her.

At first I thought she didn't hear the question. It was only when we turned into Manchester that she dug the CD out of her bag and handed it to me. I started to stick it in, but she held my hand to stop me.

"Not until I leave," she said. "I don't want you to lie if you don't like it."

Bobby smiled. "Josephine never lies."

I didn't know if this was true. I thought it probably wasn't, but I liked it when he said things like that. It made me feel older, like a person who has her own ideas about how things should be done.

"Why don't the two of you come to our gig tonight?" asked Cosima.

"Gig?" We'd seen bands before, mostly at village halls, but we'd never been to anything I thought of as a "gig."

"Can we, Bobby?"

"We'd love to," he said, to her. "But we've a ferry to catch."

"*Please*, Dad . . ."

"Sorry, pet."

Actually, I was relieved. The word *gig* shook me up as if I'd been asked to jump out of an airplane. It seemed the right moment for her to leave us after all, before we had time to stop liking each other so much.

We dropped her off in Bridge Street. Cosima tried the door, but it stuck. Bobby leaned across her to open it for her. As he looked up at her, his eyes were big, as if he had one last question to ask, but he didn't ask it. She thanked him and shook his hand. She shook my hand as well.

"Stay cute," she said to me, and jumped down.

She walked away with her fiddle slung over her shoulder. I put my hand on Bobby's arm and waited for him to wink at me, the way he did after we'd let the other girls out, but he didn't. He tilted his head to read the CD in my hand.

"Cosima Stewart and Her Goodtime Guys," he read. "*Swooning, Drinking, Loving, Lying, Getting Back on the Road.*" He looked at me. "Put it on."

Apart from the label, the cover had no pictures on it.

"It could be a bomb, Dad." I was only joking, but I could see it all the same—inserting the CD, the explosion, and us turned into a crazy ball of fire in the middle of Manchester.

"Go on," he said.

I pushed it in.

CHAPTER 2

1985

Bobby Pickering wore his handsomeness like an ill-fitting garment. If he was aware of it at all, it seemed accidental to him, a thing that had happened to end up on his face. Yet despite his handsome face, and his County Antrim accent, which made everything he said sound like a question, Bobby lacked the hubris of heartthrobs, of other musicians who used their music to entice or torment. He lacked it even though he was the only member of Slow Emotion who was under thirty (or, for that matter, under forty).

Slow Emotion was an easy-listening cover band that played every Friday night in the Tuxedo Lounge, an annex of the Better Ways Hotel, just off the A1 in Welwyn Garden City. Bobby played at the back of the stage, out of the spotlight and hard to see, like his own bass guitar—the drone beneath the melody.

If the older men were jealous, they hid it well. They chided him on his accent, his Irishness, his clothing. (Even his good leather jacket assumed the same sulky puffiness of the windbreaker it had replaced, tenting at his back rather than molding to his body.) Bobby's most vocal admirers were the wives and mothers of band members.

"Such a nice-looking lad," Dennis's wife would say every time she made a sandwich run to her garage, where the boys rehearsed on Sundays.

"Thanks a million, Mrs. Bradley," Bobby would say.

"Thanks a million, Mrs. Bradley" was one of the phrases Bobby used most, along with "Cheers, Mrs. McVeigh." Bobby liked the older women, the wives who brought him tea and Custard Creams and made him tea cozies. Sometimes they brought their friends to gigs, pilfered from the bingo or bridge gatherings, to thicken the coterie of matrons who stood at the front to make plucky heckles and join in on the choruses.

Bobby did have girls of his own from time to time. One barmaid, captured by the shadows beneath his eyes, his unkempt hair, and his large and gentle hands, sidled up to him after a gig, brought him drinks and crisps, and told him about her aunt in County Cavan. He took her home with him, but she did not come back to the Tuxedo Lounge again. Later, his only explanation was that nothing had happened. Nothing happening, it seemed, was enough to drive away a bold and lonely girl. After this, as though warned, his few fans admired him from a distance. There were murmurs in the ladies' toilet, confessions of intrigue or fear, as if there might be something dangerous in his sweetness, like hot wires smoldering in a damp pile of laundry.

Generally, however, young girls were sparse at the Tuxedo Lounge. Apart from wives and mothers, the room was speckled with commuters, on the slow route to villages in Hertfordshire or Bedfordshire. They usually came on their own and sat at the bar, their faces blank with the strain of trying not to think about the spouses who waited at home (or those who didn't). The Tuxedo Lounge was consoling with its smell of suburban tragedy.

"Welcome to Slow Emotion, for the fine 'n' mellow touch." Oliver, the lead singer, started every set with this, nearly kissing the mike to make it whisper, ". . . where even in this day and age, there are folk out there who like it nice and gentle."

Nineteen-year-old Rosalie Chapkis, an art student from Encino, California, was not one of them. Rosalie's hair was dyed black, teased to jut above her head and then down her back in a stiff plunge. Her ears were semicircles of studs, standing out against the shaved sections of her head. Rosalie was an assortment of big and luscious things: full lips, big tits, and a big bottom, sewn together by a confining blackness, by spikes and chains and fishnets that strained at her legs like barbed wire.

Rosalie's favorite bar was the Batcave, and her favorite men were the ones who went to it: chalk-white Goths in black, groin-tight jeans and hair gelled into furious points. It was her good luck to be going out with Rugg-Edd, a fellow student at St. Martin's School of Art and lead guitarist of Bastard Sex Canal. Fashionably emaciated, he looked as though he would either stab his granny or faint from an excess of speed.

Rugg-Edd doubled over his guitar with a livid agility, shrieking songs he'd written such as "The Wrath of Brixton" and "Mean Maggie T." Even offstage he spoke in lyrics rather than whole sentences, lyrics so inscrutable that Rosalie was sure they were incredibly clever.

"You can't enter the same river once," he said to her once, and she thought about it for a very long time.

And yet, one Friday evening, Rosalie found herself in her friend Louisa's blue mini in a parking lot in a suburb she'd never heard of, glaring at a squat, rectangular building with the words TUXEDO LOUNGE in neon above the door.

"Remind me why we're here again?" Rosalie asked.

"Uncle Dennis plays in a band here."

"Oh, yeah."

And yet it wasn't for the band that the girls had come. Uncle Dennis was also the unlikely provider of Louisa's hash.

Louisa was a fellow Goth, albeit a less committed one than Rosalie, for she couldn't bear to dye her hair and, for all her swearing, couldn't obscure her Home Counties accent. Secretly, Rosalie envied her friend. Louisa would always be a beauty, an English rose. Rosalie knew that whatever beauty she herself had was fabricated, a macabre glamour of paint and dye.

"We'll just stay for a bit," said Louisa. "Get the drugs, go. It'll be a laugh."

Thinking what a laugh it wouldn't be, Rosalie watched a couple climb out of their Ford Fiesta. The man wore a gray suit, the wife a Laura Ashley dress that looked like cocoa being stirred. Walking carefully across the car park, the man steered his wife's elbow as though he were still at the wheel.

"This looks like somewhere in the Valley," said Rosalie. It was true. From the outside, the Tuxedo Lounge could have been the restaurant in Sherman Oaks where her grandfather had held his retirement party. The only thing missing were the Mexicans who parked the cars.

Inside, the Tuxedo Lounge fell short in its American theme. American lounge bars were tacky, but they were big. They had booths to sit in, carpet rather than linoleum floors, and bowls of olives and maraschino cherries at the bar. This was a poky room of clashing colors—red and orange *and* purple. A low platform passed for a stage, strewn with stray wires and a cheap piano sitting off to the side. On each of the tiny tables a fake red rose in a vase held up a menu with a color promotion for a steak meal, complete with a jacket potato and a pint of lager, all for £2.99. (Chips could be substituted for the jacket potato.)

"Any place that has pictures of food on the menus is bad news," said Rosalie.

"Do you want a drink?" asked Louisa.

"Anything. Just as long as there's a lot of it."

Louisa came back with two pints of lager. Lager was the one thing that Rosalie didn't like. All of that fluid made her feel bloated, and she didn't see the point of something that took so long to get the high from. It depressed Rosalie, reminding her that she would have to travel five thousand miles to find someone who knew what she liked to drink. She went to the bar to get her own.

The band was starting up. Uncle Dennis sat at the piano, a beefy, broad-chested man with strands of red hair combed over his big, pink head. The lead singer, Oliver, was short and skinny with fine, yellow hair. He wore a peach-colored sweater that made him look like a prawn. He patted the mike, re-coiled from the feedback.

"Hello, ladies and gentlemen," he said. "Welcome, first-timers, new-timers, and old-timers, to the beautiful Tuxedo Lounge of Welwyn Garden City, Hertfordshire. We are Ollie, Dennis, and Bobby: We are, in short, Slow Emotion, your fine 'n' mellow sound."

Rosalie ordered a double whiskey.

The guitar let rip; the chords were long, loud, and mawkish. Rosalie recognized the song instantly, along with something sour in her spit. They were singing "If You Leave Me Now."

Fuck.

Was it 1975 or 1976? Rosalie was thirteen, being driven home from school in the back of a Datsun that stank of hairspray. The seats were hot and burnt her thighs. Who was on carpool? Fran Moskowitz's mother? Lisa Patterson's mother?

Dougie Feinstein's mother. Of course! Driving down Lankershim Boulevard, tapping her fingers on the wheel, singing along. Dougie Feinstein's mother, who wore tight jeans with rainbows on the back pockets and had big blond hair like Farrah Fawcett-Majors and didn't look Jewish but was. Who, for a treat, would stop at Dunkin' Donuts, where Rosalie would buy a white doughnut with colored sprinkles on it. Dougie Feinstein would say, "Do you think you should be eating that?" and his mother would say, "Leave her alone, Doug. What she eats is none of your business," though she never bought a doughnut for herself.

The song ended to a sprinkle of applause. Rosalie did not applaud, but neither did she look away.

Uncle Dennis played a few notes on the piano, plaintive and fussy, his face contorted with pathos. Ollie spoke low into the mike before singing: "I don't know why it is, but sorry always seems to be . . . the hardest word . . ."

Rosalie was walking to Taco Bell during school hours. She was twelve, her body on the verge of shape, soft like a lump of dough that hadn't found its form. She walked past a clique of girls her age, tall and leggy, a chemical smell of berry lip gloss stinging the air between them, Elton streaming from their ghetto blasters.

"Sorry Seems to Be the Hardest Word" merged seamlessly into "I'm Not in Love."

Rosalie ordered another double.

She was surprised to find she knew all the words, and that they stung her, down in the fleshy bits where puberty still lurked. Rosalie was fourteen. She was at the summer camp disco, wearing a T-shirt with a shiny bolt of lightning on it and the word ZOOM across her chest. She played Truth or Dare outside the disco walls, away from the patchouli-smelling counselors who ignored them anyway.

Rusty Edelman, dared to kiss Rosalie, wiped his mouth first and wiped his mouth afterward and said "Ugh" and ran off to brush his teeth.

When had this stopped happening? When did boys stop saying *ugh* to her? Did they still say it, behind her back?

"He isn't bad, is he?"

Rosalie jumped. She had forgotten where she was. She tried to focus on the pretty blonde beside her. Rusty Edelman would never have said *ugh* to Louisa.

"Who's not bad?" Rosalie glanced up at the stage. "They all look as though they should be on a golf course."

"In back. The younger one."

The bass guitarist stood in the back, all slouch and shadow.

Rosalie shrugged. "I can't really see his face."

There were no encores at the end of the set. Oliver said, "Thank you, Welwyn Garden City, and good night," and they started packing up.

A few minutes later, Uncle Dennis sidled up to the girls. "Enjoy yourselves, ladies?" His voice was rough and gravelly, nothing like his niece's.

"That was smashing, Uncle Dennis," said Louisa.

As if to reward her for her praise, he slipped something into her hand.

"Dennis?" It was the bass player, calling from the stage. "Dennis, have you a wire cutter handy?"

"Do I look like I have a fucking wire cutter handy?" He turned to Louisa and Rosalie. "Will you look at that Irish prat! Don't get me wrong—heart of gold—but look at him. Not a bad-looking bloke, but see how he puts himself together, he looks like old luggage."

The lights came on; stark, white light that turned the room into a lunchroom. Dennis ran onstage, shouting at Bobby, showing off for the girls.

"That last song was in G, Pickering. Not E minor. Must you always be the saddest bloke on earth? You and your fucking minor keys."

"You could have said it was in G."

"I *do* say it. Every fucking time."

Rosalie tried to get a better look at the Irish boy. She wondered if he was from Southern or Northern Ireland. She hoped he was from Northern Ireland. Her favorite band, the Implications, were Northern Irish, and she loved them. This guy was nothing like Conor Morrow or any other of the Implications, but she could see now that he wasn't, as Louisa said, bad. She tried to catch his eye, but he was lost to some inner world of tangled wires and minor keys.

The following Friday, Bastard Sex Canal had a gig at the Batcave. Rugg-Edd sang a new song he had written:

> Yvette Lacey is the bird I crave
> The girl-next-door freshly depraved
> A strawberry girl dipped in the devil's syrup . . .

It was his first love song, and it wasn't for her.

Rosalie knew Yvette Lacey, or knew of her; Yvette was the prettiest girl in textiles. Yvette was here tonight, standing at the front, vampirically gorgeous with her nose rings, navel rings, the bow-and-arrow tattoo on her shoulder, her feline eyes. If Rugg-Edd were a girl, he would look like her.

Rugg-Edd never ran, but as soon as he'd done his last encore, he ran down and wrapped himself around her or, given that she was as big as he was, within her.

Rosalie charged up to the kissing couple, but once she was there, she didn't know what to do. The top of her head came up to Yvette's shoulder. They didn't even *see* her. She thought to slap Yvette but Yvette's face was concealed behind the sinewy haven of Rugg-Edd's face and neck.

"Can I talk to you, Rugg-Edd?" asked Rosalie, but her words were eaten up by the music.

"*Can I talk to you, Rugg-Edd?*" her voice broke. She looked up to see a group of girls whispering and looking at her. Rosalie made for the bathroom, avoiding the eyes of the whispering girls.

Standing in front of the mirror, she waited for the grim completion of tears. They didn't come. A wave of shame came over her and made her face burn. Not being with Rugg-Edd wasn't the worst part. (She hardly had him, anyway; Tuesdays and some Saturdays, after his gig.) What was worse was that everyone could see. And in case they didn't know what they were seeing, they could hear about it, in the declaration of the song. That song was worse than his breaking up with her (or, as it happened, not even *bothering* to break up with her). What would it take, she wondered, to make herself "freshly depraved, a strawberry in the devil's syrup"? It would take nothing, of course. That is, nothing could do it. She would always have her mother's hips, her mother's thighs, her father's nose. She would always be a Chapkis, talking too much, eating too much, trying too hard.

Louisa came out of a stall, grinding her teeth.

"Where the fuck have you been?" asked Rosalie.

"What is it, Rosalie?" Louisa put her arms on Rosalie's shoulders.

Rosalie did cry then. She told Louise everything. Louisa listened as she'd never listened before, shaking her head, *tsk*ing at the sorriest parts. Girls were never so attentive, Rosalie mused, as when she'd just been dumped.

"And then to sing that *song!*" Rosalie recited some of the lyrics for Louisa.

"What rubbish," said Louisa. "You're just as pretty as she is."

"She hasn't got the big butt I've got."

"It isn't big. You hide it well."

"But he's seen me with my clothes off."

"Well, Rosalie, if he's that fucking shallow, he isn't the man for you."

Rosalie nearly smiled when Louisa said the word *fucking*. Louise had stressed the second syllable and pronounced the *g* so that it sounded like *fuck-eeng*. As she studied Louisa's mouth, she noticed a few grains of white crumb along her upper lip.

"Have you got drugs, Lou?"

Louisa wiped her mouth.

"I've no more coke, but Uncle Dennis said he might sort some out if I do him a favor. Actually . . . Hey, Ro, do you fancy a little ride? We can get chips on the way."

This was all Rosalie needed to hear.

They drove up the Essex Road, over the Old Street roundabout, past Whitechapel and further east. They followed signs for Bow, Plaistow, Mile End.

"Here's what it is," said Louisa. "That bass guitarist—that Irish bloke—he goes funny sometimes, takes to his bed for a day or two. The other guys have to go and sort of chivvy him along, get him back to rehearsal and things. Dennis thought that if I did it this time, he'd come back quicker."

"Why do they put up with him? Is he such a great musician?"

"He has a van. He moves all the stuff and picks them up and everything. He has no phone, though, which is a real pain."

The Mile End Road was deserted apart from a Dixie's Fried Chicken, an Oodles nightclub fronted by a solitary bouncer, and a few lanky youths at a bus stop playing football with a tin can.

"Where are we, Lou?"

"The East End. The back arse end of nowhere."

Louisa turned into Harford Street and made a right into Shandy Street. Kenneth Estate was made up of three low buildings that scowled down at the street through boxy window eyes. On some of the dilapidated balconies broken toys and bicycles stuck to the railings and laundry was draped across flimsy ropes. The estate was black with sleep apart from a television flickering through the odd window. Rosalie had never seen such poverty. Even in L.A. the ghettos had palm trees, wide streets, Spanish houses with terra-cotta tiles.

They didn't get out of the car right away. Louisa lit a cigarette and passed it to Rosalie. They watched a skinny old man come out of the middle building. He was dressed like a farmer in a tweed jacket and cap. He glanced up at one of the flickering windows, crossed himself, and climbed into a green van. He sat there smoking, oblivious to the smoking girls who watched him. Finally he pulled away, the midnight news trailing from his radio.

"I think that's his dad," Louisa said.

"His dad lives here?"

"He lives in Ireland. He just visits sometimes. He's a creepy old bloke. Did you see how he crossed himself?"

"They're Catholic?" Rosalie hadn't known many practicing Catholics, but she admired them in movies: the solemnity of priests and altar boys, the kneeling women and the rattle of rosary beads, the intimacies exchanged in dark cubicles. It was all so sexy, so furtive, so much more attractive than her own family, where people didn't confess so much as talk, all of the time and loudly.

"But why did he cross himself? I thought you only did that if someone was dead or something." She had an image of Bobby, murdered by his father like Marvin Gaye, blood trickling from his neck but his face as still as a saint's.

"How do I know?" said Louisa. "I'm not Catholic."

They trudged up the path, a bottle dancing darkly at their feet. Louisa rang the buzzer. Rosalie hugged herself, feeling her goose pimples through her clothes. She didn't feel like taking drugs anymore. She felt like being back in her tiny room with its black walls and fairy lights, her cozy satanic womb.

The hallway was vaguely lit and it was hard to make him out, the lumpy figure who opened the door. "Jesus, Louisa. It's yourself."

"And Rosalie," said Rosalie.

"Aye, Rosalie. I seen you up the Tuxedo last week."

He led them up three flights of stairs. She thought he had company, but it was the metallic chatter of his TV spilling into the hallway. The flat was one room with a tiny kitchen area, an unmade bed, a big and blaring television, and stacks of records that took up most of the floor space. Plates streaked with baked beans and sodden teabags were piled in the sink. Bobby cleared off the bed, making space for the girls to sit. He sat on his one chair with a record album on his lap. On it was tobacco, rolling papers, and a lump of hash.

"Mind if I turn this down?" Louisa perched over the TV as though she was about to clean it.

"Be my guest there, Louisa."

She turned it off.

He hadn't shaved. His hair was messy and matted from bed. "Will youse have a cup of tea? I've no milk."

"No thanks."

Rosalie sat on the bed but Louisa stayed standing. "You didn't go to the gig tonight."

Bobby licked a rolling paper and ironed it out with his finger. He loaded the tobacco onto its paper bed before sprinkling in the brown crumbs. Rosalie didn't like hash, though it was what people usually smoked in England. She couldn't get used to the big spliffs, the way you held on to them forever before passing them on, and the hash itself made her nervous and sleepy. She missed the good grass, the Thai stick or Humboldt County that made her giggle and hear things that weren't in the music.

He lit the joint, took a puff, and handed it to Rosalie. Despite not liking hash, she took it.

"Wasn't that your father I saw, Bobby?" asked Louisa.

"Aye. He's over here for a *fortnight* this time, can you believe it! He thinks my soul is dirty or some fucking thing."

"Sounds like he's worried about you," Louisa said. "Dennis and Ollie are worried, too. You didn't come to the gig last night."

Bobby stood up, clicked the kettle on. "And they thought it would soften me up, sending two wee dolls along?"

Rosalie had never been referred to as a "wee doll" before. She shifted her bottom on the bed. She handed him back the spliff. His hand was big and ruddy. She folded her arms across her chest.

"What do you do, Rosalie?" he asked. "Are you at art school as well?"

"Yes. I do photography."

"Are you that girl that Dennis was going to get along to do shots of the band?"

"She doesn't do that kind of photography, Bobby," said Louisa.

"No? More arty stuff, is it?"

Rosalie reeled at the word *arty*. The kettle clicked off. Bobby poured out the tea, slipped the cozy over the teapot. The cozy was crocheted in pink and blue, like a child's toy. "See there, Louisa? Your aunt's tea cozy's come in handy. You can tell her I use it all the time."

"You can tell her yourself." Louisa buttoned her coat. "You'll be at rehearsal tomorrow?"

"Aye."

"Because you seem all right now." Louisa sounded stern, like a mother accusing her son of pretending to be sick.

"Why? Did you think I was dead or something?"

Louisa shrugged the question off, but Rosalie wondered if this was exactly why Louisa had been sent, to see that he hadn't killed himself.

Slowly Rosalie stood up. She pried her hair from its collar. She wished for once her hair wouldn't stick together like balsa wood, that she could free it in a melee of curls like a girl in a shampoo ad. She felt suddenly glutted with her own hair dye, hairspray, gel. She wondered what he would make of her without all of that. She wondered what he made of her, anyway.

"Nice to see you, Rosalie," he said. "Pop in again sometime."

She looked at him, this pile of a boy obscured by a smoky fug. She kissed him on the cheek. His eyes flashed like mirrors, more silver than blue.

Outside the cold was shocking. The evening broke behind her eyes: Rugg-Edd and Yvette wrapped together like snakes, the old father crossing himself, the silver flash of Bobby's eyes. Chips lay damply inside her as if they'd been dropped, undigested, onto the floor of her stomach. Spittle thickened in her mouth. She doubled over and puked beside the garbage can. When she finished, she looked up at Louisa.

"Hash," she said. "It never agrees with me."

Rosalie awoke at five A.M. She'd often planned for these risings, dawn shoots when the streets were empty, peeled back to the postwar, putty-colored Britain she'd come to Britain for. She had never managed it. But today her head felt strong and clear, as though, with vomiting, she'd expelled the worst of herself. Her face empty of makeup, she headed out, her cameras dangling from her shoulder.

Rosalie didn't see much point to walking. She had a bad sense of direction and she usually got lost. But this morning she did walk. She even felt like it. She left Holborn, headed up Faringdon, turned into the meat district. She found the biggest warehouse, stood back from it, and took three photos, framing it to look like an old postcard. Then, with her Nikon, she came right up to the building, close enough for her nose to touch it. She zoomed in on one brick, down to its swirling grain, so close that it was difficult to tell what it was. It could have been an ant colony, a jug, the hide of an animal.

She walked toward Whitechapel. She shot saris, garbage, traffic lights, shoe-shop windows. She photographed an old man on his vegetable allotment, and then, close up, a rootless eggplant on the pavement.

At Kenneth Estate she couldn't tell which was his flat. She looked up to where his window would be, but in the vague new light there was nothing that marked it as his. She peered behind the garbage cans and saw her own vomit, a brown-and-yellow stain on the ground, now as dry as potpourri. She stalked the building in a slow circle. She photographed his bricks, his litter, and even her vomit, which somehow had also become his.

She shot his building from a few yards away, daunting with slum menace. She zoomed in until there was no outline, no edges, just the clay from which his home had been made. She imagined small, unsavory intimacies inside of it: undershirted fathers molesting their daughters, fat women on the toilet. And finally, Bobby, stoned or drinking tea or, most likely, asleep.

When she had finished, she stole across the street. She felt guilty and invincible, as though she had robbed him. She ran toward Bethnal Green and caught the bus, headed for a good morning's sleep, with Bobby and the grain of his bricks swirling in her head.

CHAPTER 3

1998

Del McCourys or Charlene Sweeney, music that already belonged to us.

Bobby said that Cosima seemed like a "nice wee girl," but he said that about anyone who was even slightly nice. He said it about waitresses, hitchhikers, a lady who worked at the Granada service station just outside of Blackburn. *She* was a "nice wee girl" even though she was fifty and wrinkled and big.

Two months after we met Cosima, we had a drop in County Wicklow. We had to drive all the way to Holyhead to catch the two A.M. ferry to Dun Laoghaire. It was a long journey—only 282 miles from London, but it took us five or six hours on the mountain roads.

We crossed the Welsh border at Shrewsbury. Wales was dark, and Snowdonia the darkest. The mountains looked purple and frozen in the night. My eyes were sore from staring ahead, but I wanted to stay awake for Bobby. We arrived at Holyhead at half past twelve.

"Might as well get an hour's rest on the lorry," said Bobby, and he got the beds ready in back. I bent my head against the window, looking at the shapes rising out of the bay. When I was smaller, the harbor frightened me with its smells of fish and oil. I felt that if I hadn't been sealed in by the bubble of the cab, I could slip away and be lost to the tar pudding below. Now I liked the harbor. It was the exact point where the world finishes.

"All set now, Jo. You can do your face and teeth on the boat."

I climbed into the back.

"Look away, Bobby." Lately, I didn't like for him to see me undress. In the past year, I had gone less fat around the waist but fatter in the hips and chest. Also, I had a patch of hair under each arm that seemed furry and disgusting to me, and my armpits smelled when it was warm. With my clothes on, you couldn't tell I was any different.

I climbed onto the top bunk and lay on my back. The lorry was dark, with one ribbon of light leaking in from the front. I could hear the water lapping against the dock and fishermen chatting in Welsh and loading bottles.

Bobby put on some music before climbing into the bunk below me.

"Who is this?" I asked, but then I recognized her voice.

Jessie sits in her bungalow

'Cause there's nothing so sad
As what I ain't never had
And the best that I've lived
Ain't never been lived
At least not by myself
Could it be that my life's been lived by someone else?

Her fiddle came in, a single note in the dark. Bobby sighed.

"Jo," he asked, "did you ever wonder if your life could be stolen, the way a wallet could? Did you ever wake up and think, 'Someone might have nicked my life, and now they're walking around living it'?"

"Whose life would you have, then?"

"A borrowed one."

"But if your life was borrowed, who would have your real life?"

"There might be no real life. The real Bobby could be no Bobby, just a grain in a handful of sand at the bottom of the sea."

"If you weren't really you, would I still be really me?"

"You'll always be you."

I wanted to ask more about this, but he moved on to something new.

"I wish I'd played the fiddle," he said, "rather than the bass guitar."

"Why?"

"Listen to her. Breaks your heart, doesn't it?"

Now that he said it, I could feel pain where my heart would be. I wondered if this was something to do with my new breasts, small but definitely there. Another song was coming on.

> Ain't that just like love . . .
> To come right up and stab you in the eye . . .

"That is like love," said Bobby. "Stabs you right in the eye, so it does."

"Did Rosalie ever stab you in the eye?"

"She couldn't really stab anyone, except with her jewelry maybe."

Bobby hardly ever said bad things about anybody, even my mother who I'd never met. When he did say things that were even slightly bad, I liked it, the little bit of naughtiness that wasn't like the rest of him. I laughed now, but quietly, so that I wouldn't upset the buttery blackness. My nightgown rode up into my bottom. I pulled it out and felt a fresh flow of air between my legs.

The bunk shook as he got up again. He lit a cigarette and opened a tin of lager. He had his usual nighttime smells on him: cigarettes and lager and a banana he'd eaten after supper.

"I have to sleep, Dad."

"Ah, Jo. We've a whole album to get through."

I tried to keep my eyes open, but sleep crept up to me, and I sank right in.

I awoke to a buzzing in my body. The neon butterfly flickered in my eyes. For a moment, I thought we'd fallen over the edge after all, and that these—the orange butterfly, the hum in my bones—were the first stages of drowning. I sat up quickly.

I didn't remember getting to the ferry lounge. I knew that Bobby must have carried me up from the bottom deck, weaving us through the parked lorries and cars and up the metal stairs. The idea of Bobby carrying me made me feel funny, though when I was smaller he did it all the time.

The fruit machine made the same old chimes: *clink, pedeenk.* Some men were talking about Charlton Athletic Football Club and their wives were talking about the price of duty free. Their voices were low with the middle of the night, as though they were telling secrets. Bobby sat with his pint of Guinness. He was singing, already remembering the words: *'Cause there's nothing so sad, as what I ain't never had. . . .*

Now that I was awake I wanted him to notice me. Though I hadn't liked his carrying me, I climbed into his lap like I used to do. I was too big now really, but I wriggled into it, forcing myself to fit. He didn't cuddle me. He just let me do it. I was lazy and limp, as if I'd had a hot bath. I wished I hadn't fallen asleep. I couldn't remember what we'd been talking about before; something to do with sand. I tried to fetch it back, but it was like drinking water from my two cupped hands; most of it trickled through the cracks.

CHAPTER 4

1985

pected was that the entire city would shut down, or, if the weather was good, thin out like a schoolyard after the last bell. It made Monday into a second Sunday, and she'd never liked Sundays to begin with. She despaired of too much space, too much time alone. And the few people she knew had gone for the day, to the seaside or some green place to which she wasn't invited.

At least she had time to work on her essay. She sat at her desk, arranging the tools of her work: two pens, an electric typewriter, three highlighters, a cup of instant coffee, a pack of Marlboro Lights, two fat and abstruse texts. She opened her copy of *Culture and the Urban Myth*. She tried to read the first line. It didn't go in. She read it again, aloud:

> In daily discourse, we often speak of "culture," as in the culture of a nation or an ethnic grouping, but we do not account for the more insidious culture of the individual: contradictory, multilayered, and infinitely complex.

She highlighted it with a pink marker and shut the book. She could read just as well outside. She grabbed her bag and her book and left her room, setting out into the sticky, vacated city. Yet once outside, she wanted to be inside.

It was too hot for schoolwork. She decided to go to the movies. She was in the mood for something easy and American, but the show times were wrong. She ended up at a film called *Sour Sun* about brother-sister incest in Kurdistan. The film was in hues of beige and gray, with endless scenes of a girl in a burka with sad cow eyes, herding chickens or mending a fence or sleeping with her brother or trying not to. Rosalie walked out before the end.

She fought to keep Bobby Pickering from her mind. She tried to see him as she'd first seen him, or *not* seen him—a muddle of a man, entangled in cord, a sad sack who even the old guys laughed at. Now he seemed like a dismal celebrity, a ghostly Celt: dusty and handsome and sort of *ill*. Louisa had told her that Bobby hadn't gone to the rehearsal yesterday, despite saying he would. He could be dead after all.

Back in her room, Rosalie sat before her mirror and painted her face. She put on her most flattering dress, took some of the studs out of her ears. It was ten-thirty at night, but her evening was just beginning.

Walking felt dangerous now, and not just because of the neighborhood he lived in. It seemed that boldness alone could endanger her, drawing any demon out of any alleyway, any demon but him. She took a taxi to Shandy Street. She rang the bell and waited. With the coming of footsteps, she went over her reasons for being there:

We were worried—you didn't come to rehearsal after all.

You said I should "pop round" again. Is it okay, to just "pop round" again?

The light went on. He stood in the doorway, exactly as he had two nights ago.

"It's yourself," he said.

"I'm sorry it's so late. I brought you whiskey." Her offering of whiskey sounded strange, as if she'd been invited.

"Ah," he said, but he didn't lead her upstairs. He just looked at her. She began to shrink away.

"Is it too—"

"Ach, come in. Sorry. Come in."

She followed him to his room.

"Have a seat there." He switched off the television. Rosalie sat. He reached behind the kettle and found two cups, both chipped and tea-stained.

"These are all I have." He handed them to her and let her pour. She felt strangely maternal, pouring out his whiskey in a teacup and handing it back to him. He sat on the bed, but not too close to her.

"Cheers." He sipped his drink and sat in silence, as though drinking was something that had to be thought about. Something hit the floor.

"What's this?" He picked up her copy of *Culture and the Urban Myth*.

"Oh," said Rosalie. "I forgot I had that. It's a Lacanian study of London cityscapes." Her words felt clunky, like hard candy that was too big for her mouth.

He read the back of the book. "Dead intellectual, isn't it?"

"I guess." She wished he wouldn't ask about it. She didn't want to have to explain anything to him.

"My sister nearly went to art college. She ended up going to Canada instead, but she nearly did that there art school in Belfast."

"Oh, is that the Belfast School of Art? It's supposed to be good. I thought about going there."

"Is that right, Rosalie?"

"Yeah. I think that, you know, conflict is excellent for art."

He gave a short laugh. "You think it's good to see how us 'real' people live, do you? In our own wee war zone?"

She wiped her mouth with her hand. "Oh God, that was really patronizing of me. I'm an idiot! I'm sorry."

"Don't worry." He got up, grabbed the bottle from the counter, poured

tidy one. This was a good sign, the two of them settling in, preparing their late-night picnic. She had the urge to tell him something personal.

"I'm feeling a little weird," she said. "I just broke up with my boyfriend. Just before we came here the other night."

"That's a pity."

"He was a musician, too. He was in Bastard Sex Canal. I mean, they're probably not your thing. They're not very . . . gentle."

" 'Not very gentle'? Do you think that all I listen to is the Eagles or something?"

"I didn't say that."

"Let me tell you something. Slow Emotion wasn't going to be Slow Emotion. We were Dennis and the Dividers and we were doing country covers, pure country: Dolly, Loretta, Johnny Cash, Hank Williams. Then Ollie got us this regular gig at the Tuxedo Lounge, and the manager there wanted 'easy listening,' but I'll tell you, Rosalie, there's nothing easy about it for me."

This was more than she'd heard him say at once. He sank to the floor and started going through his records until he found the one he wanted. It had a glossy picture of a man with long sideburns in a cowboy hat. He put it on, kneeling over the record player like a doting parent, waiting for the song to fill the room.

> *I used to know all my neighbors.*
> *Now I don't know who lives on the other side of my wall.*
> *I used to go to church on Sunday*
> *Until they knocked it down and built a shopping mall . . .*

Rosalie didn't hate all country music. She liked some of the new country bands like the Knitters, who used to be the punk band X. But this music was the real thing: God and horses and Bibles and bigots who burned crosses in your lawn. She wondered if Bobby was racist, or anti-Semitic. He might be anti-Semitic and attracted to her at the same time. She could tell him about her Russian-Jewish ancestors, watch him struggle with his lust and disgust.

Bobby's fist was clenched and hanging in the air. He brought it down and sang along: "But I don't need whiskey or wine to make me feel divine!"

"Are you religious, Bobby?"

"You're missing the point."

The next song was a sad one. Bobby stretched his legs out, propped his back against the wall. "This is a cracking tune," he said. "It's called 'That Old Disused Railway Is the Place You Broke My Heart.'"

"Bobby?"

"Yeah?"

"Why do you like this music so much?"

He looked surprised by the question. "It's magic, so it is."

"But so much of it is like . . . you know, racist, or sexist, or homophobic."

"I'm none of those things. Not a one."

"Okay, but . . ."

"It makes me happy. It cheers me right up. Because I haven't always been very—"

"Happy," she finished for him. "Tell me why you're not happy."

"I didn't say I'm *never* happy. Just sometimes."

"Tell me."

"It's just a mood. Hold on—listen to the chorus!"

So if you loved me like nobody's loved me, oh darling, that would mean so much. . . .

She jerked forward, let her feet thud onto the floor. He looked up, startled.

"What's up, luv?"

She didn't know that Irish people said *luv,* too. English people said it all the time, even when they were selling you apples or something. Bobby had only said it once, as if he'd saved it for her.

"I get the feeling," she said, "that you want me to go."

"Do you?"

"Well, do *you?*"

Bobby thought about it. "I don't think so. It's a nice wee surprise, having you here."

He was looking at her, smiling even. She smiled back. Slowly she leaned toward him and kissed his cheek. She pulled away to see his reaction. He was blank. Trembling, she kissed him on the lips. He didn't kiss her back. Her face burned with shame again. *Ugh,* he would be thinking; *just like Rusty Edelman, just like Rugg-Edd.* He didn't want her any more than Rugg-Edd had! She started to lift herself off of the bed.

She felt herself caught around the waist. The motion was so abrupt that she cried out. Bobby had her now. He lay her down on her back. She felt his stubble on her face, his hands in her hair. His tongue was in her mouth, so deep it nearly choked her, and then, in her ear, came his voice: "You're not getting away that easily."

cool air to slice her neck and chest. Rosalie sat up.

Bobby was fetching his joint out of the ashtray.

"It isn't you," he said.

"What is it, then?"

"I can't describe it. Everything's just . . . dark. There's a fog in my head, and there's noise. Like static."

"Now? You're like this now?"

"Now and again."

She knelt beside him, leaned on his shoulder.

"We could talk about it."

He smoked.

"*Talk to me.*" This sounded too intimate, as though she knew him better than she did. He had faint lines in his face. He looked older than twenty-four. He held her hand against his cheek, then returned it to her own lap.

"I'm not a good idea for you. You'd better go."

His face had gone inward, as though she had already left.

She picked up *Culture and the Urban Myth,* tore off a corner of a page, wrote her number and address on it. "In case you change your mind."

He didn't take it. She put it on the bed beside him.

"Will you at least call me?"

"I don't have a phone."

"You could use a phone booth."

"I don't know, Rosalie."

She walked down the stairs and into the courtyard. She looked up to see if he was standing at his window watching her. The whole building was dark, not so much as a flickering TV, not so much as a night-light.

She didn't really sleep that night. Images crowded her, too conscious for dreams but dreamier than thoughts. Bobby swam in and out of her: Bobby in his navy sweatshirt, the silver flash of his eyes on hers. Bobby the sad guitarist, idiot *mick*, gauche and rumpled, the fusty smell when he bent over, his gentle, violent, gentle voice, as husky as a criminal's in her ear: *You're not getting away that easily.* She masturbated. She drifted off. She masturbated again. She was wide awake.

At 5:15, she gave up. It was exhausting to try to sleep. What was she thinking about, anyway? What did she want to do, live with him in his slum? Move to Northern Ireland, to the ghettos of his youth? She had to admit, that part didn't sound too bad. They'd find themselves a flat in West Belfast. They'd make love all day on a spongy bed that gave beneath their weight. They'd drink tea and whiskey from the same cup, glut themselves with comfort food and heavy blankets while rainstorms or soldiers or IRA men raged outside, sealing them in.

When it finally came, the morning was soggy as old milk. Her hands were sticky. Her room, usually hot and smelling of incense, was freezing. She lay on her bed for most of the day and smoked. She wanted to call Louisa, but Louisa was still away. She waited till five o'clock, when it was late enough to call Los Angeles. Yet when five o'clock came, it seemed even stranger that she should talk to somebody there. Bobby would make no sense to anyone she knew.

When darkness fell, she ordered pizza. She turned on the TV. When she finished eating, she left the box where it was. In the darkness, her room, cluttered and smoky, was not so different from his. Her film lay undeveloped on the floor, on top of *Culture and the Urban Myth.* Why had she become a photographer in the first place? She'd taken a few photographs when she was fourteen and a few people—friends and relatives mostly—had said they were good. So what? Did *she* think they were good? Did she even enjoy it?

She turned off the TV. She took a Valium. She ran a hot bath. She lit candles and rifled through her cassettes, looking for a song to suit her mood. She put on "The Ghost of We" by the Implications. She eased herself into the bath. She closed her eyes and leaned her head against the back of the tub, melting as the song settled into the steam, turning the room to sigh and echo. Conor Morrow sang to her in his strange falsetto:

The last time I saw you, Julie
You were standing in Sugar Lane
You were waiting for Danny, but Danny never came
And while you waited in Sugar Lane
You said to me (at least, I think you said to me)
My heart doesn't break in two, you know
My heart breaks in three . . .
My heart breaks for Danny, for Julie, and the ghost of We.

There was a knock on the door.

Rosalie froze. It could have been Rugg-Edd. She realized, with some surprise, that she no longer wanted to see him. Could it have been Bobby? She was wearing no makeup! She stepped out of the bath and wrapped a towel around herself. The knock came again. Still in her towel, she opened the door.

Bobby stood there with a half-bottle of whiskey, a cheaper brand than the one she had bought for him.

"Is that where you're from?"

"No."

Slowly he followed her in. She found some glasses and poured out the whiskey. She knew she should get dressed but she felt that if she left the room, even for a minute, she could lose him.

He sat on the bed. He had something to say. He looked down into his whiskey, but he didn't drink it. Finally he began.

"It's the anniversary of my ma's death tomorrow. Five years."

"How did she die?"

"The big C."

"The big C—oh, you mean cancer?"

"Yes." He took a swig of whiskey. "I've been thinking—you know—about the last time we took her to hospital. It was the first march of the season."

"First march?"

"The first Orange March. Ma was writhing around the bathroom floor, having one of them seizures. It was only me and her in the house. When the ambulance came, she was still shaking like fuck. I sat with her in the back of the ambulance, and wouldn't you know it, we couldn't get through because of the march. All them Orangemen blocking the road with their Union Jacks. I thought that Ma was going to die right then and there with all them bastards outside singing, 'Fuck the pope! Fuck him hard! Fuck him up and down the yard!'"

Bobby gave a short laugh, but his eyes were wet.

"And there's me in the back, me holding her hand, just trying to shut it out, that scum outside, and I looked at my ma and there was this one single tear running down her cheek."

He took another sip. Rosalie waited.

"In the hospital," he said, "she seemed nearly cheerful again. The nurses propped her up with all these pillows. My sister Anne brought her flowers, great purple things. Me da was sitting there in the chair saying nothing, cap in his lap. He looked more miserable than she did. Me ma says to me, 'Bobby, go and fetch us some tea and biscuits, pet,' normal as anything. We was all dead relieved. I went round asking did anyone else want anything and I ended up taking this long order, biscuits and crisps and Cadbury Flakes for the wee ones. Everyone was there—Annie, Good Guy Mike, Norah, Adele, everyone. So I went to this hospital shop and I bought all this tea and all the other stuff and it took ages. Wouldn't you know it—I got lost on the way down—somehow ended up on the fourth floor rather than the third. Took me near twenty minutes to get back."

He drank the last of his whiskey. "When I got back, the priest was there. Me ma was gone. I kissed her cheek, but her face didn't feel like her face already. Her face was like—like rubber. I heard my da say to Anne, 'Well, isn't that typical of our Bobby, to be late for his own mother's death.'"

Rosalie's own eyes were moist, but it seemed wrong, somehow, to cry, as if she'd be taking something away from him.

"I left Ireland after she died," he said. "There was nothing to keep me there. But since then—it's a mad thing—I don't look in the mirror all that much. It's like she took my face with her."

"A shame," she said. "A face like yours."

He looked up at her. He leaned forward, looked a little closer.

"I knew there was something different," he said, "You're not wearing any makeup."

She brought her hand up to her face. "Do I look awful?"

"You look . . . beautiful."

She took his glass from him, put it on the table. She touched his arm. Ignited, he held her fast, squeezing her so tightly that he nearly cut off her breath. He looked up at her, clasped her neck, and tried to kiss her. She resisted, trying to keep the towel wrapped around herself, trying to keep herself upright for as long as she could before finally allowing herself be pulled down, thinking, *Go on, okay, drown me.*

CHAPTER 5

1 9 9 9

We never thought we would see her again. We didn't think we needed to. We had twelve songs of Cosima Stewart and Her Goodtime Guys: *Swoon-ing, Drinking, Loving, Lying, Getting Back on the Road.* When we weren't on the

three weeks and I could hardly remember what happened there, though I had the back-to-school smell in my nose already: a thickish smell of chalk and glue. Bobby said I was always miserable before school. "Ah, Jo," he said when I was like that, because he didn't have enough words to change my mood.

We were in the flat at Shandy Street. Bobby had had the Shandy Street flat since before I was born. It was supposed to be home to us, but mostly we thought of it as a waiting room, a place to sleep when we were off the road. There wasn't room in it to do much else. There was just about room for a cooker, a telly, and the two single beds.

The only good thing about London was that we got to go to the cinema. I wanted to go tonight, even though my stomach hurt. I wanted to see *I Never Loved You Anyway.* I'd seen the trailer. It was about a woman who fights for custody of her four daughters and she wins but then she gets ovarian cancer. We liked films like that, American ones, where you get to know the person and they get ill or die. Even the hospitals and the funerals looked shiny and comforting. We let ourselves cry, knowing that nobody died really, and even if they did, they weren't people we knew. We'd buy sweet and salty popcorn and mix it all together.

We saw most of our films at the Mile End Odeon, but *I Never Loved You Anyway* was only showing at the Barbican, where I'd never been. We had to take the lift to the fifth floor. Because it was more of an art-house cinema, it sold carrot cake and foreign chocolate, no popcorn or Pepsi, so already I wasn't completely happy.

When we got the front of the queue, the ticket lady pointed to the number 15 behind her. "She has to be at least fifteen to see this film."

"Why?" asked Bobby. "It's hardly sex and violence, is it?"

"Mature subjects, strong language."

"They'll show the film on telly soon," I said. "And I'll watch it then, so why can't you just let me watch it now? Especially if we're *paying* you."

But she just went on to the next person.

We stood outside the cinema wondering what to do. People were going in, in couples and little groups, and the lady said nothing when they bought their tickets.

"Bitch."

"She's only doing her job, Jo."

But this made me hate her more.

"Do you want some chocolate, anyway?"

I didn't. It was no good without the film. Bobby put his hands in his pockets, as though he could find some little thing there that would make it better.

"I don't want to go to school tomorrow," I said.

Bobby shook his head. He never believed that kids at school were horrible. To him they were all just "wee lads and lasses," but I knew they were evil bastards, the boys wearing hoods that made their heads look like oval weapons, the girls with their big hoop earrings and trousers hanging low so that you had to look at the top of their groins. Bobby didn't hear the names they called me—*Oy, Fatto; Retard; Weirdo*—and I didn't tell him, either, because the thought of him hearing those names made it worse. I usually preferred to shut them out, to remind myself that soon I'd be on the road again, back to our skies and our songs and going out for dinner most nights. All those losers had were their filthy flats and hip-hop music and drunken parents on the dole. They would end up in prison or dying from bad Ecstasy or getting themselves stabbed at some nightclub in Leyton or Romford.

"Shall we make a move, Jo?"

My feet were vibrating. Some kind of music was coming up through the floor. A man and a girl walked by us, holding hands. The man had a shaved head and he wore a silver suit and he had a big boxer dog on a lead. The girl was Chinese or Japanese and she had long black hair and a perfect flat face, her skin like paper. I watched as they went downstairs to the level below. I leaned over the rail and I saw the tops of their heads as they went down to the floor below that.

"Dead arty this place, isn't it?" said Bobby. He was reading a notice board with flyers all over it. He pointed to a cartoon of dark people clapping their hands and dancing.

"'Hungarian Gypsies in April,'" he read. "And see this one—'Castro Doesn't Believe in Tears: Cubafest in June.' Dead cheerful, so it is. See this, Jo?"

"I can *read*." I didn't feel like looking at flyers. Applause rippled through my shins.

"Let's go and down and see," I said.

"Do you not just fancy a takeaway? A bit of telly?'

Normally this would have been fine with me. But something started me walking down, and he had to follow. Levels four and three were just empty, all carpet and pillars. Level two was the same as level three, but we could hear people clapping and shouting things.

When we reached level one, the first thing we saw was the banner above the stage: DEEP IN THE HEART OF TEXAS: COUNTRY & WESTERN WEEK. Underneath, in

trucks, not of music. I wondered how many other country-and-western "events" we'd missed. I watched the Chinese/Japanese girl and her boyfriend spread out a blanket. They had two friends with them, a blond mother and daughter who looked alike. The daughter was tall and thin with orange extensions in her hair. She was probably only a year or so older than me, but I couldn't imagine looking as grown-up as her in just one year. (I thought she could get into the cinema upstairs, no problem.) The silver-suited boyfriend opened a bottle of champagne with a *pop!* that I could hear above the noise. He poured the champagne into plastic cups for all of them, even the young girl. The dog sat down at the edge of their blanket, as if taking part in their conversation.

"I feel funny," I said.

"Funny in what way, Jo?"

I wasn't sure. It was like when you have to go to the toilet, but it wasn't that.

"Listen." Bobby took my hand. His hand was sweaty, and I didn't see any other girls holding their father's hand, apart from tiny ones. He started taking us through the crowd, saying "Sorry" and "Pardon me," but getting us to the stage all the same.

"Listen, Jo!"

But the words were fuzzy. Bobby pushed us forward and at last I could see her. She was just like I remembered, but taller and brighter up there on the stage.

> *I been out of orbit so long there's mold upon my heart*
> *Got myself a slum on the wrong side of town.*
> *I've been pretty sad, it's true*
> *Drinking rum and singing the blues*
> *Your leaving me had torn me right apart . . .*

Bobby and I looked at each other, then sang along:

"So the last thing I expected was to see you in these parts!"

I took Bobby's hand again, not caring how sweaty it was. I wanted to shout to the whole of the crowd, to tell them that we knew this song better than they did. At times she sang it differently than on the record. Her voice went down when it usually went up, or she cut a word short. It made me think she was getting herself slightly wrong, but when she started on the fiddle, the tune tore out of her, happy and mad at the same time, just like it always was. I knocked into a woman. She wore army fatigues and held her little boy.

"Sorry," I said, but the woman just smiled at me. She jiggled her little boy. "It's a great song, isn't it? Would you like an orange?"

With one hand she opened her bag and the smell of oranges came from it. I thought it was clever of her to have a bag big enough for whatever her son wanted. Looking around, I saw that most of the mothers had big bags with them, and some of the fathers had them, too. Bobby never carried a bag with things in it for later. Now he stood there without anything, not even a jacket.

The keyboard player was playing on his own. He was the boy we'd seen on the motorway, the one with the bleached blond hair and lashes. When he'd finished his solo, the guitar player stepped up beside Cosima. He had long hair in a ponytail. I wondered if this was the boyfriend. He looked beautiful and bad, like the "heartbreakin' guy" from her song "Heartbreakin' Guy." She watched him play. Her fiddle teetered on her fingers as though she was daring it to drop. She shut her eyes and lifted her bow until it kissed the string. She let out one long, high note. I thought it would run away from her, but she caught it and brought it back to herself. She sped up, making a laughing sound like two fiddles at once. Her hair looked wet and the front of her shirt was wet, as though the music was making her bleed. The guitar player came in, stamping his foot so that we all stamped our feet on the carpet. I lifted Bobby's arm and put it around my shoulder.

The Chinese/Japanese girl and her friends were standing near the stage now. Cosima waved at them; she seemed to know them. She sang:

> Would you love me if I was somebody else?
> A beauty queen turning the heads of a nation
> Would you love me if I wasn't just a girl
> A nobody girl who you met at the Texaco station.

I loved this song, but now I wondered how she could have written it. She wasn't a "nobody girl." She *was* a beauty queen turning the heads of a nation. My eyes kept going back to her friends. The girl near my age, the one with the orange extensions, had a full mouth and sexy, lazy eyes that made her look like she wasn't bothered about anything.

My stomach tugged at me from the inside, wanting to make a puddle of me on the floor. Bobby's eyes were full of Cosima. I hit his shoulder.

"Steady on, Jo."

Chinese/Japanese girl, her silver-suited boyfriend, and the blond mother and daughter. The guitarist—the heartbreakin' guy—had his hand on her shoulder. The silver-suited boyfriend handed her a glass of wine.

Bobby started to walk toward the stairs, but I didn't go with him. He turned.

"What is it, Jo?"

"We've met her."

"So?"

I started walking toward her.

"Jo?" He called after me, but I didn't stop. My stomach was spiraling like a twister but I made myself do it. I went up to the bar and stepped right up to her.

"We gave you a ride in our lorry," I said. "Do you remember? We listened to Charlene Sweeney. You gave us your CD."

The girl with the orange extensions had this "What do you *look* like?" face on her. Cosima looked off to the side. She didn't say anything. I felt myself shrinking. I started to back away.

"About six months ago?" she asked at last.

"That's right!"

"I remember. Of course I remember."

"We listen to your CD all the time. We know every song."

"Really?" Her eyes went off to the side again, but came back to me. "Josephine!"

"Yes!"

Bobby was hovering at the edge of the group.

"And remember my father?" I said. "Bobby?"

"How are you, Bobby?" Cosima introduced us to everybody. Apart from Cosima, they were all English, even Katie, the Chinese/Japanese girl. They were all posh, too, except for Rick, the boyfriend, who had a London accent. Bobby said, "How's it goin'?' or "Good to meet you there" as he met each person and shook their hands. When he finally turned back to Cosima, he said, "That was dead on. Great craic altogether, so it was."

Most of the time I didn't notice Bobby's accent at all, but now a terrible thing came into my head: *stupid paddy.* (*Stupid paddy* was what kids at school called me when I said things the Irish way, like "dead on" or great craic.")

"Bobby and Josephine have the best country collection you've ever seen," said Cosima. "They have all my favorites!"

"You're our favorite now!" I told her.

Cosima reached into her handbag and took out a CD, sealed in plastic and ready to sell in a record shop. On the cover was a picture of her on a horse. Rick and Sean, the keyboard player, stood on either side of her. Sean held up a large Rubik's cube, as big as a fourth head. On top it said COSIMA AND HER GOODTIME GUYS: PUZZLE OF THE WILD WEST.

"What do we owe you for that, Cosima?" asked Bobby.

"Don't be silly," she said. "By the way, I meant to ask you the last time. Are you from Scotland?"

"Uh . . . Ireland."

"Northern Ireland?" asked Rick.

"Aye, the north of Ireland."

"Yes, he's from Northern Ireland," I repeated, wondering why he couldn't just say Northern Ireland like everybody else. Rick looked away and wiped his hair away from his face as if wiping us away at the same time. I tried not to look at Bobby now, but he was in my eyes no matter what; his jeans, his heavy shoes, his flat brown hair. I'd never hated him before, not even a little, but now I wanted him to piss right off and leave me alone with Cosima Stewart.

It was time to say good-bye to her. Bobby put his hand on my shoulder the same way that Rick had his hand on Cosima's shoulder. I shrugged it off.

"Good-bye, Cosima," I said. It came out sad.

Cosima leaned forward and kissed me on the cheek. Her breath smelled of wine and mint.

"Bye, Josephine," she said. "See you on the road."

As we walked away, I heard the Chinese/Japanese girl say, "Sweet." I knew the girl with the orange extensions wouldn't think I was sweet, but she knew nothing. She probably had to go to school every day. She didn't get to spend her days driving up and down the country, to Europe and Ireland sometimes, too, listening to Cosima all the time.

I thought it was the excitement that made my stomach tug again, a happy new hurting inside me. I ran up the stairs. When I felt the wetness between my legs, I stopped. I'd peed myself! I ran faster. They must have known, Cosima and her friends, they must have smelled it! Bobby called after me, but I ran up to the next level and into the toilet.

There was blood, not pee, all over my legs, a smell coming off it like metal. I knew about menstruation from school, but I didn't think it would happen to me already, though I was already thirteen. I wiped it up with the loo roll, but it was the cheap crunchy kind that didn't soak up so well. When I'd finished, the inside of my thighs were smeared with pink.

I wondered what the girl with the extensions had done with her first period. She'd probably talked to her mother, and her mother had cried but not because she was sad, and they'd gone to Boots and bought the stuff. I wrapped some loo roll around myself, like a nappy, to hold it all in. I turned to check myself from the back in case I was leaking.

Bobby was waiting outside the ladies' room.

"All right, luv?"

I didn't look at him. I worried that he could hear the crunchy loo roll as I walked. He took my hand, which made it worse. He was holding the hand of a body that was oozing down below with its funny smell. My hate for him had gone, mopped up like the blood.

"Let's get some supper into you," he said. "Hungry?"

I nodded, though for once I wasn't.

"What do you make of her, then? Your new mate?"

"Bobby?"

"Yeah?"

"Could I get extensions in my hair?"

"Extensions?"

"You know, to make it longer?"

Bobby looked dumb at the word *extension*. It wasn't a word he'd used before, unless he was talking about the back of a house or something.

"Why don't you just grow your hair? That would be nice."

But I knew my hair would never grow long without help. It wouldn't look like Cosima's or any of those other girls. It would always break off just below my neck, leaving the ends split and dry.

CHAPTER 6

1985

Rain: a prick of it on her ear. And then another one, dripping into the gap between the sheets. She scrunched down. Another drop. The drizzle probed her through the sheet, seeking out her bare skin.

She reached for Bobby, seeking out the nicotine shelter of his chest and breath. He wasn't there. Her eyes flickered. What could be different? The room smelled the same: of tea, of hash, of bananas and Bobby's sweatshirt. But there was a new, rude glare behind her lids.

It must have been a leak in the ceiling. No surprise there. The only sur-

Rosalie opened her eyes and sat up.

The old man faced the bed, his knees bent and crunched together. Bobby's father was flicking at her with a bottle of Dettol cleaning fluid. The fluid was white and clear, not its usual yellow. Seeing her, he pulled his hand out as though he could arrest the last drop, but it was too late. It stuck where her hairline met her forehead. She left it there, allowing it to glitter back at him.

"Jesus." His voice was croaky. "I thought you was him."

She wiped the drop away and the sheet collapsed, revealing her breasts. The old man flinched.

Bobby walked in with a bag of food. He looked at his father and then at Rosalie and back to his father.

"I didn't know you were still here, Da." He spoke carefully, lest the old man explode into worse violence. "Jesus, though, will youse get away with your holy water?"

His father pointed to Rosalie with the Dettol, holding it like a gun. "Looks like you're needing it more than ever."

Bobby's father, though old and skinny, did not look weak. He had the glinting, God-fearing eyes of someone who could do harm. He could reclaim

Bobby from her, convince Bobby of her badness. And the glare! He had opened the blinds, inviting the daylight in as his witness.

Bobby brought his bag to the counter. He took out the items one at a time: PG Tips. Hovis bread. Milk. Rizla rolling papers.

"Will you have a cup of tea, Da?"

"I will not."

"A biscuit?"

Bobby's father let out a gasp, sounding more like an old woman than a man. He left the flat and slammed the door behind him. Bobby stared after him, his mouth open as if he'd been left in the middle of speaking. For a moment Rosalie thought he would go after him. But instead he sighed and closed the blinds, letting the room darken into its familiar relief.

"Holy water," said Rosalie. "Where does a person get holy water?"

"Sure you can get it at the airport these days. In Ireland, that is."

"How did he get into the flat?"

"He has a key."

"You gave him a key?"

"He worries about me. He's going to worry even more now that he's seen a woman in my bed."

It cheered her up, being the "woman" in his bed. She looked at Bobby's groceries, hoping he'd bought enough this time. He'd forgotten toilet paper, of course. She would have to use paper towels, covered in pictures of superheroes and rough on her private parts.

Bobby was making tea. He was slow to absorb the fact that she didn't like tea. He would make it for her every time he made a cup for himself, even though her cup always cooled, still brimming, forming its scaly crust on top.

"Did he ever hit you?" she asked.

"The last time he hit me, it was because I stole the Union Jack from the flagpole at the RUC station."

He sat on the edge of the bed. He pulled a Buck Owens record cover onto his lap and lay out his rolling papers upon it along with his hash and tobacco. He arranged the items neatly, the only slice of order in the flat.

"How did they know it was you who stole the flag?"

"We were the only Catholics in the village. And I made trousers out of it, them flares everyone was wearing."

"You *wore* the flag?"

"Aye."

Rosalie laughed, and then Bobby did.

"Why was that the *last* time he hit you?"

"Because I hit him back for once."

She tried to imagine Bobby hitting his father, or hitting anybody. He lit his spliff. He put his lips to hers and breathed the smoke into her lungs.

"Shotgun," he said, liking the name of the ritual. The first smoke of the day was always the best. She sucked in, feeling her innards barbecue pleasantly. She let the smoke out. Bobby kissed her, nice and long. He lifted himself on top of her. She loved to begin their lovemaking like this, with him in clothes and her not, the coarseness of his jacket against her bare skin, his gradual unwrapping as he sank himself in. There was no daylight anymore, no buses, no books, no fathers, no bright sun with its angry white purity. Only them.

Later she lay awake, watching the shadows creep over him as he slept. She didn't know if it was dusk outside, because it always felt like dusk in here. She was itchy with unwelcome pangs, reminders of what she hadn't done. She'd been with Bobby for a month, and she hadn't been to college for three weeks of that.

She thought of Bobby's father and his holy spray. She thought about rain. She liked England because it was wet. It was wetness—the unholy spirits of whiskey—that had brought Bobby and herself together, and now it was wetness that kept them here, sticking to their hands and hair and bedclothes: sweat and booze and the surprising potency of his body.

By contrast, nothing seemed as dry and bright as the place she was from. ⸺ home, it seemed to her now, but a place of brutal light and ⸺ ⸺ ⸺ a Boulevard like skinny overseers, the sushi bars with their sili-⸺bes, the aerobics studios drowning in sunlight. It made her wonder if she had ever been loved at all, or even liked; if anyone could really love anyone in that hell of hard bodies and hard stucco where all her blemishes were exposed like carnage. Even her parents' house was a place of stony edifices; of terra-cotta tiles, of wooden floors that clicked with the approach of guests and thudded with her own, a swimming pool built to replicate the Hockney print above her father's desk, a gelatinous cube of blues.

Nuria, the Guatemalan maid, used to bring her daughters to swim in the pool. Their hoarse, Spanish voices floated up to her window while Rosalie sat on her bed and ate great quantities of secret cake washed down with Dr. Pepper. The girls had been coming here since they were little. Now they were lithe and narrow-hipped, growing into young women just beyond her room, while she stayed put and expanded.

She had always been hungry. She had always been thirsty. She'd even stolen food: from the kitchen, from Nuria's bag, from the food truck at school. She had a store of it in her sock drawer, not hard to find if anyone ever thought to look for it. Through her teenage years her drawer would be filled with edible items, though not always caloric ones. Cigarettes, diet pills, and Quaaludes would settle in among the cookies and cakes.

Even now she was impossible to satisfy. Bobby could fill her up for a while. He could spread himself over her insides like butter on a wound, though every time he left her—even to go to the store—she felt herself drain again.

She looked at him now. She didn't like to think what he did when he wasn't with her. There were no infidelities, she knew that much. Yet while she'd allowed herself to dissolve into his life like a stock cube in soup, he had grown stronger. He never missed a gig now. He was training to drive an articulated lorry, or an artic, as he called it, and his arms were getting muscular from handling large vehicles. Increasingly his conversation was peppered with lorries, sounds with an alien certainty to them: Scania, Magnum, MAN.

"I could make a fair bit of money if I'm my own owner-operator one day," he'd told her. "An eighteen-wheeler all of my own. What do you make of that?"

She didn't make much of it. All those wheels, just to take him away from her.

She wished he were awake. She wanted him to talk to her—about anything but trucks. She wanted him to fuck her again.

She considered brushing her teeth and decided not to. Earlier, while going down on him, she had swallowed. He'd been so pleased that he'd come a second time, and together they'd rubbed the semen into her breasts and thighs, rubbing him like lotion into her pores.

They didn't use contraception. He withdrew. Sometimes while having sex she imagined she could feel a fetus, left over from the last time they'd done it. She thought of a hit man she'd seen on TV. With each new murder, said the killer, you felt the last less. *You erased the murder with the one you were doing now.* It seemed possible that Bobby had impregnated her, that he had not withdrawn early enough (Bobby was never quick at anything) but that he had erased it later. Each penetration killed the last.

He was stirring now, reaching for her again. There was nothing to worry about. Nothing like a life could grow in that womb of hers, the darkest place in the world, as dark as any bottom drawer. There was only room enough for him.

CHAPTER 7

2 0 0 0

I wasn't sure about the new album. I expected it to be like the first one, and it just wasn't. Bobby said it was a mistake to try to like an album too quickly. He said I should let it simmer, like a good stew.

"You know what I think?" I asked. "I think she's letting the Goodtime Guys take over too much now."

By this I mostly meant Rick Watson, the boyfriend. "He's singing a lot more on this album than on the other one. And there's more guitar on its own."

"He's not a bad guitar player," said Bobby.

There was one song we liked straight away, and that was called "Crash." "Crash" wasn't about a real crash; it was about when your dreams come crashing down. But one day, on our way to Lockerbie, where the plane crash had happened, we played it again and again. I wanted to visit the exact place where the plane had gone down twelve years ago. Bobby said that if we finished the Tesco delivery by lunchtime, we could.

There was only a small queue to tip at the co-op, but I was warm and bored as I waited for us to tip. A wall to our right was plastered in posters, new over old, so that you couldn't read what half of them said. A new one caught my eye: COSIMA STEWART AND HER GOODTIME GUYS! A diagonal strip across it said they were playing at a club called Meg's Borderline in Glasgow. The strip was yellow and alarming, as though warning us of danger.

"That's tonight they're playing!" I looked at Bobby. "Can we go?"

Bobby looked at the poster for a long time, longer than he needed to get the information.

"We're not meant to be in Glasgow tonight. We're meant to be in Greenock."

"Greenock's not far."

"I don't know, Jo. I don't know if I'm in the mood to watch a band."

"This isn't just a *band*." I was surprised at Bobby, talking about Cosima as if she was just like the others, the Dollys and Lorettas with their sequins and big hair and Nashvilles and Atlantas. Cosima had ridden with us in our lorry. She'd given me both of her albums, her fingers touching mine as she handed those slices of herself over to me.

And yet I wasn't sure if I wanted to go myself. It had been eight and a half months since we'd seen her at the Barbican. Since then, she'd gotten better known. The band was in nearly every issue of *Country UK*. Fame might make her too busy, and less friendly to us. I wondered if the mother and daughter would be there, the daughter with her extensions. I was sure she'd still be against me in some way, in some spreadable way that would spread to the others.

But Bobby's doubt pushed out my own.

"Okay, Bobby? We'll go for just half an hour, and if we don't like it, we can leave, all right?'

"We'll see."

We drove out to Tundergarth, where most of the plane had fallen. I expected to see a plane-size gash like I'd seen in pictures, but the gash had been filled in. Apart from a hut of remembrance, there was only a church and a field.

"It doesn't feel like a plane went down at all."

Bobby didn't answer. He ran his hand over the walls of the church. Since we'd seen the Cosima poster, he'd gone inside himself. I wondered if the darkness was coming. It hadn't come for a while, and it never came before nighttime.

"Dad?"

He knelt to the bottom of the door. "See them there hinges? My uncle used to make them up in Carrickfergus."

I picked a piece of metal off the ground. "This could have been a bit of the plane."

"That's part of a rusty old pitchfork. Put it down, Jo."

I put it down. "Bobby? Do you think people would have died instantly?"

Bobby tried the church door, but it wouldn't open. He picked up a handful of grass and weighed it with his hand.

"Bobby?" I asked again. "Do you think—"

"Most of them, aye. Some might have suffered for a while."

"One day we'll go on an airplane, you and me. And we won't be frightened."

"That so."

"You don't believe me. You don't believe I won't be frightened."

"Maybe you *should* be frightened. Once something happens, that's it."

"We'll go anyway."

I waited for him to ask where we'd go. He didn't.

"Or you don't have to go. *I'll* go. I'll go to America, To the places in Cosima's songs."

"Yeah? What about the song that's based in Woking, Surrey?"

"Not the English songs, stupid. I'll go to Texas, where she's from."

Bobby closed his eyes, tilted his face to the sky. "Feel that," he said. "That's a western breeze. Comes all the way from the Gulf Stream, maybe."

"I'll go to California," I said. "Where Rosalie is."

I didn't want to see Rosalie. I just wanted him to talk to me. I was doing a bad job of it. My own words were coming out angry. He walked on. I followed him.

"It's like this plane crash never happened," I said.

"You already said that."

"Well, it's true."

"That's kind of like life, anyway, so it is."

"What do you mean?"

"You're here and then you're not. And nobody remembers you at the end of it."

"You'll remember me if I die," I said.

"I'll go first," he said. "Least I hope I will. I'm older."

"Then I'll remember you."

"Will you? What will you remember exactly?"

"Lots of things."

"Name them."

I knew there were lots of things, but right now I couldn't name them. He shook his head and gave a little laugh, as if he realized he was being daft. "Let's get some lunch."

This was a good idea. Lunch always put us in the mood to talk to each other. We got back in the lorry, back on the road.

"I want to go to the Little Chef," I said.

"It's too dear. I can't keep taking you to Little Chefs all the time."

"What about the Lough Erby caff?"

"I think we should go to the supermarket today. To buy real food, I mean."

"Why?"

"Because we're pretty unhealthy at the minute, so we are."

"We're not unhealthy. We're just normal."

"It isn't normal to eat junk food. You're a growing girl. Your skin isn't looking its best. You're putting on a wee bit of weight."

I looked out of the window. I didn't feel like talking anymore, but it was too late. He was on a roll now.

"We eat too much fish and chips and burgers and sausages and chocolate and all of that. It wouldn't kill us to eat a few grapes and bananas once in a while."

"I *hate* bananas. They make me sick. I hate the way you eat them, all yellow and slimy on your toast."

"Fine."

"They look like *sick*."

"I get the point, Jo."

We were back at the Tesco, but not to tip. We drove round to the car park where the normal shoppers parked. He opened his door but I stayed in the cab.

"C'mon, Jo."

"I'm not hungry."

He came round to my side, opened my door.

"Don't be like that."

"Why should I eat, anyway, if I'm so fat and spotty?"

"I didn't *say* that."

"You did."

He sighed, closed my door and got back in the cab.

"I'm sorry, Jo. Look, I'm being a tube."

"Don't use that word *tube*. Nobody outside of Belfast says *tube*."

He sighed again, threw up his hands.

I was slightly less mad with him now, but I wouldn't talk to him until he took back what he'd said about my putting on weight and my skin not being its best. We didn't say a word for the next sixty miles. Usually, any bad feeling between us cleared soon enough, like a bad smell in the loo, but today, as far down as Glasgow, I wasn't sure that it had.

Meg's Borderline was nothing like the Barbican. It was a narrow black pub and easy to miss, huddled between salmon-colored flats on the south side of Glasgow. We were about to go in when we saw the sign:

YOU MUST BE 16 OR OVER TO ENTER THIS ESTABLISHMENT.

Bobby put his hand on my shoulder. "That's the problem," he said, "when you want something too badly."

People were coming up behind us.

"Keep your hair on, Cos. I just meant—"

"No. Your attitude sucks as usual, Rick. It *sucks!*"

Rick came up first, a rollup cigarette in his mouth. His hair was loose around his shoulders. Cosima was behind him, yelling at his back. Katie, the Chinese/Japanese girl, was there, too, and Sean, the keyboard player. They were going in so fast they didn't see us.

"Cosima!" I called.

It took her a moment to see where the voice came from. She looked interrupted, not happy to see me.

"Oh . . . Geraldine?"

"It's Josephine."

Bobby stepped forward. "And I'm, uh . . . Bobby, remember? Bobby Pickering. How's it going?" He held his hand out to Rick. Rick took it, just about. Everyone just nodded, not saying any real hellos.

"We've come to see you," I said, which was stupid, because it was obvious.

"Cool," said Cosima, but she didn't sound as if she meant it.

Rick pointed at the sign. "How are you going to get past that?" Cosima looked at the sign, too.

"If she's with us," said Cosima, "I'm sure she'll be fine."

"How old are you, darling?" This was from Sean. He had a Liverpool accent, which made him sound more hopeful than the others.

"Fourteen."

"Dead small, aren't you? I thought you were younger than that."

I didn't say anything. I felt I'd done something wrong, just by being young.

"Shut up, Sean," said Katie. "I was smaller than her when I was her age, and I'm taller than you now." I couldn't get over how posh her voice was. I'd never have known she was Chinese or Japanese if I hadn't looked at her.

"We'd better make tracks, guys." Rick opened the door. Cosima raised her eyebrows at me and shook her head as to say *I'm sorry* before following him. Yet just as the door nearly shut on me, I caught her arm.

"We've come up all the way from London!" I said. "We've come all the way up here to see you."

Bobby started to say something, probably about us being in Scotland anyway, but I kept talking before he could. "I'm not going to make any noise or anything. You won't even know I'm in there."

"Oh, I'm sure you won't make *noise*. . . ." Cosima and Katie exchanged a look. I couldn't tell if it was an on-my-side look or a girls-at-school look, laughing at me.

Cosima held the door open with her back, let her eyes rest on my face. "Josephine," she asked, "do you ever wear makeup?"

"She's a bit young for that," said Bobby.

"I wore makeup at her age," said Katie.

"So did I," said Sean.

"We've got twenty minutes, Cos," said Rick.

Cosima's lips were pursed as if she was thinking about something.

"Twenty minutes is plenty," she said. She took my arm and looked at Bobby. "Is it okay?" she asked.

I hoped he wouldn't ask "Is what okay?" but he just nodded. Cosima and

Katie whisked me down the foyer and into the ladies' room. Cosima dragged a chair in and placed it in front of the mirror and told me to sit in it.

"The trick with makeup," said Cosima, "is to look as though you're not wearing any."

It was true that neither of them wore much, yet when they turned their handbags upside down, an avalanche of cosmetics clattered against the sink—compacts, blushers, mascaras, eyeliners, and lipsticks in slender black and silver tubes.

They took off their jackets and got to work, leaning so close over me that I could smell their chewing-gum breath and see the pale hairs along their arms. I could see how skinny Katie was, with her tiny waist and a tummy that caved in from under her white vest. She had small breasts and a long neck and long arms, and her skin was the color of a rich tea biscuit. Cosima was slim, but her hips were wider and her breasts were bigger, making her more curvy, from the bigness of her hair to her feet where her cowboy boots tapered her jeans in. When she pinned her fringe up to see me better, her eyes were so green and bright that she looked as though she was lit up from the inside.

In quick little circles, Cosima rubbed some pinkish cream into my face.

"What's that?" I asked.

"Foundation. You don't need much, just a base to even out your skin tone." Her fingers were cool, making my face full of energy. Katie held my hand, trying different eye pencils on the back of it. She kept looking up to my eyes to see which one matched.

Fragrances came off Katie and Cosima, not the heavy perfumes of older women in shops, but crisp, clean smells. I could imagine these two gliding through London (or "the Capital," as they called it on the news), Rollerblading over the Thames, swimming in indoor pools with sun streaming through the skylights, swinging their bags in Perspex buildings with glass lifts, like a shampoo ad: a world of sparkle and air and beautiful hair.

Katie stepped back, and I saw myself in the mirror.

I was standing between the prettiest girls in the world, working hard to make me one of them. I wouldn't have swapped the moment for any other, apart from one thing: me. I had never thought I was ugly exactly, but now I saw that I was. I had a small mouth and a flat nose and a hint of a double chin. I had three spots: on my nose, on my forehead, to the side of my mouth. And my body! It was a tree-stump wedge, straight up-and-down, soft from all the fried food we ate. Bobby hadn't said those things because he was in a mood. He'd said them because it was true.

Cosima snapped her compact open and smoothed powder over my face. "This will take the shine away."

I'd never thought about the shine before. Now that she'd said it, I could

see that it was very much a thing—*another* thing—to be taken away. She
dabbed on some more powder and, using her fingers, she spread it on the oily
bit around my nose. She was taking the shine away, but she'd never take my
face away.

I pulled my face back.

"What is it? Would you rather do it yourself?"

I shook my head.

"What, then?" She held the powder in the air. Both of them were staring
at me.

"What if it doesn't work?" I asked.

"What if what doesn't work, Jo?"

Her saying my name made it worse. A tear crept down my face like a
worm. I wiped it away but another one came. The idea of her touching me
seemed disgusting, disgusting for *her*.

She put her hands on my shoulders and looked at me through the mirror.
"You have a lovely face, Jo. Look at it."

"I don't want to look at it." I was surprised at how angry I sounded, as if I
was angry at her. She dabbed the corner of my eyes with a tissue. She and
Katie looked at each other again and I knew they felt sorry for me. Part of me
wanted them to feel sorry, if it made them stay longer. Cosima smiled at me
through the mirror.

"You know what?" she said. "I don't know a single woman who feels genuinely secure about the way she looks."

I didn't know enough women to agree or disagree. I just wanted her to
keep talking. To keep her standing there with her hands in my hair, telling me
things I needed to know.

"Look at Katie," she went on. "Katie is so gorgeous. She is so *boring*. The
number of times she calls me up to whine about how ugly she is or how fat
she is—"

"And don't forget my tiny little eyes," interrupted Katie.

"I don't believe you." I said.

"*Believe* me," said Cosima. "And me! The hours I've spent going on about
my big butt and my split ends and everything else you can think of. . . ."

"Yeah," I said. "Except it isn't true, is it?"

"It *was* true," said Katie. "You didn't know her when she was a teenager."

"I was a mess," agreed Cosima. "I'd much rather look like you than the way
I looked then."

All three of us said nothing, just looked at one another.

"Is it all right for us to go on?" Cosima asked.

"I suppose so."

Katie picked up another compact and snapped it open. The air was tin-
gling again, the sweet smells coming back to me.

"Close your eyes."

I closed them. While Katie did my lids, Cosima played with my hair. She clipped it and unclipped it, trying to squeeze the wiry mush into some kind of shape. Sometimes she pulled it a little, trying to get through the knots. "When was the last time you combed your hair?"

"I don't know." I didn't say that I never combed it. I sort of shoved it around with water, the way Bobby did.

"The next time you take a shower, put a lot of conditioner on it, but don't rinse it out, and when you get out of the shower, just comb it through. It'll take the frizz out."

I tried to look at myself but Cosima pushed my head down to finish my hair. It didn't hurt when she brushed now. In fact, my head and scalp felt glorious, full of tingle. When she was done, Katie pushed my head up and started on my lashes. They were almost competing over which part of me to do next.

"You have your father's eyes, don't you?" asked Katie. "Lovely Irish eyes. He's a bit of all right, your dad."

"He is totally cute," said Cosima.

It felt funny, them saying Bobby was "cute" or "a bit of all right." I realized I wasn't mad at Bobby anymore.

Cosima took a Swiss Army knife out of her pocket. She pried loose the tiny scissors. "May I?" She held the scissors up to my hair. "Just a trim . . ."

"Anything you want."

She shaved a little hair away from the top, to give me a fringe. Katie stood back with her arms folded. "You're not bad at this, Cossy."

"I never even thought about this stuff," said Cosima. "Until I started gigging."

At the word *gigging* there was a knock on the door.

"Three minutes, Cosima." His voice was muffled, but I could hear whose voice it was. Cosima picked up a lip pencil and started to paint the outside of my lips.

The knock came again. "Did you hear me? They need to do a sound check for 'Crash.'"

"I love 'Crash,'" I said. "We were just listening to it today."

But Rick's knocking and yelling had made Cosima quiet. She started to fill in my lips. Suddenly the door opened, and Rick's head was in it, handsome and horrible.

"Fucking hell, Cosima, you haven't changed or anything!"

"This is a *ladies' room,* Rick. I'll be there in a minute."

Rick just stared at her.

"*I'll be there in a minute.*"

He slammed the door behind him.

"Things okay with you two?" Katie whispered.

"Well," said Cosima, "you know."

Katie nodded, but I didn't know.

Katie started going through a big bag. She held up a top. "Try it on."

The top was black and skimpy and looked as if it would barely fit over my arm.

"It won't fit." I could feel myself getting angry, holding this scrap of a thing I was meant to shrink myself into. "I'm too big."

Cosima pushed open the door to one of the stalls. "Go in there and try it on, and if you don't like the way it feels, you don't have to model it for us."

I went into the cubicle. I was sure that I would tear it, but it went easily over my head, stretching over my arms, my shoulders, and waist. It was silky on my skin, like nothing I'd ever worn.

Katie and Cosima were waiting for me when I came out. They turned me to the mirror so that I could see what they'd made of me.

My eyes were bigger and bluer. My lips were red and as shiny as stream water. My hair looked longer, pinned on top with a red cloth rose, wisps of it coming down. Katie's top held my waist in and my chest up, like a firm hand. My breasts looked like breasts and not just swellings.

I didn't look like me at all.

Katie took off two of her bangles and put them on my wrist. She took off the overshirt she was wearing, a green silky shirt. She slid it over me, one arm at a time, and tied it across my waist in a loose double knot.

"You look *amazing*," said Cosima.

"Do you think so?"

"*Smashing!*" said Katie.

There was a pounding on the door. "Two fucking minutes!"

Cosima grabbed her bag and shoved her cosmetics into it. She kissed Katie and kissed me and said, "See you out there," and before we could wish her luck, she had gone.

I wondered if I was beautiful yet. I wondered if I was, like the girl in her song, *the most beautiful girl in this one-legged, arse-backward, tumbleweed town.* I knew that if I saw myself on the road as I was now—if I saw myself with my thumb out—I would ask Bobby to stop for me. I would want to give me a lift somewhere.

I didn't look eighteen. Sixteen, maybe. And yet nobody stopped me when I walked into the club. The man at the ticket desk didn't even charge me, probably because he'd seen me with the band. I was almost disappointed. I wanted everyone to look.

Meg's Borderline was as dark as a cave and full of little wooden tables, each lit by a candle in a Chianti bottle. Folk music played on the stereo, one woman's voice, all slow and serious. I couldn't find Bobby. I had been in the ladies' room for more than twenty minutes and I hadn't even wondered where he had got to, and now he'd wandered off. When my eyes adjusted to the candlelight, I saw his anorak across the pub, at a table next to mine. Both anoraks were folded over the chairs like people waiting for other people. Even in the dimness, they looked cheap and rubbery in a way I'd never noticed.

I had to walk by the stage to get to the table. The Goodtime Guys were setting up without Cosima. Rick was shaking a thick wire, as if he was cross with it as well. I hurried past him, keeping my eyes on his feet in their big Doc Martens. I felt a crazy energy in my chest, as if a squirrel was trapped in there. I didn't know much about him, but I knew enough to hate him.

A hand clamped down on my arm. It was Sean, the keyboard player who'd reminded me how small I was. I sucked my stomach and my bum in, preparing myself for another insult.

"You look fabulous." His own eyelashes were thick with blue glitter and I wondered if Cosima had helped him as well. "Doesn't she, Rick? Doesn't she look *fabulous?*"

Rick glanced down at me, then went back to what he was doing. He was smiling, as if my makeover made him want to laugh. Cosima came onstage then, with her fiddle. She was wearing the best outfit I'd ever seen: a suede miniskirt and a matching top, sleeveless, with fringes in a V-shape that showed her cleavage. Around her neck hung a necklace, a cross in red and turquoise, dangling into the top of her breasts. Her face was painted and she looked unhappy. She looked like a gorgeous doll in a rotten mood.

Rick held up the wire to her, as if its being broken was her fault. She took it and plugged it into a black box. She put her hand on his cheek and said, "See, babe, it's fine." She kept staring at him, even when he turned away and tuned his guitar.

I sat down with the anoraks. On the other side of the room, Katie was sitting at her own table with her boyfriend and some friends. The blondes from the Barbican weren't there, but there were other people who drank champagne rather than beer like everyone else in here. I couldn't make out what they said, but I could hear their accents, polite Scottish ones, not rough like the Scots we met on the road.

Bobby still wasn't anywhere. I wondered if I still looked as good as I had in the ladies' room. I could see why girls carried tiny mirrors to check themselves all the time. I felt as if my new face could slide away, leaving the old, plain one. I would never let my face be naked again.

A spotlight lit the stage. An announcer said, "And now, without further ado, all the way from Texas, Liverpool, and London, will you please give a warm Glaswegian welcome to Cosima Stewart and Her Goodtime Guys!"

Everyone clapped. There were more people in here than I'd realized. I wondered if Cosima knew a lot of them, and I hoped she didn't. I didn't want to have to wait ages for her to talk to me later.

Cosima slid her bow along her fiddle, sending the first note into the room. Sean hit a chord and they all came in. I couldn't believe that Bobby was missing it, that he wasn't here at the exact moment that it kicked off.

A man came toward me. He was like Bobby but younger. He wasn't wearing a sweatshirt but a white T-shirt, his arms bare. As he got closer, he became more and more like Bobby, until he was Bobby. His eyes fell to my breasts in Katie's top. They stayed there for a moment before jerking up to my face. His eyes were pale and startled, as if he'd been stung by a bee.

"Jo."

"What? How do I look?"

"You look . . . older."

I felt older. In the candlelight, with him looking so young, I nearly felt older than he was. He set his beer down, and my Coca-Cola.

"I went out and bought a packet of them Marks & Sparks T-shirts," he said. "Three to a packet."

"Watch the band, Bobby." I gestured to the stage.

And yet when he turned to look at Cosima, a part of me wanted him to look back at me again.

When the song finished, Cosima spoke into the microphone. "I'd like to dedicate this next one," she said, "to Little Jo, the belle of the ball tonight, who's come all the way up from London to see us, with her handsome truck-drivin' daddy. You're a star, darling!"

Rick gave a mighty slam on his guitar and the band kicked into "Crash." Across the room, Katie was pointing me out, showing her friends who Little Jo was. Bobby and I looked at each other. We sang along:

> *I hear that Oxford Street been hit by a bomb last night*
> *And the Jews and Arabs still ain't given up their bloody fight*
> *And I sure am glad that Berlin Wall has come down at last*
> *But here in Skelmersdale*
> *The rain's still a-pourin' . . .*
> *I'm off to the job center while my man's home a-snorin'*
> *My toddler's got the measles and the six-year-old's annoying me*
> *   and . . .*
> *Crash! Go my dreams . . .*

Bobby was right. The second album was as good as the first, not just "Crash" but every song on it. It had needed time to simmer and now it was boiling inside us both.

CHAPTER 8

1 9 8 5

Bobby's childhood was Rosalie's favorite topic, especially when it was political. To please her, he turned the volume up on his past, making himself more of a victim of the Troubles than he was. To hear him tell it, Orange Marches had no longer just marched through the village, but right past his house. It was not a cousin who had been grazed by a plastic bullet, but Bobby himself. He even had the scar to show for it (rather than a pimple that had become infected). Most heroically, Bobby had refused an "invitation" to join the IRA. (The true story was that Bobby had once "applied," on a drunken sixteenth birthday, to a Republican acquaintance of his uncle's, and, much to his own relief, had been advised to "go on home, lad, and look after that mother of yours.")

He wasn't entirely lying. He'd seen his share of Orange Marches. He'd been an unwitting witness to bonfire nights where stuffed popes tumbled to their pyre deaths. Three times—in Kilkeel, and Kilminster, and Portadown— he'd met gangs of boot boys who called him *taig* and threw sticks and bottles at him. But most of the time, the worst of the Troubles was filtered through newspapers and television. Secretly, he was envious of the more downtrodden Catholics from Ardoyne or the Bogside or the Falls. His own village, the farming community of Drum, was not without bigotry, but it was expressed without violence and mainly in the marching season, when his otherwise benign Protestant neighbors dressed up for the 12th of July. (Mr. Anderson even banged the Lambeg drum at the back of the march; Mr. Anderson, whose nice wife Lois had taken Bobby to the hospital when he'd broken his leg.) It seemed a shame to Bobby that he had been reared in one of the most fractious corners of Europe and yet lived a life as banal as baked beans.

"Tell me again," Rosalie would say, "about the boot boys."

And Bobby would, enhancing his story every time, surprising himself with his memory for detail that hadn't happened.

What Rosalie didn't seem to like was when he talked about his actual day. Routine and work were a betrayal to her, a nuisance to their world of bed and sex and Terrible Beauties. Her own plans seemed to be forgotten, left to float around the room like dust motes. Bobby had been with Rosalie for seven months now, and for most of it, she had not even stepped out of doors.

So when Rosalie turned up at a Slow Emotion rehearsal in Dennis's garage, it took Bobby a few seconds to place her. There was something reptilian in her paleness. She had shadows under her eyes, and she'd put on weight around the hips. Her hair was straggly, with her lighter roots growing out from the darker ones. Ollie and Dennis stopped playing. They lit cigarettes and stared at Rosalie with a smirking disdain. Bobby longed to hide her.

"What have you done to her, mate?" It was Ollie, daring to claim her plainness out loud. But then he gestured, in a hoarse whisper, to her stomach. "Looks like you've got her up the duff."

It was true that she was broader than she used to be, but she wasn't *up the duff.* The fact that Ollie—gormless Ollie, in his argyle cardigan—had spotted it made it seem especially untrue.

Bobby pulled her behind the large speaker. "All right, pet? Not well?"

"No." Her voice was high, like a five-year-old's. "I think I have the stomach flu."

And yet, two hours later at the clinic, the nurse asked Rosalie how far along she was before she even undressed.

Rosalie was five months pregnant.

Back at the flat, Bobby unearthed a clean sheet his mother had given him. For the first time in six months, he changed the bedclothes. He made a cup of tea for Rosalie that she did not drink. Outside the sky was muddy. Snowflakes shot against the window and turned to instant dirty water on the glass. In the five hours they had been out (one for each month, he thought) everything had changed, even the season. Winter was upon them, and she was heavy with his child.

When Rosalie awoke, the room was different. Smoke and the smell of hash had been stripped by bleach and air freshener. Bobby was at the counter, arranging cleaning fluids into a rigid line, like soldiers: Ajax, Vim, and Dettol (the real Dettol, in yellow). She was surprised he'd known which ones to buy.

"Will you roll me a joint, Bobby?"

"Best not." He had changed his sweatshirt and brushed his hair. He sat beside her, but he did not merge into her. He held her wrist as a doctor would.

"Listen," he said. "We never used any—watchmacallit—contraception? We never used any."

"You're Catholic."

"I'm not *that* fucking Catholic."

"We were careless."

"We were careless, aye, but given that we were the both of us careless, I mean, is it possible that we weren't careless?"

"What are you saying, Bobby?"

He hesitated. "What if we wanted it? What if we wanted this to happen?"

Rosalie was surprised. To Bobby, life seemed a random, sleepy place. Feelings were fine; he could talk about his black moods for as long as he had them. But when it came to what lay beneath, he was mute. "Too much psychology for me," he would say when she tried to analyze his darkness. Yet here he was, spouting "psychology" without her help.

"If we wanted it," she asked, "how come I managed to get this pregnant without either of us noticing?"

Bobby raised his chin, and she knew he was thinking about it. "I don't know."

She thought of how her mother, who was a psychologist, might answer her question. *A person struggles with ambivalence. A person may want two things, and be caught in the space between them.* But this kind of thinking was new to Bobby, who thought the unconscious was just something that happened when you slept.

"You're not very big," he said finally. "You don't look all that pregnant. The nurse said the fetus might be smaller than normal."

"Which means I might be able to have a normal abortion. They won't have to induce me."

Bobby stood up at the word *abortion*.

Rosalie had had an abortion two years ago. She had found the experience quite pleasurable. She'd awakened, still woozy from the anesthetic, in a tangerine-colored room with a melee of similarly relieved girls in single beds. Together they had watched *General Hospital* and eaten Double Stuf Oreo cookies and cheerfully avoided the topic of sex.

Bobby was back at the counter. He tilted the Dettol to one side and back again. The top wasn't screwed on properly, and it looked like it could go everywhere.

"What are you thinking?" As soon as she'd asked it, she knew it was a stupid question. Asking men what they thought only made them think of nothing.

"Nothing," he said, but when he turned toward her, a tear was running down his cheek. "It's *your* body, so it is." He put his jacket on. "I need a bit of air."

He opened the door and went out.

Bobby never went for a "wee bit of air" if he didn't have to. Things like fresh air didn't really occur to him; everything he did conspired against it. He'd probably gone to the pub.

That was fine. It gave her time to prepare a speech for him. She couldn't have a baby. She was young. She was an artist. Her life wasn't confined to this bed, though she couldn't seem to get out of it right now. This was a wakeup call—time to crawl from her bottom drawer once and for all, to give up the grim security of Bobby's arms. She thought of the things she would do: finish college, do an extra term if she had to. She was only eighteen!

At midnight, Bobby still hadn't come back. The pubs had been shut for an hour. There was an Irish pub, further away than his local, that drew the curtains and stayed open illegally, "the auld lock-in." She hoped he hadn't gone there. If he had, he would come home drunk. He would stand at the foot of the bed, bleary-eyed and swaying, only pretending to listen and doing a bad job of it.

At one A.M., the room was twitching with his absence. She looked for his hash and couldn't find it. She rehearsed her speech out loud, but her words felt starchy in the newly bleached air. *Career* and *future* were pompous words, really. A year ago, they had been givens. Now they were like buildings too tall for her to see the tops of. What was her *career*? Photography. What was *photography*? The only pictures that came into her head were snapshots of his building, bricks holding her captive to his absence.

At two-thirty she went through the trash to see if he'd thrown away his hash. Finding nothing, she got back into bed. What if he had done something to himself? Extinguished himself, before she could extinguish their child? If only they had a phone! But who would she phone?

At three-thirty he still hadn't returned. She turned on the TV but it was only Muzak, and a picture of a little girl playing tic-tac-toe with a puppet, its button eyes blank and sinister. Some fucking country! They couldn't even gather up a few reruns to broadcast in the middle of the night!

She stood at the window in her robe, watching a figure walk into Kenneth Estate. The figure walked with a stoop, like him. With his approach, he became a fatter man with a short red Afro; not him.

She thought of her parents. They were five thousand miles away, but something like this would bring them over in a hurry. There would be raised voices and remonstrations. How could she throw her life away? Did she want to be forever connected to this man, a sweet boy, a *mensch*, but with nothing to show for himself? (And a gentile, slovenly in the way that only gentiles were, though this would not be said.)

And yet, seeing them now with their furrowed brows and shaking heads, she could only say: "I love him!"

At four o'clock he still wasn't home.

What had upset him the most? Was it the abortion? Was he "that Catholic" after all? Did he really shun his father's holy water, or did he privately revere it, which is why he'd given his father a key? Was that why he had scrubbed his room with the *real* Dettol, a store-bought holy spray, to cleanse their souls and save an Unborn Child?

She imagined him facedown in a heap of rubble on the Isle of Dogs. She imagined him floating in the Thames.

The dawn leaked through the blinds. Her eyes stung with exhaustion but she wouldn't close them. If the abortion bothered him, it wasn't because of fathers or Fathers. It was because of his mother. His face changed at the sound of her name. He would not murder the grandchild of Josephine Pickering.

Rosalie could imagine him with a child. She could see his big, ruddy hands, adept at driving, at making cups of tea, turning to diapers, baby formula, the construction of cribs and playpens.

It was five A.M. The reek of bleach remained, but there was nothing of him. Her skin was dry. Her hair was dry. She felt herself shrivel and harden like a sponge ignored by the tap. Why had she been so flippant? Couldn't she see that the two of them—the three of them—might be, at last, totally filled, fully fed?

She didn't know what time it was when she fell asleep. She felt him warming himself against her back, smelling of pavement but not of drink. She spooned herself inside his body.

"I want to have it," she said.

"What's that?" he asked, though she knew he'd heard.

"I want to have it. And I want you to marry me."

He lay still, and then his arms tightened around her. They lay in their own fetal station, marinating in slow arousal, before making love for the rest of the day.

CHAPTER 9

2001

Cosima's fourth album came out on my fifteenth birthday, the fifteenth of April. For the launch, she was doing a bigger gig than she'd ever done before, a proper concert in a stadium with a warm-up band and everything.

The launch, however, was in Texas.

Cosima and Her Goodtime Guys were releasing their latest album in America. It wouldn't even be in the English shops for another four months. There was an article about it in *Country UK*, as well as a picture of the band leaning on the sign for Route 66, and the heading SCOTT DIDIUS TALKS TO

COSIMA AND HER GOODTIME GUYS ABOUT FRIENDSHIP, LOVE, AND MAKING IT IN
AMERICA. The article was three pages long, but it didn't say much about love or
friendship. Scott Didius seemed mostly interested in making it in America, as
if England was just a place to rehearse in and America was where the real
show was. Cosima said that the band had struggled to find a market over
there. I didn't like the article, with its talk of "market" and "over there." The
band had started in England after all, and they wrote songs about England as
well as Texas and Kentucky and California.

Bobby and I talked about America sometimes. I said I wanted to go there
when I was cross with him, but really I didn't feel much of a need to go. I felt
as if we'd nearly been there anyway. It wasn't to do with Rosalie, who was
nothing to do with us. And it wasn't just because of our music. Nearly every
time we turned on the television, we'd be staring at cops in New York or black
boys on crack or white girls with anorexia in Minnesota or somewhere. It was
hard to avoid America no matter where you were so long as you had a telly.

We looked up Texas in Bobby's atlas. "You could fit the whole of Britain
into that," he said.

The only atlas I really liked was the *Motorist's Atlas of Britain,* with its red
for small roads and green for the main arteries, and beige and white shadings
for towns and villages that even we had never see the whole of, making Britain
seem big to me. In the atlas proper, Britain was a just a pear-shaped island, its
craggy edges sealing us off from the sea and the rest of the world.

It wasn't just the Texas launch that bothered me. I didn't like it happening
on my birthday. In the past we'd let the road decide what to do for my birthday. My thirteenth birthday was easy. We were on a job in Alton, so we went
to Alton Towers to ride the roller coasters. On my fourteenth we were in
Tambill, Suffolk, so we ended up in a church hall watching a local band called
the Outlaws of King's Lynn. They weren't very good, but the old farmers
were funny, line dancing with their wives. They all wore black satin jackets
with tigers sewn on their backs and the words TAMBILL TIGERS. The people
weren't all that friendly—Suffolk people weren't—but we enjoyed it anyway.
Bobby didn't even mind the warm beer and we bought half a dozen cheese-
and-onion rolls for only 35p apiece.

Two days before my fifteenth birthday I told Bobby I didn't want to leave
it to the road this time. I wanted to plan something to make up for my not being at the launch. I wanted us to go to dinner, to a proper place. On the CB
we'd heard some drivers talking about a steakhouse called the Old Moat, three
miles from Worthing Wellton. Bonsai Brian, a driver we knew from Glouces-
tershire, had taken his wife there for their anniversary. He said the place was
"dead smart, with seats soft enough to sleep on, and it don't break the bank."
I even rang the restaurant and booked, which was something I'd never done.

There was one more thing.

"If we're going out for a smart dinner," I said, "I want a new outfit."

Bobby was making good money compared to what he used to make, but we still shopped as though we didn't have much. So far I'd made do with the little things. I had enough makeup to wear it every day. At the end of the Glasgow gig, Cosima had given me a cowboy hat. It was too big on me, but if I kept my head tilted back, I could get away with it. Bobby bought me a pair of cowboy boots to match. But as for dressing up, I had nothing apart from Katie's green silk top. And I had grown five inches in the past year.

On the morning of my fifteenth birthday we went to the Brent Cross Shopping Centre. Not in the mood for shopping—because he never was—Bobby would have been happy to sit on the second floor of the mall all day, smoking fags and reading the *Mirror* while the shoppers milled around him.

Today I didn't mind him stalling, because it gave me a chance to look at the shops we didn't usually go to: Jenny K. Next. Head Girl. Benetton. Bliss. Every window display made me think I ought to be wearing what the mannequin wore; *this* miniskirt or *those* boots or *that* belt. I held my own private survey, watching the prettiest girls to see which shops they went into the most. A lot of them went into Jenny K.

I stood over Bobby. He sucked on his cigarette to get the final juice out of it, and stubbed it out in the stand-up ashtray.

"Right then, Jo? Marks 'n' Sparks, is it?"

"Marks & Sparks" was short for Marks & Spencer, which was where we did most of our shopping. We sat across from it now, the biggest shop in the mall, with an entrance so wide I could see to the back. I looked in and saw two granny types helping a fat little girl try on a purple cardigan. I could tell which was the real granny because the other one had the M&S tag on, but they could have swapped places, they were so similar. Even the little girl looked old.

"I want to show you something, Bobby." I pulled him up to the window of Jenny K. The mannequin wore a plastic miniskirt and a top with her midriff showing. Bobby was blank, as if he'd never seen a girl in a miniskirt.

"Wouldn't be too well made, that stuff, would it?"

"How would you know?"

"Jo, you're not really built— I don't think you're quite the right build for—"

"I'm not going to buy that *particular outfit*."

In fact, I *had* hoped to try on the skirt, but he'd ruined it for me. Without asking him, I went into the shop, and he had to follow. Straightaway I saw two dresses and a pair of trousers I liked the look of.

The dressing room was open with no separate cubicles. It was chattering with girls, mostly in twos and threes, in different stages of dressing and undressing. They tried on turquoise tops, pink blazers, black trousers, plastic miniskirts, tartan miniskirts, scarlet bras.

On either side of me, two of the girls, both slim, looked surprised to see each other.

"All right, Ange? I saw you in that magazine *She* the other day."

Ange was as tall as a mannequin herself, with short, dyed-red hair and slanted eyes and a sleek, unfriendly look. She wore a short skirt, high-heeled sandals, and an ankle bracelet with tiny hearts that tinkled. "Yeah, I'm going to Prague tomorrow," she said. "For the FCUK shoot."

Ange tugged off her skirt and pulled on a pair of gold trousers. She had the thinnest, longest legs I'd ever seen. My legs were three times the size of hers. I quickly pulled the first pair of trousers on.

All around us, the girls kept chatting, changing as they talked, hanging things up, slipping on things and folding old ones up; good at it, used to it. With the mirrors surrounding us, there seemed to be four times as many girls as there were.

"So we had a few days of not talking to each other at all," said one of them, "not a bloody word, until I buggered off to Santorini on my own."

"What did you fall out about?"

"Long story. *Long* story. I'll tell you over lunch."

At Marks & Spencer I took a size-twelve trousers, but these twelves weren't having any part of me. I pulled them down. One of the mirrors showed me from the back; my rippled thighs, my sausage legs. If I didn't have panties and trousers to keep my arse in, my arse looked as though it would spill everywhere.

"We were only friends out of history, you know?" said the Santorini girl. "Not for real reasons."

The first dress was complicated, with several openings and sashes. I pulled it over my head but I got stuck in the armhole. When I finally got my head through, my hair was wild and frizzy. I smoothed it down and looked around to see if anybody had seen. One girl was looking. She was on her own, and bigger than the other girls. I had a feeling that the reason she had looked at me was because she recognized me as the other bad-looking one. To get back at her, I stared at her as she tried on a short skirt. I didn't think she'd get away with it, but she did. She had a round stomach but her legs were skinny. Even she had it better than me, with her fat in better places. Another girl came up to her; she wasn't alone after all.

"That's really flattering on you, Jenna," said her friend. "That's one of them Lycra blends, isn't it?"

The next dress fit me better. It was snug on the hips, but when I tugged at it, it loosened up. I felt a rush of air around my thighs. Someone's mobile phone went.

"Yeah . . . yeah . . . great . . . wicked . . . I'll see you in town later, yeah?"

I wondered if later they would all go clubbing or to the cinema with their boyfriends. That was what they were probably here for, to buy clothes for tonight. I was also buying clothes for tonight, but I was the only one who'd be having dinner with my father in a steakhouse in Bedfordshire.

"All right, Jo? Can I see?"

Without seeing his face, his voice was loud and coarse and bog Irish. I rushed out of the fitting room. "Do you have to stand so close to us?"

He looked at me. "Not so sure about that dress, Jo."

"Why not?" I hadn't been sure myself, but his saying it made me want it.

"It looks kind of tight around your . . . hips, so it does."

"It's supposed to be like that."

"Just around your hips there . . ."

"It's a *Lycra* blend. It's supposed to be close-fitting—"

"Just round your hips there . . ."

"Stop saying 'round your hips there'! I heard you the first time. The whole shop could hear you."

"You're the one who's yelling, Jo."

I forced my voice down. "Listen," I said, "do you think I could shop on my own for a while? I'll meet you at that café upstairs, at the Place to Eat, in, say, an hour?"

"I don't know." He folded his arms. "I don't think I should give you money for a dress that's too small for you—"

"I won't buy this dress. I *agree* with you, basically, that's what I'm saying. I'll buy something else. I promise. It's *my* birthday!"

He had to say yes when I said it like that.

Bliss was on the level below. It didn't have so many bright and sparkly things, but the clothes were cheaper and there was a section for bigger-built girls, though I didn't like the idea of buying something from that section. The fitting room at Bliss had separate cubicles. I heard girls talking from somewhere, but they were hushed as if they were in a library, and their talk was of clothing, not boyfriends or friends they'd fallen out with in Santorini.

I kept thinking about the Santorini girl. I wondered what she meant, that she and her friend had only been friends "out of history"? What were the *real* reasons for being friends with someone? What I mostly wanted to know was why they'd fallen out in the first place. I never would know, because I wouldn't be having lunch with them. I thought about her other friend, the one she was shopping with now. Was she a real friend or was she out of history, too? I'd never had a friend at all, real or historical. At school, the girls didn't look so cheerful together. Most of them just stood around and whispered about other girls and looked offended all the time. A best friend one day was always a "bitch" or a "slag" the next day. The girls in Jenny K looked happier, apart from Ange, the really beautiful one. Maybe if you were that beautiful you didn't have to *look* happy. You just were.

At least this fitting room was kinder. In the tan light I didn't have as many ripples in my bottom and thighs. And when I tried the dress on from the bigger-built section, it was too big for me by far.

This wasn't even the best thing.

When I went back out to look for a smaller size, I saw the outfit. It was a suede skirt and a suede top with fringes all along it, exactly like the outfit that Cosima had worn at Meg's Borderline (apart from Cosima's being real suede and this one imitation). I took it into the cubicle. The skirt was longer on me than it was on her, but it fit. The top looked exactly the same as her top did. It even gave me a cleavage I'd never had.

But then I looked at the prices.

The skirt was £30, and the top was £24. This was £14 more than I had. I was trying to work out what to do when I felt something dig into my back. I twisted the waistband of the skirt and found the antitheft device, a clip that set off the alarm if you tried to take it without paying. And yet the top didn't dig into me at all. I ran my hands over myself in it, and there was definitely no clip. No alarms would be set off by taking it.

My pulse began to race.

I tried talking to myself as Bobby would: *Put it back, pet. We'll find you something else.*

But I didn't want something else! If I put on my normal clothes over it and walked out and got caught, I could say I'd forgot I had it on. A person could forget something like that, couldn't they?

I looked at myself in the mirror, watching to see what my reflection would do. I watched myself take the skirt off and put my jeans on. I pulled my jumper over the top. My mirror-self was slower than I was, hanging things and folding them, careful as a mother. I didn't even look that nervous; I didn't look the way I felt. But I thought of the staff in their red Bliss T-shirts, watching me through some hidden camera, waiting for me to come out so they could pounce on me. I stuck out my head to see if the sales assistant was there. She wasn't.

The queue took fifteen minutes. The salesgirls asked each person who bought something:

"Do you have a Bliss card?"

"Did you know that if you spend more than fifty pounds you get a free perfume?"

"Do you want to keep the hangers?"

When I finally got to the front, I answered the questions in advance.

"I don't want a Bliss card, and I don't need the hanger."

She rang the skirt through, took my money, and put the skirt in a bag. But just when I thought it was over, it wasn't.

"There's a top that goes with this. Have you seen it?"

"Uh . . . yes. It's too big in the chest."

"I know what you mean." She looked down at her own chest.

Leaving was the worst part. I'd seen the security guards earlier, big black men in navy suits with shiny buttons. In a moment, two of them would take my arms—one on either side—and march me back into the shop. I would be held in the back room until the policemen came, who would be whiter, smaller, and meaner than the security guards. I thought of the phrase they said on the news about criminals: "held for questioning." Josephine Pickering would now be "held for questioning." They might even send me to prison. The worst thing was the idea of Bobby's face, his startled, bee-stung face. Even yelling would be better than that, but Bobby didn't yell.

I kept my eyes on the other side of the mall. I went through the exit. The alarm in my head was so loud that I was sure I could really hear it. I jumped onto the escalator, expecting the big black men to grab me, but nobody did.

Bobby was at the Place to Eat, finishing his meal and reading his *Mirror*.

"I went for the all-day breakfast," he said. "Bit of a rip-off, so it was. One poxy slice of toast, one egg, one rasher of bacon, one sausage, one wee little pudding, baked beans, and it cost me nearly seven quid." He swallowed the last of his food and glanced at my bag. "Well. What did you get?"

"I'll show you later."

"Why not now?"

"I want to get out of here. I'm boiling up."

It wasn't a lie.

On our way to the restaurant, we passed the Worthing Welton truck stop. We'd been to most of the truck stops, though we avoided the dodgy ones when we could. We'd heard there were strippers up in West Thorrock, and once, at Wolverhampton, a prostitute ("Lot Lizard," they called it on the CB) banged on our window late one night, though she got a shock when it was me who rolled the window down. Mostly, the truck stops were just places to sleep and shower and buy a bacon buttie. I wasn't old enough to go to the bars.

Primrose Hardy, Bobby's boss, said that when I turned eighteen, she'd take me for a drink at the Worthing Welton bar and "a spot of the ol' karaoke." I wasn't mad on Primrose, though I liked her lorry well enough, a gleaming orange Magnum that she cleaned more than she cleaned herself. In my eyes, Primrose was a barely a woman. She was big and brick-shaped and she laughed at her own jokes, which weren't really jokes but things said loudly. I once asked Bobby if she was a lesbian but he said he'd never seen her out with anybody, male or female. Mostly, we saw her while getting our orders. We didn't take part in her social life, which happened in places like Worthing Welton truck stop.

We were getting near to the restaurant. I had on my new outfit, but

Bobby hadn't seen all of it because I kept my jumper on over my top, which made me feel I was still in the middle of stealing it.

The Old Moat was in a Tudor-style building with a heavy wooden door. The moment we stepped inside we were met by a stuffy smell of heat and cauliflower, but it looked fancy enough. A skinny, frowning man in a suit came up and asked if we'd booked. I said we had. He checked a list and said, "Right this way." Bobby followed him to the rear of the restaurant, but I went into the ladies' first. I took my jumper off. I brushed my hair hard to get rid of the knots. I put on Cosima's hat and touched up my face. I put my necklace on, a cross of my own that dipped into my chest. I backed up to take in the whole of me. Not bad, I thought; pretty sexy really. I looked nearly thin.

Classical music was playing when I came out of the loo. Men stared at me as I walked by. Even the host smiled at me. I tried to keep my back straight and my head back, so that Cosima's hat wouldn't fall off. I felt like the star of an American movie. I was the girl who used to be unpopular but was now transformed into a beauty queen, sailing into her school prom and about to win over the popular boy who'd taken no notice of her before.

"Jesus," said Bobby when he saw me.

"Don't you like it?"

"Oh, you look . . . dead on, but do you not want to maybe put your jacket on?"

I looked around the restaurant. It didn't look the way it had a moment ago. Really, it was a fancy version of the Little Chef. There were pictures of food on the menus, including kiddies' specials and special meals for old-age pensioners. Most of the customers were old, just staring at me the way old people did. It wasn't classical music that was playing either, but a Muzak version of "Something."

"I don't want to put my jacket on. It doesn't go with the outfit."

"But—will you not be cold?"

"Why do you have to ask it in a question? Why don't you just say, 'I'd rather you put the jacket on'?"

"Uh . . . okay, then. I'd rather you put the jacket on."

I hated my jacket, which matched nothing I owned or wanted to own, but suddenly I did want to cover myself up. There was no point in showing my cleavage off to a bunch of old people. I took my cowboy hat off as well. Bobby and I both ordered the steak special, with jacket potatoes instead of chips. Bobby ordered a Guinness and I had a Coke.

"That necklace," he said. "Where did you get that?"

"Aunt Anne gave it to me when I was nine."

"My sister Anne?"

"Who else would 'Aunt Anne' be?"

Apart from when I was a baby, I'd only met my aunts once at Christmas, six years ago. When Anne had given me the cross, I thought I'd never wear it. But now that I'd seen Cosima with her red-and-turquoise cross, this was the closest thing I had, a little cousin to her better one.

"Bit religious, isn't it, Jo?"

"I'm not wearing it in a religious way."

"But I mean, it's a bit . . . cheesy, so it is?"

"It's horrible on purpose."

"Why would you want to be horrible on purpose?"

It was getting harder and harder to talk to him. We used to have plenty to talk about. Even if we said the same things again and again, the things felt different in different places and on different days. And if it was quiet sometimes, that was fine, too, each of us tucked inside our own heads like cats in separate pools of sunlight.

I took a sip of Coke and tried to think of something to talk about. Bobby looked odd in his jacket and tie, like a man who should be sitting behind a desk in a bank. I was suddenly embarrassed that we were all dressed up. The violins in "Something" whined all over us and made it worse.

The food came. I was pleased for something to do with my hands, but the potato was mushy and the meat was tough. I wondered how the pensioners managed it, with their teeth or lack of teeth.

"What do you think of the steak, Jo? Nice, isn't it?"

The song changed. Bobby looked up, as if seeing the song in the air. " 'Sorry Seems to Be the Hardest Word,' " he said. "I used to do this with Slow Emotion."

"You've told me that a million times."

"I was just reminded again now."

"I can't imagine any of Cosima's songs being turned into Muzak."

"We weren't really a Muzak band, Jo. In fact, when we first started out, we were a country band called Dennis and the Dividers—"

"I *know*, Bobby."

He didn't say anything. I wasn't doing a very good job of keeping us talking.

"Do you think that Cosima's on right now?" I asked.

He looked at his watch. "It's only 2:45 P.M. there. She could be getting ready, though."

I thought of Cosima getting ready, halfway across the world. I took another stab at my steak. "Dad?"

"Yes?"

"Why does Britain have only one time zone? Along with Ireland? I mean, Ireland's a completely different country, and it's still in the same time zone."

"The land mass is tiny, so it is. America is vast."

"Do you think Americans think about us as much as we think of them?"

"I wouldn't say so, no."

An old couple were leaving. The old woman had a Zimmer frame and it took her five minutes just to stand. Her husband and the waiter stood behind her, their arms held up as though expecting her to fall. I looked out of the window. In the back of the restaurant, there was no fancy old-style stuff, just a block of concrete. Beyond that was the motorway.

"Bobby?"

"Mmm?"

"Can we go to Worthing Welton? The bar, I mean?"

"You're not old enough."

"I wasn't old enough to get into Meg's Borderline, but I got away with it, didn't I?"

Just then the waiter came up with a piece of chocolate cake and a candle in it. The lights went down and the waiter started singing "Happy Birthday." The pensioners joined in and Bobby sang the loudest of all. I blew the candle out and pretended to be pleased, but what I wanted was for everyone just to stop. I didn't want dessert either, even though it was my birthday. I was speedy suddenly, my hunger all jammed up. I kept glancing toward the motorway with its distant wash of cars and the lights that had gone on for nighttime.

It was early, and the bar at Worthing Welton was empty. Empty and ugly. It wasn't even as good as the bars on the ferries, with their happy lights and jukeboxes and the sea that rumbled like hunger in your tummy. It was just a tatty pub with brown-and-white carpet and ashtrays bursting with fag ends. A karaoke machine sat at the back of a low stage, like a squat, forgotten person. The only actual person, apart from us, was a big lad, his face buried in the latest *Truck & Driver.*

"Spoiled for choice," Bobby said, motioning to all of the empty tables. I found a table in the middle and I put my hat on it. Bobby rattled the change in his pocket. "What will you have, Jo? A Coke?"

"Can I get it? And can I get your Guinness as well?"

"What if they suss your age?" he asked, but he gave me the ten-pound note anyway.

A wooden sign above the bar: ALL THIS WORK IS GETTING IN THE WAY OF MY DRINKING. The barman had three chins and he wore a Leeds United football jumper. He watched *Match of the Day* from a telly fixed to the wall. I could hear the fans with their muddy voices, singing their football songs.

"Pint of Guinness, please, and a Bacardi and Coke," I said, as if I'd been ordering this for years. Still watching the football, he poured half of the Guinness and let it settle. Then he poured the Bacardi and Coke.

Bobby had given me a sip of his beer from time to time, but I knew he'd say no if I asked for my own drink. I knew that a lot of young girls drank Bacardi and Coke because Bacardi wasn't supposed to smell on your breath. I put lots of ice in it so that it looked like a normal Coke, and I took a swig to get the first taste over with. It had a sharp chemical taste that reminded me of cologne. I went back to our table.

"Cheers, pet." Bobby took a sip of his stout and leaned back in his seat. He let out a long sigh. "You know, there's no comparison. A pint in a pub beats a pint in a restaurant, every time. Got your Coke all right there? Do you want crisps or anything?"

"No. Coke is fine."

"Can I have the change?"

"It's my birthday. You have to let me keep the change."

"Uh, I don't think that's quite—"

"Bob!" I knew who it was before I saw her. Nobody else called him Bob. The guy hidden behind the *Truck & Driver* was actually Primrose Hardy. She looked bigger than ever, just a puny head on this building of a body. The only girly thing about her was her eyes, which were like the eyes of a doll, twinkly and pretty and out of place with the rest of her.

"It's yourself, Primrose," said Bobby. "Come and join us." He seemed pleased to see her. I didn't want to spend any part of my birthday with her.

"There you are, there's little Jo!" Her voice was horrible, stacked with those Somerset *rrrrr*'s that went on for miles.

"Her birthday today."

"Blimey! Tell you what, you look a good few years older than fourteen!"

"I'm fifteen," I said. "And do you have to shout?" I motioned toward the bar.

"Oh, right," she whispered, but her whisper was nearly as loud. She shoved in next to Bobby. She wasn't fat so much as wide. You could have put two of Bobby into her. It was hard to believe that Primrose was the same species as Cosima, not to mention the same sex. If every woman in the world was on a road the width of Britain, with the plainest to the east and the prettiest to west, Cosima would be in Anglesea and Primrose would be in the Fens. I tried to work out where I'd be. Tonight I might be in the middle, Midlands, maybe. I still had a way to go before reaching Cosima, especially if she kept moving. She'd gone so far west now, she'd ended up back in America.

The start of "Billie Jean" cut into my thoughts. A young lad was onstage with the karaoke machine. He turned a switch and the music stopped, hanging mid-air so that my head wanted to finish it.

Some drivers came in and took up the biggest table. Though there were only five or six of them, they drowned out the whole bar with their London accents and Geordie accents and their swearing, but Primrose didn't seem to notice. She turned the pages of her *Truck & Driver* until she found something she wanted to show us.

"'Ave a look at this."

At the top of the page it said TRUCKFEST, PETERBOROUGH. It was the usual Truckfest spread: winners standing in front of their lorries, showing off their ribbons and medals. But in this spread, Primrose was there as well, her meaty hand on her Magnum. A gold ribbon hung across the front of her lorry. She read out the caption to me, as if I couldn't read it myself: "'It's nice to win thrice! Primrose Hardy, owner of the cleanest Magnum in Britain, says you could eat off her engine!'"

Laughter broke from the table of men. One of the younger ones went up to the karaoke boy and handed him a sheet of paper. He was slim and in his twenties, and he wore tracksuit bottoms and a black T-shirt. Jutting his chin back and forth as if he was dancing, he walked back to where his mates were sitting.

Primrose was still going on about Truckfest. "You wouldn't believe how many times those judges check under the lorry to see if the bottom is clean! They wouldn't even do that to a horse in a horse show. They wouldn't be checking underneath a horse six or seven times to see if its bits are clean."

"You won, Prim," said Bobby. "That's what matters."

"The thing is, Bob, I'm always winning for best-kept owner-driver vehicle, you know what I mean? And once—this was before you came working for me— I won for best large fleet. But it'll be a cold day in hell before I get a prize for, say, best customized, and she's a handsomely put together old thing, isn't she?"

"She is, right enough."

She turned the page and showed us a lorry painted top to bottom with Madonna.

"Dutch, that bloke was. Them Europeans always win for murals and paintwork. I bet you it's a damn sight cheaper to get a paint job on the continent, that's all I can say."

"You got to admit, Primrose," said Bobby, "a lot of work went into that."

"We've got some fine murals in our very own fleet! Fickle Phil's new lorry? _Bladerunner_. One end to the other, just _Bladerunner_. You seen Tiny John's? _ET_. I mean, ET looking more realistic than the actor what played it."

A guitar twanged into the room, good and country: Hank Williams's "Your Cheating Heart." Bobby winked at me. But when the voice came in, it wasn't Hank's. It belonged to the guy who'd handed in the sheet earlier, the one in the black T-shirt. He had nice skin, smooth as if he didn't need to shave, and a cheeky face that looked as if it would find the funny side of everything.

"Fancy a drink, Primrose?" I asked.

She looked up from her _Truck & Driver_. "Uh . . . okay, I'll get a round in. What are you drinking, darling? Lemonade? Do you want some scampi fries or something?"

"I'll get it. Just give me a tenner."

Back at the bar there were quite a few men now. There were two female truckers as well, but they were as plain as flooring panels. The only glamorous female truckers I'd seen were from Europe. I didn't understand why the women didn't make more of an effort here. Sometimes Bobby let me drive at North Weald airfield. The place was always deserted, but even so, driving made me want to show myself off, to be more beautiful than I already wanted to be. If I was driving all the time, I'd always want people to look at me as I flew past them.

I got the drinks and sat back down. Primrose was still reading to Bobby from her *Truck & Driver*.

"'The new Superspace DAF gives you more room to live in.'" She looked up to see what we thought about this. "Room to live in, my arse. Room to live in if you're a welcome mat or something."

"Primrose? That you?"

"Guilty as charged." She turned around to see who it was. It was the guy in the black T-shirt, the one who'd been singing "Your Cheating Heart."

"Tom! Fucking 'ell." She batted her arm at us. "Tom, this is Bobby, and this is Jo, whose birthday it is today."

"Many happy returns, Jo," he said, and he turned to Bobby. "I seen you before, mate. You have a little girl, don't you?"

"Little girl?" asked Bobby.

"There's your 'little girl,' Tom." Primrose pointed at me.

"Oh!" Tom laughed. "I thought she was—you know—"

"You thought she was Bob's girlfriend, did you, Tom?" Primrose let out one of her mad laughs.

"Shut up, please," I said.

"Jo," said Bobby, but his own face was red.

"Sorry, mate." Tom didn't look as embarrassed as he should have looked. He looked at me. "You've grown a bit, haven't you?"

"Who are you here with, Tom?" Primrose stood up to look at his friends. "Oh, you're with that lot. There's Nick and Bonsai Brian. I'll come and join you, shall I?"

She went off with Tom. Though I'd hated having her here, she'd left a hole at our table by leaving it. Tom thinking I was Bobby's girlfriend had left a cringey feeling inside me. I didn't look at Bobby and he didn't look at me. He stuck a finger into his pint and lifted a hair out of it. "There we are, Jo," he said, which was what he said when he couldn't think of anything to say.

I got another round in. I had almost eight quid extra because Bobby kept forgetting to ask for his change. The pub was packed with people now. The windows steamed. I set our drinks on the table and sat down.

Bobby started to say something, but the singing rode right over him, rough and loud. Three guys, one of them Tom, were onstage singing "Jolene." The whole pub was singing along, apart from Primrose, who had her *Truck & Driver* open for one of the lads at her table. "Jolene" was a Dolly Parton song about a girl begging another girl to stay away from her man. Bobby looked surprised at first but then he smiled at me. I smiled back. It was funny to hear a group of men singing it.

I leaned across to him, not even caring that he might smell Bacardi on me. "Bobby?"

"Yes, pet?" His eyes were sleepy. I decided I would never be cross with him again.

"Do you remember exactly fifteen years ago? When I was born, exactly?"

He looked around for his cigarettes. He found one burning in the ashtray, and he took a drag of it. "Have I not told you before?"

"You know you haven't." He'd never told me because I'd never asked him. It wasn't something he would just bring up on his own, because it involved Rosalie. But now I wanted to hear about it.

"Well?"

A sheet of paper was shoved in front of my drink. Tom was back, standing close to me. "Pick a favorite, luv. A favorite song from the birthday girl."

"There's no way I'm singing."

"You gotta sing. House rules."

"You can't make her sing," said Bobby.

"Okay, okay. Pick a favorite, and *I'll* sing it. A little birthday gift."

The list was long and I needed to be quick about it. I'd asked Bobby a question and I didn't want him to wander off in his head. But then I saw it.

"Look, Bobby!" I held it up. " 'Rather Be.' Look!"

"So it is. Nice one."

"That's Cosima and Her Goodtime Guys. They're friends of ours." I ticked it off. I'd look forward to hearing that, even sung by a stranger who couldn't sing.

"Right you are," said Tom, and he left us alone.

"Cosima must be getting famous, right enough," said Bobby, "if she's made it to karaoke level."

"Do you think the band is on yet?"

He looked at his watch. "Sound check, maybe." I liked this, Bobby knowing about sound checks as well as the time zones of places he'd never been to, all these Bobby-type things.

"So go on," I said. "About when I was born."

"Well . . . you weren't well at first."

"Did I nearly die?"

"No, not really—"

"I did really, didn't I. Did I?" I found it exciting, that I could have nearly died.

"Like I said. You weren't well."

"Did you love me even when I was sick?"

Bobby opened his hand on the table, palm up, as if waiting to catch a ball from the air. "You were a gift to me, Jo, from the start. That's it. A gift."

"Yeah?"

"Yeah. I mean, on the day that you were born—"

The voice was so loud it hurt my ears.

"Josephine Pickering! Whose birthday it is today, is going to sing 'Rather Be,' by Cosima Stewart and Her Goodtime Guys!"

Tom was onstage. He said my name again, so close to the microphone that it was followed by a shriek of feedback. I froze. Someone was banging a pint glass on the table. I looked over and saw that it was Primrose. One of the guys joined in, and then another, and then all of them. Tom looked at me, made a "C'mere" gesture with his arm.

"Come on up here, girl!"

I shook my head.

"C'mon!"

Tom came down from the stage and grabbed my hand. Bobby stood up to face him. Tom was the taller one.

"That's not fair," said Bobby. "She said she didn't want to."

"It's just a bit of fun, mate."

"It's not fun if she doesn't want to."

Tom held his hands up, surrendering. "Okay. If you really don't want to, that's fair enough."

The start of "Rather Be" was coming on. If I didn't go up now, the song would go on without me and I would look even more stupid than I looked right now. Bobby and Tom were looking at me, waiting for me to do something. I couldn't decide, and yet suddenly, I was standing up. I was thinking, *I will not I will not*, but I was walking toward the stage. Then I was up there, facing an audience of men, so many more men than there'd been even a few minutes ago. Tom handed me the mike. I felt the Bacardi swirling in my head and circles in my eyes, like the brown and white circles in the carpet. I thought I would fall backward, but I was still standing, trying to stop the circles. The singing part was about to start. I knew the words of this song, but not one of them came to me now. On the screen, the words were up there anyway, with a bopping ball to tell me where to go.

> *I'm a grungy stranger to your flawless beauty . . .*
> *Trailer trash to your Italian sports car, so classy and quaint . . .*
> *I'm out of here tonight, and you'll hear no more from yours*
>   *truly . . .*
> *Cause I'd rather be the gal that I am*
> *Than the man that you ain't!*

I could hardly get my voice out. The music sounded slower than it did on the record. The men were all clapping along slowly, but Tom was looking worried. My voice went altogether and the rest of the verse played itself without me. Tom came up beside me and whispered in my ear, "Take a deep breath."

"What?"

"Deep breath!"

I took a deep breath. I felt my body unclench slightly. I was extremely hot. I let my jacket fall to the ground, leaving my arms and shoulders bare. All of the men cheered. A wave of cool air surfed along my arms. I waited through the fiddle part and came back in on the chorus:

> Give me some rollin' tobacco and a bottle of cheap Frascati
> Give me a stained mattress, my bad old tomcat, a tumbledown
> shack and a bucket of paint

I let my hips loosen. I started walking up and down the stage—not quite dancing but strutting, sort of.

> All the riches I need are right here in my body
> And I'd rather be the gal that I am than the man that you ain't!

I looked into the eyes of men I didn't know. I was doing it. I was singing "Rather Be" even before she was tonight, and the men were all smiling at me, except for Bobby. Bobby was looking down into his pint. I tried not to look at him. If he wasn't here, I could really let rip. I could dance for the boys, the way she did.

I started on the third verse. *Just don't look,* I told myself, but this only made me look again. His eyes were flashing round the room now, as if searching for someone else he knew.

He stood. He came toward me. My throat seized up and I fudged a lyric. I had never been frightened of my father, but now I felt myself freeze, waiting for him to arrest me in some way. I didn't know whether to sing or stop or what. There was a sudden shattering of glass, and then his voice: "Sorry, mate, so sorry about that."

He'd bumped into somebody's table. He knelt to the floor, gathered up some broken glass and, still holding the bottom of the glass, headed for the door. From the back, he looked like an older man, ashamed of himself for spilling another man's drink. His jacket bunched up at his neck, a hump of air where it should have been smooth.

The boys went mad when I finished, but I could only think of Bobby, who was no longer there. I wondered if he'd cut himself on the glass. I thought of him walking around the car park, his shoulders stiff against the cold. He hadn't gone dark since before Glasgow. If he went dark now, it would be my fault, and because it was my fault, he might not share it with me, or tell me about it. He might even walk away and not let me know how long he'd be. I ran out to look for him.

He wasn't in the car park or the lorry.

I went into the ladies' room and splashed water on my face. Looking at my reflection pumped me up again. My hair looked wild and long, as if it had grown since I'd sung that song. My face was flushed. I really did look like "the most beautiful girl in this one-legged, arse-backward, tumbleweed town, with lips a cherry pink, breasts ripe and winter white." Of course, that girl also had "a head as scrambled as a fun fair," but I didn't think about that now. I wished Cosima was here to see me tonight. But then, if she was, I wouldn't be the most beautiful girl, because she would be.

Tom was waiting for me outside the ladies'. His face was pink and he smelled of lager. He didn't say anything. He took my hands and eased me back against the wall. I'd never been kissed before. There were girls younger than me who not only kissed men but had sex with them, but the idea of a kiss, tongue and all, was still disgusting to me.

Yet there was something natural in the way he put his hands on the sides of my face. He didn't put too much tongue into my mouth, just the tip of it against my lips. When our tongues touched, it wasn't disgusting, just warm. It made me feel like I was in the middle of everything, a girl that things happen to.

"Josephine?" The cold air rushed in from outside. Bobby was watching us. I pushed Tom away. I didn't know how much Bobby had seen, but from the way he looked at me now, I thought he'd seen it all.

"I was just looking for you," I said.

His eyes slid away from my face, and I knew he didn't believe me.

I lay in bed in Bobby's old T-shirt, the one with HARDY'S HAULAGE on it and a picture of a lorry just like ours. We were parked close to the bar. I could still hear the shouts and singing from inside. The sweat had cooled on my arms and neck though my mouth tasted of Bacardi and Tom's warm tongue. I kept thinking of the song I'd sung. I imagined myself singing it again and again and each time I was better than before. I'd be doing more of a dance or even playing the fiddle, cheered on by Tom and the lads.

Bobby lay below me, smoking.

"Are you angry with me?" I asked. It was a strange question, because I'd never asked it.

He didn't answer straightaway. I wondered if he'd fallen asleep with his cigarette burning. I peered over to look.

"Why would I be angry?" he asked.

I thought about the things I'd done, all in one day. If I hadn't stolen the top, I wouldn't have worn that outfit. If I hadn't worn the outfit and looked sexy, I wouldn't have been forced to sing and get all that attention, and I wouldn't have been kissed.

"I don't know," I said.

Bobby just smoked.

"You were telling me about when I was born," I said.

"I wasn't telling you. You asked."

I heard him put his cigarette out, a *ssssht* against the ashtray.

"Will you let me drive tomorrow?"

He turned over on his side.

"Please don't go dark now," I said. "Please don't do that."

But there would be no more talking tonight.

CHAPTER 10

1986

Bobby and Rosalie were on time for the registry office, but the registry office wasn't on time for them. They had to sit on a bench outside of Parking Permits and Fines, waiting for the wedding before them to finish. It did finish, finally, to lusty applause and a racket in some foreign language. The doors burst open and a dozen dark-eyed children threw confetti, making a blizzard of the bride and groom.

"No confetti inside!" The registrar, a ponderous West Indian woman, stood in the doorway with her hands on her hips, like a chaperone on a school outing.

"Save your confetti for *outside*, please!"

The wedding party ignored her.

"Greek, are they?" Bobby whispered to Rosalie.

"Or Turkish, maybe."

The registrar approached Bobby and Rosalie. She held a large clipboard. "Pickering? Chapkis?"

"That's us."

"Where are your witnesses?"

"Witnesses?"

"You need two witnesses."

Bobby and Rosalie looked at each other. It hadn't occurred to them to invite other people.

"Well," said the registrar, "you'd better go and get some."

On the steps of Camden Town Hall, the Greeks or Turks were shouting their farewells to a convoy of honking cars. The newlyweds gave a long honk and turned onto Marylebone Road, curly pink ribbon trailing from their car.

Bobby approached one of the waving couples.

"Excuse me? We were wondering where youse lot were from? Greek, are you?"

"Ask them about the *thing* first, Bobby!" said Rosalie. "We haven't got time to—"

"We're not Greek," said the man. "We are Armenian."

"Oh, aye, Armenian. That's interesting—"

"*Bobby!*"

Bobby looked at Rosalie and back at the Armenians. His face was red. "Look, we were also wondering, me and the girlfriend here, we're supposed to be married—"

"Like *right this minute*—" cut in Rosalie.

"Aye, right this minute—"

"And you need witnesses," said the Armenian woman.

Bobby laughed. "Aye!"

"Okay," said the man. "But first we clarify—we are not Greek."

"Of course. My mistake."

Satisfied that the error had been righted, the Armenian couple followed them inside. They introduced themselves as Burt and Lisa.

"Those are your names?" said Rosalie. "Burt and Lisa?"

"Sort of," said Lisa. "You might not be able to say our real names."

The walls of the registry office were paneled in dark wood. Two maritime landscapes hung on the wall above a heavy, lacquered desk. The registrar stood behind the desk, on which lay a signature book and a vase of pale flowers that looked fake but weren't. She read from a sheet in front of her, and when it was over, they all signed the certificate, and a clip of Beethoven's *Pastoral* piped into the room. The wedding was over in twenty minutes.

Out on the steps again, Bobby took a photograph of Rosalie with Burt and Lisa. Rosalie took a photograph of Bobby with Burt and Lisa. Finally, a stray Armenian from the former wedding took a photograph of the four of them. When it was time to say good-bye, Lisa hugged the bride and groom. Burt shook their hands. The Armenians stayed on the steps and waved to the newlyweds as they had waved to their cousins half an hour earlier. Heartened by the sendoff, Bobby and Rosalie felt like any just-married couple walking down Judd Street, on their way to a honeymoon in Majorca or the Canaries, their immediate future mapped out through traveler's checks and travel guides and itineraries for rail and sky.

In fact, there was no honeymoon, but there were plans. Bobby had just received his Class 1 license for driving an articulated lorry. His first job—his "first tip," he called it—was on the very next evening. Bobby wanted Rosalie to come with him to Hardy's Haulage in Colindale, to meet his boss and his lorry.

"Sure, we'll stop at Mothercare on the way," he said. "Buy a cot and a pram for the wean."

Rosalie thought it was cute that he said "wean," as well as "cot" and "pram," but she wasn't in the mood to shop for them, any more than she was in the mood to stand around a parking lot in the cold. But Bobby was making a proper day of it, as if this *was* a honeymoon. In Mothercare, he lingered in every aisle, asking Rosalie questions she had no answers to. Which pushchair was the most durable? Was it better to buy wood or plastic? Which cot was easiest to assemble?

"They're all the *same*," she said.

Bobby chose a blue-and-red cot that he would have to assemble himself. He looked forward to laying out the parts until the flat was a clutter of cheerful plastic pieces, before jigsawing them into a structure as bright as his new lorry would be.

Afterward, their arms stretched by unruly shopping bags, they made their way to Hardy's Haulage. They walked slowly onto the lot, dwarfed by a fleet of lorries as long as city blocks. Rosalie shrank back, as though one of them would escape. It would only take a wheel of a truck like that to squash her.

"Have a look at these, Rose."

But it was the trucks, with their boxy, shiny red faces, that seemed to be staring at her.

"See these Magnums? Aren't they lovely?"

"Is this the kind of truck you want to buy?"

"Ah, no. Didn't I tell you?"

Bobby had been doing his homework. Copies of *Truck & Driver* were piling high by the side of the bed. He liked Scanias the best. He even loved the word Scania, the only Swedish word he'd ever said.

"I'll tell you what, Ro," he said now. "What I really fancy is one of them Scania R143 Streamliners. In fact, we saw one yesterday, near the registry office, do you remember?"

She shook her head.

"Dead comfy, better than a caravan. I could take you and the wean anywhere with me, no problem."

"How much do they cost?"

"How much do they cost?" Bobby had a habit of repeating the question before answering it. She used to like it, but right now, with her nausea coming in waves from the bottom of her stomach, she was overwhelmed by irritation.

"They're dear, all right," he said. "Forty, fifty grand."

He'd never make that kind of money, and even if he did, she didn't like the idea of riding around Britain in one of these things. All she could think of was the noise of the road, and the effort of trying to sleep over it.

The office was easy to miss, a square, skin-colored building that could have been a public lavatory. Primrose Hardy, the boss, filled what space there was. Primrose was a mammoth woman with a tattoo of a lizard on her left shoulder, a scar on her forehead, and ruddy cheeks like the cheeks of a happy person in a child's drawing. She gave Bobby's hand a hearty shake.

"Good to know you, Bob. Have you met her, then? She's on the far end. Waiting for you."

"*Who is* waiting for him?" asked Rosalie, who would not be ignored.

"This is my wife," said Bobby. "This is Rosalie."

Primrose nodded at Rosalie. Her eyes fell to her swelling stomach.

"How far along are you, darling?"

Rosalie held up six fingers.

"Six. Very good. Now, Bob, c'mere to my desk while I sort you out."

Primrose talked him through his wages and his first drop-off point. "You'll be tipping at Preston tonight, Purfleet tomorrow. You know what I mean by 'tipping'—that's unloading."

"Aye, I know what tipping is."

"And don't be getting any ideas about that tacko. That tackograph stays where it is. Last year we got in trouble because this tosser we had working here, he was fiddling with the fuses to free up the tackograph."

Bobby blinked. Now, what the fuck was a tackograph? He'd heard the word quite a few times while training, but he couldn't think of it now.

Primrose was studying him. "You from Belfast, mate?"

"Antrim."

"How do you find England? Do you find it friendly like?"

"Eh . . ."

"I love the old hills of Antrim myself—for driving, that is. Is there much trouble up there at the moment?"

"Not much." Apart from the baby, Bobby had thought of little but his first lorry. He'd imagined the first touch of chrome, a particular sheen in its texture that would let him know it was his. What he had not expected was a woman boss with a West Country accent who would hulk above him and ask him so many questions. And where had Rosalie had got to?

Primrose took him to the far end of the yard. She opened the door of a lorry and told him to climb on up. This lorry was bigger than the one he had trained in, and the steps felt narrow under his feet.

"Must be dead slippery," he said, "in the rain."

"Up you go," she said simply.

Once in the cab, everything was wrong. He was too low in the seat, too far from the windscreen. He looked down at his new boss.

"Is there no air suspension in the seats?"

"It's only them new lorries that have that. Old-style lever you got there. Pull it back to move the seat forward."

He did as he was told.

"Pull that other one to raise it."

He couldn't find the other one. She climbed up on the sideboard and the truck leaned dangerously with her weight. She yanked the level up.

"Good, lad. Reverse."

"Reverse?" He had the key in the ignition but he did not turn it. "It's just that it's a wee bit different from the one that I—"

She turned his fingers on the key and started it up for him, then leapt down, allowing him to shake back to center.

Reversing was the worst. He was sure he would scrape the other trailers as he squeezed himself out of the row. When he was finally in the clear with space around him, he wiped the sweat from his forehead. He spotted Rosalie. She was sitting on the steps of the office, odd-shaped shopping bags all around her. He was about to call out to her when his door swung open. Primrose was on the sideboard again, her neck and head strong against the sky.

"Okay. Remember: tipping in Preston tonight. Job's a carrot."

"Job's a what?'

"Piece of piss. Easy-peasy."

She handed him the order sheet with the address on it. He looked at it, but it was hard to concentrate with her staring at him.

"You ready, then?" she asked. "You know where you're going, when you're going, and why you're going?"

Bobby nodded.

"That's more than you can say for the rest of us!" Primrose laughed. Bobby tried to work out the joke in it. She leaned into him.

"And make sure that woman of yours is eating her greens. She don't look too well." She leapt down and went back to her office. She reminded him of a rubber soldier doll he'd played with as a boy; bouncy and unbreakable no matter how hard you threw it.

He breathed in the smells of the cab, of well-worn leather and diesel and a faded whiff of someone else's cigarettes. He sought out Rosalie in the side mirror. From this angle, she looked small and lopsided. She looked as though she was partly lying down. He didn't like her to lie on the cold pavement, not with the baby inside her. He wouldn't say anything because she would only yell at him, the way she did these days. It was true that she didn't look healthy, but when had she? He had seen her look good, or even great, but health had never come into it.

That night he drove to Preston. It was alarming, at first, to be so high up off the road. He felt he could fall from his perch into some whirling pandemonium. Yet as the minutes stretched into miles and hours, he began to enjoy the rhythm of the road. He hadn't worked out how to speak into the CB yet, but he liked the burbling of other drivers, their voices bronchial and intimate inside the box. He liked the anonymity, the towns and truck stops: South Mimms and West Thorrock and Night Owl. Evil Knievels were motorcycle cops. Puddle-jumpers were vans, or rigid lorries. Weekend gypsies drove caravans. Car drivers were skateboards (or simply arseholes in cars).

The lorry had a sound system, a good one. At home he no longer played his music. Rosalie didn't like it. He'd learned to use the headphones, to shrink the songs to the space between his own ears, and even then, he had to watch the volume. Nine miles north of Watford, he slipped in the Dale Mitchell Band. The banjo came in—a "can't wait" pluck to it—and, right on its tail, the nasal exuberance of Dale's voice, fueling the flat English landscape, making it mighty, making it *big*. Bobby raised his seat a notch. Seeing a police car, he turned the music down, thinking he'd be arrested for simply enjoying himself. The police car slid by, indifferent. Bobby laughed at his own caution and turned the volume up:

> *Now honey, I'm just barely standing*
> *I work like a dog, but you keep demanding!*
> *I aint' got no money, I don't have no fun*
> *I'm all fed up, my honey, and I'm going on the run!*
> *Don't need no bags*
> *Don't need no hat*
> *Got a tank full of gas, and I ain't coming back*
> *Oh sweetie-baby, you'll never lose a better man than me!*

The sky was gleaming. The road wasn't just England, with its tidy patches of greenery, its roadworks and fumes and Granada service stations. It was the space in between. It was everywhere, and all of it. It was the silvery foreverdom on every side of him.

———

Rosalie was throwing up into the kitchen sink. There was such fury in her retching that it seemed as if she would expel the baby itself into the yellow mash below her.

"Rosalie! What the fuck is going on!"

Bobby, just back from Exeter, didn't take his coat off. He grasped the handle of the new pushchair he had made, and held it so hard that his knuckles went white.

Rosalie crawled on her knees toward him. The smell of puke and booze rose from her like smoke.

She clamped her hand onto his and tried to push the pushchair across the room. The pushchair crunched along an inch or two, but Bobby kept his hand on the handle.

"Wipe your face," he said.

She looked around for something to wipe herself on. He went to the counter, threw a roll of kitchen towels at her. Still on her knees, she dabbed at her mouth, missing most of the puke.

"Stand up." His voice seemed strange even to himself, this flatness of anger. She lunged at him, somewhere between a strike and an attempt to get him to hold her. Managing neither, she collapsed. Bobby lifted her onto the bed. He picked up his headphones and his Walkman. He sat near the door.

"Come to bed with me, Bobby."

"I will not."

She flipped onto one side, then the other.

"You brought it on yourself," he said. "Drinking. How could you be *drinking?*"

She groaned. She flipped onto her back and closed her eyes.

Bobby put on his headphones, but he didn't push the PLAY button. He looked at Rosalie's stomach. Still not much there. He didn't know if he was imagining it, but it looked as though there was even less there than a week ago, when he'd done his first job to Preston. But that was ridiculous; you couldn't puke a baby up! Still, she could have hurt it, taken bits out of it. It could come into the world with toes missing, a leg missing, part of its head. It wouldn't walk or talk or even think. What would he do then? What would Rosalie do? Drink, probably. Take drugs. He'd have to quit his job, look after the pair of them. He imagined the three of them in day-care centers, in hospitals, in that dole office down the Mile End Road, grim as a gulag.

He pressed PLAY and turned the volume way up.

Rosalie was in the desert, but she didn't know which one; she could have been in Nevada, she could have been in Israel. She was walking and starving. Walking and starving and hollow with thirst. She passed an oasis but the water had dried. She tore off a piece of cactus but the spikes made her mouth bleed. She came to a deserted Texaco station. From one of the defunct gas pumps, a song was playing: "There's So Much You've Yet to Learn About My World, Little Girl." She opened her eyes but the song went on; a diminished version, as though played down the phone over a great distance.

Bobby was sitting in the chair, listening to Ronnie Ray Jergin on a pair of headphones. He had played Ronnie Ray for her when they first got together. He'd made her read the sleeve notes on the album. She'd tried to like it, but really, Ronnie Ray was just a wizened old codger with a voice as rough as a bad road. Sometimes, Bobby put his mouth to Rosalie's stomach to sing "There's So Much You've Yet to Learn About My World, Little Girl."

"Why do you assume it's a girl anyway?" Rosalie had asked.

"It's only a song."

But that was just it. Bobby had shrunk her life to the size a song, and a dirge at that; not even the whiskey-swilling, gun-toting variety. As it said on the sleeve notes, Ronnie Ray had found God. He'd given up the bottle. And Bobby wasn't drinking much either these days, "to keep her company," he said. A cruel thing, this abstinence was. If only he would come to bed right now, she could do without the whiskey or the hash—or at least, with less of it.

His eyes were shut, and he was mouthing the words. He sat by the door with his jacket on, as though he would leave at any moment. She went to him, wiping her mouth to make sure there was no vomit left. She put her arms around his neck. He twitched. She kissed him on the lips. He opened his eyes, but he didn't kiss her back.

"Please," she said. "Please make love to me."

From his headphones leaked the words "Lady, you only think you know me . . . but Jesus knows I've too many sad stories for your pretty little head to hold . . ."

She fumbled behind his head. She tried to pull the headphones away but they were tangled in the back.

"Turn it off," she said. "Please turn it off."

He didn't turn it off. He looked waxy and inanimate. She wanted him to fuck her right now, fully clothed, composed as a cop making an arrest. He would never do it; he would never inflict such sordid authority on the baby. She sat in his lap.

"It's been a month."

"It hasn't."

"It *has*."

She had tried to woo him back into bed. She had been good! She'd agreed to name the baby Joseph or Josephine, after his mother (though the name reminded her of librarians and she hoped, in time, it would be shortened to Josie). She'd even cooked him an Ulster Fry to celebrate his mother's namesake, with all the things his mother used to cook for him: soda farl and potato farl, bacon and sausage, black and white puddings. Beer was permitted, too, a little. But sex stayed absent, like a guest who'd forgotten to come. Rosalie's body was still waiting when Bobby lay snoring beside her, comatose from eating too much greasy food.

"You won't hurt the baby," she said now, "if you make love to me."

"I won't hurt the baby, aye, because you'll beat me to it."

She knew he must be deeply angry, not to use her name. Even the absence of swearing made his anger seem more angry. The kettle clicked off. She hadn't known it was on. Tense but careful, he eased her off his lap. He began his tea ritual: a spoonful of real tea, an inch of milk, three sugar cubes.

But this time there was just one cup.

"What about me?" she asked.

"What about you?" He stirred with his back to her.

"I think we both know," he said, "that you never really liked it."

CHAPTER 11

2002

We didn't do anything for my sixteenth birthday. Bobby was the worst I'd seen him. It was like the chat had been stolen from out of his mouth. I stopped asking how he was all the time. It only annoyed me, the way he answered—*Och, I'm grand, Jo*—the way he lied so badly. Sometimes he told the truth. He'd say, "The static is bad," which meant that nothing, no conversation or music or anything, could cut through it. When the static was bad, I had to stay in my own head more, rattling around as though trying to find my way around a house that was too big for me.

In May we had two days' work in Northern Ireland. Though Bobby was from Northern Ireland, he called it a "desperate black hole." Personally, I didn't think the Troubles were such a big deal. Less than four thousand people had died, and that didn't seem very many to me, not in thirty years. Nearly that many had died on September 11.

To me, Northern Ireland was really just a place of people who sounded angry and friendly at the same time, of flags and murals and the Ulster fry, of once-in-a-while soldiers and black-and-white cows—spanking-clean cows that looked as though they'd been scrubbed—and the mountains of Mourne with its peat-burning smells.

And this time we had a treat waiting for us. Cosima and Her Goodtime Guys were doing an Irish tour, starting in Belfast.

We'd booked a sleeping cabin on the Liverpool-to-Belfast crossing. Unlike Holyhead-to-Dun-Laoghaire, there were mostly lorry drivers on this ferry, not too many wives or children. I liked it this way; all of us lorry folk cozied up at sea together.

Everything was normal as we drove to Liverpool, over the industrial bridge, into Bootle Dock and down into the belly of the boat. We parked on Deck C and we climbed the metal stairs along with the other drivers. We had steak and kidney pie for supper and we didn't talk too much. The ferry was crowded and we had to share our table with an old hippie driver. Everything about him was long, from his long head to his ginger hair. He read his book as he ate, holding it high so that rather than facing us, his book did. On the book was a picture of a Red Indian, and the words *My Stolen Horizon: The Journey of Thomas Fire Lake, a Native American.*

After supper we had a drink in the bar. I didn't even hide my Bacardi and Coke now. I knew Bobby didn't like it, but he didn't say anything about it. He drank his usual Guinness. I watched the other drivers at the blackjack table, the girl in a black cocktail dress taking their bets. The hippie driver sat on his own, drinking some kind of red drink and reading his book.

"I seen that driver," said Bobby.

"That hippie guy?"

"He drives for Clifford's Keyboards."

"Oh, yeah. *You Keep the Beat, We Beat the Clock.*"

"That's it. Little rigid, he drives. I didn't remember him till just this minute."

"Why would you remember someone who drives a rigid, anyway?" To me, rigids were only half-trucks, with little half-men in them, though this guy was quite tall.

"Maybe he hasn't got a license for an artic."

We were quiet after that. We went to our cabin at eleven. I slept on the top bunk and Bobby slept on the bottom, just as we did in our lorry.

In the middle of the night I woke up. I couldn't hear him snoring, or even breathing. There was only the slurp of the sea against the cabin wall.

"Dad?"

I jumped down. His bunk was empty. I put on my jeans and coat and left the cabin. Last month a driver had fallen overboard on the Fishguard–Rosslare crossing. His body was found weeks later off the Isle of Man. Bloated as a stuffed trout, they said, and the fish had eaten his face away.

My feet made a muffled thud on the carpet as I ran down the corridor. I ran upstairs and out on deck. The cold tore into my chest and ballooned my clothing out from my body. I forced myself to peer over the railing to where the foam gnashed against the bottom of the boat. I didn't know what I thought I'd find out there; that lather would suck up anything.

In the bar there was nobody apart from the old hippie driver still reading his book. There was no noise or music, just the fruit machine tinkling into the dead, smoky air.

"I can't find my father!" I said to the hippie driver. "Have you seen him?"

He looked up at the ceiling, his neck strained as if he was searching for the answer up there.

"When I'm absorbed in something," he said, "I find it hard just to *see* things in, for lack of a better word, the 'ordinary' world. This individual"—he patted the Red Indian on the cover of his book—"is the only man I have been *seeing*. A robbed and pillaged man on his long journey from Montana to Minnesota. Extremely disturbing story, extremely powerful."

I started to run away.

"Hold on! You!"

I stopped.

"I was toying with the idea of having a sauna. I don't suppose you'd care to join me?"

"Fuck off."

I'd never said "Fuck off " to a grown man or anybody. I hated him, talking his hippie bollix while the foam gnashed against the bottom of the boat. But then, the old perv had done me a favor. I had forgotten that this ship had a sauna.

The sweet wood smell hit me as soon as I opened the door. Bobby was slumped next to the smoking coals, wearing only his socks and underwear. His eyes were closed. There were lashes of sweat across his pelvis, making him look as if he'd wet himself. I sat down beside him.

"What are you doing in here, Bobby?"

He opened his eyes but he didn't look at me. I tried again.

"Bobby, what on earth are you—"

"I could just disappear," he cut in. "Steam myself away."

My own chest, too, was beginning to sweat.

"What about me?"

He looked at me. "Why aren't you in bed?'

"I *was* in bed."

"I fancied a wee steam. What's wrong with that?"

"C'mon, Bobby." I took his hand. I led him out and down along the corridor. As the cool air hit us, I caught a whiff of him, an underarm-y sort of sweat he didn't usually have.

"When was the last time you showered, Bobby?"

He didn't answer. It was strange that I couldn't remember. Normally he showered every day. We passed the bar, where the hippie driver was still reading his book. The blackjack girl was there, too, running a lint comb over the table. Her head was framed by a round window, a disc of navy that could have been sea or sky.

I slept on the bottom bunk so that I could hear him if he got up again. I listened for his snoring and was pleased when it came, though even his snoring sounded different. Bobby was a smoker, but these sounded like the snores of an older man. At the end of each one, his breath rose up as if it was begging.

I usually liked the cranes of Belfast harbor, but this morning the fog was as thick as phlegm and we couldn't see much. We docked for an hour while breakfast was served. The lack of sleep rattled in my head and made every sound loud and clanking, and the smell of fried food made me feel sick. Yet when Bobby said he wasn't hungry, I said we should eat. Bobby never missed a breakfast.

"It's free, Dad," I reminded him.

"Have some yourself."

I loaded up the plates for both of us. He ate half a slice of toast.

After breakfast I carried our bags down to the parking decks. The stink of fish and diesel stung my eyes, and I couldn't remember if we were on Deck C or D. Finally I found the lorry, and we sat in the queue waiting to be guided off by the man in the yellow windbreaker. On the deck above us, lorries hammered down the ramp, and my head vibrated every time they did. The day had only just started, and I didn't know how I was going to get through it.

Whenever we disembarked in Ireland, we played one of Cosima's Irish songs. She only did two, and she did them in a country style. Bobby liked "Eileen McMahon" the best. "Eileen McMahon" was a ballad about a lonely maid who appears before a stranger to say that she is "forced as an exile to roam, far away from her home in Killarney." Bobby didn't like Irish music, but he liked this one because his mother used to sing it.

The cab was a mess, but I tried to find the CD with "Eileen McMahon" on it. I went through all of the tapes and CDs.

"What did you do with Cosima, Bobby?"

"What?"

"The *Pure Country* CD."

"I did a wee spot of tidying."

I saw no proof of tidying. I saw only CDs that weren't there.

"I'll find it later, Jo."

But later would be too late; we were disembarking *now*. Still, he wasn't looking his best, so I let him concentrate on getting us off the boat and away from the docks. We drove east toward County Down. Just outside of Banbridge we passed five or six soldiers on foot patrol. We rarely saw soldiers in Northern Ireland these days. They used to stop us, asked to see our load. They weren't usually nasty, more often bored; young guys with Yorkshire or Lancashire accents. Now I almost wished they *would* stop us, give us something to talk about. One of the foot soldiers wasn't bad to look at, a blond-haired bloke with fuzz on his lip, not quite a mustache. I caught his eye through the window. He winked at me.

"He was young, wasn't he?" I asked. "Only eighteen maybe. That's just two minutes older than me.'

Bobby jerked his head. "What?"

"I mean two years."

"I don't care how old they are. They're all British bastards."

He'd never said anything like this before. Usually he said, "They don't know any better, really" or "They're only young lads" or something like that.

"*I'm* British."

"You're fucking not."

I didn't argue. As we drove into the mountains of Mourne, rain slammed down on us, cutting into our windscreen like long glass knives. Bobby pulled into a viewing spot, though there was nothing to view. We sat staring into the smear of greenery around us. The rain finally cleared, leaving a drizzly fog. Bobby looked at me. His face was covered in stubble and his eyes were rimmed with pink.

"You look like my ma just now," he said.

I'd seen photos of his mother at Aunt Anne's house. She was pretty when she was young. She was Josephine Pickering, same as me. I didn't mind talking about her when we were driving or eating, but not when we were just stopped like this with places to go to. We had to get to Kilminster and Warrenpoint and back to Belfast, all in time to see Cosima.

"C'mon, Bobby. 'Job's a carrot,' like Primrose says. We'll do the round and have lunch in Rostrevor."

Rostrevor was on the sea. There was a café we liked there, not our usual thing but a bistro that looked French. If the weather cleared up, we would sit at the window, watching people stroll up and down the seafront.

"Bobby?"

"I think you'd better drive, Jo."

"What?"

"You'd better drive."

"You're having me on."

When Bobby let me drive, it was something I asked for, a treat in a place where nobody would see us. But this wasn't the North Weald airfield or a sleepy little road near the New Forest. Here, even the country roads were busy with vans and tractors and herds of cattle that took forever to cross.

"The roads are fine," said Bobby, as if he could hear my thoughts. "I used to drive my dad's tractor down here when I was a lad."

"No, Bobby."

"My head's dead funny. Static's bad."

"How bad?"

"Like pylons, like . . . hissing, crackling."

"But what if the RUC stops us? Or the 'Police of Northern Ireland' or whatever they're called these days?"

"Sure, they have better things to do than go looking for teenage girls in their fathers' lorries."

I wanted to say that that young soldier back there had been quite happy to look at a teenage girl in her father's lorry, but instead I opened my door. We changed places. I piled two coats to make me high enough, but then I was too tall and I took one of them away. I'd grown since I'd last driven. My foot reached the pedal easily. When I started the engine, I nearly expected the lorry to refuse me, to bleep or flash some light it hadn't flashed before, but it didn't. I switched on the high beams, though all I could see was a blur of road right in front of me. Slowly, I drove. After a mile or so, the mist began to lift, showing patches of mountain, yellow and brown and buttery as suede.

"You're doing well," said Bobby.

"I'd do better with Cosima on."

The rain began to fall again. I clicked the wipers on. We'd done this route a dozen times, but it looked different to me now, all wet and smeared.

"Jo!"

A rush of fur lit up in the headlights. I jerked the wheel to my left and skidded to a stop.

"Look, Jo."

The deer was looking at us from the side of the road, its head to one side as if trying to work out why we'd nearly killed it.

"Fucking lovely, that," he said.

"It came out so fast. I didn't see it."

"It's *beautiful*." There was a sad blame in his voice as if I had killed it, as if we were gazing into the eyes of its ghost now.

"Listen, Dad, I don't think this is a good idea."

Bobby just stared at the deer. I started up again. The sky was growing blue, with streaks of leftover cloud. It seemed to be playing with me, this weather. We drove through a wooded area and a sign for Dundrum. The lake began to our right.

"I used to fish here," said Bobby. "And I used to come here with my first girlfriend."

"Maire, she was called."

"That's it."

I rolled down my window. The rain had left everything smelling of peat and wet pencils.

"Over there," he said, pointing. "That's where me and her made love for the first time."

"I don't need to hear this bit!" I hadn't meant for it to come out so loud. "Where is Maire now, anyway?"

"Fuck knows."

"Should we try to find her?" I didn't really want to find her. I just wanted to keep him from talking about static or the sex he had when he was a teenager.

"Sure, she's probably married some farmer and living in one of them American-style bungalows."

"Like Aunt Anne's."

"Like Anne's, that's it."

As we reached the edges of Kilminster, there were strange sounds, like voices in a tunnel. We passed a wooden sign nailed to a tree, written by hand as if a child had done it: THE WAGES OF SIN IS DEATH.

Traffic was bad for a Sunday. We crawled through the town. On one side of the High Street the curb was painted in red, white, and blue. Union Jacks flew from the streetlamps. On the other side the curb was red and green and white, and Irish Tricolors flew instead of the Union Jacks.

"Gutted like a fish, this town," said Bobby. "Worse than Belfast. Prods one side, us taigs on the other."

"I thought you didn't like that word, *taig*."

As we inched toward the harbor, the tunnel voice got louder. It sounded like a man burbling underwater. At a broken traffic signal two policemen directed traffic.

"Bobby! They'll see me."

"They're too busy to notice."

He was right. The cops waved us through and the traffic lightened. We passed a Presbyterian church and McCroom's Ballroom Wear, established 1946. We passed a derelict pub and a mural of William of Orange crossing the Boyne.

This drop was on a long jetty and we'd done it before. It was a bastard of a drop, not really a "carrot" at all, because there was no forklift and the jetty was too narrow for articulated lorries. We had to park at the bottom and walk up to the warehouse and wait for John Loughlin, the foreman, to come down with his van and help us handball the gear ourselves. Sometimes John Loughlin wasn't there and we'd wait forever, holding our breath because the harbor stank of sewage and rot.

The jetty was usually deserted, but today it was jammed with parked cars. I was suddenly tired, thinking how long it would take us to tip and get out of here.

The moment we got out of the lorry, a fierce wind hit my ears and droned in my head as we walked. We walked up the jetty past a derelict building, its windows smashed. We passed a tank, a net entangled with seaweed, a van missing all of its wheels. In the dredge below us a water rat dragged a sausage roll into a rat-sized tunnel. I felt a taste in my mouth like moss.

The megaphone man was louder now. A crowd of people was standing on top of the jetty.

I was surrounded by eyes.

All of the parked cars had people in them, facing the megaphone man. Some had children in the back, not fighting or talking but just sitting. We passed a blond couple, their eyes glazed and staring ahead as if they were at the cinema.

Some of the megaphone's words were clearer now: "God," "repent," and "redemption." As we came closer I could see the backsides of the ladies in their flowery dresses, and the necks of men in their suits.

Through a gap I saw the megaphone man, a tiny booming man in a big white collar. He stood on a concrete island, separated from the others by a strip of estuary. The megaphone blocked the bottom half of his face.

"He who defiles himself," he shouted, "defiles every single one of us!"

I wanted to stay and watch but Bobby turned toward the warehouse.

"Who are those people?" I asked.

"Prods. God squadders!" It wasn't Bobby who answered me. John Loughlin stood there with his hands on hips. Loughlin was a small, balding bloke with a potbelly and a high-pitched voice. We hadn't seen him for a year, but he always talked to us as if we'd just nipped out for a cup of tea.

"Fucking Bible thumpers!" he went on. "Hellfire and damnation and all that shite. Have they not got perfectly decent homes to go to? More decent, I might add, than the likes of yours or mine?"

"Why aren't they in church?" I asked.

"Oh, don't you worry, darling, they do church as well. These Born Agains never miss a chance to pollute the air with their manure. Kingdom of Christ, me arse. They don't drink or smoke or swear, they're not human, and they can't relax unless they annoy all us with their witnessing ceremonies."

"What's a witnessing ceremony?"

"This. It's where they get together and pray for salvation and freak out about the apocalypse or some fucking thing. Tell you what, I'd *approve* of a fucking apocalypse if I didn't think those bastards would be the only ones to survive it. Like cockroaches."

Loughlin stopped hating Protestants long enough to look at me. "Anyway, sweetheart, what about you? You're looking very tall, so you are."

Bobby looked at me as if noticing for the first time. "She's tall, right enough."

We drove down in the van, John Loughlin nearly—but not quite—scraping some of the Protestant cars. Handballing the gear didn't take too long after all. By the time we'd got away, I didn't even mind taking the wheel. In fact, as we cleared the town and sprung ourselves back onto the mountain road, I wanted to. Something slid against my toe. I leaned down and picked up *Pure Country* and slipped it in. "Mojave Desert Girl" came on. Bobby hummed along, but I went for it:

> *Your skyscraper is so high*
> *It cuts the sky and makes it bleed*
> *You eat sushi for breakfast, lunch and dinner*
> *But what part of you does it really feed?*
> *You can keep your golden ghetto*
> *Leave me with my lizards and my Joshua tree*
> *The Mojave Desert's the only place for me!*
> *Now you've got your Jacuzzi and your private plane—*

The RUC man stood in the middle of the road with his hand up. He was looking straight at me, shaking his head. I pulled over, my heart pounding. He marched toward me and motioned for me to roll down my window. He wasn't old, but he looked as though he didn't find many things funny. "Jump down."

I jumped down. I was much smaller than him now.

"In my opinion," he said, "you couldn't be anything *resembling* twenty-one."

"My father's not well enough to drive. It's only been a mile or so."

He glanced at Bobby, then leaned into the cab to speak to him. "What's wrong with you, son?" he asked, though he was younger than Bobby.

"He was sick in Kilminster," I said. "He ate some dodgy sausage. He threw up all over the cab, and it took me forty-five minutes to clean it up." I was surprised by how easy it was to lie. I didn't even stammer.

The RUC man sniffed. "I can't smell anything."

"I cleaned it well."

He looked at me again. "What's your name?"

"Josephine Pickering. My father is called Bobby. He's from Drum."

"Drum in Antrim or up Tyrone way?"

"Antrim. We live in England, though."

"Pickering, did you say?"

"Yes."

"Right. Tell you what. Get him out the cab, and change over. I'll pretend I never seen you, but you can't be driving your da's lorry. Jesus, sweetheart, you mustn't be more than eighteen."

"Okay."

I thought he was going to leave, but he stuck his head in the cab again. "Listen, son, you ought to know better, letting your wee girl take over for you. Can I have your word you won't let this happen again?"

Bobby didn't say anything.

"What was that, son?"

"Say it, Bobby."

"I won't," said Bobby.

"Am I deaf, son? You won't *what?*"

"I won't let her drive again."

"Away you go, then." The RUC man waited for us to swap over.

Bobby looked as though the last thing he could do was drive. He was smushed into himself, like a pile of clothes that had been left somewhere. But with the RUC man watching, he pulled himself to the wheel. The man gave us a single wave. I tried to let go of my breath but it stuck in my chest. We started off.

"RUC bastard," said Bobby

'Aren't they called something different now? 'Police of Northern Ireland' or something?"

"Aye, they're called cunts. He only let us go because he thought I was a Prod."

"He thought I was eighteen," I said. "Do you think I look eighteen?"

Bobby didn't answer.

We made it to Belfast by 6:45. We stopped at a petrol station just off the A12 so that I could change into my suede outfit. I took no longer than twenty minutes, but Bobby was dozing when I got back into the lorry.

"Aren't you going to change, Bobby?"

He opened his eyes suddenly, as though he'd been caught doing something bad. He started the engine, reversed and drove us onto the A12, heading for Belfast. The closer we got to the Empire Music Hall, the more I checked my makeup in the visor mirror. We exited, drove through Sandy

Row and onto the Lisburn Road. Halfway up the Lisburn Road, Bobby pulled over.

"Listen, Jo—"

"I don't want to drive again. We're nearly there."

"No, it's— I'm not feeling too clever, so I'm not. I don't think I'm going to be able to make it—"

"*We're nearly there,* Bobby."

"I'm sorry, I just don't think—"

"*What* don't you think? After I drove all that way and got you out of trouble with that RUC man? I wish he did arrest you, except then we'd *definitely* never get there!"

I waited to see what he would do, but he wasn't even looking at me. He was looking in the rearview mirror, probably at something not even worth mentioning, some stupid cat or tree.

"Your woman," he said. "See your woman running? She looks like Cosima."

"Where?"

"Just there."

He was right. A woman was running in our direction, and she was the spit of Cosima. She even wore a cowgirl hat, which bobbed up and down on her head as though it wanted to fall off. I opened my door. Her eyes were big and round with terror. It was her.

"Thank God, it's you guys! We've had an accident. My phone's not getting a signal!"

She climbed up beside me as if she'd done it many times before.

"Can you turn around?" she asked Bobby.

I thought Bobby would never do a U-turn on the Lisburn Road, but he signaled, made a wide arc of the road, and managed to do it without even one person honking at us. About a quarter of a mile toward the city center, she yelled at us to stop.

"It's there!" She pointed to a van that had crashed, head on, into a lamppost.

Bobby pulled over, killed the engine, and jumped down from the cab. Cosima and I followed him.

Rick was collapsed at the wheel, his hair spilling over his face. He looked dead, but when Bobby checked his pulse, he groaned. I had never seen Bobby carry a grown man, but he lifted Rick and carried him to the cab.

"Get in, you two," said Bobby.

We got in. Bobby draped Rick across us as though he was a travel blanket to keep our legs warm. Rick stank of rum and looked annoyed even while he was unconscious. Bobby started to drive.

"Are you hurt yourself, Cosima?"

"Not physically."

As we drove toward the Royal Hospital, she turned to look at the skid marks on the road, at the place where it had all turned bad.

We waited in casualty for the doctor to come. I expected a man, but when she finally did come, the doctor was a short Indian lady in a sari. She spoke with a Belfast accent.

"Only a few cuts and bruises," she said. "Nothing major." Bobby and I smiled and nodded as though we were Rick's family.

But then she spoke only to Cosima. "Miss Stewart," she asked, "do you think I can have a wee word?"

Cosima looked at Bobby. "Will you wait for me?"

"Surely, aye." He watched her as she went with the doctor. Bobby seemed his old self again. The accident had made him nearly cheerful.

"Dead polite, that wee doctor," he said.

"Why wouldn't she be polite?"

"I mean, her accent. One of them Malone Road accents."

"It's funny seeing a Paki with a Belfast accent."

"Don't say 'Paki,' Jo. It isn't nice."

"Why not? They say it at school."

"I don't care what they say at school. I don't like it. I don't think she's Pakistani, anyway. I reckon she's Indian."

Bobby and I went quiet again. We looked up every time someone came into the room, then looked away when the person wasn't Cosima. The "wee word" with the doctor was taking a while.

We drove Cosima to her hotel. Her eyes were red and inflamed.

"I'm sorry you couldn't do your gig tonight," I said.

"I don't care about that," she said. "He's going to be charged with drunken driving."

"Maybe it's for the best," said Bobby, "if it'll keep him off the road when he's on the gargle."

I used to hope that we would find Cosima in trouble one day so that we could rescue her. Now this exact thing was happening, and neither of us had the right words for her.

"I don't want Katie or Sean or any of those others around me now," she said, as if we were about to find them and tell them. "I just want to be on my own."

"No problem," said Bobby. "No problem at all. We'll leave you off wherever you want us to."

But when we drove up to the Europa Hotel, she changed her mind about being alone. "Come in," she said, more to Bobby than to me. "Don't leave me now."

"Whatever you say, sweetheart."

I couldn't believe the way he'd just switched back to his old self, his best self. If he could switch himself back for her, why couldn't he do it for me? I nearly wished we were alone again so I could ask him about it.

Her room was white and spotless, with a king-size bed and a ringing phone that we could hear before she even put her key in the door.

"Shut up," she said to it, throwing her jacket on the floor. She sat on the bed and put her face in her hands. Bobby picked up the jacket and folded it over the back of a chair. The phone kept ringing.

"Fuck off!" she shouted at it.

Bobby slipped his hand down the wall and pulled out the cord. "Did you know," he asked, "that the Europa is the most-bombed hotel in Europe?"

Cosima lifted her face, took her hands away.

"I think I did know that," she said.

"Nobody told me," I said.

"It would be funny if they erected a wee plaque saying that," said Bobby.

"A place of tragedy." Cosima reached for a pillow and hugged it. "A center of conflict. Just like us."

"Just like you?"

"Just like us. We were fighting when we crashed. So it's my fault, too."

"It was him that got into the motor with a bellyful of rum," said Bobby.

"And coke," she said. "He had a bellyful of rum and coke."

"Coke doesn't neutralize the rum."

"*This* kind of coke certainly doesn't neutralize the rum." She slurred the word *neutralize* so that it sounded like *neuralize*. She wiped her nose and hugged her pillow harder. I realized that she might be a bit drunk herself. She kept looking at Bobby and not at me.

"Will you put me to bed, Bobby?"

Bobby took a step toward her and stopped.

"I'll do it," I said. I knelt in front of her and started to take her shoes off. She giggled. She put her hands in my hair.

"Geraldine."

"Josephine."

"They're the same name really." She put her hand under my chin. "You're so cute."

"I am not."

"You are. My cutest fan. You're the cutest fan of all my fans. *Intercontinentally.*"

I wished her shoes were more complicated than they were, so I could stay longer on the floor and tend to them. Slowly, I peeled off her left sock. I peeled off her right one. Bobby was up at the desk, looking at the hotel stationery.

"Cosima?" I asked. "Have you noticed my outfit?" I leaned back to show her. "It's like yours, only it's not real suede like yours."

She fondled the fringe on my top. "Oh, yeah . . . You little magpie."

"I wore it on my birthday, and I sang 'Rather Be' at the karaoke, and everyone said I sounded like you."

"Really? Do you want to be a musician, too?"

"I don't know. I can't play the fiddle or anything."

She touched my cheek. "So adorable." Her eyes were moist. "It's a dead-end situation, Jo, you know what I mean?"

I nodded, though I wasn't sure I did.

"He punishes me. He punishes me with his moods, his silence, his depression, his sulking . . ."

"I think he's an arsehole."

"That's enough, Jo." Bobby had chosen the worst time to stick his stupid voice in. Cosima looked up at him, like a blind person who can suddenly see again. "Bobby?" she said. "Come and put me to bed."

"*I'm* putting you to bed," I said.

"You can both put me to bed."

Bobby cleared his throat. I had to get out of the way for him to get to the bed. I stood up and folded my arms against my chest. Cosima stood up, too, and let her dress fall, leaving just her underwear and bra. I could see Bobby trying not to look at her.

The sheets were tucked in tight and he had to wrestle with them to yank them back. When he finally did, she lay down looking up at him. Bobby quickly pulled the blanket up to her neck, and stepped back.

"What you were saying just there?" he asked. "About your man's moods—about Rick's moods, you know?"

"Yes, Bobby?"

"It's just that . . . I know what that's like . . . them black moods. . . ."

"But you always seem so serene."

"He isn't serene," I said. "You should have seen him earlier today."

"She's right," he said. "Like I say—I have them moods. I just want to say that, you know, just because *he* has them moods, that doesn't mean he doesn't love you. What I mean is, it's probably nothing to do with you."

It was odd, hearing him compare himself to Rick. If he could talk that way to her, why couldn't he talk that way to me anymore?

"Anyway," he said, "it'll all look better in the morning."

I thought this was a bit useless of him. He put his hand on my shoulder. He started moving us to the door.

"You're leaving?" she asked.

"Aye," said Bobby. "Gotta get Jo here to bed."

"Get *yourself* to bed," I said.

Her eyes were swimming around. "Jo . . ." she said, nearly singing it. "I love Jo. Don't you love Jo?"

"Jo's my girl."

"I just *love* her."

I was going red but I didn't mind really.

"Give me a hug, Jo," she said.

I went to her. She put her arms around my neck and she hugged me tight. When she'd finished, Bobby was there, waiting his turn. He went to hug her, but she grabbed the back of his neck and kissed him. It wasn't exactly a smoochy kiss, but it wasn't a peck, either. I'd never seen Bobby kiss a girl, not to mention her. I felt cringey inside, more than when Tom had thought I was Bobby's girlfriend.

Not looking at each other, we moved toward the front door. Just as we were nearly out, Cosima called to us. "Hey, you guys!"

We turned to look at her.

"You're on the guest list, you know what I mean? Any gig. You're on my guest list forever. You're on the guest list of my *life*."

She fell back on the pillow and shut her eyes.

I thought we were at sea again, because the bed was rocking.

I opened my eyes. We weren't at sea, but the truck was turbulent. Music was coming from down below, too small and strange for me to tell what it was. I strained to hear it: Cosima, singing "Every Color of Love."

I heard his breath and then a silence. He gasped in a muffled way, as though he were trying to hold it in. I didn't know exactly what he was doing; all I knew was that I didn't want to know. I pulled my T-shirt down over my knees as far as I could stretch it, to make myself into a bag of something separate from him and the bed. I heard him roll over. Soon his snoring came, but "Every Color of Love" kept going through his headphones and through the bunk, and when the song finished, it started again.

CHAPTER 12

1986

Bobby no longer knew what he'd find when he got home, but the one thing he did not expect was to find Rosalie absent. He was the absent one these days. He was the one covering longer distances, the road slick beneath his wheels: the M4, the M1, the M-anywhere-but-here. It was Rosalie who was always waiting—and whining, and crying—at home.

Bobby had been on his first overnight to Calais when he came home to an empty flat. Recent signs of her were strewn across the bed, haphazard intimacies: her nightgown, her underwear, a damp towel. Her hospital suitcase sat by the door; he had packed it himself. It was five-thirty in the morning. He stood in the middle of the room, exhausted by what he didn't know yet.

The buzzer shrilled. He ran downstairs. Rosalie must have locked herself out. That would be typical! She'd have gone to the all-night chippy, probably still in her slippers and dressing gown, and forgotten her keys. She could have been down there for hours in the cold, with only the junkies and stray dogs to help her.

Yet when he opened the front door, it was a young punk who stood before him. He was a head taller than Bobby, his fringe a shock of pink that added another four inches to his height. He was so skinny that his ribs protruded through his T-shirt, on which there was a sketch of a lynched man and the words BAS-TARD SEX CANAL 1984: SUMMER BEACH TOUR. He looked as though he would growl rather than speak, but when he did speak, his voice was high, nearly girly with panic.

"Rosalie's gone into early labor! She's at the Homerton!"

Bobby ran upstairs, fetched her suitcase, and ran back down. Together, they drove to the hospital. Bobby was quick and agile, like any good man in an emergency. Yet with every efficient jolt and slam and acceleration, he was aware of a grim calmness in his body. The emergency was no stranger than the petrified, pinkified bearer of news who sat beside him now. Bobby had been waiting for something like this, or even this.

Five minutes from the Homerton, Rugg-Edd started flapping his hand.

"If you don't mind," he said, "I won't actually go into hospital. I don't want any . . . trouble."

"What do you mean?" asked Bobby. "You two been doing drugs? That why she's gone into labor?"

"It was she who phoned me! She asked *me* round."

"It was you who had the coke."

"She didn't tell me that she was pregnant."

"Could you not fucking *see* that she was pregnant?"

"It isn't my way to tell people what to do!"

There was a yellow light up ahead. Bobby floored it but didn't make it. He thought about running the red but stopped at the last second, causing the wheels to screech. "I think," said Bobby, "that you should get off here."

With a manic jerking of his head, Rugg-Edd took in his surroundings. "Could you not drop me off at Hackney Central? I can get a train home to Chelsea."

Bobby rubbed his forehead. Another man would have hit this man. Bobby might have hit him himself, if Rugg-Edd had seemed more like a man and less like a rat.

"Having given drugs to my wife when she's seven months pregnant," said Bobby, "I think you can fuck off and take the *bus* home to Chelsea."

In casualty Bobby was told to sit and wait. The wailing of strangers and the fluorescent lighting added to the horrible calm inside of him, as if nothing that had ever happened to him could be quite real. Dawn had come, but the drunks sang and shouted as if they'd just been jacked out of the pubs. Flannel-shirted twins—their wounds fresh from the same fight—called for nurses who didn't come. Bobby sat beside a girl in an acid-green miniskirt who held her boyfriend's bleeding hand.

"I'm so sorry, Tim," said the girl. "I'm so sorry." She kissed the wound four or five times.

"How could you do it, Kerry?" But the boyfriend—Tim—lifted their two hands and kissed hers back.

What women do to their men, thought Bobby.

When the nurse appeared at last, she asked whom Bobby would rather see first, his baby or his wife.

"Wife?" he repeated.

For the word *wife* was even stranger, now, than the word *baby*. A *wife* would not snort those powders, expelling her baby—*their* baby—like a constipation she'd been trying to break for months.

"The baby," he said, and then, as if he'd said something wrong: "If that's all right."

The nurse took him along the corridor, up a lift and down another corridor to the Premature Baby Unit. In the glass between Bobby and the incubator, Bobby's own reflection bounced back at him. He had to raise his hand to block the glare. The infant looked like a wrinkled fish, openmouthed and jerking in place as it fought for breath. The whole baby was barely bigger than his hand. Its face was covered in tubes. It wore a hat and gloves like a ridiculous doll.

"What's its weight?" he asked.

"Just under four pounds."

"Why has it got all that on?"

"To keep the heat in." The nurse touched his shoulder. "Will I ring somebody for you?"

He shook his head.

"Have you any family? Your mother, perhaps?"

"She's passed away."

"I see."

They stood together and tried to look at the baby, who was hard to look at. The nurse was young, but her hips were wide and generous, as though she'd recently given birth to a fat, full-term baby of her own. Her name tag said Brid.

"You're Irish," he said.

"From the west."

"Galway?"

"Clare."

"Ah."

"Yourself?" she asked. "The north?"

"Aye."

"Ah well."

The exchange comforted him. He'd had the same one, more or less, probably forty times since leaving Ireland. He'd had it with Irish women and Irish men, with young ones and old ones, on buses or in bars or trains. He didn't always enjoy it. Yet it was these words now that made his eyes well up, rather than the crisis that awaited him. He gazed back into the incubator.

"Thank you, Brid."

She touched his hand, the way his mother used to do. His sister Anne used to do it, too, sometimes. Rosalie did not touch him like that, ever. How could he not have seen it? She'd sucked him into herself and, while she was at it, cooked up their child only to crush it within her own body, pushing it out while it was too weak even for the air.

———————

Two floors up, Rosalie slept. Out of danger, she stayed under, feigning sleep to avoid the nurses in their starched skirts and hard collars. The way they *looked* at her! Even the Irish nurse—the one with the quiet voice, the one with the big ass—tightened her lips in some sanctimonious way, always saying "Now" when she brought her meals or fixed the sheets. "Now," she would say, but she was really saying, *What's to be done with you?*

The two English nurses were worse. They were pasty and skinny and hardly spoke to her at all. Rosalie had seen their equivalents in Van Nuys or Reseda, the poorest reaches of the Valley, with their bleached drugstore hair and their bony legs and their petty moralities.

And yet, the more Rosalie feigned sleep, the more awake she felt. Without drugs or booze she was sensitive to everything: to a crumb of bread digging into her thigh, a fly buzzing in the corridor, the moral superiority of skinny nurses. She felt a pang when they called each other by name. She was jealous of the names themselves, as if these working-class sounds had rendered them as cute and blameless as the teddy bears they (undoubtedly) still kept on their beds at home: "Get them Jaffa cakes, Sandra?" or "Seeing Nick at the Tally Ho tonight, Kelley?" Worse, she knew they would treat Bobby with disgusting pity. Girls like that needed to have a good person and a bad person, and all the better if the good one was a doe-eyed male, sweetly absent from the scene of the crime. Meanwhile, she, Rosalie (spoiled brat, Jewish princess!), had brought it all on herself: her throbbing pelvis, her lactating breasts, her broken baby.

"I guess you need my milk," she said to Kelley, in one of her few moments of honest wakefulness.

"To be honest with you, we ain't too happy about *your* milk."

She longed to explain. To tell Kelley that it wasn't badness that had made her milk poisonous, any more than it was badness that made her call her ex-boyfriend. It was loneliness, a loneliness so pungent it stank. Bobby was away all the time. He never made love to her anymore. He'd pumped her full of his seed, a seed that had grown like a creature in *Alien;* meanwhile, she had shrunk and shrunk until she'd felt no bigger than the maggot who'd burst out of her.

She never said actually this to Kelley. Nor did she say it to Sandra. She knew they would hate her even more, roll their eyes over her head like girls at recess.

When real sleep did come, it was black and dreamless. When she awoke, she was out of breath. How long had she been here? One day? Three days? However long it was, Bobby hadn't come to see her. She gulped for air. Though she'd probably destroyed that other life, she had the right, at least, to breathe her own breath, didn't she? She consoled herself with what her mother would say if she knew: *It isn't about bad and good or right and wrong. You're too much of a baby to have a baby and I don't mean that in a judgmental way!*

"I'm sorry, Mommy," Rosalie said out loud. And she could hear her mother reply to her, as if she was there at the bedside: *Come home with us, honey. Come home and rest. You'll start again. We'll help you!*

And they would. For while her parents had been inattentive in her growing years, ritually failing to notice her binges and failed exams and illicit substances, they were good in an emergency. Money would be spent, airlines and hotels booked, and later, shrinks would be enlisted, with liberal prescription pads. Rosalie thought of her bedroom in Encino; the real Frank Stella hanging above the bed, the eucalyptus tree outside her window. She'd always found the bed too hard and the room punishing with light. Yet when she thought of her room now, the bed seemed big and clean and crisp with its crescent of pillows to prop her up. And, once installed in her clean, crisp bed, she could watch as much TV as she wanted to (all night, because something would be on *all night!*) and in the afternoons, after work, her mother, energized by crisis, would come and talk to her. She would bring her magazines, hot chocolate with marshmallows, onion bagels with cream cheese. Her mother would bring her a black-and-white cookie. A black-and-white cookie! It had been years since she'd had one of those.

Anger was too personal a thing to feel, and Bobby would feel none of it for Rosalie. He visited her every day while she slept. He didn't visit her because he wanted to. He simply would not give her the satisfaction of thinking she was wronged in any way by him. He was relieved, always, not to find her awake. She was nothing to him now, a stranger who'd entered his life and left him with a fetus rather than a baby.

But then, his use of the word *fetus* dizzied him with guilt. This "fetus" had become the point of his months and weeks and driving jobs, of his twenty-five years on earth. He spent most of his time with it. He willed it to grow, to fill the shape of an actual baby. He made himself use the word *baby*, and further, *his* baby.

The baby rewarded him by gaining an ounce. The twitching abated, and its eyes opened, slightly. He went to tell Rosalie, to wake her if he had to. He wanted her to know that the baby could live.

Yet the sight of Rosalie already awake was a shock. She was even sitting up, brushing four days of bed from her hair.

"The baby's put on two ounces," he told her. Adding the extra ounce made it seem true.

"That's good," she said.

The contest was etched in the air between them. Rosalie's indifference was matched by Bobby's will for the baby to live. And now, with her new, stand-up strength, she looked as though she could win.

"I'm being discharged," she told him. "My parents are flying over."

"Your parents?"

"That's what I said."

"But . . . you don't like them."

"When did I say that?"

Bobby didn't answer. She'd never *said* it, not exactly.

"It's L.A. I don't like," she said. "Their way of life and everything. But my parents . . . my mom . . ." Her eyes brimmed. "I miss my mom."

It was an accusation: *I miss my mom.* It was his fault that she missed her mother, that she might go back to a life she didn't like.

"So you're going back with them? You sure that's what you want?"

"I'm not sure of anything."

He looked at his watch. The few minutes with Rosalie seemed an act of theft from the baby. He started to leave.

"Bobby!"

He stopped.

"I don't know how to pray," she said. "But if you want me to, I'll pray."

Pray for what? he thought. *For the baby to live or die?* Bobby would *not* pray. Prayer was a disease left over from childhood. It would only make him long for his mother, or create a sickly bond with his father, who'd had the cheek— the filthy cheek—to outlive her.

Instead of praying, he willed the baby on. He willed it to breathe and grow and suckle at Brid's bottle, the milk of a good Irish nurse. He devised a system for it. He thought of the tackograph, the paper disc that tracked his speed and hours and number of rest stops. He devised his own mental tacko-graph, gauging the baby's age, its every day and hour.

Born, he thought, *at minus eight weeks old.*

But at minus seven weeks exactly, the baby worsened. It was yellow with jaundice and looked as slack as a dead pigeon on the ground. He stared at it for as long as he could bear to, wanting two things at once: to touch its blue veins through its yellow head, and to run away and never look at it again. He nearly hoped the baby wouldn't make it. If it did make it, it would surely be damaged. He thought of its pruned brain, its vegetable eyes. A bit of broken-ness he could tolerate, relate to even. This much would kill him.

Every night he slept in the waiting room, and every morning he awoke to the squeaking of a stranger's chair or cigarette. He prepared himself for the doctor or, worse, the priest. And yet, with each new dawn, there was nobody. There was only this pale space, a space as forgotten as the battered old walls. He wandered along wards that were nothing to do with him, comforted by the illness of other patients and the nurses who administered to them: folding sheets for the new arrivals, emptying bedpans for the incontinents, preparing syringes for the cancerous. Then, finally, his own journey down the corridor: up the lift, right turn, left turn. Every day he taught himself a new rule. He must not walk too quickly, lest he shock the baby back into spasm. He would refuse the lift if it was lit by a red arrow rather than a green one. (He must not go down in order to go up.) Once he reached the Premature Baby Unit, he took twenty steps to the ward—no more, no less. He was not a superstitious man, but this magic was vital to him now.

Returning to the flat for a shower and a change of underwear, he found Rosalie packed and dressed to leave.

"My parents are at Claridges," she said. "I'm going to fly back to California with them."

The three big things she had mentioned—the most expensive hotel in London, the distant notion of California, and the airplane that would take her there—exhausted him. He collapsed onto the bed, already unused to soft surfaces. He was afraid to even blink, lest he fall off into sleep for a hundred days. (Too much of his own sleep and the baby would be deprived of it.) He tried to concentrate on what she was saying, but his head could contain nothing bigger than the baby.

"I don't know what to do." Her voice was suddenly loud and weepy. "I've made them promise to come to the hospital tomorrow and see the baby."

He sat up at once. "What? *You've* hardly even seen the baby! As a matter of fact, *have* you actually seen the baby?"

"We'll all come."

"I don't care what you do." He knew that she was staring at him, but he didn't look back. When she finally picked up her bag and coat, he fought the urge to call her back.

Yet the next morning, he was excited. The baby's eyes were open and its arms were playing with the air. Its hands even looked like hands, tiny fists rather than snails.

"You're having visitors today," he told it. He thought of Rosalie and her parents standing there with him. He thought of how he would explain it all to them, how the baby had progressed each day of the past week: how it was breathing, how much milk it could tolerate, how still or spasmodic it had been. He wondered what Rosalie would do. Weep, perhaps; she was good at that. Confess her love for the child and for him, her new family. But then he thought of the way she'd looked when he'd fetched his lorry in Colindale, her pregnant self sprawled on the pavement, funny-shaped shopping bags on every side of her. He thought of the Armenians, kissing Rosalie's cheek in turn, and the tear she'd been left with under her lash, one lonely tear, like a drop of rain on a leaf. Was she wrong to be just a wee bit lonely? He had been away for so much of the time, away on the road with his music so loud and his head empty of her.

Something new came into his mind.

What if her parents *wanted* the baby? Or to take the baby *away* with them? He conjured up meetings in his mind: nurses, social workers, the police, maybe. Brid would be pulling for him; so would Kelley and Sandra. *No fucking way were they having the baby!*

He waited all morning. Apart from the nurses, and another baby's mother and father, the ward remained soundless.

"They'll come," said Brid, passing him in the foyer for the sixth time.

But they continued not to come.

He tried to speak calmly to the man behind the desk, but even Bobby was jarred by his own voice, as though a bigger, angrier man was speaking through him. The concierge at Claridges punished him with courtesy. "I'm terribly sorry, sir. The Chapkises left for the States early this morning."

"She can't fucking just *leave!*"

"I'm afraid they can do what they like. And there's no need to swear, sir."

Back in Shandy Street Bobby parked with a shriek of his brakes, nearly hitting the lorry in front of him. He let himself into the flat, thinking he might find her, in the bath, on the bed, in bed even. But Rosalie was gone. She had taken every book, every shred of clothing, every cream and crazy color dye and bottle of hair goo.

Bobby had never struck a woman. The idea of a fist against a female face only made him think of his mother's face, and his eyes smarted. Yet he would like to hit Rosalie now, to hear the crack of his palm on her cheek. For her not to even *look* at the baby, not once!

He opened the blinds. He looked through the filthy window, as though the grungy East London air would produce her. Rosalie and her parents would be on their airplane by now—first class—gazing down on Scotland and Northern Ireland before inclining over that glacial orb, the top of the world. Bobby had never been on an airplane, but the atlas was his favorite book. The Chapkises would have been to all of those places he'd studied in his atlas, and they wouldn't have known hardly anything about them. They would have gone to those places for holidays, for weddings, for Jewish things: Bar mixers? Bar Mitzvahs? Now, right this minute, they would be eating their nuts and drinking their martinis. He was a nobody to them, and so was his child. Nobodies to Mr. and Mrs. Chapkis. The Chapkises.

Cunts.

His eye was caught by a glint of blue from the road. The sun bounced off the lorry he'd nearly hit. It was a tractor without the trailer, about 22 feet across, a spanking blue. A Scania R143 Topline, the kind he'd always been going on about to Rosalie, if she'd ever been arsed to listen to him. His own lorry, a mucous color from too many motorways and ferry crossings, looked ashamed of itself before this new blue one. There was one blemish on the Scania, a parking ticket, fluttering in plastic to protect it from the rain. *Serves it right*, he thought, *flaunting itself there*. Yet the ticket looked strangely big, even from here.

He walked downstairs and into the street. The ticket was almost festive. It reminded him of the Armenian wedding cars with their trailing flutters of ribbon.

The envelope had his name on it. He knew her writing immediately.

Bobby . . . We were going to give you this in person. It isn't my parents' fault. I couldn't face it. I am no kind of mother. The keys are in the mailbox. —RC

RC? Royal Catholic? What madness was this now?

Rosalie Chapkis, of course. He laughed at his mistake. And yet this could be another hoax, a final act of sadism. She had proven herself capable of any cruelty now.

He went into the building and unlocked his postbox, taking slow steps and being careful, as he was with the infant, not to upset the possibility that it was true.

The keys chimed as he fetched them out of the box. They were attached to a key ring, a patch of suede with the Griffin emblem in silver, the Scania mascot.

He went out to the lorry again. He touched the chrome. He unlocked the cab and climbed into the driver's seat. He was higher up than he was in the Magnum. He felt odd rather than great, naked and chilly and covered in goose bumps. He remembered what Primrose had said about the new lorries and their air-suspension seats. He pushed the button and felt himself begin to rise.

Eleven months ago, he'd met a girl. Now she'd replaced herself with a baby and a lorry. He was amazed at the magic in it, how she could appear and disappear, turning him into a father with a big blue lorry, a proper flying machine, better than any airplane. A truck that was *his* truck, a child that was *his* child, and nothing to stop the three of them—himself, his child, and the truck—from driving forever.

When the baby was zero days old, Bobby brought champagne to the hospital. He watched as the nurses removed the baby from its plastic cage and laid it in a tiny basinet. It weighed five pounds and ten ounces, nearly normal. On one side of its head Brid put a little brown bear. On the other side Bobby placed a tiny blue lorry that he'd found, incredibly enough, in the hospital gift shop.

"Have you decided on a name yet?" asked Kelley.

He looked at the baby. Having been around so much longer than the other babies, it looked wise. Its eyes were steady, its cheeks hollow. A layer of yellow fuzz had settled upon its head.

"I have."

He raised his glass in a toast, although he knew that the nurses, still on their shifts, couldn't drink it.

"She's called Josephine," he said. "After my mother."

He felt a shiver, not just at the name, but at the word *she*.

"That's lovely." Kelley was moved enough to take a real sip. "Did you decide just now, then?"

"To be honest with you, Kelley," said Bobby, "deep down, I've always thought of her as that."

CHAPTER 13

2003

When I was seventeen, Cosima and Her Goodtime Guys won the Best New Band on the Country Brit Awards. We stayed in Shandy Street to watch the awards. I made the flat as comfortable as I could for it. I shoved our beds together and lit candles all over the room so that we didn't have to sit under the one bare bulb that showed up every insect and tea stain. It was cold for May, so I got out the old three-bar heater. It gave off a smell of scorched dust, but it was worth it. We ordered an Indian takeaway and when the food came, the place smelled of nan bread and chicken korma, which made it even better.

"Dead comfy, Jo," said Bobby.

Before the award was presented, a video of "Rather Be" was shown. The video started off with Cosima on a horse, galloping on the beach. Way behind her, Rick was riding a horse of his own, trying to keep up. He didn't look like he usually looked. His eyes were wide and he looked almost nice, like someone who might actually be pleased see you. In the next scene Sean was driving a Porsche down Sunset Strip, his sunglasses mirroring the palm trees and billboards. He was obviously supposed to be the rich person she'd rather not be.

"Why did they make that video in Los Angeles?" I asked. "Is it because they're spending so much time there?"

"I don't know, Jo."

"Do you think Rosalie still lives in Los Angeles?"

"I don't know." He said it in a final way that told me he didn't want to know. It wasn't that I was so keen to talk about her, either. The idea of Los Angeles just had her in it. I had an image of her hanging around while they made that video, a Goth girl among the shoppers and cars and palm trees, just another speck in the Sunset Strip of Sean's sunglasses.

When the video was over, the band went up to collect the award. They looked taller and beautiful, like any famous band we'd never met. Cosima wore a strapless dress and she was crying, not enough to smear her makeup; more like she had diamonds in her eyes. She thanked a long list of people.

"She could have thanked us," I said, "for helping her after the accident."

"I'm sure she doesn't want the whole world knowing about that."

After the awards we flicked around for something else to watch, but there wasn't anything good. The room was cooling with the hour. I didn't like it when Bobby finally switched off the TV. I felt as though somebody had left us with our dying food smells and each other.

It was hard to sleep off the road. A normal bed just didn't feel right. It was bigger and softer, but it didn't mold to me as the lorry did. Bobby felt the same. I could hear his crunchy movements as he tossed around all night.

I kept thinking about Rick. The last time I'd seen him he'd been draped, passed out, over our laps. Even unconscious, he'd looked cocky, as though he thought he was better than us. But tonight, stumbling along the beach on a spotty brown horse, he looked kind and awkward, like a different man.

I wished Bobby would fall asleep, because I wanted to be alone with my new image of Rick. At least in the lorry we couldn't see each other. Here, we were side by side, with barely a foot between the beds.

When I woke up in the morning, both of my hands were in my private parts. Bobby was sleeping but he was facing me, his mouth opened as if he'd fallen asleep talking. I pushed back against the wall, putting as much space as I could between us.

The next night, Cosima had a gig at the Tempo Bar, just off Tottenham Court Road. I didn't know whether Bobby would come with me or not. For the last few months, I had a drink on my own from time to time, usually at the truck stops while Bobby slept in the lorry. I liked drinking alone and having blokes come and talk to me, though I was never completely calm in the back of my mind. I would wonder if Bobby was asleep or just lying there deep in his head, or if he'd remembered to put his cigarette out before drifting off.

But when I asked Bobby if he'd come with me to the Tempo, a part of me wished he'd say no. I kept thinking of the Europa Hotel, and how if he hadn't been there, I would have had Cosima all to myself. So when I asked if he was coming and he said, "Surely," I sank a little. It was mad that the thing I wanted most—for him to be light again—was the thing I didn't want on this very night. He even made supper before the gig, whistling "Rather Be" as he grilled our fish fingers, making my heart hurt with my own awfulness.

What neither of us expected was that the show would sell out.

The man at the door didn't look as though he wanted to keep us out. He had a beard and a thin, gentle face and he looked like he cared about trees and animals. "It's that award," he said. "The phone's been ringing off the hook here. You need to book these days."

"But we're friends of the band."

"Maybe you're on the guest list?" He checked the list for our names. I saw a Bobby, but that was a Bobby Levine from Virgin Records.

"She said we were on her guest list for life," I said.

" 'For life' is good. But she'd need to know you were coming tonight."

"But we always come!"

"That's not strictly true, Jo," said Bobby. "We had to miss that gig in Plymouth because Primrose couldn't—"

"Hush, Bobby."

"Look." The bearded man picked up a notepad and a pen and handed it to me. "Why don't you leave a note? I'll try to get it to them."

I wrote it quickly:

> Cosima—
> You said we would be on the guest list for life but I didn't know I had to let you know first and anyway I don't have your number. Can you get us in? We are outside.
> Love,
> Josephine and Bobby

The bearded man took my note, folded it, and put it in his pocket. I didn't like it in there. It looked like something he might forget until he undressed later that night. He asked now, in a nice way, if we could step aside. There were people queuing up, people who'd known to book or were smart enough to be on the guest list. Bobby was hanging half in, half out of the foyer, but I wasn't ready to get out of the way.

"Are you getting the note to them now?" I asked.

"Soon as I can. Why don't you go for a drink while you're waiting?"

"Make sure *she* gets the note," I said. "Not Rick or Sean."

"I'll do my best."

We went into a pub on the other side of the alley. We bought our drinks and sat down near the window so that we could see the entrance to the Tempo Bar. I took one of Bobby's cigarettes.

"You'll kill yourself, so you will," he said, but he didn't stop me. I looked at the long queue snaking out of the club. Some of the people were quite attractive. Perhaps I wasn't attractive enough to be on Cosima's guest list, though she'd said I was "cute" and "adorable."

"Bobby? Does 'adorable' mean 'attractive'?"

"Sorry?"

"You heard."

"The thing is, Jo . . . when she said that about us being on her guest list for life . . . She'd had a drink or two when she said that."

It took forty minutes for the whole queue to go in. When they did, I stood up. "Let's go and see now."

As soon as we opened the door to the club, I heard the band starting on "Yesterday's Full Moon Is Just a Thumbnail in My Sky Tonight."

"They've *started*," I said to the bearded man.

"Yeah, there's no warm-up band tonight.'

"But did they get the note?"

"I got it to them."

"But did they read it?"

"That I cannot say."

"Will we make a move, Jo?" Bobby zipped his jacket up halfway.

"No."

"Look, even if we do get in, we'll probably miss half the show, anyway."

"But I can still *see* her, get her phone number so I can arrange it properly the next time."

He kept fiddling with his zipper as if that was all he was interested in.

"You go on, Bobby," I said. "I'll be all right."

He looked up at me. "It's London, Jo. You've never even been on the tube on your own at night."

"I'll take a taxi home. Give us a tenner."

"Jo . . ."

"*Please.*"

He thought about it. Finally he brought out a twenty-pound note and handed it to me. "Take this. Just in case." His put his hands back in his pockets. His eyes were heavy. He looked like a man who had been mugged, who had twenty pounds less than he had a minute ago. I thought about going home with him after all. But I stayed where I was.

Once he had gone, I didn't know what to do. I was half-cold and half-hot: hot on my right side, which faced the club; cold on my left side, which faced the door and the street. I stayed in my half-hot half-cold place through all of my favorites: "Chevy Surprise," "Crash," "101 Here I Come," "I Never Thought I'd See You in These Parts," "Rather Be," "Summerfly," "Every Color of Love."

After eighty minutes I heard the crowd clapping and stamping and shouting, "We love you, Cos!" and "Moooore!!!"

Someone dashed into the foyer, fast and blurry, a white-blond head on leather legs. He swooped down on the bearded man. It was Sean. By the way he panicked, I thought she must just have got the note and sent him out to fetch me.

"Got anything for me, Rob?"

"Might do." The bearded man—Rob—reached under the desk and brought out a Shania Twain CD. I couldn't believe Sean would want to listen to a rubbish singer like that, even running out during the encore to get it. But Sean winked at Rob and shook the CD at his ear, as if he could already hear it. "You're a star, babe," he said, and I didn't know if he was talking to Rob or Shania.

Just as he was about to run back into the club, I grabbed his arm. "Sean!"

He looked surprised, and then his face crinkled. "Get off."

"I've been waiting all night," I said. "I was supposed to be on the guest list."

Sean looked at Rob. Rob shrugged. Sean turned back to me.

"You're that trucker girl," he said. "Look, I don't have time." From inside the club the stomping was louder. I didn't let go of his elbow.

"Come on, then." With me still hanging onto him, he tore us into the club. He leapt upon the stage and left me standing in front of the crowd. I was close enough to see Rick glare at Sean, and to hear Sean say, "Sorry, sorry."

The club was hot. People stood in their vests or shirt sleeves, their skin and hair silvery in the stage light. Bottles rolled on the floor, and the smell of something other than cigarettes was strong. The crowd cheered and clapped and stomped. Rick gave a mighty "One, two, three," and the band went into "Let Me Touch You for Awhile." I was all fired up. I didn't mind anymore that I'd had to wait at the ticket desk for so long. They were all smiling up there, even Rick. After "Let Me Touch You," they waved good night and went through a door on the stage. I ran onto the stage and followed them. Nobody stopped me this time.

Backstage, there were lots of people I'd never seen before. Cans of lager were passed around.

"That's the business!" someone yelled.

"Way to go, guys!" said someone else in an American accent.

I couldn't see Cosima. Katie and Sean and Rick were all standing separately, each in their own circle of people. I said, "Hi, Katie," but she didn't seem to hear.

Sean tapped Rick on the back and handed him a beer. As Rick turned to get it, his eyes flickered onto me, just a quick up-and-down.

"Child of the road," he said. He looked as though he found this funny, but he didn't want to make the effort of laughing. "Who let child o' the road in?"

Sean raised his chin at me. "Oh, you again. What are you doing back here, pussycat?"

"I was confused," I said, "about what I was allowed to do and what I wasn't."

Sean laughed. "I always feel that way." He was definitely in a better mood than he'd been before. "Have you said hello to Cosima?" He took my hand and led me to her.

She was sitting at the dressing table, surrounded by a wall of standing people. Sean broke us in. I waited for him to say something like "Here's little Jo, hasn't she grown?" but someone else said, "Great show tonight, O'Don-ahue," which started him talking, saying that the sound man was crap and had made everything too echoey. He still held my hand, but he'd forgotten about it. Whenever he made a gesture, my hand flew up with his, so that our two hands were like one bird making shapes in the air. Finally I pushed forward toward Cosima.

"Hello," she said. "Are you on your own?"

"Yes." I didn't know whether to hug her or not. She'd hugged me the last time, but with all these people around, it seemed odd. "Bobby went home. We couldn't get in." I waited for her to apologize for us not getting in, but then Katie came up and whispered something in her ear and Cosima laughed.

The backstage crowd was thinning. Rick came up to Sean and said, "What's the story?" and Sean just held up the Shania Twain as if Shania Twain was the answer to everything.

I didn't ask anyone if I could go with them. I just followed them into Rick's van and nobody stopped me. I sat in back with Sean and Katie. Cosima sat in front, next to Rick.

"I thought you weren't allowed to drive anymore?" I asked Rick, but Sean shot me a look as if to say *Don't ask about that.*

Sean's flat was the pinkest place I'd ever seen. It was lit by a pink neon cock-tail, a neon New York City skyline, and three lava lamps that made swirling patterns on the walls. On each wall was a huge movie poster—*Dust Be My Destiny* on one wall and *Barbarella* on the other, both with wild-haired women thrusting their tits at us. There was one shelf just for cowboy dolls, posed in different positions as if they were dancing.

I went to the window and looked down on Oxford Circus. I could see the Saturday night people, the lager louts and the tourists and the couples. Some of them waited for the night bus. I wondered if it occurred to them, as they set off for their homes in Tooting or Ealing or Dulwich, that someone was watching them from a flat right here in Oxford Street, in the middle of every-thing. I turned back to face the sitting room. Rick and Cosima were cuddled up on a settee shaped like a pair of lips.

"Margarita time!" Sean was in the kitchen area, fresh oranges rolling on the counter. He clicked on his remote control and the room filled with fiddles. Cosima tapped her knee and even Rick, who was rolling a joint, tapped his foot. I was about to say how much I liked this music, but then another sound came in. It was like the music kids listened to in school, drum'n' bass or jungle or whatever it was called. Sean swiveled his hips to the beat as he put oranges and rum in a blender. He poured the drinks into long glasses, tiny paper um-brellas on top of each one. When he handed a drink to Rick, Rick plucked out the umbrella and said, "Hold the frilly bits, mate."

"I'll have it," I said.

"You get your very own umbrella, pussycat." Sean handed me a drink with a green umbrella. I loved the way it looked against the orange froth.

Katie, who hadn't talked to me so far tonight, was staring at me now. "Hold on," she said, "I know where I know you from. You're that little girl we gave the makeover to."

"She's not so little now," said Sean. "You've grown about a mile, haven't you, kitten?"

"I still wear your top," I said to Katie. "I used to wear it as an overshirt, but now it's small enough so that I can wear it like a proper top."

"I gave you a top?"

"Too many chemicals, Katie," said Cosima. "They've addled your mem-ory. Speaking of which . . ."

She looked up at Sean. Sean ran to his coat and came back with the CD.

"Do you really like Shania Twain?" I asked.

"We love her." Sean dropped to his knees in front of his coffee table. He opened the CD with great care, as if opening it clumsily could cause Shania Twain herself to break. Everyone was quiet as they watched him. In the CD case, there was no CD. Sean fished out a tiny envelope. At first he looked like he was praying, but he was emptying some white powder onto the glass table. With a credit card, he cut it into lines. He rolled up a fifty-pound note and sniffed one of the lines. I'd seen this done on the telly and I knew it was probably co-caine, but I hadn't thought it would come in a CD case. All I knew was that peo-ple became addicted and that Daniella Westbrook, from *East Enders,* had lost the bridge of her nose.

Sean handed the fifty-pound note to Katie and she snorted the second line. When Katie was finished, she handed it to Cosima. Rick didn't want any.

I was panicking. What would I do when it was my turn? I didn't want to lose my nose! I would just say no. But when Sean was about to do his second line, I realized he hadn't even offered me any.

"Don't I get to have some?"

Sean looked up at me. "I'm sorry, pussycat. I didn't know if you—Okay, sure. Here you are."

"Wait," said Cosima. "Jo, have you done this before?"

"Yes."

I took the fifty-pound note from Sean. I put my hair behind my ears. I wished I hadn't lied about doing it before, in case I did it wrong. I snorted. It soared up my nose and into my head. I threw my head back and sniffed again. My mouth was numb and my whole head tickled. It wasn't bad, though I wasn't sure it was good. I felt awake. My skull seemed to be getting bigger.

Everyone had changed their seats. Rick sat in the corner with his guitar. Katie and Cosima were whispering on the settee. Sean and I stayed on the floor beside the coffee table.

"Did you enjoy doing your "Rather Be" video in L.A.?" I asked him.

"I did," he said. "But you know that Porsche I was driving? Well, I tell you, they made more of a fuss about that car than they did about me. They kept touching it up between takes. It would be like: 'Cut!' Makeup girl comes out to dab the shine from my nose, and then the props guy comes out and spends three times as long dusting down the Porsche, as if I had dandruff and I was flaking all over the bonnet or something."

"Oh. But you had a good time in California generally?"

"Absolutely, defo, but you know, I've been there loads of times now." He rubbed his finger along the coffee table, gathered up some loose crumbs of cocaine, and rubbed it along his gums. "Hey," he said, "I'll show you something. Come with me."

I followed him into the bedroom, which wasn't pink so much as furry. Leopard skins covered the floors and the wall and the bed. I wondered what it would be like to have everything matching. It was hard to think of anything matching in the lorry.

"Sit down there."

I sat on the bed. Sean took down a photo album that was also coated in leopard skin. He opened it to a photograph of the video, of him in the Porsche that got so much more attention than he did.

"They wanted me to dye my hair brown to look more butch. They're really dead conservative, these record company people. Now that we're getting fans from places like Texas, or Nevada, from people who like, carry guns and go to rodeos—well, God forbid there should be a peroxide princess like me in the band, a faggot playing country-and-western songs!"

"So . . . you don't like it in America?"

"I like it well enough. In fact, everything I like about it can be summed up in five letters, and I'll bet you'll never guess what they are!"

I couldn't guess.

He turned the page carefully, as if lifting a curtain. The next two pages were full of photographs of a guy about twenty years old, lounging by a swimming pool. He was blond, but a natural blond, and slim and beautiful the way that girls are supposed to be.

Jamie spelled out the letters. "J-A-M-I-E. What do you think of him? Spitting image of Jude Law, isn't he?"

I nodded, though I couldn't remember quite what Jude Law looked like.

"My beautiful boy. I'll tell you something—he hasn't been exactly what you'd call a good boy. In fact, he's doing my head in, if you must know."

"Oh. So he's your— I mean, like your boyfriend?" I felt funny saying this.

"He's my boyfriend, he's my best friend, he's my everything. I even got him on the video as a dancing cowboy."

"I didn't see any dancing cowboys."

"They cut that bit—they said it was too poofy—but he was there." Sean took my hand and put it to his heart. "But most of all, he's in here."

"But how can you see him if he's in America?"

Sean leapt up and opened his top drawer and waved a brochure in the air. It was a program from *Les Miserables*.

"You're going to see that?"

"He's going to be in it! Of course, it's a bit doolally, because just after he gets here, we'll be going back for the American tour—"

"You're doing an American tour?"

"Southwest. California, New Mexico, Arizona. We're thinking of relocating there, the band, I mean. Then I get to be with my baby all the time. Once he finishes *Les Miz*, that is."

I felt my face going cold, especially the tip of my nose. If I was going to lose my nose, I wondered if this was the start of it. Also, I needed to go to the toilet and it was a number two, but if I stank up Sean's pink flat, I would definitely mess up my chances of friendship with him. Because now I needed to become his great friend, to be the best friend he could ever have—someone he couldn't get through a day without talking to—so that he wouldn't be so keen to move to America. And he'd persuade Cosima and Rick that staying here was better for them as well.

When he got out Shania Twain again, I cheered up. It was a Christmas sort of feeling, watching him cut the little white rock into lines, rolling up another fifty-pound note because he'd left the first one in the sitting room. He seemed so settled and cozy right now, it was hard to believe he'd ever want to live anywhere apart from here.

"Will you still use this money?" I asked.

"Of course," he laughed. "Give it a good dusting, or I'll make some shopkeeper very happy, so I will."

The way he said those words—*so I will*—sounded Irish. I thought of

Bobby asleep in the flat. He was as far away as he'd ever been from me. I thought of going home to him.

From the next room, voices rose, sudden, angry ones.

"What's going on?" I asked.

"Oh, Cos and Rick are rowing, as usual."

"Rowing? Why?"

"Who knows? Rick's just being Rick, probably. I am so mad with Rick. He's been saying bad things about my baby. He thinks he's being clever and ironic, but I think he's being plain nasty."

"Rick doesn't seem to like most people," I said.

Sean sniffed his line. When he came up, his eyes were big.

"That is correct. Rick doesn't like most people, and it is a tragedy, Jo, because you know the person he really doesn't like? The person he feels the least amount of love for?"

"Himself?"

"That's exactly right. Himself."

I rubbed some crumbs of coke along my gums, the way I'd seen him do. I liked this new taste of me, this Jo who got it right. I didn't even have to go to the toilet anymore.

"Powerful weapon, this self-loathing," said Sean, "because even though it's himself that Rick despises, he can make others feel very inferior, very less-than-him. It's all locked up inside this arrogance. Do you know what the recipe for arrogance is, Jo? Arrogance equals low self-worth combined with grandiosity."

"So . . . do you not like him, then?"

"I don't like him, no, not at the moment. . . ." He hesitated. "And yet my antipathy notwithstanding, I do *love* him. He is a pied piper of the prairie, and a deeply hurt creature. I love *all* deeply hurt creatures—Rick, Cosima, my baby boy in L.A. All deeply hurt beauties, and me heart bleeds for every one of them."

From next door, the voices were loud again. Cosima sounded so loud and hoarse, she didn't sound like herself. "Go fuck yourself, Rick. *Fuck you!*"

The front door slammed.

"Was that both of them leaving?" I asked.

"I think so." Sean put his hand on my shoulder.

We listened to the silence.

"They're always at it," Sean whispered. "It's tragic. She loves him. But a person can love a person too much, you know?"

I nodded. "Cosima didn't talk to me tonight."

"Sometimes I wonder," he said, "whether Cosima really *talks* to anyone. She speaks, she sings, but whom does she really *speak* to?"

"Rick," I said. "She talks to Rick a lot."

"Yes. She talks to the one person who is incapable of really listening. That's why they are a perfect pair. Perfect in a fatalistic way, of course."

A samba tune rang out beside the bed. I jumped. It was Sean's mobile phone. He answered it and began to swivel as he did before, as if he was dancing. "Phil, you fat-arse poof, where have you been keeping yourself?"

I waited for him to say good-bye to whoever was calling him so late at night, to come back to our conversation.

"Okay . . . now? I don't know, I'm kind of— Uh all right, go on then, see you there."

Sean rang off. He put on his jacket, stuffed his phone in his pocket.

"Where are you going?"

"Heaven."

I didn't know what Heaven was but I knew I wanted to be in it. "Can I come?"

"Uh, I don't think it's really— I'm not sure it's really your scene. It's kind of . . . boys only tonight."

Suddenly I didn't want to go, anyway. A blanket of exhaustion fell over me. All I wanted was to be in bed for a hundred hours, with Bobby sleeping nearby.

"It's okay," I said.

"You sure? Well, do make yourself at home! And help yourself to alcohol. And, there's *taramosalata* in the kitchen, and Dolly Mixture."

"Right."

"And in case I don't see you, have this."

He handed me a card. It was pink with gold lettering. It said "SEAN O'DON-AHUE, PERCUSSION: *I will rock your world.*"

I put the card in my pocket. At least I could get hold of him now. Next time, I wouldn't have to wait outside the club, hoping only to be found by accident.

CHAPTER 14

1987

Bobby found it odd when people said the baby looked like him. It wasn't that he didn't want her to look like him. He simply didn't want to be reminded that there was another person for her to look like. At least she didn't look like Rosalie. Her skin was pink rather than olive, her eyes a jesting blue. It was hard to know what Rosalie's natural hair color was, but whatever it was, Josephine's wasn't it.

At nine months old Josephine came into full delightfulness. She fattened into a pert and perfect baby, her name shortening cheerfully to Jo. Strangers admired her at service stations, in parks, in shopping precincts. The old ladies were the best gushers. Bobby even forgave them for glancing over his shoulder in search, most likely, of some nappy-buying, damp-breasted mother.

The other lorry drivers were more doubtful. "How do you manage, mate?" they asked, some of whom went weeks without seeing their families and didn't seem to mind.

"We drive. Just like yourself."

It was as easy as that. They stopped for food or sleep or nappy changing. Jo was a good passenger. She wasn't a baby who cried for the sake of it. She cried when she wanted something. When Bobby couldn't work out what it was she wanted, she seemed to want to help him. Sometimes she'd stop crying mid-complaint, her eyes shiny with tears, before downshifting into a steady whine to coax him along: *Not the rattle, the bottle!* or *I'll have my nap now, I know it's earlier than usual, but the mountains of Snowdonia make me woozy, you know that.*

"Such a happy baby," said the white-haired Irish woman who sold them Linctus for Jo's cough.

"Happy enough, aye."

Jo gave her "happy enough" smile to the old woman. The woman clasped her hand to her chest. "Will you look at how she *smiles* at me!"

"All smiles," he agreed.

The woman laid a hand on Bobby's arm. "I have four young grandchildren in Mayo. I miss them to bits but it's better, so. They have dogs and fields to play in. Do you get back much yourself?"

"Not much."

"There's no mistaking that face of hers. She's an Irish baby all right."

Bobby did not think of Jo as an Irish baby. She wasn't an English baby exactly, and she certainly wasn't American. She was simply *his* baby. And yet people needed to insist on where the two of them *must* be from, where their home *must* be.

One day Primrose had a new order for Bobby.

"Bob, I'm sending you home to Antrim. Twenty tons of peas need a home in Ballymena."

Bobby wanted to say that while peas might need a home, a person did not. To tell her that Antrim *wasn't* his home, because he'd never felt at home there. Primrose would give the job to somebody else if he asked her to. But he didn't ask her yet, because he didn't want to have to explain. He wasn't even sure that Primrose, who appeared to have no family of her own to avoid, would understand.

In the lorry, he talked to Jo about it. "Will I change it, Jo? Get her to send some other punter up to the Glens of Antrim?"

Jo made a spit bubble.

"That your new trick, is it?"

Surprising himself, Bobby decided not to change it. He even felt a strange high at the thought of returning to the place he'd avoided for six years. It was like passing an open window and deciding to jump, knowing that something— his lorry, his beautiful child—would catch his fall.

On the M6, bound for Liverpool, he told Jo about stealing the Union Jack from the RUC station.

"I was never in any trouble as a boy, except for the that. Me and Cousin Mickey. We cut it up and made flared trousers, you know like they had in the seventies?"

Jo listened with her head inclined.

"And didn't I go and wear them? Didn't I fucking wear them to school one day!" Bobby laughed, and so did Jo.

What he didn't say was that he'd been pleased to be caught. He'd liked the headmaster who'd admonished him, the solemn Methodist from Edenderry. He even took comfort in his punishment, staying late in the classroom with its smells of pencils and chalk. The best part were the hours away from farm duties, and from his father.

"It was then," he said now, "that I first starting thinking. About leaving Ireland, I mean. I wouldn't have left my ma though, no way. Not with that miserable auld bastard."

And now he was going back, knowing he could get away again, though not before showing off the child he'd made without its help. Big Primrose—reassuringly un-Irish Primrose—was sending him to the mildewy clutches of his youth, only to oversee his return with a gurgling baby and an empty tractor, ready for the next delivery to someplace those Antrim *culchies* would never have heard of.

They took the Liverpool-to-Belfast overnight ferry. As they sailed west through the late summer's evening, Bobby took Jo on deck for her first sight of the sea. The sky was starry and motionless like the set of a play, but far below, the sea sucked and frothed and made angry swirls. He stood at the rail, holding Jo so tightly that she seemed a part of his own body. He leaned them over, just enough for their faces to tilt into the fury below.

"Twelve seconds," he told her. "We just have to look for twenty seconds, and then we can go back inside where it's warm. It's been six seconds already."

The sea spat up at them, tickling their faces with spray. Jo made a sound, a half-cry, half-laugh.

"Sometimes," he said, "and this was before you came along, I'd be doing a run to Dublin or Calais or somewhere, and I'd think about jumping. Not to kill myself, like. It was more like I thought the sea would pull me in whether I wanted to or not. You know what I mean, like? That you'll do it even if you don't want to?"

A second spray flew up. Jo let out a proper cry, a cry that made her sound not like herself. He drew back from the railing altogether. When he took her inside, there were faint pink welts on her arms from where he'd been holding her too tightly.

"Jesus, I'm sorry, baby. No more outdoors for us."

Bobby had booked a cabin for them to sleep in, but Jo preferred the bar. She was transfixed by the drivers with their pints, the girl in the cocktail dress who worked the blackjack table. He rocked her to sleep in her pram, though the motion of the sea made her drowsy anyway. Yet when she did fall asleep, he wished she would stay awake with him to enjoy their first night at sea together. When his own eyes shut, lonely places awaited him: seagulls following a ship off to war, the deep green intestines of the sea.

The ferry docked at 6:40 A.M. He woke to the sound of real seagulls and the creaky grunts of anchoring. Breakfast smells hit him in an assault of old comforts: the Ulster Fry. And with it all, the lads, emboldened by their return home, piped up:

"White pudding too, aye, and easy on the mushrooms, sweetheart!"

"Jem, what about ye, ye fat fucker! Haven't seen ye for a wee while."

Even the ferry had changed this side of the sea. The bar had become a caff, the English pint replaced by the Ulster Fry. He looked through the window, and there it was, the sooty Belfast Harbor, that old plutonium sky.

Something was wrong. For the first time in ten months, he hadn't awakened to the thought of the baby. *Where the fuck was the baby?*

There she was, a few feet away in her pram, and there was a lad with his big, bald, head dipped into it. The lad came up, his mouth an awful grimace, his hands waving behind his hammy ears, the blue-and-white Rangers scarf coiling like an eel around his neck and down into her pram. Bobby grabbed the handle and yanked it closer, but the scarf stayed stuck inside, strangling her!

It was Jo, he saw now, who was clutching it with her little hand. She was smiling, and not the good-enough smile for the old ladies, but the ecstatic one she usually reserved for Bobby.

The lad chuckled. "A lovely wean, so she is." His accent was broad, every word as sharp as a profanity. "She likes me. Och, she's beautiful all right."

"How do you know she's a she?" Bobby made himself sound as English as he could.

"She's wearing a dress."

"Billy!" His friends were calling him back. (Billy was the big lout's name; of course it was.) "Fuckin' Freddie'll have yer breakfast if ye don't get yer arse over!"

Billy blew a kiss down to Jo. "See you later, gorgeous."

He grinned at Bobby and went off to join his fellow Ulstermen, back, most likely, from a stag night or a football game in Liverpool or Manchester. They sat around a table of filthy ashtrays and empty cans of Tennents lager, the detritus of last night's piss-up. Some of them were reading copies of *The Sun* open to page three, to the naked bimbo with her mane of hair and bare breasts eyeing Bobby up from across the room. From here, too, he caught their sulfurous smells, their eggs and flatulence and last night's beer venting from their pores.

"Don't ever be fooled," he said to Jo, "by the laughing sounds in their voices."

As if on cue, a shout of laughter came from the next table. Bobby picked Jo up and held her to him. She needed to be changed.

Then again, the lad had meant no real harm, had he? His only crime had been to admire his baby, and who could blame him? He was a Prod sure enough, but England too was full of lads like these. England had *invented* them, as England had invented *The Sun* and Tennents lager. And yet, it was the extras that marked Billy and his mates out: the *what-about-ye*'s and *no surrender*'s (or *fuck the pope*, when the occasion called for it) and *Will ye ever remember Marty Bradley, rocket man, him!*

Back in the lorry, with Jo clean and changed, they drove through the checkpoint. The soldier made Bobby pull over. He made Bobby unlock the tractor so that he could have a look at the cargo. It took twenty-five minutes in total. Jo smiled at the soldier. The soldier did not smile back at her.

"British bastard," said Bobby as they drove west.

Jo let out a cry. He glanced over at her.

"Too warm, are you? Sure, it's not as cold as it looks."

He pulled over to remove her cardigan. He kissed her. Grateful, she spoke. "Aroo."

"Aroo yourself. Fancy a bit of music, Jo?"

He slipped in the Dale Mitchell Band.

> How I long for East Kentucky
> For my old banjo and my sweet-eyed Jan
> Oh, I'm longing for the bluegrass mountains
> 'Cause I'm a down-home country man!

Jo waggled her legs to the music.

"You like that song, don't you? That your new favorite?"

They drove west past Banbridge and into Mourne.

"Look at them mountains, Jo. Aren't they good? Aren't they lovely?"

Their first stop was in Kilminster, at a derelict-looking jetty that stank of waste.

"Hold it there, pal!" The foreman stood halfway up the jetty, waving his arms. "I'll come down to ye!" A minute later he drove down to Bobby in a dirty white van and jumped out. He was short and fat, with a shrill voice and an anxious County Down accent.

"Loughlin's the name, tinned peas are the game."

Bobby unlocked the tractor, but Loughlin was in no hurry to help him handball the gear. He lit a fag, put his hands on his hips, and looked around as though keeping an eye out for the enemy. "How are things," he asked, "on the British 'mainland' like?"

"They're fine, thank you." Bobby opened Jo's door to give her some air.

"Who's that there?" Loughlin darted over to have a look. He grinned at Bobby and back at the baby. "Fine wee ba', isn't she?"

Jo gave her real smile to Loughlin. She wasn't put off when he gawped back at her, showing three dirty teeth and three dirty gaps between them. She would have to start saving her smiles, Bobby thought, if she was to have any left over for him.

"The ma at the fat farm or something?"

"There is no mother."

Loughlin shook his head, assuming, as Bobby wanted him to do, that the mother had died. "Fair play to ye pal, fair play to ye."

Bobby said nothing.

"You'd be from up Ballymoney way, I'd say, are ye?'

"Drum."

"Not many of our kind in that place."

Bobby was tempted to ask how this fellow—a country runt, no less—knew what "his kind" was, with Bobby's Protestant-sounding name and all. The fact that Loughlin was right only annoyed him more.

When they had finally handballed the goods, Bobby reversed out of the jetty. Keen to wipe out the last of Loughlin, he put on Loretta Lynn's "Don't Come Home a-Drinking with Loving on Your Mind."

They drove through the Giant's Causeway.

"See that there, Jo? The earth here sits on these things called tectonic plates. That's what makes them rocks so choppy. Beautiful, aren't they? See that one there? Does it not make you think of a chocolate cake cut in half?"

They headed west and then south at Portrush. They passed McCallister's farm. They passed an Orange Lodge, led, funnily enough, by lodgemaster Jerry Adams.

"I'd forgotten about auld Jerry Adams," said Bobby. "Jerry with a J." He began to grow cold, deep in his chest as though he was actually getting a cold.

He hadn't told Anne that he was coming. People didn't really phone each other anyway, round here. Even when Adele came back from Canada to visit, she just turned up. Of course, that was when Bobby's ma was still alive, before they'd even had a telephone. But Bobby was still like his mother. He didn't have a phone to this very day, and pay phones alarmed him. He hadn't learned the language of speaking into a wire. He'd always felt his voice swallowed up by a black tunnel, and he never knew quite what he was saying.

"Fuck it. We won't go." But his wheels were taking him inland, along the B62 toward Cloyfin and finally to the sparse granite town of Drum. His primary school stood at the crossroads, and the Union Jack topped the flagpole he'd once stolen it from.

It was only when he pulled up to the old house that he wondered if he was lost. The house had been renovated to look like a Texas mansion, though it was too small to be a real mansion. An awning topped the doorway, a Western-style facade. On either side of the doorway two copper-plated lions, regal and ridiculous, guarded the place.

"Take a look at that, Jo. Sure, you'd be expecting horses and Marlboro men, wouldn't you?"

Jo had her dummy in her mouth and she didn't feel like talking. Bobby hopped down and walked up the path, his feet crunching on the stones. He rang the bell. He looked up to the upstairs window, where his old room had been. It hadn't occurred to him that nobody might be here.

Bobby had three sisters. The youngest, Anne, was eight years older than he was. Anne had helped to raise him, and he knew her the best. Yet if she answered the door now, he wasn't sure he would know her from Adele or No-rah. He remembered more about what kind of people his sisters were, as his aunties gossiped about: *Well, you know that Norah, she would be the stubborn one now, always has to do things her own way. Or Adele, with her traveling ways, doesn't she need to be the big girl in the big picture? Annie would be the sensible one, aye, though she wouldn't suffer fools, so she wouldn't!*

He could nearly hear them now; Auntie Niamh and Mary, a duo of thick-waisted widows with permed hair (one head of black dye and one head of beige) living together down Newtonards way, with their Jesus and Mary stat-ues and endless cups of tea and Custard Creams and talk of who was this way and who was the other way.

Bobby climbed back into the cab. "Will we wait, Jo? Or will we head back to Belfast?"

Jo had fallen asleep.

Bobby tried to remember more. What was the name of Anne's husband? Everyone liked him, even though he was a Prod. Thinking about it now in fact, was he not the nephew of Jerry Adams, master of the Drum Orange lodge? Jerry Adams had been at the wedding. He'd made some speech about both sides coming together, and Uncle Noel had whispered in Bobby's ear: "Aye, and let's see how fucking *cross-denominational* he is on the twelfth of July."

"Mike his name was! Protestant Mike. That's it!"

But Jo didn't rouse herself for this.

How quickly his thoughts had converted into this other currency! If a driver in England was getting married, you'd never hear anyone say, "A Protes-tant he is actually; kicks with the other foot, you know." No, in England, you'd never even *think* a thought like that.

"Born into the wrong family, that lad," Aunties Mary and Niamh had said.

So eager were the Pickerings—and the McMillans, on the ma's side—to adore their new honorary son that by the time of the wedding, Mike was known mostly by his nicknames: Good Guy Mike or Good Man Mikey, the gentle giant with the large hands. Good Guy Mike who played the flute but not for marches, no, who played *traditional* Irish music, which was more than any of them ever did! And didn't the Red Hand Commando go and threaten him because of it, issuing him a threat to "declare an embargo on whistles and fiddles"? *But did that stop our Mikey?*

He had had only had one real conversation with Good Guy Mike. Bobby had been seventeen, hiding in his room the way he did, listening to Buck Owens. His brother-in-law stuck his head in the door.

"Doing a few tunes with the lads later," said Mike. "Fancy coming down?"

"I don't play traditional."

Mike stepped into the room, picked up the Buck Owens cover, and shook his head. "See you've been well sucked into the American machine."

"It's not a crime, is it?"

"Too many Irish are listening to this rubbish. It's up to lads like us to get the old tunes going back up here."

"Lads like us?"

"There used to be great sessions up here. All of us together, Catholics and Prods."

"Sure I know all about that," said Bobby, who didn't, really.

Mike sat on Bobby's bed. "You know what my own ma said first time she heard me play the tin whistle?"

"No."

"It's awful Catholic, that's what she said. 'Awful fucking Catholic! 'Fenian music,' she called it. But we *all* played that stuff once. Even those god-awful Orange tunes come from traditional ones. Ironic or what? Troubles have wiped it all out! Some fucking place!"

"True enough," said Bobby. "Ever thought of getting out of it?"

"Oh, I would never leave it. Because for all that, I fucking *love* this place."

"I've no love for it, Mike."

"Then you'll always be chasing someone else's music."

But this didn't sound too bad to Bobby.

Don't get sucked into the American machine, Mikey had said. And now here he was, living in a phony prairie house, as if he'd stepped off the set of *Dallas*.

"Bet he doesn't do the auld diddly-eye these days," said Bobby now, but Jo was fond of her nap today.

A Peugeot crackled onto the drive. The driver was a curly-haired woman with a turned-down mouth. Her hair was speckled with gray and she looked older than he thought Anne would be.

He had thought to surprise her, but of course, Anne was never surprised. She got out of the car and appraised him as if he was an electrician awaiting orders. She came toward him, her feet making a brisk sound on the pebbles. Behind her, two tall, skinny teenagers skulked toward the house.

"Bobby," she said, "did you not think to ring?"

"Adele never rang."

"Adele *wrote*."

She turned to call after her children. "Ring your father, Duncan, and tell him you won't be going to football because your ankle's still bothering you. I can see that it is, there's no point in arguing. Pamela, check you've got all that dog shite off your shoe."

She wore jeans and a heavy anorak, ready for the rain that would surely come now, as if the weather would adjust itself to her. She spoke in that unshockable tone that middle-aged women had up here, a tone that always seemed to say, *Well, that's just the way things are.*

Feeling suddenly too young to have a child himself, Bobby lifted Jo out of her seat. Jo's hat fell off. Annie lifted the hat from the ground, wiped it on her jeans, replaced it on the baby's head.

"Da's told me about this one."

"Sure he's never even seen her."

"So? She doesn't need the old bastard."

"Where *is* the old bastard, then?"

"Pilgrimage at Croagh Patrick. Banning the snakes out of Ireland as usual."

Jo opened her eyes then, and seeing her aunt for the first time, let out a cry.

"She's cranky," said Bobby, "after her nap."

"Fair enough," said Annie, and followed her own kids into the house.

"New, that piano," said Bobby. "When did you get that, Annie?"

"Duncan plays it." Annie hadn't stopped since they'd come home. She'd dropped her daughter at swimming, bought some fertilizer, and penalized her son for some earlier rudeness by confiscating his Walkman. Now, while she prepared supper in the kitchen, Bobby settled Jo in the sitting room. Too restless to play with her usual toys, Jo found an old crisps wrapper that she scrunched in her fist and released over and over, delighted by the noise she could get out of it.

"Look at these, Jo." Bobby pointed to the photos on top of the piano. He picked up one of all three sisters, all with feathered hair and glittery tops and bright green eyeshadow.

"That was for the disco in Cloyfin, that time, was it not?" he called to Anne. "I was sat in your room watching the three of you torture your hair with that curling iron. I always wondered why youse never burnt your heads with it."

Anne couldn't hear him, or she wasn't listening. Bobby studied the photograph up close. He remembered the lip gloss they used, the fat pink tube that made the room smell of cherries. He remembered Gilbert O'Sullivan's "Alone Again (Naturally)" playing from the eight-track tape. He loved to watch them get ready, but the best part was after they'd gone, when he got to stay up late and snuggle into his mother's lap, watching Z-Cars on the old black-and-white. His father watched too, but he sat in a wooden chair, hunched forward as if at any moment there would be chickens to feed or calving to be done.

"Rest, Brendan," his mother would say. "Relax yourself."

But Brendan Pickering wouldn't. Rest was for mother and son, curled up together and slowly making their way through a plate of Jaffa cakes and a pot of milky tea.

"Supper!" Anne called now.

They all sat down at the kitchen table. "Mike's away in Cushendall all day," said Anne. "We'll meet him up at Mullen's later. They don't mind if you bring the baby. Remember that place?"

Bobby didn't.

"Ah, you do. Always a music session there. Traditional. They shut it down when the Troubles got bad, but it's back now." She handed him a plate of fish fingers, peas and sweetcorn.

Even dinner was hurried. Bobby wished he could keep eating after the food had gone. He hated not having something to do with his hands. The last time he'd seen Anne, they'd shared a cigarette. He looked around for his Bensons now.

"I know you're wanting a fag," she said, "but we haven't spent a fortune getting the house to look like this to stink it up with smoke."

Bobby nodded as if he didn't mind. "So Mike's doing all right, I gather?"

"Not too bad."

He mashed another fish finger for Jo, though she was less hungry than usual. She was mesmerized by the older kids, jerking her head at their forks on their plates or, too soon, their trainers on the linoleum as they left most of their food.

"Do they not want to play with their new cousin?" he asked.

"Sure, they're used to babies. They've dozens of cousins. Not that you'd know yourself."

As if to make up for the barb, Anne spooned the last of the vegetables onto his plate and took a look at her niece. "She's pretty enough, I'll give you that. She's the spit of how you were."

Still smarting, he didn't reply.

"Mind," she said, "I never saw the mother. The mother would have been dark, would she? A Jew, is that right?"

"Yes."

"Was she a Catholic Jew or a Protestant Jew?" This was from Duncan, who was up at the sink now.

Annie laughed. "That's as old as the hills, Duncan. What's that you're doing?"

"Washing my Walkman. You got grease on it."

"And why are you not doing that in the bathroom?"

"Pamela's in there, as usual."

Duncan went upstairs.

"He's mad with me for not letting him go to football." Anne seemed impressed with her son's teenage display. "But did you see the limp on him?"

Bobby didn't want to talk about his nephew's limp. For the first time in nine months, he wanted to talk about Rosalie. To let his sister know that Bobby had had a child with the kind of girl that Anne would *never* know.

"She wasn't a bad-looking girl, Jo's mum," said Bobby, but Annie was already clearing the table.

As soon as Bobby walked into Mullen's pub, the smoke and stout and sweetly rotting wood flooded him with something like memory, though he couldn't exactly remember being here. The pub was packed with tweed-capped farmers smoking Majors and drinking stout chased by whiskey shorts, but there were also students in their black jeans and Doc Martens, rolling their own cigarettes by the real fire. A collective spiral of smoke coiled up to the ceiling.

Good Guy Mike was the only person that looked as Bobby remembered him looking. He played the flute in the middle of the session, and when he saw Bobby, he raised his hand to greet him.

Anne put a hand on Bobby's shoulder, presenting him to everybody. "All right there, Fintan? Siobhan? You'll remember this brother of mine? See our Bobby, with his lovely ba'?"

"Sit and have a wee chat with us, Annie," said Bobby. But it wasn't until her third drink that she settled down with him at the back. She fixed the hat on Jo's sleeping head.

"Out for the count," she said.

For the first time since he'd arrived, his sister smiled at him.

"You must be relieved," she said, "that the old man isn't around. All he ever did was make you depressed."

"It was Ma getting ill that made you actually go."

"Well, you was always, you know, a wee bit out of sorts."

He shrugged.

"I still think of you," she continued, "out on the farm with him. All on your own, all dreamylike. He used to yell at you, she used to cuddle you. We used to talk about it, Adele and Norah and myself, about you being the only boy, and such a different lad than himself. And not to mention one of the only Catholic boys at St. Christopher's—that was when you started to go dark—"

"It was *Ma getting ill* made me go dark, Anne."

"It was Ma going that made you actually *go*. Nothing to keep you here, you see. But you were always a bit—you know, wrapped into yourself. We blamed him for being a miserable bastard with you, and her too, for spoiling you."

Bobby looked away from her. It wasn't that she was wrong. It was just the way she always seemed to know something he didn't, something she'd discussed with the others and worked out in his absence. He looked around the pub, as though these people, too, knew something he did not.

"You say I've been to this pub, Annie?"

"You have."

"He's too young to remember." The old farmer was on Bobby's left side, listening to the conversation.

Bobby looked at Anne. "Who's that?"

"That's Ricky." Anne was suddenly louder, censoring any further secrecy between them. "Bobby, surely you remember Ricky? From Cushendun?"

"He won't remember me," said Ricky. "Like I said, he was only small."

Bobby wanted Anne to explain and not Ricky. If he couldn't remember it himself, his sister's memory was the only thing he had.

"Your ma was in that session there," said Ricky. "She was a great singer."

"She sang?" Bobby didn't remember his mother singing, not in the house or the farm or anywhere.

"When did she sing, Annie?"

But Anne was shouting across the room. "Deirdre! I'm sat here! Come and meet the long-lost brother!"

Bobby looked up to see the woman who was Deirdre, a ginger-haired sack of a woman. Deirdre mouthed, "I'll come over in a bit," before sitting down next to Mike.

Old Ricky kept on. "Your mother sang here until the mid-sixties. She would sit over there, where your woman Deirdre sits now."

"Why did she stop singing, Annie?" asked Bobby. "Why did she not sing at home?"

Just then, Jo let out a groggy *aroooo*.

"Awake, are you pet?" asked Bobby, but he wasn't ready to let this go.

"I remember the last night she sang in here," said Ricky. "You must have been about two year old. She liked the sad songs."

"Oh, yes," Anne said. "Ma loved a good sad song."

If Bobby had been two, Annie would have been ten. She would remember it well, while all he had were these old pub smells to tease the edges of his mind.

"I hear you moved to England," Ricky was saying, "to join a country-and-western band?"

Bobby was in no mood to explain that Slow Emotion had been a country band for six weeks only. He thought of his guitar in Dennis's garage. It had been there for nearly a year.

"These days," said Bobby, holding the baby up, "the only thing I play is cassettes. Isn't that right, Jo?"

Jo wrapped her arms around his neck. Bobby wondered if she might prefer to leave now, to be tucked up in her seat and back on the road. They could catch the late ferry back to England. If he didn't have a drink or two in him, he'd do it. He'd line their best tapes up on the dashboard. They'd start with Johnny Cash.

A shushing quelled the room. Bobby stiffened for the speech, a toast to his return perhaps. Instead, the woman called Deirdre began to sing a capella. She sang with her eyes closed, as if she thought she was as beautiful as her voice.

> On the deck stood a handsome young lady
> With features I ne'er saw before
> And she sighed for the wrongs of her country
> Saying I'm banished from Erin's green shore . . .

Erin's green shore me arse!

How he hated it, all of it! The sad songs and the misty eyes of everyone from the students to the shandy-drinking fishwives. It was all very well to blubber after a jar or two. Even his father might start keening after a pint, but he'd be miserable enough the next day, making Bobby till the shittiest fields in the sleet and rain, or counting the biscuits to see that none had been eaten between meals, as mean a Puritan as any Prod.

Bobby gave Jo a little shake, wanting her to cry, to give a real baby *wah!* Instead, her eyes moistened, as if she, too, was keening.

"This was one of Josephine's songs, you know," said Ricky.

Bobby looked at Ricky, then back at Deirdre.

"You're having me on," said Bobby.

"No," said Anne. "He's right."

Late that night he lay in Duncan's room, the room that used to be his. The pub smells were still on him: fags and Guinness and sweetly rotting wood. Jo lay on the floor between her blankets.

"If I knew she liked that stuff," he said, "I would have played along with her. Even the diddly-eye, I would have done a wee riff." He reached down and touched Jo, but Jo turned on her side and sighed, like a wife who had been ignored all evening.

Bobby closed his eyes and tried to see his mother singing. He added touches to her, making her hair tawny rather than gray, shaving the weight from her hips, filling in the stonework of the pub. He painted Ricky—a young admirer—to one side of her, ten-year-old Annie on the other, and in the middle, young Bobby, listening as if he understood the words:

> My name it is Eileen McMahon
> My age it is scarcely eighteen
> I thank you, kind sir, for your kindness
> You don't know how lonely I've been.

CHAPTER 15

2003

It was strange to find myself alone in Sean's flat, but not bad. I decided I would help myself to another drink, eat Dolly Mixture while looking at the rest of Sean's photo album. I took the album into the sitting room.

But I wasn't alone.

He was like a statue of himself. Rick was sitting where he'd been sitting before. He had his guitar in his lap, one arm draped over it but not playing. He held a joint in one hand and a glass of whiskey in the other. His eyes were narrow on mine, as if he'd caught me stealing. I lifted the photo album up to show him.

"I was just going to look at this," I said. "Sean and I have been looking at it already."

He didn't answer. I knew I couldn't eat or look at photographs with him watching. I felt him wanting me to be gone.

"Or maybe I won't," I said. My coat was on the chair near the window. I put it on and swung my handbag over my shoulder, trying to look easy about things, as if I'd just changed my mind naturally. I went to the door.

Just as I was about to leave, he spoke. "Have a whiskey if you want."

I turned around to look at him. He didn't look any nicer than he had a moment ago. But then, Rick was never really nice, which meant he might actually want me to have a drink with him. I went to the kitchen, found a glass and rushed back to him, as though he might change his mind if I took my time. He poured me some Jack Daniel's. I'd never had Jack Daniel's before, but it seemed the right drink for him. He looked like his face should be on the bottle. I was gritting my teeth. I was cold, though I couldn't tell if the room was cold or if I was just cold in my bones. I looked around the flat.

"Sean must have a lot of money," I said.

"Or a rich old man."

I'd never thought of any of them having families.

"Sean says you're all going to California."

I thought he was nodding, but it was just a small motion forward, a dip of his chin as he leaned into his guitar. He began to strum.

"I know that song," I said. "What's it called?"

He kept playing.

"I definitely know that song," I said again. "What is it?"

"'Blackbird.' Everyone knows it."

"Well done, by the way, for winning that award."

He didn't answer. I wondered if he was thinking of Cosima and the row they'd had. I felt stupid with him not answering my questions. I wondered if he knew that I'd held him in my lap after his accident.

His hand slammed down and tore a riff out of his guitar.

"Did you write that?" I asked.

He slowed the tune down and made it sad again. "I wrote this when I was in India."

I tried to think of something to say about India. "Was it hot?"

He didn't answer. He sang:

> I been on every mountain from Boulder to Nepal
> I swum in every sea
> I found no difference between them all
> But I found a difference in me. . . .
> Time changes you, ready or not
> You never know what time will do
> But the only thing that hasn't changed
> Is I never stopped loving you.

It wasn't a song I'd heard the band do. He screwed up his face as he sang, making him look like he'd hurt himself.

"Did you write that for Cosima?"

He stopped strumming and carefully laid his guitar on the floor. It felt different with the guitar not between us. He could see too much of me. I gathered my knees together, tried to make myself look slimmer. I looked around the room again, pretending that I'd only just noticed the lava lamps and the *Barbarella* poster. When I looked back at Rick, he was looking at me.

"Can I ask you something?" he said.

"Go on."

He licked the papers and rolled his joint, taking a long time to actually ask me. "What do you want?"

It wasn't a question I'd really been asked. Bobby had asked me something like it, but it was more often about particular things, such as: *Fancy chips, do you, Jo?* or *We'll stop here, will we? Want* wasn't a word we used, not on its own like that.

"You mean right now?"

"Right now. Tomorrow. In ten years time. What do you *want?*"

Whatever it was I wanted, I felt he had the power to give it to me, somehow. If I didn't get it right at this very moment, I would never have another chance.

"I want what Cosima has."

He reached for his guitar again. I had disappointed him. I had to talk before he started singing again, putting his songs about women and India between us.

"But I can't sing," I said quickly. "And I can't play the fiddle. I can't do what she does."

"So why do you want to be something you're not, Jo?"

He'd never said my name before. I was surprised that he even knew it.

"Anyone would want to be her rather than me."

"What you want should come from the person you already are."

"But I don't know what that is. I mean, not quite."

He leaned toward me. I could feel heat coming off him. He lifted his hand to my face, wiped something from my mouth.

"You have coke on your lips," he said.

I should have been embarrassed, but I wanted him to do it again. He leaned back, took a drag on his cigarette.

"I suppose nobody really knows who they are," he said.

"But some people do things well," I said.

"There must be something you do well."

"There isn't."

Three chimes sounded from somewhere. I looked around but I couldn't see from where.

"That's the church down the road," said Rick. "It's three A.M."

Three A.M! I thought of Bobby. I wondered if he knew I wasn't with him, even in his sleep. But thinking of Bobby reminded me of something.

"There is something I can do. I can drive."

"You can drive?"

"I can drive a Scania 143. That's our lorry. I drive for us all the time now, even though I'm not legal yet."

Rick smiled, almost. "Well," he said, "that doesn't sound too bad to me."

"It isn't, no. When I'm eighteen, I can drive a rigid, but what I really can't wait for is to be twenty-one, so I can train for my own artic."

I had said too much. He didn't care about artics and rigids. He stretched his arm over his head. He looked bored.

But just when I thought he would stand up, he leaned forward and kissed me on the cheek. It was a short kiss, but after doing it, he kept his face close to mine. It was better than when Tom kissed me. It wasn't just my face that tingled. I was hot and cold both, all over.

He was pulling away now. In a moment he would stand up, stretch again or even leave. I had to do something. What had Cosima done the first time he'd kissed her? I remembered how she'd kissed Bobby in Belfast. How she'd put her arms around his neck, pulled him to her and just kissed him.

I brought my face close to his. I kissed him on the lips as if I'd kissed many men before. I braced myself for him to push me away, but he kissed me back. He put his tongue inside my mouth. He didn't seem sure. He didn't put his arms around me. I was losing him. He pulled away again.

"I don't think it's a good idea," he said.

"Are you worried she'll come back?" I asked.

"It's not that."

I kissed him again. He kissed me back. This time he did put his arms around me.

"I just don't think," he said, "that we should sleep together."

In a way, it pleased me to hear him even use those words. To be a girl—a woman—he might consider sleeping with.

"Can't we just lie down on the bed? Just for a while?"

He looked at me again. His eyes weren't so narrow now. They were wide and open, like they'd been when he rode the horse in that video. I waited for him to say no. He didn't say no. He took my hand and led me into Sean's room.

It was odd, the two of us in Sean's bed, but once we were under the bed-clothes, there was no pinkness, no leopard skins, just the two of us mixed up together.

I didn't know how to have sex. It just seemed right to keep unpeeling myself, to spread my arms, my lips, my legs; to open everything for him. I lay as still as I could while he made his way down my body. I felt his tongue on my neck, in my breasts, on my belly (it tickled but I managed not to laugh) until finally, down below, his tongue went inside me. It seemed about the weirdest thing a man could do to me, and yet it was right because it was him doing it. I thought of him doing it to Cosima and I could see nothing bad in it, no bad smells of piss or arse or anything like that, just the two of them lovely and close, and him doing it to me made me feel I had no bad smells or ugliness in my body either, and when I finally touched him down there, he wasn't sticky the way I thought a man would be, but smooth and dry. He lay on top of me and I felt his parts go hard against mine.

He looked into my face. "Jo," he said, "is this your first time?"

"No."

"You're pretty young. . . ."

"I'm not." I touched him and he went hard again, but I couldn't open myself down there. Slowly, he put himself in. I tried not to tighten up. I looked up at him. I couldn't believe it was Rick here loving me, about to love me totally, and yet I couldn't unfold myself for him.

"Relax," he said.

I tried to relax and but I tensed up even more.

He touched my face. "Do you want me to stop?"

"No!"

"Relax, then. You're lovely."

I took a deep breath and breathed into myself. He drew the tip of himself to my opening again. He entered me, sharp. I didn't mean to, but I shut my eyes. He went in another time, and a shock of red lit up my lids. I opened my eyes. He looked worried, but I smiled at him and he went in again. With the third stroke, I pushed myself up into him, inviting the pain in. I was learning how to do it. I was learning how to be the woman he thought of when he swam in his different seas and went to his countries and sang his sad songs, the woman he'd love all of the time even though *you never knew what time will do.* The fourth stroke was perfect, with him right up inside me. Even the pain was good.

CHAPTER 16

2 0 0 3

Bobby woke up to nothing there. Somebody had died but he didn't know who. There was a smell in the room like old tobacco, the last cigarette the dead person had smoked.

"Jo?"

He flicked the switch and the room flared up. A cockroach shot across the floor. In the lorry there were no cockroaches. A bluebottle in summer sometimes, hard to get rid of. Or a ladybird; nice. Only London had this vermin.

Her bed was empty.

His head was like a broken radio, the odd word fighting to get through the noise. Bobby never took a drink in the morning, but now he fumbled around the kitchen in search of it. He found nothing in the fridge apart from half a banana and a can of Tango. They rarely ate here, apart from takeaways, and there was no booze in this flat.

Or was there? His mind strained at some fuzzy long ago: Rosalie at the door late one night with a bottle of whiskey—the surprise of it! Skittish as a cat for being uninvited. That had been the beginning, the beginning of Jo.

He looked under the sink and there it was: the bottle. (It wasn't the first bottle—they'd done away with that soon enough—maybe not even the second or third, but a bottle sure enough, older than Jo herself was.) He took it to bed with him now.

"Teenager," said Bobby to the bottle, and he took a slug. Jo was a teenager, too, who'd stayed out last night, all night. She'd watched him leave the club. Her shoulders were bare and her eyelids were purple. She'd jutted her hip to one side and clutched her handbag as if her plans for the night were sealed up inside it along with her cigarettes and twenty pounds of his money.

"Go on now, Bobby," she'd said. "I'll be all right."

The static wavered. It crackled along the walls of his skull and made its way along the walls of this room. This was a *desperate* room. Why had he never noticed just how desperate it was? There were fat lines of dirt in the cornicing, scabs of peeling paint all over the wall.

He tried not to wonder where she was. He listened only for the distant groan of traffic. Traffic eased the pain sometimes. There wasn't much now, a siren heading east, for Plaistow, Barking, Bow. He lay back. He thought of Jo aged four, somewhere up the northeast, Sunderland or somewhere. A dusk had coated them both like velour, and she was too awake for any child's bedtime.

"Daddy, do the cars go off the road at night?"

"What do you mean, Jo?"

"Do the cars go off the road at night?"

"Look, there's a car, a nice C-reg Corsica for you, still on the road."

"No, it's not the same; it's different at nighttime."

"Aye, well Jo, I can't argue with that."

When had she started to jut her hip out like that? To fold her arms, to paint her lids the color of plums?

Go on now, Bobby. I'll be all right.

He closed his eyes. His hands fell to his underwear. He hadn't had an erection for a long time. He thought of the Europa Hotel. Cosima had been lovely that night, a weepy doll, her breath on his neck, her lips feathering his. She'd wanted him to stay. Why hadn't he stayed? Because of Jo, of course.

It was Jo, now, who stayed out all night.

He took another swig and lay back, breathing in the duvet and smells of that other time: of Rosalie and sex and strong hashish. What had she said in her note? *I'm no kind of mother.*

He put the headphones on, flicked back to Cosima singing "Eileen McMahon."

Sleep covered him up.

———

The guitar shocked him awake.

She stood over him. Big hair, big bosom, big legs; as big and tall a girl as ever there was. She held the Discman close to her pelvis as if she'd given birth to it, but she'd left the headphones on him, making Rick Watson's guitar shriek inside his head. He pulled them off but she caught them and put them on herself. She backed to the center of the room, the squeal coming from herself now. Her hair was tangled. Her top was wrongly buttoned, leaving too much of her chest and neck showing.

"Where have you been all night, Jo?"

"I can't hear you."

"Where have you been?"

She took her headphones off. "If I had a mobile phone, you would know."

"What?"

"Name me one driver who doesn't have one. Something could happen to one of us, and how would the other one know?"

"But why, if we're hardly apart?"

She shook her head at him, made a clicking sound with her tongue. "You need a shower," she said.

He didn't tell her that the shower frightened him these days, the force of the spray, the wet menace that seemed to want to *whish* him down the drain. But he went now, to get away from her and her talk of mobile phones. And today, it wasn't so bad. The warm water eased the bruising in his body and the hissing in his head. He let the sweat and the booze ebb off until he was ready to reverse the morning, to make a new one for them both. They had a ferry to catch, to Dublin. She liked Dublin: the buskers in Grafton Street, a drink at Grogans.

Once he was clean, she seemed less clean. She smelled of cheap perfume and tobacco and some kind of metallic sweat. A better father would punish his daughter right about now. He couldn't think of how.

"Aren't you going to have a shower, Jo?"

"Why? Do you think I'm dirty?"

"I didn't say that."

Jo didn't wash. Instead, she arranged herself, tucking her top in, pinning her hair up, making herself as neat and narrow as possible, ready to extract herself from the room.

They were quiet for most of the way up the M1.

"Looking forward to Dublin?" asked Bobby.

"Mm."

"We'll have two days this time."

"Uh-huh."

Barely in Milton Keynes and already they'd run out of things to talk about. He slipped in the CD, skipped it to "Eileen McMahon." Jo put it one track forward. The guitar screeched through the cab. Bobby put the CD back to "Eileen McMahon."

"My *ma* used to sing this song," he said.

"I know. We've heard it a million times."

"I want to listen to it again."

"Fine. Listen to it."

But he couldn't listen to it, not with her wanting it over.

"There was a time," he said, "when you never hated anything I loved."

She had no reply to this. When the guitar came on again, she turned the volume up.

In the Safeway bay in Birmingham, as the load tipped slowly into the warehouse, she asked for his wallet. He gave it to her, hoping that whatever she wanted to buy would make her in the mood to talk to him. When she came back an hour and a half later, she had a chunky box with the Virgin logo on it. Back on the road, she played with the smallest phone he'd ever seen, reading the instructions and keying in the numbers of people he didn't know. Once, in Warrington, she made him stop. She said she had to go to the toilet, but he knew she was calling someone.

On the boat, she did shower, for a long time. When she came out of the bathroom she wore a red dress he hadn't seen. Her hair was brushed big and it had gold glitter running through it. Her lips were painted red to match the dress.

At least she was nicer to him. "Are you ready to eat, Bobby?"

"The head's bad."

She sat down on the bed. "Do you want me to stay?"

He did, of course. But to do what? To want to be elsewhere?

"I'll be all right," he said. "Go and have your supper."

"Will I bring you something to eat?"

He smiled. She'd asked the question the Irish way, saying "Will I" rather than "Shall I." She'd even asked it with a touch of an accent, a sensible Antrim one like Anne's.

"No. You're all right, pet."

For a minute she didn't go. He wondered if she would stay after all, if she might even want to. Then she stood up, leaned down, and kissed him on the cheek. She opened the door.

"Try to rest," she said, and she left him there.

He lay down. The static began to drill into him, probing the edges of his skin. He got up, found his bag, and took out the bottle, the bottle that was older than Jo. He took a swig, letting it wash over him in a lovely tide. She'd put that same CD inside the Discman, and brought it here. He picked it up, skipped it back to "Eileen."

> Last night as I lay on my pillow
> A vision came into my view . . .
> Of a ship sailing over the ocean
> And the wind it tremendously blew.

He yanked the headphones off. Jo hated it. She hated it! She was as big as a woman now, and she sounded like a woman, a woman who hated the song his mother used to sing. He had Josephines on every side of him and they had never met each other, and neither of them was with him now.

He should have married Nurse Brid. He hardly knew her, but he should have done it; Lovely Brid, with her Galway accent and her childbearing hips, who had taken him, for the very first time, to Jo. She knew how he felt; he didn't even have to tell her. How he wanted to go to the baby, to touch her blue veins through her yellow head. How he wanted to run away and never set eyes on the creature again.

He threw the blanket off. He took a swig of whiskey.

Brid thought the baby wouldn't make it, though she hadn't said as much. But Bobby had had his rules: not to walk too quickly, lest he shock her into coma. Not to take the lift if it was lit by a red arrow rather than a green one; he must not go down in order to go up. Once on her floor, he had to get to her in twenty steps—not one more, not one less. Twenty steps to where she'd lain, limp as a dead pigeon on the pavement.

But then there was that day, when her eyes were open and her fists were playing with the air!

He was burning up. He had to get out of here.

Coming into the bar, the first thing he saw was the thick long girl with thick long legs. He saw the red dress, the mass of glittering hair, her back bare in its backless dress.

It wasn't Jo.

It was.

She was half a sea away from him, or half a floor away. She had a big man to the right of her, a big man to her left. The bigger of the two—a skinhead wearing blue and white, the Rangers colors—was handing her a drink.

So the Orange fucker had got her after all!

He took a step toward her. He was nowhere near. He forced himself on. He touched her shoulder. She turned around smiling, but when she saw him, her face turned to thunder.

"Bobby! Fucking hell! What are you doing!"

"I was going for a wee wander."

"Who the hell are ye?" said the skinhead. He was Scottish, not Irish.

"Focking care in the community, 'nt it?" said the other one. Jo yanked Bobby away from the men.

"What is *wrong* with you! What do you *look* like, walking around with hardly anything on!"

She took the bottle from him, leaving him without anything to hold.

"Jo—it's like—Christ, it's like—yellow dots, little wasps, black and yellow, wee wasps . . ."

"It's all in your head!"

"That's just it, they're in my *head*. . . ."

The Scot stepped between them. His eyes were solid black, no pupils at all. He wasn't laughing anymore.

"He bothering you, sweetheart? He giving you hassle?"

"I'm fine," said Jo.

"Look, pal, she's having a drink with me, you get it? Will youse pick on some lassie your own age?"

Bobby waited for her to say, "He's my father," but she didn't say anything.

"I'm talking to you, son. You fucking deef or something?"

"I'm," said Bobby, "I'm her—"

"It's okay," cut in Jo. "I know him."

Bobby took a step back. His stomach tossed up bits of old food, of body parts, a whiskey burp that tore like acid through his throat. If he didn't hold himself in, his insides would spill out of him, over the carpet, over her.

Jo took his arm. He let her guide him down the stairs, through the foyer, back to the cabin. She opened the door and drew the coverlet back. He sat on the bed, still hugging himself.

"Lie down," she ordered.

He toppled onto his side. He drew his knees up to his chest.

"Not like that. On your back. Stretch yourself out."

He lowered his legs and turned on his back. It wasn't too bad, with her showing him how.

"Close your eyes."

He closed them. The static was in his head, but it was just an *sssss* now, like the gas left on.

"Take a deep breath."

He did as he was told.

His mind began to drift, to fill with the color green: the hills of Antrim, the smooth intestines of the Irish sea. He waited for his mattress to sink beneath her weight as she sat on his bed. He waited to feel her hand on his forehead, cool as his ma's, keeping him from school, even when he wasn't so ill.

There was no weight on the bed. When her voice did come, it was from far away.

"I might not be here forever, you know."

He opened his eyes. She was still standing in the doorway.

"You don't know me as well you think you do. You don't know what I want. I may go to America. You don't know what I'll do."

He said nothing.

"I want you to promise that you'll stay in bed. Promise me."

He kept his eyes on the bunk above.

"I want you to *promise* me," she said again.

"All right."

She opened the door, letting in a sliver of light before shutting it with a switch-click sound and leaving him in darkness.

He doubled over to quell the pain, this eating himself alive. He took another deep breath, just like she'd told him to, and straightened himself out. He threw the sheet off. He stood up. He dressed, put his shoes on so she wouldn't hate him again. The box from her mobile phone was at the foot of the bed. There was a phone number at the bottom; her new phone number. He took it with him, along with the Discman. He opened the door and let it shut behind him, locking him out. He went upstairs, crossed the landing, turned left into the bar.

She wasn't there.

"You all right, mate?" It was a driver he'd seen before, a hippie bloke with a long face. He was in the wrong bar. How had he ended up in the wrong bar?

"You're looking a bit rough," said the long face.

"I'm looking for Jo."

"Looks like you could do with a chat. You can have some of my cider."

Bobby didn't want to stay, but he was dizzy. He crumpled into the chair beside the long face.

"What's it all about? Girl trouble, is it?"

"Jo's my wee girl."

"That tall girl? Ah yes. I've seen you two before. I do this crossing twice a week. Guess you could say I'm a sage of the sea, know what I mean? I see a lot of life on this ferry. Great big chunks of it."

Bobby nodded.

"I have a daughter and all. She lives in Swindon with her young man. I don't see much of her these days."

Bobby jumped, grabbed his own neck. A spider had landed on him, something from the ceiling. "What's that!"

Long Face brought his hand to Bobby's neck and extracted the wire, dangling down Bobby's front. "It's your Walkman, isn't it? Or Discman, whatever it's called? Where's the machine?"

Bobby ran his hand over his back pocket. As he took out the Discman, something dropped from his lap. Long Face picked up the box.

"You're all over the place, mate. What's this you have here? Oh, it's for a phone. Did you lose your phone?"

"It's my wee girl's phone?"

"Well, mate, if you can't find her, why not ring her? Have you got a phone?"

Bobby shook his head.

"We can have a go on mine." Long Face took a phone out of his pocket. He read the number on the bottom of the box and dialed. "It's ringing." He looked hopeful. "Hello? Hello . . . hello?" Long Face waited, then looked down at his phone.

"It's no good. I've lost her."

Bobby wrapped his arms around himself, sank his neck into his chest.

"Listen, old son, you don't look all that well." Long Face pushed his drink toward Bobby. "Have a sip of my cider, mate."

Bobby took a sip. It was sweet and horrible. "Can we try ringing her again?"

"You won't get a signal. Why not leave it for a bit? It's like I was saying about me own daughter. . . . I let her go, she moves on. They don't need us anymore. Regeneration. Rebirth. 'And as summer turns to winter and the leaves fall from the trees, the child I swaddled in my arms now stands tall above me. . . .' Do you know that song?"

Bobby picked up the Discman. "I have to go." He put the headphones on. He didn't look at Long Face. He took himself away, walking sideways to steady himself. Long Face called after him, but he didn't hear him anymore.

He crossed the landing and went onto the deck. The wind was spitting black spray. He turned the volume up on the song.

> It was then that I awoke from my slumber
> I looked for my Eileen to see
> There was only the face of my mother
> As she gazed with a fond smile on me.

A disk of light drew his eye. He pressed his face to the round window and stared into the bar. It was the right bar, the one he couldn't find before. He made out shapes of gold: a packet of Benson & Hedges, golden pints of lager held by men with shiny heads.

And then, entering the circle, there she was, big and glittering, Jo again, surrounded by Orange men.

Go on now, Bobby. I'll be all right.

He sidled left, running his hands along the damp wall, trying to find the door. Then he went back to the right. There were no doors. There was only the disk of gold and a bar of gold things and Jo, who couldn't see him now.

The first time he'd taken her on a ferry, she was nine months old. The Liverpool-to-Belfast. He'd booked a cabin but they never stayed in it. They stayed in the bar, and the sea had rocked her to sleep.

Now he was colder than he'd ever been—the tips of his hair, his nose, his lips, his cock, his knees—and yet his body flushed hot and he knew he was in fever. The song kept on—"for the want of employment in Erin, I am forced as an exile to roam. . . ."

He moved to the railing. The roar of the sea drove the music away. It gushed and whooshed and whipped his head, washing the static away and all. He leaned over, forced himself to look below. Sixteen years and four months ago, she had stood here with him.

Twelve seconds, he'd said to her. *We just have to look for twelve seconds, and then we can go back indoors where it's warm.*

Twelve seconds to look at the sea. Twenty steps to the Premature Baby Unit where she'd lain, the blue veins clear in her yellow head.

The wind kept whooshing, the cold running like a dagger through him. His head was bursting clean.

He lifted himself onto the railing. The metal was oily, slippery. He hoisted himself up with one foot, the sole of his shoe clinging to the rail. The other leg hung behind.

But then came that day—her eyes were wide open! Her wee arms playing with the air!

He thudded down on deck again. His veins were fat with poison. He was bust to bits inside.

Dear God!

He raised himself up again, both feet on the railing.

One.

The air sliced through him.

Two.

I do love you, Jo.

That isn't—

The headphones clinked against his ear as he tumbled.

Part *II*

LET ME TOUCH YOU FOR A WHILE

CHAPTER 17

2 0 0 3

His last kiss was long and groggy at the door. I pressed myself to him until I felt him stiffening against me.

"Best not." He pulled himself back, peered into the hallway as if somebody was coming. Nobody was. He kissed me on the forehead.

"Be a good girl."

He kissed me on the lips. He sent me off full of his sleepy eyes and the last graze of his stubble. I trotted down the stairs and into Oxford Street. The shops were still shut. Only a few people were on their way to work, men in suits and women in heels which made cheery *click-clicks* against the pavement. In the bright new space I drank in the just-now-ness of him. He was in my new woman's breath and my new walk and the new ache between my legs. I could still feel him down there, not even dry. I wouldn't wash until tonight.

I was alone as I waited for the tube, just me and two mice playing in the tracks. I watched the mice diving in and out of Coke bottles and sweets wrappers, as though trying on clothes that didn't quite fit them. I'd taken his guitar pick. I felt for it now in my pocket. It was the same texture as his fingernail. It lay against the card that Sean had given me.

I'd never liked the tube before, the non-lorryness of it: no daylight, no windows, no driver you could see. But now I enjoyed charging through the ground with strangers who read newspapers or stared into space. Across from me, a large, light-skinned black woman read from a book called *Poems from the Fat Black Women's Press*. Standing over her was a skinny white guy with dreadlocks and a dog on a rope.

At Liverpool Street the tube emptied. Even the dog guy got off. I was the only person going all the way to Mile End. I came up through the station and into the street, my teeth rattling in my head from the drugs I'd done last night. As I dragged myself along the Mile End Road with its stinky, honking traffic, the lovely soreness of him began to fade. I groped in my pocket for Rick's guitar pick, but it wasn't enough to fill the hole.

I wondered if Cosima had come back to him by now, if they'd made up or made love. If they'd made love, or were about to make love, would he wash himself first? Would he still have some of me on him? I didn't know how to think about Cosima now. I was jealous of her for having him, but it wasn't just her I was jealous of. I was jealous of the me that was younger by three or four hours, the me that still had him to look forward to.

I turned left into Harford Street, right into Shandy Street and into Kenneth Estate. I'd never noticed just how ugly our building was. Even the sunshine didn't help it today, heating up the rubbish and making the crushed lager tins glare on the pavement. The bins stank. On top of the rotten vegetables and pizza boxes and KFC wrappings sat a crooked teddy bear, its stuffing pulled out from the top. I went into the building and up the stairs, my chest heaving *no* with every step.

The smell hit me as soon as I let myself into the flat. He was twisted in a sheet and he looked like a hanging man lying down. His face was twitching, caught up with some worry even in his sleep. He hadn't washed for days. Could the lorry smell like this and I hadn't noticed? Could *I* smell like this? Rick wouldn't have come near me if I had.

I stood over him and pressed PLAY on his Discman. Rick's "Wildfire" charged through him. He sat up suddenly, shielding his face as though I was about to hit him. He wore two sets of socks which made his feet look enormous. He had been drinking whiskey.

I put the headphones on my own head, letting Rick's guitar drown him out.

Usually I looked forward to leaving London. I particularly liked to hit the roundabouts of the North Circular and make the final shove onto the M1, with Cosima's "You May Be Going Down But I'm Headed North" ready to go.

And because he'd showered and freshened himself up this morning, Bobby was up to driving.

But once we were on the motorway, I wasn't as keen as I usually was. London wasn't just Mile End anymore. It was Sean's pink flat in Oxford Street. It was the bed where Rick had made love to me. It was the Tempo Bar, where, in ten hours time, the band would do another gig, a gig at which I wouldn't be.

Bobby usually let me choose the music, but today all he wanted to listen to was "Eileen McMahon." I used to like that song, but there was something about the way Cosima sang it on her own, bare and hurt-sounding, that bothered me now. It was as if she knew what I'd done.

I looked out of the window. Only a few hours ago Rick had lain on top of me, his hair sliding into my breasts. He'd put his tongue in my mouth and my lower parts. He'd been inside of me. What if he wanted to ring me right now? He wouldn't be able to, because I didn't have a phone. *Be good*, he'd said. If I had a phone, he could see for himself how good I was being.

At the ATM machine in Birmingham I checked our bank balance. We had more than ten thousand pounds in savings. Though Bobby had been his darkest over the past year, we had made the most money, probably because I'd done so much of the driving.

After I bought my phone, I went into the Wimpy bar and ordered a black coffee. It was awful and bitter but Rick liked it; he'd had two cups of it this morning. I imagined us drinking it together over breakfast while reading real newspapers like *The Guardian* or the *Financial Times*, not *The Mirror* over cups of milky tea. I sipped my coffee and made my first call on my new phone, to Sean. After three rings, he answered by saying, "I'm *asleep*."

"Sean, it's Jo." My voice quivered. I rubbed his card in my pocket, reminded myself that he was my friend now.

"Jo?"

"From last night."

"Heya."

"Listen, I just wanted to thank you, for your hospitality and everything."

He paused for so long that I thought he'd forgot about our talk. Or worse, that he knew what I'd done with Rick.

"What time is it?" he asked.

"It's ten past one. I just wanted to say thank you."

"Oh. Well. No problem."

"And Sean? Rick gave me his number, he said I could have it to get on the guest list next time?"

"Uh-huh."

"And I've lost it."

He let out a noise like he was stretching. "I don't think he's here. Probably gone to find Cosima, patch up row number 3220."

I felt a pang in my chest when he said this. I tried again. "Well, could I get his number off you?"

"Oh . . . okay, if he gave it to you . . . it's 07989 324666—or 5, is it? No, it's 6."

"You're sure?"

"Try 5 if 6 doesn't work." He sounded more awake now. "And if you do speak to him, tell him to get his arse to sound check by seven!"

After I'd rung off I took a sip of black coffee. I dialed Rick's number. His phone rang four times before I heard his voice. I thought it was him, but it was one of those messages.

Speak after the tone. I'll probably get back to you.

He didn't sound the way he'd sounded with me this morning. He sounded like his old self, not even almost nice. The bleep went.

"Rick—it's Josephine—Jo. I just wanted to say that I'm thinking about you. I hope you're not too tired. I'm tired myself, but in a good way. I have a phone now, you can phone me. Here's my number—oh wait, I have to read it off the box—here it is." I read out the number, then repeated it. "And oh, yes, before I forget . . . Sean said to remind you to 'get your arse to sound check by seven.'"

On my way back to the lorry I went over the message in my head. I was pleased that I'd remembered the thing about sound check. I thought of Meg's Borderline two years ago, when Rick kept yelling at Cosima to hurry up with my face so they could do the sound check. I thought he was being unfair, but I should have known better. Cosima definitely should have known better.

Bobby was at the caff, his plate smeared with egg and baked beans from his all-day breakfast.

"Where's your *Mirror*?" I asked.

"I didn't buy it today."

It bothered me, the idea of him eating on his own without a newspaper. I paid for his breakfast out of his wallet.

Back in the lorry, we threaded our way through the lunchtime traffic, past a power station.

"Have a look at that, Jo. They look like wee rubber springs. What can they be making there?"

"You always ask me that. What makes you think I know this time?"

I put on Rick's solo again. I wondered what he would think if he phoned me now and heard his own music when I answered. He might say something like, "Well, somebody's got some taste around here." Most likely he wouldn't say anything. He'd pretend not to hear it, but I knew he'd be pleased.

Bobby's voice slopped all over everything.

"Guitar's dead ropey in this bit, so it is."

"What?"

"He's a wee bit ropey here."

"He's a wee bit *fucking fantastic*."

The road was thinning and the sky glowered, wanting to rain. We drove through the West Midlands. I kept staring at my new phone as if by looking away, I'd miss his ring. My phone had a camera in it. Next time I saw him, I would take a photograph of him, so that when he did ring, his face would flash across my screen.

We had three more drops that afternoon. By the time we'd got to Warrington, it had been four hours since I'd left my message. I gripped my phone, trying to squeeze a ring out of it. *Relax,* I said to myself. Rick had said that to me early this morning: *Relax.* I took a deep breath and breathed into my lower parts.

In the loo I rang Rick again. "It's me, Jo. I just wanted to say that I may have given you the wrong number before. This is the right number." I said the number slowly and repeated it again. "Ring me if you can, even if it's just for a minute. Bye."

When I came out, the car park was dark with rain, and Bobby was just a dark shape behind the windscreen. If it was yesterday, I'd have been asking about the static, trying to work out the thing that would help: Paracetemol, aspirin, a hot-water bottle. I'd be looking forward to when he could have his evening Guinness; that usually put some chat back into him. But at this moment, I couldn't be arsed to even ask.

We boarded just after eight and went straight to the cabin. I showered, soaping lightly on my private parts. As the hot water hit, I caught a whiff of me and Rick, coming up warm and yeasty. I had a little red dress from Miss Selfridge. I hadn't paid for it, but it had been easy to take. I had a pot of glitter to make my hair sparkle. With my new dress on and my face done up, I looked good. I looked like what I was; a girl just recently not a virgin. I wanted to hurry up so I could go and drink with other drivers, to see if they could tell the difference.

When I came out Bobby was sitting on the bottom bunk with his head in his hands. He didn't want to eat. He looked up at me. He stared at my dress, my legs, my hair.

"You don't like the glitter," I said, touching my hair.

"I wasn't thinking that."

I kissed his cheek and got out of there.

The jukebox was playing "New Kid in Town." This was one of the songs that Bobby used to play with Slow Emotion. It was that easy-listening, *who-cares* seventies rock, but it seemed exactly right when I walked into the bar. All the guys looked up at me because *I* was the "New Kid in Town" who everybody loves. I bought myself a large rum and Coke and sat waiting for the boys to talk to me. It wasn't long before one did, a big Glaswegian with a Rangers scarf and a shaved head. He looked like a hard man, but he was nice for a Glaswegian. His name was Trevor.

"In Dublin fay' long?"

"Two nights."

His friend came up with pints for both of them. The friend was fat but he was called Slim. Slim said, "What's your tipple, then?" and he went and bought a large Bacardi and Coke for me.

"New Kid in Town" finished. Horrible rock music began coming out of the jukebox. I said so.

"Do you not like Bryan Adams?" asked Trevor. "I was the one who put him on."

It was hard to respect him now, though when he gave me some pound coins to play something better, I took them. I chose Johnny Cash's version of "One." When I came back another drink was waiting for me. We'd been chatting for half an hour when I felt a hand on my back. I turned my head, expecting to see another bloke who wanted to buy me a drink.

Bobby stood there in his boxer shorts. His shoulders were slouched and he looked smaller than he'd ever looked. Gray hairs stuck out from his vest. He had a bottle of whiskey in his hand, most of it drunk. I grabbed the bottle from him.

"What the fuck are you doing, Bobby?"

"I was going for a wander—"

Trevor came right in. "Who the fuck are you?"

Every guy in the bar was looking now, not just Trevor and Slim. Looking at Bobby, I could see what they saw: a drunken old Irish pervert trying to hassle a girl half his age.

I pulled him downstairs and along the corridor. Bobby was clutching his stomach, bent over like a crab. I unlocked our cabin and took him inside and made him lie flat on the bed. He swallowed. It was a small, gulping sound, a sound a baby might make.

Be nice, I said to myself, but the need to be horrible hadn't left me yet. I was all crunchy inside.

"You're pathetic," I said.

Lying down, he looked fuzzy, the edges of his body blurring into the dark. He was like a man out of focus, except for the whites of his eyes. My eyes began to prick, but I blinked it back.

"I want you to promise," I said, "that you'll stay in bed now. No more 'wee wanders round the ship.' Promise me."

He didn't promise at first. I had to ask him twice. I left him there, shutting the door behind me.

When I got back to the bar, Trevor had another drink waiting for me. I'd been in a hurry to get back, but I couldn't stop thinking about Bobby. He'd never come looking for me like that, not so long after he'd gone to bed. I decided to go back to him, just to check he was asleep. I was just about to, when my phone went. I answered on the first ring.

"Is that you, Rick?"

I heard a man's voice but it faded. I ran out on deck but I still couldn't hear. The words MISSED CALL flashed on the screen. I pressed 901 but no message came. The wind smacked my hair and made my nipples hurt. I made a fist around my phone. I could imagine it slipping from my grasp, sliding down the deck and into the sea. That would be typical, to lose it now! But it wasn't going to happen. I had my lovely little phone and a message waiting for me on land. I was perfect and happy, with my new red dress and a call from my lover and the lads in the bar waiting to keep me in Bacardis. I went back inside.

"Popular lassie," Trevor said. "Lads ringing you this time of night. Boyfriend, was it?"

"It was, actually."

The jukebox was playing "I'm Not in Love."

"My dad used to play this with his band." I didn't tell them that my dad was the same man who'd been here less than an hour ago.

"Aye? Your dad a musician?"

"Not anymore. He drives for Hardy's Haulage."

"Oh, aye, Primrose Hardy. Not a bad old egg, is Primrose. Good worker, is he?"

"He is. He's a great driver." I was about to go back to the cabin, but the boys wanted to buy another drink for me. I let them.

It was after two when Trevor walked me downstairs. I was too tired for his questions, but he kept asking them: Did I know people in Dublin, would I be coming back on the same ferry? Halfway along the corridor, he put his hand on my elbow.

"This is my cabin."

"Oh."

"Slim's sleeping in it, too."

I was pleased to hear this. I didn't want to have to come up with a reason of my own to not go in there. But Trevor began to move in on me, pressing me toward the wall. I didn't want him to kiss me but I felt I should let him try, after all those drinks he'd bought for me. He brought his face up to mine.

"Go on. Give us a wee lumber."

"I know that word lumber. It means kiss in Belfast."

"It means kiss in Glasgow as well."

"Well, I can't really give you a lumber."

"Because of your boyfriend?"

"That's right."

"Big bloke, your boyfriend?"

"Bigger than you." I thought of Rick onstage. Onstage, he was bigger than every man.

"Well, I have a girlfriend and she's bigger than you. So give us a kiss. Just one."

I turned my face and gave him my cheek. He put his lips to my cheek, then he snuck one on the lips. When he pulled away, I could still feel the wet on my face. I slid out from under him, walked back toward my room. I felt him looking at me from behind. *"C'mon, doll."*

But I'd had enough of Trevor. Glaswegians made me tired after a while, the way they never stopped talking, and everything they said sounded like the punch line to a joke. And now that I thought about it, I'd never been so tired. It wasn't a bad feeling. I was melting toward my room, the carpet sliding under me like a drowsy orange road. I looked down at my phone but there still wasn't a signal. I wondered what Rick would think about me tonight. Had I been "good"? Maybe I'd been naughty, slightly. I wished I could be alone in my cabin. I would lie naked on top of the covers. I would think about Rick, do things to myself as he would. If he was on top of me now, I would let him enter me and there would be no pain.

I put my key in the lock, preparing myself for Bobby's smell. He wasn't on the bottom bunk. He wasn't in the top. I knocked on the bathroom door.

"Bobby?"

The bathroom was empty. I left the cabin again. He wasn't in the sauna. He wasn't in the little bar. He wasn't in the big bar. He wasn't in the public toilets. I went out on deck. I made myself circle the ship, despite the wind and the cold.

In the reception area, I met the night steward.

"What's up, sweetheart?"

"I can't find my father. His name is Bobby Pickering."

"What does he look like?"

"Brown hair, blue eyes. He was in bed the last time I saw him."

"Does he walk in his sleep?"

"No," I said, though now that he'd said it, I could imagine Bobby half-asleep in some corner of the boat, listening to "Eileen McMahon." "I've checked everywhere. The gents', the ladies', the bars, the deck, the sauna."

The night steward lifted his pager and mumbled something into it. I couldn't hear what he was saying, apart from the words "duty manager" and "stewardess." A few minutes later a plump, middle-aged woman walked up to us. Her clothes were crisp and clean but she had crumbs of sleep in her eyes.

"This here's Edith," said the steward. "She'll look after you."

"Would you like a cup of tea?" asked Edith.

The night steward walked away.

"Where's he going?" I asked. I wanted him instead of Edith. He seemed older, wiser than she was. With him here with me, Bobby seemed more likely to turn up soon.

"To find the duty officer," said Edith.

"Why?"

"So they can notify the search team."

"Search team? You mean they're getting lots of people to look for him?"

"It's just a precaution."

"WILL BOBBY PICKERING PLEASE COME TO THE RECEPTION LOUNGE! WILL BOBBY PICKERING PLEASE COME TO RECEPTION!"

"What's that? Who's saying that?"

"Don't worry, luv. That's the duty officer. Why not just sit down here with me?"

"I don't want to sit down."

There was a sudden clatter of feet, heavy ones stamping toward us. Seven men and one woman, all in thick blue jumpers, thudded into reception.

"Toilets!" shouted another.

"Deck C!" shouted the woman.

"Deck B!"

"Stairwell!"

"Bars!"

Each one ran in a different direction.

"I want to look, too," I said. "I want to go down to the lorry."

Edith put her hand on my back. "You're not authorized to go down there. Best let them get on with it. You sure I can't get you a cup of tea? A biscuit, maybe?"

I shook her hand off. I waited for the blue men and woman to come back with Bobby. I waited fifteen minutes and still, they didn't.

I thought the ship had hit something, so loud was the screeching, but it was a siren, a *WAWAWAWAWA* that sounded like it could kill you all by itself. Cabin doors slammed open and shut. Men, some with their shirts open, came up from the cabin floor. Trevor was one of them, and the hippie rigid driver with the long face. Their eyes were bulging.

"What the fuck's happening here?"

"Have we hit something?"

"Man overboard!"

A searchlight shot through the window. I ran outside. Beams of light criss-crossed over the sea. Edith ran out after me. "Come back inside," she said. "Please!"

I heard the helicopter before I saw it, flying just above the mast of the ship. I looked over the railing, but the sea spat out nothing. When I lifted my head again, the night steward was there.

"Any joy?" Edith asked him. He shook his head.

Just then my phone rang. The night steward smiled at me. It was a lovely, gap-toothed, old-man smile, an everything'll-be-all-right smile.

"That'll be him now," he said. "Probably trapped in some old broom cupboard."

I answered the phone, yelled *Hello!* as loud as I could. There was a pause, and then an automated voice saying, "You have a new message. Please stand by." Another operator, this time with an Irish accent, spoke to me: "Welcome to Telecomm Eirann, your Irish phone network. Please dial this number to speak to a service representative."

Red spots were flying at my eyes. I clung to the railing to hold myself up.

Dublin Port was drawing closer. A halo of light lit up the sky around it. At the harbor was an Irish police car, the *Garda Siochana*, waiting, I knew, for me.

CHAPTER 18

There were two detective guards, Fogarty and Staunton, a man and a woman. They were around thirty years old, maybe thirty-two. They gave me coffee and apologized for the state of the interview room, the grotty walls and the sandwich crusts in the ashtrays and other things I wouldn't have noticed if they hadn't pointed them out.

"We know what you must be going through," said Fogarty (the man), which was funny because a few minutes later, Staunton (the woman) said, "I can't *imagine* what you must be going through."

They took turns asking me questions.

"Jo," said Fogarty, "how often would you say your father and yourself visit the north of Ireland?"

"Every six months or so."

"What do you deliver there?"

"Metal sheetings, mostly. Canned goods from time to time."

"Anything else?"

"Microwaves. Roofing materials, once."

"Has your father ever had any dealings up in Northern Ireland—well, anything that might not be strictly aboveboard?"

"What do you mean?"

"Any kind of weapon, perhaps—guns or explosives—"

"You mean like, for terrorists or something? He hates that lot!"

Staunton rolled her eyes. "You're all right there, Josephine. I think my colleague's a bit out of date, so."

"I *know* they're on ceasefire, Tricia." Fogarty sounded hurt. "But there *are* still dissident paramilitaries, as you know yourself."

Staunton ignored him. "Jo," she asked, "has your father had a row with anyone, including yourself, recently?"

"Not a row, no."

"But . . ."

"Well, last night he came into the bar when I was drinking with some blokes there . . . he was a bit upset."

"Why?"

"There wasn't really a reason. . . . He gets a little bit sad."

Staunton nodded as if she understood. "Would you say your father was depressed, Jo?"

"Depressed" wasn't a word we used. Of course there was the darkness, but he never stayed in bed all day. He'd never been in the loony bin or taken antidepressants.

"No."

Staunton looked at Fogarty and back at me. "We've spoken to your father's boss. She thinks he may have been slightly depressed."

"About what?"

"We were hoping you might know. I mean—let's pretend he was depressed, just a little, just for the sake of argument, like. What do you think he'd be depressed about?"

I looked at Staunton. She had a small face with a tiny nose and a sprinkling of freckles around her nose and mouth. She had curly brown hair to her shoulders and she looked like a little girl and a teacher at the same time. She wasn't pretty, exactly, but she had a face that made me want to tell her things.

"He might be depressed about me," I said. "I stayed out all night the night before last."

"The boyfriend, was it?" This was from Fogarty.

I nodded. Even with everything that was happening, that word warmed me on the inside. *Boyfriend.*

"Well. It's not the biggest crime in the world, so," said Staunton.

"And," said Fogarty, "if your father wasn't all that well to begin with . . ."

"Why do you keep saying *wasn't?*"

"The thing is, Jo," said Staunton, "they've checked every inch of that boat. They've checked every lorry and automobile as well."

"It's easy to sneak into a trailer," I said. "Particularly if it's a curtain-sider, you could just cut yourself in with a Stanley knife. Primrose had refugees once, a dirty great family of them. Kosovan."

"But even if your father did that," asked Fogarty, "where would he have gone?"

"If I knew that, I'd be there with him."

"You seem very calm, Jo."

"Is that bad?"

"Jo," said Staunton, "You do realize . . ." She said "realize" in three syllables, like *re-a-lize*. She looked to Fogarty for him to finish her sentence.

"We were thinking," Fogarty lowered his voice, "that there's a possibility that your father may have jumped overboard."

"He would never do that."

"Why not?"

"Because he can't swim."

They just looked at me.

"He likes to go for a wander," I said. "Sometimes he goes for a wander."

"But why would he go for a wander in Ireland?"

I shrugged. "He's Irish."

"He's from the north, so."

"He never liked the north. He liked the south better."

After the interview they asked for a photograph of Bobby to e-mail to the missing-persons division and to the English and Irish papers. The only photo I had was in my wallet, the two of us with Aunt Anne and Good Guy Mike, eight years ago. Staunton took it to send off. When she came back she told me that she'd just been speaking to Primrose Hardy. Primrose was coming to Dublin tomorrow to take the lorry back, and me with it.

"I could drive it back myself." I said.

"We're sure you could," said Fogarty, "but it's against the law."

"Who has to know?"

"We *are* cops, Jo," said Staunton.

"You're not. You're guards."

They laughed, as though I'd said something funnier than I had.

Later they took me to supper at a restaurant called O'Hanlon's Steaks. We all three of us ordered burgers and chips and Fogarty and Staunton didn't mind when I smoked afterward. Staunton even had one of my cigarettes.

"Tell us about this boyfriend of yours," she said.

"He's in a band." I said.

"Ah, you want to watch them," said Fogarty.

"Watch who?"

"Lads in bands. They get about."

"Don't listen to him," said Staunton. "He's only jealous because he never got to be in a band himself." She leaned toward me. "And he knows they get all the pretty girls."

"Are you two going out together?" I asked.

Staunton laughed. "Himself? Sure, I wouldn't touch him with yours."

"*Tricia,*" said Fogarty.

And yet to me they did look as though they could be together, especially now—a mother and father taking their daughter out to supper.

After dinner I went home with Staunton to a suburb of Dublin called Stillorgan. We changed into our nighties and watched *Newsnight,* which was about Iraq and the weapons of mass destruction that nobody had found. There was also a section about a little Iraqi boy who'd had his arms blown off.

"What a state the world is in," said Staunton, shaking her head.

Usually, *Newsnight* bored me, but it was nice to watch it with Staunton while we drank hot chocolate and ate the best Madeira cake I'd ever tasted, cake she told me her mother had made.

At eleven-thirty, she fixed up her settee for me to sleep on. I wasn't sleepy but when she pulled the covers back for me, I got underneath.

"Is it all right?" she asked. "The bed, I mean?"

"It's lovely."

She looked at me as though she had something to say but she didn't know quite what it was. "It'll all come right in the end, so," she said finally, and she touched my hair before saying good night and turning out the light.

After she'd gone I lay thinking of Bobby. I wasn't missing him, because I felt him close to me. I could imagine him in a pub right now, a lock-in, listening to the songs his mother used to sing, and maybe even that music he'd always said he hated; the flutes and fiddles, "the auld diddly-eye."

What a state the world is in, Staunton had said. I wondered why Staunton didn't have someone to hold her in her bed, to make her feel better about the state of the world. She deserved that, I thought, a girl like her.

The next day, Primrose came to take me away from my new friends. We were having lunch in the refectory, the three of us, when she came bumbling through the door.

"I want to stay here," I said, without saying hello. "To wait for Bobby."

"But who would you stay with, chicken?"

"Staunton."

"I'm afraid you can't, Jo," said Staunton. "As much as I'd like you to."

"And look," said Fogarty, "if Bobby's going to turn up, wouldn't he do it in London?"

He was right, but the sight of Primrose kept me from saying so.

We took the day ferry back to Liverpool. Primrose stayed in the big bar reading *Truck & Driver,* so I went into the other bar to eat crisps and read *Country UK,* looking for pictures of Rick. I didn't find any, but it kept me from having to talk to her, or from going out on deck and feeling my eyes pulled down below.

We left Liverpool at three. Primrose drove our lorry and I hated it. She looked too big for our cab.

"The gears are bollixed these days," I said.

"I got it."

"Don't *jerk* it like that. They stick if you do."

"Jo," she said, "I may not know much, but I know about lorries. It was me who put your father in his first lorry."

On the M6 our silence was long, with the road snoring through us. I tried not to look at her because every time I did, she said "All right?"

Of course I'm fucking all right, I wanted to tell her. *The only not-all-right thing is that you keep asking me if I'm all right.*

"You know," she said, "maybe it's best that you stay with me for a while? You've never been to my house, have you? It's up near Biggleswade. Nothing fancy, but nice enough."

"What would I do in Biggleswade?"

I don't know, I just thought . . . "You all right for money, chicken?"

"You know we are."

"He worked hard, your daddy did. He left you well provided for. . . ."

"What do you mean, 'left me'?"

She didn't speak for a moment.

"Them cops," she said, her voice bright, "they say you got yourself a young man?"

"I might have."

I tried to sneak a look at Primrose without her noticing. Her eyes were watery, like blue marbles. Her face looked rounder now that she wasn't laughing, a fleshy circle with big eyes and bristly short hair. If she grew her hair and lost about five stone, she wouldn't be that bad. She could move further west, to Buckinghamshire maybe, on my map of women.

She caught me looking.

"What are you thinking?" she asked.

"Nothing."

Primrose wouldn't leave the lorry with me. She said it had to go back to Colindale.

"Promise you won't let anybody else drive it," I said. "Not even you."

"What if I have to move it?"

"You can drive it to move it, but that's all. I'd rather you didn't even *touch* it. And if you have to clean it, clean it only on the outside, not the inside."

"But promise me something and all. You'll talk to the police when they come round, won't you? That family liaison team or whatever it is they call themselves?"

"Okay."

"Jo?

"I *said* okay."

I was pleased when she dropped me off, but as I stood at the window and watched the lorry—*our* lorry—signaling toward the Mile End Road, I began to lose my balance. Not having the lorry was like not having a floor or ceiling.

I phoned Rick again, but I just got: "Speak after the tone. I'll probably get back to you."

I didn't speak after the tone. I thought he might call me if he knew my father was missing, but I wanted to tell him in person. But if I told him in person, wouldn't Cosima wonder why I was going to him and not to her? I decided to go to Sean's. Sean said they rowed all the time; perhaps they'd just had another one, and Rick would be on his own, as he had been three nights ago.

Yet once I was dressed up and ready to go, it didn't feel right to leave Shandy Street. Bobby could come home at any time. I found some paper in my school things, along with a big red marker. I wrote:

CALL ME NOW BOBBY! HERE IS MY NUMBER.

I taped it to the cupboard with industrial tape. I stood back and looked it. It looked lonely against the dirty kitchen unit. I wrote another one. I liked the smell of the marker. It smelled of a new project, of a plan that could be organized and made to happen. I wrote two more notes. The more BOBBYs I wrote, the sooner it seemed he would come. I wrote four more. I taped the notes to the refrigerator, to the chair, the window. When I left, the flat was fluttering with his name.

It was a warm night. I came out of Oxford Street tube behind a group of young people around my age, all talking and laughing. They went into a bar across the road from Sean's place. A few seconds later I could see them behind the glass, pulling out chairs, sitting round a table.

I rang Sean's buzzer but nobody answered. I sat on the front step of his building. There was a ratty fear in my stomach. If Sean came back, would he be happy to see me? Did he know about Rick and me? Twenty minutes went by. I watched two of the girls come out of the bar, smoking and having what looked like a private conversation. I wondered if they'd heard of Cosima and Her Goodtime Guys, or if they'd heard of Rick and thought he was tasty. I tried Rick but I got the voice mail again.

Finally I phoned Sean himself.

"Jamie?" he said.

"It's Jo."

"Jo?" I heard glasses clinking behind him. A girl was laughing.

"We were just talking about you," said Sean. "We *heard*."

"What? What did you hear?"

There was a blast of music and finally, a woman's voice in my ear.

"Jo? Are you there?"

"Cosima?" This was the first time I'd spoken to her since that night. I stiffened up, waiting for her to yell at me or hiss at me or hang up on me.

"We heard about your father," she said. "Are you okay, honey?"

"Yeah." I didn't mean it to, but my voice came out in a sob. It wasn't a sob of sadness; more like relief. She sounded so happy to hear from me, as if she'd been wanting me to phone her as much as I'd been wanting Rick to phone me.

"Why don't you come and meet us?" she asked.

I looked at the two girls all lit up with the bar behind them. They looked like an ad for the Gap with their khaki trousers slung low on the hips. They were slim and stunning, but I had people who cared for me.

Cosima gave me the address of her private club, a place called Cake. I had to walk up Frith Street four times before finding it. The entrance was down a metal flight of stairs, one level below the street. I rang the bell. The door was opened by a tall black woman who looked like Naomi Campbell.

"You're not a member, are you?"

"I'm here to see Cosima and Rick and Sean."

Looking as if she didn't really want to, she let me in. "In the back room."

I walked past the bar, purple and dark, where hushed and lovely people sat on high bar stools. I went down another few steps. The smell of hash hit me first, along with the *chooka-chook-chook* of a reggae song. The room was drenched in yellow light. It wasn't like any pub or bar I'd been to. There were only soft furnishings to sit on, like armchairs and settees. A sunset was painted on all four walls so that wherever you sat, you sat in front of it. A couple sat in one of the armchairs, wrapped up together and kissing. I couldn't tell which was the girl. Both had bleached blond hair and both wore leather jackets. On the floor beside them a bloke was rolling joint.

Katie was the first person I recognized. She sat on the arm of a big, deep settee, drinking something red and fizzy in a champagne glass. As I moved closer to her, I saw Cosima and Rick curled up in the settee. Rick didn't even seem to notice I was there. Cosima looked at me, but her eyes were heavy. Her eyes didn't match the voice that had talked to me twenty minutes ago.

"Hey," she said. "Sit down, babe. Would you like a drink?"

"Have this. I've had enough." Katie handed me her drink. There wasn't really anywhere to sit, so I stood and took a sip. The drink fizzed against my tongue, tart and sweet at once.

"That's delicious. What is it?"

"Kir Royale."

"God, Katie." It was Sean, sticking his head out from the snogging couple. I recognized the other person now. He was the boy that Sean had talked about; his five-letter reason for loving America.

"Only Katie would order Kir Royale in this place," said Sean. "Katie wants to be back in her native Soho House, don't you, darling?"

"I wouldn't mind going to Soho House," said Rick. "I mean, how eighties is this place?"

"Yeah?" said Sean. "And how seventies is your ponytail?"

"He's got you there, Rick," said Cosima.

He untangled himself from Cosima and went to sit on the floor beside the guy who was rolling a joint. Cosima looked lost. She kept her eyes on him the whole time.

"He's got no sense of humor about himself," said Sean's friend.

"You're Jamie, aren't you?" I said to him. "I've seen you in Sean's photo album."

Jamie gave a flutter of his lashes, as if he was posing right now.

Cosima lit a cigarette, crossed her legs and turned to me. She wore a gauze skirt that picked up the light and made her legs shimmer like a mermaid.

"Well, Jo," she said, "I don't know what to say. I didn't know your father was . . . in trouble."

"In trouble?"

"That he was . . . unstable . . . or depressed . . ."

It was odd, her using that word, too.

Everyone was looking at me, apart from Rick, who was still talking to the guy on the floor.

Katie touched my arm. "I really know what you're going through," she said. "My father took his own life. In Hong Kong. When I was five."

"How *are* you feeling, Jo?" asked Cosima.

"I don't know."

"She's in shock," said Sean.

"Actually," I said, "the Guards think he might have stowed away on one of the other lorries."

"He's left her either way. Suicide is abandonment." This was from Jamie. I would have preferred it to be just the original people, not this other American who wasn't even with the band.

"There was no suicide," I said.

"Yeah, shut up, Jamie." Sean turned to me. "Jamie here fell off the insensitivity tree and hit every branch."

A refrain went through the reggae: *It's okay, it's okay, it's okay, you know it's . . . okay . . .*

"It's okay," I said. "I love this drink."

"Would you like another?" Katie asked.

"I'll get it." Rick stood up. "We need another round here, anyway."

"Don't be ages, Rick," said Cosima.

"What do you mean by that?"

"I mean don't go to the bar and chat to everyone you vaguely know for three-quarters of an hour while our drinks get warm."

He turned and left.

"Let him do his own thing, Cos," said Katie. "We don't need him to talk to each other."

"You know what?" said Cosima. "You're right. Here, Jo, sit here, where Rick was sitting before."

I sat next to her. The spot was still warm. I was right in the middle now. Sean and Jamie even brought their armchair closer to me.

"You know, Jo," said Sean, "I had an uncle Max whom I was terribly close to. He died of AIDS only last year. It was a devastating experience for me, just devastating. But you know? At the same time, I didn't really grow up until he died. I think that for the first time in my life that I really looked my own mortality in the face."

"It must have been awful," I said. "It must have been like—you just couldn't believe it."

"That's exactly what it's like when you lose someone really close," said Katie.

It was the best conversation I'd ever had with anyone outside of Bobby. In fact, it was sort of like the conversations I used to have with Bobby, back in the days when we'd stay up together and he'd talk to me about the words of a song or say that his life might have been a thing misplaced by someone else. This was just as good in its way, talking about sad things over fizzy red drinks with the reggae going *It's okay, it's okay.* I was beginning to wonder if Rick was the one person I didn't need. My new friends were beautiful. Their faces glowed against the painted sunset. They cared about me.

"You know, Jo, I have been thinking about you," said Cosima.

"Really?"

"Really. I've been wondering—what kind of future do you see yourself having?"

"What do you mean?"

"I mean do you want a career of your own? Do you want to go to college?"

"I was never very good at school," I said.

"Neither was I," said Sean. "I mean, we can't all be like Katie here, with her Oxford degree."

"I hated Oxford," said Katie.

"But we had music, Sean," said Cosima. "That was *our* university, if you know what I mean."

"I have music," I said.

They all looked at me.

"I mean, I don't play it, but I listen to it all the time. I listen to you all the time."

"But how will you earn your living?"

"I'll drive."

"You'll drive?"

"When I'm eighteen, I can train to drive a rigid, if it's less than seven and a half tons. And when I'm twenty-one, I can drive the Scania if I get an HGV license. That's Heavy Goods Vehicles, in case you don't know."

"What's the money like?" asked Jamie.

"Gosh, you're rude," said Sean to Jamie.

"It can be good if you're your own owner-driver. We made thirty grand last year, after taxes. Mind, we're lucky, because Bobby never had a lease on the truck, he just owned it outright. And we drove more than we were supposed to sometimes, fiddling with the tackograph and with me driving as well. Don't tell anyone."

"Thirty grand. Not bad, is it?" asked Sean.

Though I'd always known it, I'd never laid it out this way. Suddenly my whole life, like the road itself, was rolling out in front of me.

"Respect!" said Katie. "Give me an articulated lorry over Oxford any day."

"You can drive our equipment around," said Sean.

"Forget that," said Cosima, "you can drive *us* around!"

At one o'clock we were still talking about my lorries and my future. I had had five Kir Royales but I didn't feel anything apart from amazing. When the Naomi Campbell woman started clearing glasses and saying, "Drink up, everyone," nobody wanted to drink up. Everybody wanted to carry on sitting in the soft chairs, talking about me.

Yet as I walked up to street level with the others, the street began to sway. The lights of Soho came at me like a swing and I had to clutch the railing to steady myself.

"We need to get you a taxi home," said Cosima. "Rick?"

Rick was still talking to the guy I'd never met. Cosima held my elbow, but it was hard to stay standing.

"I don't want to go back," I said. "I want to come home with you."

"Rick?" she said again.

His voice came from far away. "I don't think it's a good idea."

He came nearer, but his face wasn't clear. It was amazing to think I'd ever loved him. He was just a tall and mean and blurry man now.

"Please," I heard myself saying. "I'll just sleep . . . I won't talk about . . . I'll just go to sleep."

"What's that, honey?" asked Cosima.

"Look," Rick said. "Wouldn't you rather just get a taxi home? I mean, we'll give you the money."

The word *home* made my mouth thick with spit. The only home was my lorry and that was in Colindale and it was no kind of home without Bobby sleeping on the bunk below. Stripes splashed in my eyes like a scary version of the painted sunset. I bent forward and puked in the doorway. I wished the others weren't there to watch me, that I could do it in private like an animal who needs to die alone. Yet I needed them to see as well, to see how sick I was.

"For God's sake," yelled Cosima, "get her a towel!"

Naomi Campbell rushed up and handed them something. Cosima and Katie mopped me up as best they could with loo roll. I felt nearly restful, relieved at my new emptiness. Cosima walked me to the corner, where Rick was waiting for us in a black taxi.

Cosima's flat wasn't as flash as Sean's, but it was better because it belonged to her. The front room was smaller but it had big sash windows and wood floors and bookshelves of CDs. Three fiddles stood in their cases, like friends welcoming us home. Cosima took me into her bedroom and gave me one of her own T-shirts to change into. She tucked me into her bed, plumping the cushions behind me so that I could sit up.

"You shouldn't drink on an empty stomach," she said. "I'll make you something to eat."

I listened to the sounds she made in the kitchen, pots and dishes and running water. I heard Rick tweaking his guitar. After twenty minutes, she came back with a bowl of black pasta topped with dried-out-looking tomatoes, grated cheese on the side, and a glass of 7-Up; flat, she said, for my dodgy tummy.

"I didn't know if you like sun-dried tomatoes."

I tried one. It tasted like food that had gone off, sour and soggy.

I picked up a forkful of pasta. "Why is it black?"

"It's squid ink. Don't worry, it doesn't taste of it." She took a mouthful herself. "It's actually pretty boring. Have some."

She was right. I liked the blandness. It soaked up my gut and anything bad that was left over down there.

" 'Night, honey." She got up to leave.

"Cosima?"

"Yes?"

I searched my mind for a reason to make her stay. "Do you like Sean's friend from America?"

"Oh. I guess so. He's gorgeous, isn't he?"

"Like a girl."

Cosima got up again.

"Cosima?"

"Uh-huh?"

"I'm sorry to be so much trouble."

"You're no trouble."

"Can I stay here for a while?"

She sat down again. "Jo—haven't you got other friends? Friends of your dad's or something?"

I shook my head.

"It's just . . . we're going to the States soon. We've got the California tour. . . ."

"I'm sorry," I said, and suddenly I was. I was sorry for losing my virginity to Rick, and for not being able to tell her about it. I was sorry for puking in front of Cake, her special club. Mostly I was sorry for how I was now, for being my vomitty, sniveling, stupid self, in her clean white bed eating her black pasta.

"Maybe," she said, "for a day or two."

"Really?"

"We'll have to see."

I knew that "We'll have to see" meant she would ask Rick, but I didn't want to ruin it. I lifted a forkful of pasta, but I didn't put it in my mouth. "I don't think I can eat anymore."

"No? All right. I'll leave it here in case you change your mind." She took the bowl and put it on the side table. She pulled the covers up to my chin, the way Bobby used to do when I was small. She kissed my forehead.

"It's going to be okay, Jo. I can't say how exactly, or when, but I know it's going to be okay for you."

"You know that?" I said. "You know it for certain?"

Her eyes went off to the side and then came back to mine.

"Yes," she said. "I know it for certain."

CHAPTER 19

When I opened my eyes I didn't hear anything. There was no guitar, no talking from the other room, no noises from the street. I put on my trousers and walked into the sitting room. Sun streamed through the blinds and made patterns across the unmade sofa bed. Rick came in from the bathroom in his shorts and vest. He sat where his guitar was waiting for him.

"Sleep okay," he said, not like a question.

"I did."

My mouth and hair were grimy. I wanted to go and clean up, but I didn't want to miss my chance for us to be friendly again. As I sat down across from him, one of his bare feet crept back and I noticed how spiky his big toes were. He began to roll a cigarette. I wished I had something to do with my arms. Only four mornings ago, they'd been wrapped around him. His knee twitched now, as though my memory had disturbed him. "The thing is, Jo . . ."

I tensed up the moment he said my name.

"I know that Cos said you could stay for a few days, but we've been talking, and we both feel it isn't a brilliant idea."

His words were bad, but having him inches away made me feel there was hope. The last time he said something wasn't a good idea, we'd ended up making love.

"It's because of before," I said. "You and me."

He didn't say anything.

"I won't tell her," I said.

"That isn't the point." He lit his rollup. "Look, about before . . . Well, that shouldn't have happened. It's my fault. It shouldn't have happened."

"But didn't you like it?"

"You're a nice girl. But we're incredibly busy, you know, we've got the California tour coming up. . . ."

"I don't expect you to look after me," I said. "I just—I mean—I just want—"

"*What* do you want, Jo, what? Cosima isn't going to be your mother. And I'm not going to be your lover. Those things will *not* happen."

We heard a key in the lock. Cosima came into the flat with a bouquet of flowers. I waited for her to come to me, to rescue me from being thrown away from him. But she went to the sink and filled a vase with water.

"I have the most spectacular headache." She put the flowers in the vase and started to arrange them. She looked up at us. "What's up with you guys?"

We didn't answer.

"Rick, have you been talking to her? I thought you were going to wait for me. Make me a rollup, Rick."

She opened the blinds and the room filled with light, a yellow valley of light. I looked out at the sky. It was a cool driving blue, a blue to head north in.

"I don't expect anything," I said. "I only expect you to be my friends."

Cosima sat beside Rick. "We *are* your friends," she said. "Aren't we, Rick?"

"Mm."

She glared at him.

"*Yes.* I said yes."

Then there was silence, or near silence; the flick of his lighter as he lit her cigarette, the sound of her inhaling. I saw myself going home, a bad rerun of four days ago: the tube, the mice in the Coke bottles, the stairs to the flat, nobody there. How could I have hated Bobby just for smelling of a bad night's sleep?

"He won't be there," I said. "Bobby won't be at the flat."

"Haven't you got somewhere to go?" Rick asked. "Haven't you got aunts or grandparents or anything?"

"Not really."

"Well, we're very sorry about what's happened to you. We really are. But we've got to go to Bristol. In like an hour."

"No you don't. Your Bristol gig isn't till tomorrow."

Cosima stood up. "We're going down early."

"You didn't say that last night."

"We're seeing friends."

"Which friends?"

"Friends we met when we—"

"Fuck sake, Cos, we shouldn't have to explain our every move!"

"Okay, Rick! You know, she's pretty vulnerable. . . ."

"I *know* she's vulnerable. That's why she's got to get sorted out, see a counselor, go to a bereavement place, go anywhere but to fucking Bristol with us!"

It was the longest thing I'd ever heard him say.

Chalcot Square was lovely in the daylight, with wedding-cake houses in pink and white and baby blue, a lush green square in the middle. We walked to

Regents Park Road, where we were met by sweet smells: coffee, flowers, fresh bread. Even the pavement smelled delicious, baking in the early summer. People sat at cafés and ate pastries and drank coffee out of tiny cups. The road was clogged with cars, but the moment Rick put his hand up, a taxi floated up to him. Rick opened the door for me. I scrambled for the one last thing I could say that would keep me from being sent away.

"I could help you," I said. "I could go on the road with you. Help you move things, like Sean was saying."

Cosima kissed me on the cheek. "Go on home now, honey. I'll call you later."

"What time will you call me?"

"I'll call you at five."

"Can't I just stay for today? Just a day?"

"Get in, honey. I'll call. I promise."

I got into the taxi. Rick handed me a twenty-pound note. Just as he was about to close the door, Cosima leaned in and hugged me. I hugged her back as tightly as I could. When she finally did pull away, I grabbed her hand. She squeezed my hand back and gave me a little laugh. "You're going to be fine," she said.

Rick gave me a wave that looked more like a salute. He shut the door. He put his arm around Cosima's shoulder, and I knew he wasn't being affectionate. He was stopping her from changing her mind.

"Where to, luv?" asked the driver.

"What?"

"Where are you going?"

"Kenneth Estate, Shandy Street, E1."

He started off by going the wrong way, and I didn't tell him otherwise. He drove halfway up Primrose Hill Road with its picnickers and kids and dogs and kites lapping up the breeze. But then he made a U-turn and cruised back over Regents Park Road, past the shops and the people sitting outside of cafes with their tiny cups of coffee. To our left Cosima and Rick were walking arm in arm. Both had their leather jackets on and both had their hair in ponytails. The taxi sped up and I looked behind and watched them get smaller behind me.

We turned right at the bridge, past the Pembroke pub where girls and their boyfriends sat round a wooden table with wine and olives. We drove down Gloucester Avenue, with its big old trees and white terraced houses that sparkled in the sun, up Parkway, thick with fumes and traffic, past the Odeon where even at midday people were going to the pictures. We passed Camden Town tube with its crusties and punks sprawled on the ground selling the *Big Issue*, their skinny dogs on long ropes. North on Camden Road, the traffic was smelly and the houses were shabby and there weren't so many people, just mangy skateboarders taking the arc in Cantelowes Park, and finally, to our left, the red-bricked snore of Holloway Prison, with slits rather than windows. We turned right into the Holloway Road, pensioners creeping along with their heavy shopping, a black girl with her arse sticking out of tight white trousers, a dumpy white mother with a mixed-race baby coming out of Right-Style Furniture, then the industrial bridge shouting with graffiti—I'M FUCKING JENNIFER— and then rap music blasting from the Hen and Bucket, MC Revel yelling, "YOU DONE ME WRONG, MAMA, YOU MADE ME FEEL LIKE SHIT ON A SHOE, LIKE A PAIN IN YOUR HEAD, AND NOW I HATE YOU, MAMA, I WISH YOU WERE DEAD!" An ambulance nearly skimmed our side, barely able to wail through the traffic. We crossed the roundabout, northeast onto St. Paul's Road and Balls Pond Road, where everything narrowed. A sad-looking Turk stood in front of an empty kebab shop, in front of his window with its raw chips and chunks of raw meat. After Babs' Unisex Salon for Afro & European Hair the shops were few. We went east through Hackney into Tower Hamlets and onto Mile End Road with its evil-looking chavs in their hoods playing footie with a broken bottle, behind a Bengali woman in her sari, four dark children at her side. We took a right onto Harford, left on Shandy, and into the Kenneth Estate. The cabby said, "That'll be thirty-one pounds please, luv," and I had to use eleven pounds of my own money.

Only a few days ago I'd wished Bobby wasn't waiting here for me. I'd wanted to erase him, as though he was nothing but a speck of dirt on my window and Rick was the flannel that would wipe him out. He must have known it. He'd gone away because he knew.

As I climbed the stairs I began to lift with a creaky hope. Bobby always went away in his head, and he always came back. He could be back! He would shower, washing away the darkness that had made him run, and then I would shower, washing away the man who'd made me mean. We'd fetch our Scania and get ourselves back on the road. We'd forget about Cosima, find other songs to sing along to. We didn't need Primrose Hill or California. We could go to Cumbria. How Cumbria would look—not dog-running city hills but real valleys, gleaming lakes! *Have a look at that, Jo*, he'd say. And I would. I would never be a Londoner. I would never be an anything-er, apart from a driver, a daughter, a truck driver's daughter. The refrain from last night came into my head again: *It's okay, it's okay, it's okay, you know it's okay. . . .*

I opened the door and I saw his name. It fluttered from the cupboard, the window, the bed: BOBBY, BOBBY, BOBBY CALL ME, BOBBY, HERE'S MY NUMBER and another one that simply read: BOBBY WELCOME HOME.

He wasn't home.

I went to the window. The glass was too filthy to look through. I went to the kitchen and found a bottle of Dettol. The expiry date said 1986—the year I was born—but there was nothing else to clean with, so I rubbed it on a tea towel. I went back and pushed it around the glass. I looked outside through circles of smudge. It made me feel hopeful to see the street outside. But Bobby wasn't walking down Harford, or turning into Shandy Street. Nobody was.

At 2:20, I had two hours and forty minutes until Cosima rang. I didn't know what to do with myself in the meantime. I thought of going to the cinema, but I could hear Bobby's voice saying, *You're not going alone, are you, Jo?* He was right. I didn't want to sit by myself in the cinema. I found the number I had for Fogarty and Staunton. I hoped Staunton would answer, but I got Fogarty.

"Jo! How's yourself?"

"I'm okay."

"We're just after talking about you while we were eating our lunch."

I'd been to the refectory where they ate their lunch. Fogarty had eaten a Shapers lo-cal sandwich because he was trying to watch his figure, and Staunton had said, "Well, someone's got to," and she'd winked like a man at me, pleased with the joke.

"What were you saying about me?" I asked.

"We finally managed to get hold of your aunt up there in Drum. Your aunt Anne."

"And?"

"Nothing. No trace of him."

"He doesn't much like it there."

"I wish I had better news for you, Jo. We both do."

"I could come back to Ireland," I said. "We could all three look for him together."

I heard voices behind him. I listened for a female voice but didn't hear it. One of the men said "Heya, Cormac, how's the craic?"

"Listen, Jo," said Fogarty. "I'm going to have to make a move here, but we were just wondering, me and Tricia, are you on your own there? I mean, have you at least had a call from the Family Liaison team?"

"No."

"What's that, Oisin? Oh, right—sorry about that, Jo. I've gotta get going. I'll ring you later. Be good."

Be good. Another man was telling me to be good, but I didn't know what that meant now. Would it have been bad to ask to talk to Staunton? I was suddenly exhausted. I lay on Bobby's bed. I belched and last night's Kir Royale came up, a fading fizz on my tongue now. I closed my eyes and nonsense words came into my head: *Klagel . . . gorby . . . jit.* Was that what static was? If I could make my brain full of static, would my static find his static, the way one CB user found another through the squelch? I felt myself melting, spreading out like cheese on toast. I slept.

I woke at 5:17, which was seventeen minutes after Cosima had said she would ring. I rang Sean to ask him for her number, but I got his voice mail. Was Sean in Bristol, too? I decided to go to his place and wait to see if he came home. I thought of us talking about Cosima and Rick last week, of him telling me all his truths about the way they were.

It was 7:10 when I went down, two hours and twenty minutes past the time she said she would ring. As I came out of Oxford Circus, I looked down at my phone again. There was a little envelope, a message for me! I listened:

"Hello, Jo, it's Cosima. I'm just calling like I said I would, to see how you're doing. I hope you got some rest and stuff. Look, I'll give you a ring later in the week. Lots of love. Oh, Katie says hello."

I listened to the message three more times. I checked the missed calls button and saw the number she'd called from. I copied it into my phone.

But there were things about her message I didn't understand. Why did she say she'd phone me later in the week? Why not tonight? And I didn't understand why Katie had only said hello, not sent her love as Cosima did. The most confusing thing was that she hadn't asked me to phone her back. Most likely she didn't want Rick to know she'd rung me. Rick was probably talking about me right this minute, saying bad things to these friends they were staying with. He'd tell them that I'd thrown up in Soho in front of everyone. He would tell them in a funny way that would make them laugh and she wouldn't even want to ring me after that. He might even say that I had made a pass at him at Sean's and he'd said, *No fucking way*. She definitely wouldn't talk to me then!

I expected nobody to be at Sean's, but he buzzed me in straightaway, as if he knew it was me. As I climbed up the stairs, I heard dance music coming from his flat.

"It's open!" someone called.

I went in. There were four boys in Sean's front room. They were draped over his furniture and drinking creamy yellow drinks from straws, special straws with plastic ladies stuck to them. Jamie ran up to me. He wore leather trousers and a white T-shirt that showed some of his stomach.

"We thought you were the drugs!" he said.

Sean ran up, too, but stopped when he saw me. "Oh. It's you. We thought you were the drugs."

"I'm sorry."

They just looked at me.

"A friend of mine lives down the road," I said. "I've just been to see her. I thought I'd come and say hello."

"Oh," said Sean. "Fair enough, I suppose. Would you like a drink?"

The lie came so easily that it felt like the truth. I looked around for a place to sit. The only empty seat was the beanbag chair. I sank down as gracefully as I could, though my bum sank low and my legs stuck up stupidly from the floor.

"I'm sorry if I was insensitive last night," he said. "You know, about your father."

"That's all right."

I looked around at the boys. They were all as pretty as girls. Some were so skinny that their hipbones showed through their trousers, though their arms and chests were full of muscle.

"Have a piña colada." Sean handed me a creamy drink. He clapped his hands to get everyone's attention.

"Boys," he said, "this is Jo, and I want you to be nice to her. She's had an incredibly hard time recently!"

"Are you suggesting that we're not nice to people, Sean?" said one of the boys. He was Oriental-looking, but not like Katie. His eyes were rounder and his skin was darker.

"*You* certainly aren't nice to people," said Sean. "You're a bitch."

"He *is* a bitch," Jamie said to me. "To think I thought Phil was so sweet and nice when I met him. Really spiritual, *Tibetan* almost."

"Would you mind not calling me Phil?" The Oriental boy turned to me. "My real name is John. They call me Phil because I'm Filipino. Don't you think that's racist?"

"You love it," said Jamie. "It's that coquettish kind of racism that you just *love.*"

Phil ignored him. "Tell me your name again?" he asked me.

"*I* remember," said Jamie. "Don't tell me. It's . . . Josie."

"Are you at school, Josie?" asked Phil.

"She's a truck driver," said Jamie.

"Really!"

I was about to explain that my name was Jo and that it was my father who drove the lorry, but they all said "Ooh!" and Phil clapped his hands together so I let myself be Josie the Truck Driver. I loved my pina colada, coconuts and bananas swimming happily inside me. Sean started bringing out food. As he put each dish on the coffee table, he announced it as though it was a person: couscous with tagine, aubergines and feta cheese, rolled grape leaves, walnut-Roquefort salad.

"How do you all know each other?" I asked Phil.

"We're all in *Les Miz* together."

"We're not *all* in *Les Miz.*" This was from a tall boy with ginger hair, lying on his side across the lip-shaped settee.

"Oh," said Phil, "that ginger tart on the lips is Swan Lake. We call him that because he's in an all-male production of *Swan Lake*. So we're not just *Les Miz* here, though he's more 'miserable' than the lot of us together!"

The buzzer sounded and Sean went downstairs and came back with a small parcel.

"Finally!" said Swan Lake and Jamie at the same time.

Money was handed over and pills were passed around.

"Do you want an E?" Phil asked me. "They're nine quid."

"Oh, just let her have it. I'll pay for it." Sean gave me the pill. "You deserve a little bit of happiness, sweetheart, if only for a night."

"Thank you." I swallowed it with a sip of piña colada.

"Nine pounds for an E," Jamie said. "I can get it in L.A. for like four dollars."

"Try going to Italy," said Swan Lake. "They just about *give* them away."

"I've never been to Italy," said Sean.

"Don't be *ridiculous*," said Phil.

Swan Lake let out a long sigh. "I love your flat, Sean. It's kind of like Venus puked and it all came out Dolly Mixture."

"I do have some Dolly Mixture, as it happens."

"Oh, yeah," I said. "I forgot you had that." I wanted some now, but the boys were standing up and swinging bottles of water.

"Let's go!"

"Sean, can you take a bit longer fucking around with that food, please?"

"But I only just put it out!"

"Where are we going?" I asked, but nobody answered me. I didn't see why we had to go anywhere when we had everything we needed right here. But I followed them downstairs and into the back of a big Metro taxi. It was eleven o'clock and the sky looked playful, like a dark woman's face with glitter on it.

In Old Compton Street our group cut right to the front of the queue, and though the rest of the queue made *tsking* noises, the bouncers let us through.

The club was throbbing. Rainbow lights made psychedelic patterns over the floors and walls, and a big screen showed the dance floor from different angles: the floor, the ceiling, the side. In golden cages above us muscular men danced with their shirts off.

I didn't know if the drug had hit me yet or not. All I knew was that when Sean and the boys went to dance, I danced with them, though I'd never really danced before. I looked for myself up on the screen, but all I could see were boys, boys, boys—from the top and from the bottom and from the sides. I liked it that I was the only girl, until I realized I wasn't. I thought they were two men dressed up to look like girls, because they were so tall. But they were real girls, sliver-thin ones, Italian or Argentinean or something like that. Their faces were dark and uncaring, as if to say, *We're so gorgeous we don't have to bother with men who are not gay.* I felt big and lumbering dancing so near to them.

But then Swan Lake danced up to me. He tickled the back of my neck with his fingers. The lights changed, green and pink and orange paisleys all across our bodies. Words I'd never used zipped through my body, like *curlicue*. It was a great word really. It was everything that twisted or curled itself through things, which was quite a lot of things when you thought about it. I let the curlicue of my body twist me around, tug me down into the pounding *DUM DUM DUM* and up into the *wee-wee-wee* of the disco siren. For once there wasn't anything bad inside me like blood or shit or vomit, just the green-and-orange snail shapes. I was dancing with Swan Lake. I was dancing with all the beauty in the world and all the beauty in the world was dancing with me.

"Will you check out the Muscle Marys," shouted Swan Lake, pointing at the men in cages.

"Fancy themselves, don't they?" said Phil.

"Tell you what, though," said Swan Lake, "I wouldn't kick that one out of bed for eating crisps." He pointed to a bald black one in leather shorts.

"Too 'Tia Maria' for me," said Phil. "Give me a Malibu any day." He moved closer to Jamie, but Jamie held out his hand to me. He pulled me toward himself and Phil. The song slowed down and changed to something slow: "Sorry Seems to Be the Saddest Word." The screen showed a video of Elton John singing with four young guys in silver suits.

The boys—my boys—let out a whoop.

"I love you, Anthony!"

"I love you, Duncan!"

"I love you, Blue!"

This was one of the songs that Bobby had done with Slow Emotion. I tried to imagine him up there on the screen, playing his bass guitar, when Sean danced up to me and held my face in his. He was so close I thought he would kiss me.

"Are you enjoying yourself, Josie?"

"Oh, yes, Sean!"

"Well, that's all that matters."

Kylie Minogue was on a big screen now, driving her silver sports car through a silver space world, singing "Can't Get You Out of My Head." We danced faster. I wanted to make love. I wanted to fuck. I wanted to have a man inside me—Rick, Sean, Swan Lake, John Loughlin of Kilminster even. But at the same time, it didn't matter if I fucked or not. Dancing was a kind of making love, anyway. I looked around at my new lovers, Swan Lake and Sean. Where were Phil and Jamie? I wanted us all to be together. I went to the toilet.

In the toilet the sliver-thin girls came out of a cubicle together, throwing their heads back and sniffing out of their long noses. I went into the cubicle they'd just come out of. I sat down to pee and realized I didn't have to. I came out and stood in front of the mirror and looked at myself.

You're not so bad. You are a lovely girl.

My hair was as long as Cosima's and my eyes were as blue as Bobby's. I had a nice curve to my breasts, and real strength in my hips and legs.

You can dance. You are loved.

Feeling like I'd sorted something out, I came out into the club, ready for more dancing.

When I came out of the ladies', the music had gone ravey and violent. Two men were kissing against the wall. As I came closer, they looked like Jamie and Phil. I couldn't tell for sure because the strobe lights started, flashing so fast that nobody looked like themselves; just flickers of face and arm and hair.

I went back toward the dance floor, but it wasn't the same. I was having tremors, peppy little heart attacks. Sean was dancing by himself.

And then it was closing time.

We couldn't have been here three hours! And yet we had. It seemed wrong that anything had to close, that doors had to be locked or loving had to stop or that some of us had to wander off in ones or twos, not just stick together in one big group that danced on and on and on.

Back at the flat, Sean dimmed the lights. He put on a band called Zero 7. The music was oozy and dreamy, like cocktail bars in seventies movies.

Jamie and Phil were whispering to each other on the floor. Swan Lake sat on the lips settee with his eyes closed. I sank down in the beanbag chair again. Sean brought out a pot of mango-and-cinnamon tea and I didn't think I would like it but it felt good, the warm fruitiness going down my throat. It seemed unfair that I'd always been so mean about fruit.

My stomach was rumbling. I hadn't eaten all day. The fancy foreign food was still on the coffee table, but I wanted something sweet in my mouth.

"Sean," I asked, "do you have that Dolly Mixture you were talking about?"

"Good idea!" Sean seemed pleased to have another thing to do. He took a big glass bowl out of the cupboard and filled it with the tiny cubes. He placed it before me on the table.

I took a small handful. The sweetness was so good; it was everything. Even before I'd finished swallowing, I wanted more. I offered the bowl to Phil and Jamie, but they shook their heads.

"God, you English and your sweets," said Jamie. "I've never seen candy like the kind you guys eat here. No wonder your teeth are so bad."

"Uh, excuse me, Jamie, but do you see any bad teeth in the room?" asked Sean.

I wondered if my teeth were bad. Bobby hadn't taken me to the dentist all that much, but he'd always told me to brush my teeth. When Bobby came back, I decided, we would go to the dentist more often.

Sean sat beside Jamie. "You are so out of date," he said, "in your attitude toward the English. Have you failed to notice not only a marked improvement in teeth but in our culinary standard?"

"I was only *teasing*."

"I'm just bored of your 'teasing,' the way you always put us down. It's like we're a nation of cute and silly dogs or something."

"I never said you were cute."

When Sean didn't laugh, Jamie put his hand on his knee. "Oh, chill. Just chill! Look, just to make you happy, I'm going to eat some of this—what's it called—this *Dolly Mixture*. No matter how revolting it is. Josie, hand me over that bowl."

I handed it to him, but it was too far to reach.

"I'll bring it to you." I hoisted myself out of the beanbag. As I moved toward him, I hit my shin on the corner of the coffee table. Everyone said, "Ooh!" but it was too late. I fell and landed on Jamie's lap. All I could see was the floor, with the overturned bowl and the Dolly Mixture all over the pink rug.

A hand patted my bum.

"Oh, my. Someone needs to lay off the Dolly Mixture."

I lifted myself up as quickly as I could. I stood up. I was boiling hot, but I made myself look at him. "What did you say?"

"Nothing. I didn't say anything,"

"You said I need to lay off the Dolly Mixture."

'Well, you know, that stuff goes right to your hips. Forget it! It was just a joke."

"Everything's 'just a joke' with you, Jamie." Sean turned to me. "Don't listen to him. And you know what? I think you've lost a little weight. You've lost some of that puppy fat."

He was trying to be nice, but it made everything worse. "Have you been dieting?"

"I don't diet."

"I think that's wonderful. Sod what society says and all that."

"Excuse me," I said.

In the bathroom I stared at myself in the mirror. I was back to my true self again, my worst self. My arse was as big as two of their arses. I wasn't a beautiful girl who was loved by beautiful boys. I was a fat, ugly, sweaty girl who ate Dolly Mixture instead of salads with foreign names. I looked like someone who smelled bad.

When I finally came out of the toilet Zero 7 was still playing, but nobody was in the sitting room. I wasn't hot anymore, but numb and cold and wanting my bed. I put on my coat and looked around for my handbag. I found it on top of a pink chest of drawers, just before the door. One of the drawers was open. It was filled with matchbooks from Tokyo, New York, and Brussels.

There were cigarettes, foreign money, condoms, and keys. Some of the keys had labels attached: MUM. CHARLOTTE. JAMIE. KATIE. And finally: RICK & COS.

I picked up the keys marked RICK & COS.

I could hear Bobby's voice in my head:

Put them back, will you, Jo?

Just then the moan came. For one crazy second I thought the moan was Bobby's, a moan of disappointment, of sorrow. Then there was another sound from the other room, a noise that could have been sex or laughing. I put the keys in my pocket. I let myself out, down the stairs and into Oxford Street at dawn.

CHAPTER 20

When I woke up I was still dressed from the night before. I hadn't even made it under the sheets.

There was no air in the room. I got up and shook the window until it rattled. Plaster came loose from the top and crumbled into my face. I fetched a hammer and the knife from the kitchen and set to work on where it was painted shut. Finally I forced the window up and felt the first crack of air against my face. I took in East London and the traffic sounds. Two of the BOBBY notes fell to the floor.

I needed to think about breakfast. Bobby wouldn't like it, but my days of the Full English had to be over. I went to the Safeway. I didn't know how to diet, but as I walked through the aisles, I chose things I thought Cosima would like: tofu and muesli and skimmed milk. I even liked the idea of giving things up, as if sacrifice could be a sort of treat.

Two hours later the flat was stocked with healthy food and laundered clothes. With a spray of Citrus Surprise air freshener and the real air coming in from outside, even this hole smelled like hope. Yet once I'd eaten my muesli and yogurt and put everything away, I didn't know what to do.

Sean would see Cosima later on. He would tell her about last night, and I didn't know which part—that we'd all danced and fallen in love with one another, or that I'd fallen on Jamie's lap with my arse in his face.

But perhaps I was wrong to feel so bad about it. Those boys had teased each other all night. I'd even heard Phil say to Swan Lake, "Move your fat arse, cupcake," when Swan Lake's arse was in no way fat. I wondered what Bobby would say about it. I didn't really know what the rules were for those boys. We never really talked about poofs, though I could imagine Bobby saying "Don't say *poof*, Jo," the same way as he said "Don't say *Paki*."

If only I could only talk to her, I could tell her how the night really was, how close I'd been to the boys! But when I tried to picture her now, I saw Rick. I saw him standing between us and holding open the taxi door, his head dark against the sunlight.

The phone was ringing. I jumped up to get it.

"All right, Jo? I was just wondering how you're getting on."

Fuck you, Primrose!

"I'm fine."

"Have you been eating properly?"

"I had some pasta. It was black."

"That sounds a bit dodgy."

"What do you want, Primrose?"

"I was just thinking, chicken. You know Bert, the transport manager? He's off sick, you can come in for him if you like."

"Why? To tell people to go to all the places I can't go myself?"

I thought of her in Biggleswade, looking big and stupid at the other end of the line, and I nearly felt guilty for hating her. She couldn't help it that she wasn't Cosima.

"Right you are. Your friends, though? They looking after you?"

"I'm going to see them again tonight. They're doing a gig down in Bristol. Speaking of which, I have to catch a train now, so good-bye!"

I hung up. I was pulsing, suddenly. What I said sounded perfectly fine and true. I'd never had a bad night at one of their gigs. Afterward, I always had time alone with Sean, or Cosima (and, of course, there was that one time with Rick, though that had worked against me, really). I rang the Bristol Sound. This time I made sure to book.

I caught the train from Paddington at 5:40, my Shapers sandwich in front of me (260 calories) and the newest issue of *Country UK*. I sat by the window and watched London turn to farmland and the West Country. There was an interview with Cosima in *Country UK*. The heading said: SCOTT DIDIUS TALKS TO COSIMA STEWART: THE THINKING MAN'S COWGIRL. On the opposite page was the strangest photograph I'd ever seen of her. She was sitting against a big white cross on top of a hill painted in bright colors. Sprawling out from under her legs were the words GOD IS LOVE in bulging pink and red letters, and below that was a big red heart and the words: JESUS I'M A SINNER COME UPON MY BODY AND INTO MY HEART.

I read:

"I'm an American in self-imposed exile. There is so much I hate about the place. Yet at heart, for all my beliefs, I'm still an American sentimentalist."

So says rising country star Cosima Stewart. Cosima is proud to be an atheist, a pacifist, and a campaigner against the war in Iraq. Yet during her last U.S. tour, she insisted on conducting our interview not in the cool shade of the Chateau Marmont (her rustic-chic West Hollywood hotel), but here in the sweltering heat of the Imperial Valley, on a bizarre evangelical landmark called Salvation Mountain.

"It's ironic," says Cosima. "It's only since I left this country that I have a fascination for slices of Americana, these wild and wonderful relics I ignored when I lived here: hotcakes in the all-night diner, the sound of Johnny Cash in some honky-tonk bar off the Interstate 101. And only here would you have a place like this one, Salvation Mountain."

I ask her to tell me more about Salvation Mountain.

"Seventeen or eighteen years ago, in Vermont I think it was, a man called Leonard claimed to hear the calling of God. He moved three thousand miles west to inhabit this hill, and he has been painting it with his vision ever since. It's as good as any Warhol, any Hockney. I come here every time I'm in California. I climb to the top just to sit and think. And something about it—the gaudiness, the vulgarity even—well, it stimulates me. It infuses my world with color—literally."

I looked out the window to see what colors I could find. It was mostly green, apart from an old farmhouse or tractor.

The Bristol Sound was on the river Avon. I had time before the gig, so I bought a Bacardi and Coke and sat by the river. I didn't recognize him when he first walked out. He looked smaller and paler in the evening sun. For a moment, I thought he was an actor I'd seen on the telly. But then I realized who it was, with his skinny hips and his boy-girl face.

"Jamie!"

"Oh, hi, Josie." He came over with his glass of wine. He didn't look unhappy to see me. I offered him a cigarette and he took it.

"Are you looking forward to the gig?" I asked him.

"Not really, if you want to know the truth."

"Why not?"

"Well, I know they're supposed to be this neat ironic sort of band, but I still have this automatic reaction to country music—racist, homophobic and just plain white. Totally white."

To me, Jamie looked as white as you could possibly be. But we were having a good conversation and I didn't want to ruin it. "Have you told Sean how you feel about it?"

He made a waving motion. "You have to watch what you say around Sean these days. He's totally incapable of taking a joke."

I wondered if he thought snogging Phil was a joke. If it was, then his Dolly Mixture remark must have been a joke, which meant that I wasn't really fat, which meant I could get some crisps, because thinking about it, I was starving. But just then the announcer came on to say the band was starting.

As we were going inside, Jamie ran up to a small group of people, calling: "Tamsin! Briony! Brent!"

I waited for him to introduce me to Tamsin, Briony, and Brent, but he didn't. The band was coming on, so I pushed forward until I was so close to the stage that I had to crane my neck back to see them all. Sean waved to Jamie. Rick tinkered with his guitar. Cosima looked over the audience. Her eyes grazed over where I stood but she didn't seem to see me. She lifted her fiddle and went right into "Mojave Desert Girl."

And yet I couldn't enjoy it. I kept thinking of Jamie and the friends he hadn't introduced me to. Or Cosima and the way she hadn't looked at me just a moment ago.

After "Mojave," Cosima sang a song I'd never heard before. It was about a Mexican girl who works in a burger place in Pacoima, California, for $1.80 an hour. The girl's husband and three children are still in Mexico, but they smuggle themselves over the border in a freight container. By the time they reach California, they have died of suffocation. After the song Cosima spoke into the mike.

"That's called 'Where Is Home for a Girl Without a Country?,' and I want to say this isn't a true story. It's a *lot* of true stories! I hope that gives you all something to think about."

It was a lovely song and I wanted her to know I thought so. I tried to catch her eye again. She looked at other people—smiled at some of them, even— but she missed me every time or skimmed over to the person behind me.

I couldn't bear the encores. When there was another encore and then another, my nose blocked up as if I was being pushed under by the crowd. The only thing that would make it better was if I could talk to her alone.

When the encores finally finished, I ran back to where Jamie was going backstage with Tamsin, Briony, and Brent. But just as I was following them in, a man at the door stopped me.

"Are you on the guest list?"

"I'm a friend of Cosima's!"

"If you're not on the guest list, I can't let you through."

"I'm her good friend. I spent the last few days with her and the band."

"Can you step away, please?" He waved through the girl behind me.

I went outside to get a signal on my phone. I rang Cosima but I got her voice mail. I walked around the building until I found an alley. A van like Rick's was parked here. I went up to see if it was his, but I heard people talking and I jumped back. Katie was coming through the back door with her boyfriend.

The door opened again and Sean's voice flew out before he did. "You're only saying we were great because *I* said we were crap—"

"No," said Jamie, "I thought you were *genuinely* good."

Cosima and Rick came out last, along with Tamsin, Briony, and Brent and two other people I'd never seen before. They spilled into the alley, taking up all the free space.

"Crap!" Sean was yelling. "Total crapness, don't argue with your lover—"

"*I* thought you were great," I said.

Nobody heard me. They just kept talking loudly, interrupting one another. Cosima threw her hair back and laughed at something someone said. That was when she saw me. She stopped laughing. Slowly she walked up to me.

"Jo."

Suddenly Rick was there too, on the other side of me.

"We hear you went to Sean's last night," he said.

"There were lots of people there. He said it was okay."

"Sean's a good-hearted guy," said Cosima, "but I don't think he has a sense of how fragile you are at the moment."

"I'm not fragile."

"Jo," said Cosima, "do you have a mom? Is your mom alive?"

"She's in California. I never met her."

Rick and Cosima looked at each other. Everybody was staring at me now. In a way, it wasn't bad. It made me feel that something was going to happen, something that would make them care for me, like they had in the Cake club the night before last.

"We'd like to help you—" said Cosima.

"But we can't help you." Rick went up to the van, opened the sliding door with a loud noise. "What we *can* do is give you a lift to the train station."

"Wait a minute, Rick." Cosima put her hand on his arm. "There must be *someone* we can call? A friend or something?"

"Only you."

Rick put his hands on his hips. "You'd better get in."

"You don't want me to get in, Cosima, do you?"

"I *do* want you to get in." But her voice stayed nice.

"C'mon, Jo." Rick was waiting.

I got into the van. Rick and Cosima got in the front. As we drove away I looked at the others to see if they were watching, but they'd all gone back to their conversations.

I hoped it was too late for trains, but the 12:10 was waiting on platform two. Rick went to buy my ticket, leaving Cosima and me with just a minute to ourselves.

"Rick will pay for the ticket," said Cosima.

I knew that already. Rick enjoyed paying for things when it came to getting rid of me. Before I could say anything else, he came back and handed me the ticket.

"Rick," I said. "Please can I stay? Just for tonight."

He was quiet, as if he might be thinking about it.

"No," he said.

"Get on the train, honey," said Cosima.

They watched until I did. I walked fast along the carriage, found a seat beside a window. Cosima and Rick were still standing on the platform watching as the train took me away.

CHAPTER 21

On the 12:10 to Paddington there were no hopeful green fields at my side. There was only a low, wheezy chugging and a blackness outside, broken by a streetlight or a factory or a car with its beams on.

When I walked into the flat, his name was everywhere, as if the notes had reproduced themselves: BOBBY on the floor, the shelf, the telly, the counter, the walls. I didn't remember writing more notes. I did remember leaving the window open, knowing that nobody would scale this building, climb into this pit where there was nothing to steal. Yet I felt I would nearly welcome the company of a burglar now. Whatever he would do to me, at least he would pay me some attention, not make me disappear as Rick had done and made her do.

I stripped down naked and got into bed. A lorry passed outside. I'd always liked lorries passing as we slept, the friendly roadquake that told me I would soon be moving again. But now a long horn sounded, followed by *I'll kick your fucking head in, wanker!* I sat up and lit a cigarette. The shouting got louder. I grabbed my Discman and put on Cosima to drown it out:

It's been a long time coming
As you shed a lonely tear
Now you're in a wonderama
I wonder what you're doing here
The flame no longer flickers
You're feeling just like a fool
You keep staring into your liquor
Wondering what to do . . .

If the song were a real situation, with she and me in it, I wondered which one of us would be at the bar. Most likely it would be me. I would be alone and staring into my liquor. She would be the one to come in, to sit down beside me and say, *I don't hardly know you but I'd be willing to show you, I know a way to make you smile. . . .*

Or it could be she who sat at the bar first. She might have had a row with Rick. I'd come in, or maybe Bobby and I would come in together, and we'd find her, the way we had in Belfast. She had wept in our arms that night. She'd asked us to stay. Why hadn't we stayed?

I fell asleep still wondering.

The ringing lit up my dream as if a lightbulb had been screwed into it. I got to my phone just before it stopped.

"Hey, Jo. Fogarty here."

"Fogarty?"

"Have the Family Liaison team been onto you yet?"

"Who? No."

"I was concerned you might be spending too much time alone. Jo. They could give you some support."

"I don't want 'support.' I want my father."

"Yes, well . . . I'm afraid I've still no news for you."

I hated the way he said, "I'm afraid there's no news for you." It sounded so casual, like a waitress saying, "I'm afraid we're out of soup."

"A person doesn't just disappear!"

But his silence was full of the people he hadn't found. There were voices behind him again, something to do with cheese and salad. Those Irish Guards seemed to be always eating, drinking cups of tea. No wonder they hadn't found him.

"Is Staunton there?" I asked.

"She's on a job. Will I have her ring you?"

It occurred to me that he might not get her to ring me, any more than Rob the ticket guy had given Cosima the note at the Tempo Bar.

"Look, Jo . . . there's a very real possibility— I mean, you've got to prepare yourself for the very real possibility—"

"Yes?"

"We think he's jumped, Jo."

"Why would he do that?"

"Who knows why a person might take his own life?"

My finger answered before my head could. I cut him dead.

His words hung in the air: *We think he's jumped*. I sprayed Citrus Surprise through the flat, making it smell so sweet that there was no room for Fogarty's doom and gloom. I rang Cosima. Three rings went before she answered. I stood up straight to talk to her, as though she was there in person.

"Cosima."

"Yes?"

"I don't mean to bother you. I just wonder if you could help me. You know that Irish cop I told you about, Fogarty? He thinks Bobby jumped overboard, but I think they would have found the body by now if that was true, don't you?"

"Jo . . ."

"I need some help on this. Let's say a person does jump. How soon is a body found afterward? How would I find out?"

"You could try the Internet, but—"

"I don't even have a computer. You have a computer, don't you?"

"Yes, but we're down here for the next few days."

"You're doing another gig? Where are you doing it?"

"We're just driving around Bristol and Bath, seeing friends. . . ."

"We never liked Bath, Bobby and me. It's full of Americans. Not Americans like you, real ones, tourists, I mean."

"I'm really sorry, Jo. I'm going to have to go."

"Maybe you can phone Fogarty for me? You can ask him things in a more clever way, you know, the way you do?"

"Oh, honey, I'm so sorry for you, but I've got to go."

"Can I come see you? When you're back?"

"I—I don't think so."

"Why don't you think so? Is it because of Rick? What do *you* think about it? Can't you think for yourself on this?"

"Forgive me, Jo."

And then she was gone.

But she couldn't be *gone*. Only three nights ago she'd been tucking me into her bed with a bowl of black pasta and a can of 7-Up, flat for my dodgy tummy. She had kissed my forehead and told me that everything would be all right, for certain.

It was better not to phone her for a while, not with Rick and maybe Katie standing there and telling her not to talk to me. I decided to write to her. A letter would be harder for her to throw away. She could read it, think about it, come back and read it again. From my school things, I got out a notebook and an envelope. I wrote:

> *Dear Cosima:*
> *I'm sorry if I have been a lot of trouble these past few days. I have been*
> *very upset and distressed by the happenings in my life which I know you*
> *will understand. Please tell this to Rick and to Sean. And maybe Katie too.*
> *I am very sorry.*
> *Jo*

I took the tube to Chalk Farm and walked to Primrose Hill. Yet by the time I put the letter through the letterbox, I knew I hadn't given her enough words, or enough of the right ones. I'd said I was sorry, but I wasn't sure what I was sorry for. *Sorry* was a funny word, anyway. Jamie had said sorry for being insensitive about my father, but he'd never said sorry for telling me I was fat, which was worse. Cosima was sorry for letting Rick be horrible to me, but she also felt sorry to him when she wasn't strict enough with me.

Also, I'd said nothing in the letter about wanting her to ring me or write back. She'd think I was saying good-bye. The worst thing was that she wouldn't get the letter till she got back to London, and I didn't even know when that would be.

I found an Internet café in Regents Park Road. It was empty apart from a plump man in an apron eating a piece of carrot cake at the counter. He had slept-in hair and he looked like he was about twenty-six.

I sat in front of one of the computers.

"Do you need some help?" asked the apron man.

"I'm not very good on computers. I've used them in school, but I'm not very good on the Internet or anything."

He came over to me. "Luddite and proud of it, huh? What are you look-ing for?"

"Stuff about ferries."

"Travel information?"

"No. Like if you jumped off of a ferry, how long would it take them to find you?"

He raised his eyebrows. "You're not planning on trying that, are you?"

"No."

He typed in something and a list of ferries came up. "There's nothing about safety that I can see. I think you'll have to send them an e-mail."

"I don't know how to do that."

Apron Man tapped in something else. He asked me to think of a password and something called a user ID. In fifteen minutes I had my own Yahoo e-mail address. It took him another ten minutes to show me how to use it. It seemed so easy for him to be nice to me. I wondered why it wasn't that easy for everyone else.

"I'm no expert or anything," he said, "but I imagine if you jumped overboard, they'd find you in about a day or so. I mean, the sea washes everything up on shore, doesn't it?"

"That's what I thought!" I was suddenly in a great mood, the best mood since dancing.

"Can you Google?" he asked. He brought up the Google Web site. "Just type in what you want."

I couldn't really type and I felt awkward with Apron Man watching me, but I keyed in the letters one by one: Cosima Stewart and Her Goodtime Guys. Apron Man clicked "Search." At the top of the listings it said there were forty-nine thousand Web sites.

Apron Man went to serve a customer. I clicked on the word "gigs." A list came up, starting with the Barbican four years ago: *Deep in the Heart of Texas: Country & Western Week*. I went through that day in my head, starting from when we couldn't get into the pictures. I'd been jealous of the girl with the extensions and I hated Bobby for being too Bog Irish, and I hated getting my first period and it being so messy I had to stuff loo roll down my trousers. I'd been full of stupid worries, but worrying was the stupidest thing of all. How lucky I'd been just to be with Bobby, and for Cosima to kiss me on the cheek and give me her CD and for Katie to say how sweet I was. As it said in her song, *I envied the gal I was in those days . . .*

I scrolled down the the gigs list to the Tempo Bar. I'd even have settled for that night rather than this one. I'd do it all again—not sleep with Rick, have Bobby with me still.

I clicked on "Contact Us." An e-mail box opened up. My typing was slow, but with every word I felt myself moving closer to her.

```
Dear Cosima:
You say, in your song "Express Yourself" that "if
you don't express yourself you repress yourself and
soon you depress yourself and you wonder why you're
all alone." I wrote you a letter already but I
wasn't able to express myself like I needed to.
Please ring me. I'm very sad and upset. I can't ex-
plain it here. It isn't your fault but we need to
talk. Here is my number again.
```

My words looked important on the screen. It seemed impossible that she wouldn't write back. But when I pressed SEND, I had a funny feeling, like dropping a coin from a tall building, a coin that could gather strength in the

air and fall on someone's head and hurt them or kill them. I went up to
Apron Man.

"How long will it take for the e-mail to get through?"

"Straightaway, or the next time they check."

"They? You mean they'll all read it?"

He grinned. "Oh, I know. You just want to write to that Rick Watson. My
girlfriend completely ignores me when their video is on."

"Actually, I find Rick quite arrogant. But Cosima's a really good friend of
mine."

"In that case, haven't you a personal e-mail address for her? You don't
want to send it through the Web site. They probably have people to do their
reading for them. She might not get it at all."

Apron Man had put me in a good mood, but now he'd chipped away at it.
I sat down again and wrote out, on notepaper, the same letter I'd just
e-mailed. I walked to her flat and put the letter through her letterbox.

Back in Regents Park Road, I sat outside a Russian cafe and ordered something called a Rogalicky with nuts. At the next table a young girl was reading a
book called *Civilization and Its Discontents* by Sigmund Freud. She was going
down the page with a yellow highlighter pen. She looked about my age, but
everything else about her was different. I imagined she lived in a house with
paintings in it, paintings of mad shapes or lines that didn't look like anything.
She'd be one of these girls who liked classical music. There were one or two
like her at my school. They'd usually just moved from somewhere else or
were about to move somewhere else. Sometimes they spoke languages.

I started thinking about my e-mail. If Cosima did get it and *then* the letter,
she'd get the same thing twice, which was daft. On the other hand, if the
e-mail didn't reach her and she wouldn't be in London for days, she'd get nothing and that would be worse.

I phoned her and got her voice mail.

"It's Jo. Can you check your e-mail, the e-mail on your Web site? I've sent
you an important note. Let me know when you've checked it."

I went walking on the hill. I passed a young couple lying on the grass next
to a bottle of Frascati and some grapes. The girl lay on top of the boy. She had
big red hair that flamed out in the sun. Her top fell down and showed some of
her breast.

One day Bobby and I would have a flat in Primrose Hill. We'd eat our
breakfast in the Russian café and read books about civilization and not feeling
content. We'd have a big golden retriever and I'd take it out on walks so that it
could jump up on people and I'd have to run up behind it saying, "Sorry about
that. Come here, Hank!"

Two little girls, twelve years old maybe, were giggling and writing a text
message. Everywhere you looked you saw kids texting each other, but it had

never occurred to me to do it. I sat down on a bench. I found the letters on my phone. It took a long time, but I finally managed to type it out:

```
Cos . . . Wrote to you, you may not have got it. We
have to speak. Ring me. Jo.
```

I walked down the hill. I looked at the FOR SALE signs, most of them put up by Blackman's Estate Agents. Blackman's itself was easy to find, a shiny little office with a black-and-silver door. Inside a tall, yellow-haired man in a suit sat behind a desk.

"My father and I are thinking of getting a flat," I told him. "We like Chalcot Square."

"I see," he said, but he didn't look as if he did. "If you don't mind me asking—where is your father now?"

"He's working."

"What was he thinking of spending?"

"Whatever it costs."

"Mmm . . ." He took out a notebook and began leafing through it. "Well. . . . I have a lovely attic flat in Chalcot Square, two-bedroom. Just renovated, no occupants. I have the keys. Would you like to view it now?'

"Yes, please."

He took me around the corner. We walked up two flights of stairs and into a flat that smelled of fresh paint. There was no furniture, just wood floors and light streaming through the windows. The bedrooms were tiny and the sitting room wasn't much bigger than Shandy Street. Yet in this fresh, sunlit space, I knew that Bobby would never go dark. The best part was that we were across the green from Cosima. I stood at the window, trying to look into her living room, but her blinds were drawn.

"I have a friend who lives over there," I told him. "Her name is Cosima."

"Cosima Stewart? We sold her that flat."

"You *did*?"

"Yes. I have to admit, I'm not a country music fan, but even I was rather taken with their new album."

"What's your favorite track on it?"

"I don't really listen to the individual songs. It's just nice to have it on when you're making the evening meal or something, you know?"

"You don't listen to each song?"

"I'm more of a music-in-the-background chap. Anyway, what do you—"

"Did you meet Cosima's boyfriend when you sold her the flat? Did you meet Rick?"

"I think so, yes. Not quite as friendly as Cosima."

"That's what I think. He doesn't like people talking to Cosima too much.'

"Possessive, yes. I could well imagine that. Anyway, listen, I've a five-thirty viewing. What do you think of the flat?"

"How much is it?" I wondered if it was against the law to pretend to be able to afford a flat.

The estate agent scratched his temple as though he couldn't quite remember. "He's asking four hundred grand."

"Four hundred thousand?" The most expensive lorry in Britain wasn't half of that. "That's unbelievable."

"It's believable," he said, opening the door. "It's Primrose Hill."

The Partridge wasn't one of the trendy pubs. It smelled of tobacco and damp carpet and it was full of middle-aged pipe-smoking geezers playing chess. From the west-facing window I could see her front door, so I bought a glass of wine and waited there. The difficulty was that every long-haired girl looked like her for a second or two, and every van looked like their van.

By nine-thirty, I'd drunk three glasses of wine. By nine-fifty, I'd had four. I felt for her keys in my pocket. I thought of Bobby's face, his bee-stung face. *Ah, Jo. No.*

If he was here in person, I might have listened to him. But he wasn't, so I wouldn't.

I walked out of the pub. I walked across the green and up to her building. I didn't think the keys would work. I wasn't sure I wanted them to. If they didn't, I'd get the tube back to Mile End, buy a bottle of wine and a bag of McDonald's, go home and switch on the telly. I'd give up for the day because really, this day had gone on long enough. But when I put the first key in it nearly guided me, turning my hand to the right with a click. Up a flight of stairs, I tried her door. It worked a treat.

The flat felt smaller without her. There was a smell of burnt toast and jam, the last breakfast they'd eaten. I twisted the blinds and the moon made a silver strip across the floor. I sat on the settee. Every sound from the street—footsteps, the bark of a dog, the rev of a car—made me stiffen.

Her answerphone flashed the number 8. I pressed PLAY. As each message played I made a note in my notepad.

"Ricky—Everton—Arsenal, 2-1, you Gunner cunt! Anyway, ring me when you've had a good cry in your beer. Oh, by the way, in case you hadn't realized, it's Adrian, your bezy mate."

I wrote the word *Arsenal* next to *Rick*.

"Hello, Cosima, it's Helena here. Just to confirm with you, darling, your shoot with *Vogue* is at ten on Friday morning at Hanover Square. See if you can nick a Versace for me, will you?" Helena had a deep and gravelly voice, an important-person voice. I wondered if she was the person who read their e-mail.

After all eight messages were over, I pressed the button and listened to them again.

It was eleven o'clock. I thought about ringing Cosima from her own phone. She would answer in a hurry when she saw her number flash across the screen! I didn't do that, of course. I rang from my own phone.

"Hello?" She was in the middle of laughing.

"It's me."

There was a shuffling sound, and muffled voices. Rick's voice cut into my ears.

"What do you want?"

"Can I speak to Cosima, please?"

"Cosima's busy."

"She wasn't too busy to answer the phone."

"Leave us alone, Jo." He hung up.

I walked fast around living room. I picked up a cushion and scrunched it up, trying to force the bad feeling out of me and into the cushion. I thought about hurting myself. I went to the window, but it was too low. I would fall with a thud and break both my legs. I'd be stuck on the ground all night and paralyzed by tomorrow, and nobody would want to know me, ever. I wouldn't be able to drive. No boy would kiss me. Nobody would come to see me in hospital apart from Primrose, and I wouldn't even have the legs to walk away from her.

I thought of stabbing myself, not enough to die but enough to bleed all over her furniture. She would come home and see what her own knife had done to me.

We had spoken earlier today, me and her; we had spoken properly. I went over every word I said and every word she said. She'd sounded worried, as though she wanted to talk but somebody was stopping her. Even that estate agent said Rick was possessive. I thought of telling Cosima what had happened with me and Rick, but she might hate me then. And she might hate him. If she hated him, the band would be over, unless she found another man who could play the guitar as well as he could. Maybe she could get a woman to play. I could learn to play!

I found his Jack Daniel's in the kitchen. It was under a board with photographs of the band and a big note that said *C—We need bread, love, R.* I took the bottle back to the living room.

I could say he'd raped me.

She'd never believe it. Rick wasn't enthusiastic enough to rape anybody, and if he did, he'd do it to a beautiful girl. If I was one of those supermodels who weigh six stone and look like they cry all the time, she'd believe me then. I wasn't pretty enough even to be raped. I was an unrape-able girl who couldn't get people to notice me even if I jumped out of the window and broke both my unbeautiful legs.

I took the longest swig of whiskey I could. It burnt going down, but it blurred the shame. I had no Bobby voice in me now, telling me what not to do. I went through her CDs. The CD on top of the stereo said APRIL DEMO on it. I slipped it in, pressed PLAY. It sounded like they were just hanging around the studio, talking. Sean said, "Don't bogart the joint, Rick," and then Cosima laughed in a sleepy way and started singing "101 Here I Come" with the guitar tweaking behind her:

> I been round the world again
> Got stuck somewhere right near Big Ben
> Now I'm used to driving on the left side of the street
> I'm right at home with all you Brits
> I love sticky toffee pudding and your scathing wit
> But at times I wonder, is this really me?

I'd never thought about this song, but now I listened to every word. It made me wonder if maybe she wasn't so happy in England. Rick didn't make her happy. She'd cried in Bobby's chest and told both of us just how much he didn't make her happy. I'd been annoyed with Bobby that night for taking up her attention. If I hadn't been annoyed with him, would he have stayed with her then? She could be married to him now. They would both be here with me right now.

I turned the music up. I went into the bedroom and opened the door of her wardrobe. I picked out some of her outfits and draped them over the bed, including the suede one. I took off my clothes and stood in front of her mirror. I turned to the side and pulled at my stretch marks. Only pregnant women were supposed to get stretch marks, but I'd had them since I was fourteen. Up close they looked as though someone had made gashes in my hips with a penknife. Looking at myself from behind was the worst. My arse was like the arse of a sixty-year-old woman, riddled as though I'd been sprayed with bullets. I turned to look at myself again. It wasn't guilt that kept Rick from wanting to see me. It was shame that he'd fucked a body like mine.

Cosima was singing "Wish Yourself on Anyone."

> When I was just a girl
> In a lonely childhood world
> I'd sing to keep the devils at bay
> And invent sweet lovers to come and play all day with me
> And now that I am older, my world is bleak and colder
> But I still sleep in my childhood bed
> Taking pills to stuff the voices deep inside my head
> But sometimes they come up anyway, crying . . .

I pulled the suede top on. It was tight in the waist, but at least I could get it on. The skirt was harder. It snagged on my hips and made my legs look like sausages. I pulled it off and tried on the gauzy skirt, the one she'd worn at the Cake club. The fabric flowed over my bum and my lumps. The skirt was nice to swish around in. I found a silk scarf to match and wrapped it around my neck.

I tripped on one of her shoes and let myself fall back onto the bed. I'd had too much to drink and I was sick from trying on clothes. I stripped back the covers and lay down.

> *Who will love you*
> *Who will want you*
> *Who will hold you tight*
> *Who comes here at night to keep you warm*
> *But it's okay, girl, it's all right*
> *You're better off alone*
> *You wouldn't wish yourself on anyone*

Rick's guitar rode through her voice, rough. I put my hand between my legs. I hated Rick but I wanted him inside of me, harder than he'd been before with his breath in my hair and him fucking me (like a man I'd seen on Channel 5, late at night one time) saying, *You like it, don't you.* I rubbed myself to make my hand like his thing that could cut me in two, driving all the hunger out of me, and the yeast and heat rose up from my parts, hurting but in a way that made me want to go on and on. I cried out. I was soaking wet down there.

When he'd finished with me, I couldn't move. I thought of Cosima tucking me into bed, pulling the covers up, kissing me on the forehead, saying, "Sleep now, honey," and turning out the light but leaving the bedside lamp on, and the music kept on:

> *It's okay, girl, it's all right*
> *You're better off alone*
> *You wouldn't wish yourself on anyone*

CHAPTER 22

The new day hit me with a bright and instant terror. I got out of bed and faced the damage. Heaps of her clothing were tangled with my clothing all over the floor. CDs were scattered all over the sitting room and the empty whiskey bottle lay on its side on the rug. I went to the corner shop and bought another bottle of Jack Daniel's and poured some of it out so that it was the same level as Rick's had been when I'd found it. I made the bed and put away the clothes and CDs and smoothed the wrinkle out of her cushions. Just when I was about to leave, I saw something sticking out from under her bed. I went back and picked up the silk scarf I'd worn last night. I noticed that it was torn on one side, quite badly. It was this that gave me the idea.

V. Cornelia was the first posh shop I saw in New Bond Street. It was a small shop with a shiny white floor and two slender salesgirls who looked like each other in reverse. One was blond and the other looked Indian or Pakistani but both had tiny noses and straight hair to their necks and accents as posh as Katie's.

"Can I help you?" asked the blond one.

"I'm looking for a scarf for my friend."

"What's she like?"

"She's a country singer, but she's smart, nicely dressed. Classy, like."

"I'm not getting an image."

I looked at the dark one to see if she was getting an image. She didn't seem to be listening, even though she was actually folding a scarf. It was silk with blue and green circles rimmed with gold. When she held it up to the light, it shimmered.

"How much is that?" I asked.

"It's ninety-eight pounds. We just got it in from our Milan shop."

"Ninety-eight pounds! You could get five of those at Top Shop for that."

"Yes, well, perhaps you'd better go there."

They were bitches, so I went and did just that. And yet, because I'd seen their scarf, Top Shop was ruined for me. The Top Shop scarves had cheerful patterns that stayed the same no matter how you wore them, not flags of silk that shimmered in the sunlight.

I'd checked our bank balance in Birmingham five days ago, but I went to the ATM to make sure. We had money. But ninety-eight quid for a scarf! Bobby would never spend that even if he was a millionaire. It would be one of the few times he'd say absolutely *no*.

I went back to New Bond Street and into V. Cornelia. The dark girl was on her own now, talking on her mobile phone. She was laughing and saying, "Oh no, Didier, how annoying is that." She turned her back to me. The beautiful scarf was on the top of the pile. I didn't give myself time to think. I grabbed it and ran. I didn't imagine the alarm this time. It shrilled at my back, followed by the clatter of high heels and her voice calling, "Hey!"

I turned into Oxford Street and lost myself in the sea of shoppers. I ran into WH Smith and waited in the back until I was sure nobody that was following me. Because I'd gotten the scarf for free, I spent nine pounds on a card and ribbon and gift-wrapping paper. Seeing how out of breath I was, the saleswoman was nice. She was so nice, I felt like I hadn't done anything wrong. She loaned me scissors and tape so that I could clip off the tag and wrap the scarf right there in the shop.

In the card, I wrote:

> *I'm sorry if I caused you hassle. I'm feeling better now and I bought you this gift to say how thankful I am for all of your care. Jo.*

Once I'd put the gift through her letterbox, I did feel better. She would definitely be in London tonight, because she had her photo shoot with *Vogue* tomorrow. I kept my phone in my pocket, ready for her to come home and find the gift.

The next morning I still hadn't heard from her.

I got to Hanover Square at twenty minutes to ten. I found a doorway to stand in across from Vogue House. At ten minutes past ten, a woman tore across the square, a dry-cleaning bag flapping over her arm. By the time I realized it was Cosima, she was a blur through the turnstile. I had to wait another thirty-eight minutes before something else happened: Katie, this time, gliding into Vogue House. I wasn't happy to see her. It was going to be harder to talk to Cosima with Katie around. Katie's eyes were as cold as stones.

They came out of the building together at 1:45. I waited until they were in Princes Street, and then I went after them. They hailed a black taxi and I heard Katie say, "Tate Modern," to the driver. I hailed the next one.

It was a great day. The clouds were fat and friendly against a brilliant sky. African music burbled out of the cabby's radio, making me think of ads I'd seen for package holidays—hot sands and safari parks and blue-black men in bright shirts laughing. As we crossed the Thames, the Houses of Parliament bounced up from the rippled mirror of the river.

The museum was crowded, which made it easy to follow them down the ramp where an indoor sun met us, a yellow ball that looked bigger than the real sun. Steam came off it in a yellow mist. Some people lay down on their backs to look up at it; *a lovely vibe,* as Bobby would say. I wouldn't have minded staying for a bit, but Cosima and Katie were moving toward the escalators. Keeping my distance, I followed them up.

On the third level Katie flashed a card to the girl at the desk, and they went through the doors marked UnBelievable without handing over any money, though I had to pay £7.50 to be let in. I'd never been to an exhibition before, apart from in school when we went to the British Museum, but then it was all Egyptian things, boring things, nothing like this.

The first room was full of photographs, some nearly as big as the walls they were hung on. Each showed a different person holding a gun. In one of them a man with a child on his shoulders held a rifle, slanted up so that the barrel pointed at his child. In another two elderly women were drinking coffee and comparing handguns as though they were lipsticks.

I read the plaque on the wall:

> BRANT ADAMS SEEKS TO DEPICT THE HORRIFIC
> EXUBERANCE OF GUN CULTURE IN AMERICA.

I kept my back to Cosima and Katie, but I could hear them talk.

"The thing that amazes me," said Katie, "is how obtuse these people are. I mean, does it not occur to them that they're going to be gawped at by lefty artist types in London? It's like they think we're going to be on *their* side."

"London doesn't exist for them, anyway," said Cosima. "Nowhere does, except their own little Wal-Mart world."

I waited a few minutes before following them into the second room. In here, the walls were bare. In fact, there was no art at all that I could see. There were no people, either, though I could hear the sound of voices coming out of boxes tall enough to stand in. I read the plaque on one of the boxes:

> IN THIS INSTALLATION, ROLLY COSTIGAN EXPLORES THE
> COMPLICATED TEXTURAL RELATIONSHIPS BETWEEN TIME,
> DEGENERATION, REGENERATION, AND GRIEF.

I went inside and stood in the middle of four screens. Each showed a different film of the same woman. She was about fifty, with a friendly face and her hair cut in a brown bob. In one of the films she wore a flowery blouse and she was standing in an aviary, telling the interviewer about the red-bellied parrots flying around her. In another she was eating breakfast in her home. She had a single parrot on her shoulder, and sometimes she stuck a piece of toast into its beak. In the third she was in bed without any birds at all, explaining how therapeutic the parrots had been since her husband's death. The fourth film showed just a kitchen clock.

I spun around to look at the different films, trying to take in everything that she was saying. It made me dizzy, but for a moment, I forgot what I'd come here for. I turned again and found myself staring into a real woman's face. Her eyes flickered with the screens. Her scarf, too, caught the changing light—the scarf I'd bought for her! By the time my eyes had adjusted to her, she'd seen me first.

"What are you doing here, Jo?"

She was hard to hear. Her words sounded like part of what the lady was saying.

"I've come to see the art," I said.

I've named this one Dorothy Parker, because she has an answer for everything, don't you, Dorothy?

"You followed me here, didn't you?"

"No."

When Paul died, it wasn't just the grief that got me, it was the isolation. My daughter said I needed to get out more, meet new people. . . .

"Can't you just tell me the truth?"

"I like this lady."

And yet I've always felt that Dorothy understands me more than most people do. Dorothy is a truly Chekhovian parrot; she has a high sense of the tragic.

"Can we go somewhere?" I asked. "Can we talk?"

Cosima's scarf—my gift—fell on the floor. I picked it up and held it up to her. "You like this, then? I made the right choice?"

She took the scarf but she but didn't put it on.

"Listen to me." Her voice was suddenly loud enough to drown out the parrot lady. "We are all very sad about what's happened to you. But I'm not in a position to help you. Do you understand? We're going to America next week. We're running around like headless chickens trying to get ready—"

"If you're running around like headless chickens, then why are you spending a whole afternoon looking at art?"

"Jo, I'm going to ask you to do me a favor." She spoke even louder and slowly, as if I was hard of hearing. "I'm going to ask that you don't follow me anymore. Can you do that for me?"

She didn't wait for me to answer. She left the box and yelled, "C'mon, Kate!" I stepped out and saw the two of them walking quickly into the third room. I went after them but knocked into a man, except he wasn't a man but a life-size sculpture of a man with a penis where his head should be. The security girl yelled, "Stay behind the line, please."

I went through four more rooms but I didn't see them. By the time I'd found my way out of the exhibition, Cosima and Katie had gone.

I left the Tate and sat by the Thames. All around me, under the real sun, people were Rollerblading and chatting and laughing as if they'd never been sad or embarrassed in their whole lives. A man wearing sandals played the didgeridoo. A little girl ate Maltesers, her lips rimmed with chocolate. On the river a boat took tourists to Greenwich, and I knew that every one of them was happier than me.

I went over the last hour bit by bit. She'd liked the art. She'd liked the guns the best. I walked back into the Tate, to the gift shop this time. *Gunning for Glory*, a collection of photos by Brant Adams, was too heavy to steal, so I bought it. Inside, I wrote:

> *I am so sorry that you thought I followed you. It was a coincidence, really and truly. I also enjoyed this art and like you I felt the guns interested me the most.*
> *Love,*
> *Jo*

It was fifty-six minutes later when I got to Chalcot Square. The book was too big to put through her letterbox, so I left it on her doorstep. I went into the Partridge and sat at the window to make sure it didn't get stolen or that rain didn't fall on it. Twenty minutes later, I went across and rang the buzzer, but nobody answered. I waited five minutes and rang it again. I went back into the Partridge and sent her a text message:

```
I am sorry for annoying you. There is something on
your doorstep I think will make it better. Jo.
```

Seven minutes later my phone rang. Her number flashed across my screen! But it was a man who spoke to me. His didn't say hello or say my name. He sounded like a man talking to another man.

"Rick here. This is the last time I'm going to ask you this. It is time for you to leave us alone now."

"But did she get the—"

"She got the book. We think you need to save your money. *Get some help!*"

"I was only trying to say sorry—"

But he was gone. I shook all over. I rang back and got her voice mail.

"It's me," I said. "Honest, I didn't know you'd be there today. Please ring me back. I'm sorry I upset you. *Please ring me back.*"

How had they gotten the book without my seeing? I went to her flat. I rang the bell: one, three, five times. I went back to the pub.

At eight-thirty she came out of the flat with Rick. Her hair wasn't brushed and she kept looking around. I wondered if she was cross with him for saying what he'd said to me. I walked out of the pub. I crouched behind a parked car, close enough to hear them.

"You're being alarmist, Rick."

"*You* stay here, then. You stay and listen to the buzzer all night."

They got into the van and drove away.

I let myself into her flat. *Gunning for Glory* was on her coffee table. It looked good, like something she would have bought herself. I pressed PLAY on her answering machine. There were sixteen messages on it, ten from me. I didn't remember ringing that many times. I hated my voice; it was one long whine. I pressed the button and erased the lot.

I put on *Let Me Touch You for Awhile*. I ran a bath and poured her Molton Brown Seamoss Stress-Relieving Hydrosoak into it, leaving the door open while the whole place filled with her expensive smells. I opened the fridge and found a bowl of pasta, normal white pasta, and I took it into the bathroom, along with his whiskey. I ate and drank while sitting on the edge of the tub, waiting for the bath to be ready. The mirror steamed.

I'd made the bath too hot but I forced myself to stay in it, to steam the last of my panic away. I began to lose the sensation in my skin. I liked the nothing feeling; it was like a holiday from myself. I dried off and covered myself in her talcum powder. Wearing just her towel, I went into the sitting room. On a chair were two music books, one of Bob Dylan songs, the other a collection called *Songs for the Road*. I picked up *Songs for the Road* and a piece of paper fell out of it.

Cosima and Her Goodtime Guys Southwest Tour

10 June
   TOWN: *Bakersfield, California*
   VENUE: *Buck Owens' Crystal Palace*
   ACCOMMODATION: *Best Western Hotel, Buck Owens Boulevard*

11 June
   TOWN: *Victorville, California*
   VENUE: *West Coasts Roots Bluegrass Festival*
   ACCOMMODATION: *Apple Ranch, Victorville*

12 June
AM: *Interview with KCVR, Victorville*
AFTERNOON AND EVENING: *Break*

13 June
TOWN: *San Diego, California*
VENUE: *La Jolla Dome*
ACCOMMODATION: *Ramada Inn, La Jolla*

14 June . . .

I copied the list into my notebook; every date and hotel from Bakersfield, California, to Austin, Texas.

I looked around. The flat was messy. I was never much for cleaning, but now I wanted to make her surfaces shine with my own hands. I found Windolene and furniture polish under the sink. I swept. I hoovered. The more I tidied, the more I felt I was tidying my own head, mopping away the last of my bad feelings. The big note was still in the kitchen: *C—We need bread, love, R,* but under it now was another note: *R—Fucking buy it yourself—Love, C.*

I went to the shop and bought a loaf of Hovis bread along with a bottle of Citrus Surprise air freshener. I also bought a bouquet of pink and purple flowers. Back in her flat, I put the flowers in a vase and put the vase on top of *Gunning for Glory.* I put the bread on the block and I sprayed every room with air freshener. I was wondering what to clean next when I heard the key in the lock. I ran into the bedroom.

There were at least three voices coming from the sitting room.

"That's typical, Rick. You worry your head off and then you don't double-lock the door."

"I thought I did double-lock it."

"Smells like a brothel in here," said Sean. "Or me auntie Minnie's in Birkenhead." He laughed, but the others didn't.

They were all quiet for a minute.

"Rick," said Cosima. "Did you buy flowers?"

"Since when do I buy *flowers?*"

I heard the bleep of an answerphone and an automated voice: "You have zero messages."

"Fuck," said Rick.

"What is it?" asked Sean.

"Call the police."

"Over flowers?"

"Hold on. She could still be here."

I ran into the wardrobe. I scrunched as far back as I could, into the furry blackness. An arm thrust through the clothing. I held myself so tightly I thought I would creak like a piece of wood. Finally the arm pulled out.

"Nothing in there," said Sean.

For minutes I couldn't hear anything. I could barely breathe, stuffed behind a fake fur coat, so I pushed to the front.

In the next room Cosima was on the phone, her voice fazing in and out as if she was pacing. "Then she cleaned the flat, and she bought us flowers . . ."

Suddenly she slammed the phone down.

"Asshole!"

"What did he say, Cos?"

"He said, 'Flowers? Cleaning your flat? I wish *I* had a stalker like that!' "

"Bastard."

"And he asked me why I wore the scarf she gave me."

"Good question."

'I *liked* it, Rick. It's exactly my taste. It's not like *you've* ever bought me a scarf like that!"

I thought they might have a row then, but they didn't seem to. I waited five minutes. She made a noise like she was crying, and Rick spoke to her in such a quiet voice that I couldn't hear what he was saying. I waited five more minutes. Patsy Cline began to play; not loud. I tiptoed to the doorway. Rick and Cosima were alone. They were slow dancing, her head in his shoulder, his face in her neck. Their eyes were closed. All of a sudden, I wanted them to see me. I would have rather they had screamed at me or frightened me than danced like that, all wrapped up in one another.

I walked into the sitting room but I kept my feet on the rug. They didn't see me. I crossed the room to the door. I opened the door and a breeze from the hallway hit me. My heart was pounding and my skin was cold and nasty. I didn't look back. I went down.

When I rang the next day, I didn't get an answerphone. I got an automated voice: *This phone is no longer in use.* I rang her mobile and got a dead tone. I wrote her another letter.

> *Ask Rick what happened between him and me that night at Sean's flat.*
> *I had been a virgin before that night. Ring me and we'll talk about it.*
> Jo

I put the letter through the letterbox and waited in the Partridge. I knew she would ring now, if only to be mad with me.

At 10:20 P.M. a cop came into the pub, making the old pipe smokers look up from their chess games. The cop stopped when he saw me.

"Josephine Pickering?"

"Yes."

"I'm Detective Inspector Angus McFarlane. Can I have a word?"

He sat across from me before I could answer.

"We've reason to believe that you have been harassing Miss Cosima Steward and Mr. Rick Watson."

"I haven't been 'harassing' them."

"Haven't you?"

"He doesn't want me around because he had sex with me."

"They say you alleged that."

"It's true."

"Well, Miss Pickering, even if it is true, having sexual relations with a seventeen-year-old, while possibly immoral, isn't illegal. And it doesn't permit you to harass them."

"I was just trying to talk to her about it. To tell her I was sorry."

"Well, call me old-fashioned, but in my book, pursuing her in an art gallery, staking them out from their local pub, and breaking into her flat are hardly appropriate methods of apology."

"They gave me a key. Did you visit them in the flat? Did it *look* like I broke in?"

He shook his head as if he was bored with the whole thing. "Listen, my love, I have better things to do than warn besotted young girls to stay away from pop bands."

"They're a *country* band—"

"So I'll make a deal with you. You stay away from them, I stay away from you. You don't ring them. You don't ring their buzzer. In fact, you don't drink in this boozer or come to this part of town at all."

"It's Rick who is harassing me," I said. "That's why he always knows where I am. Not only that, but they gave me drugs. Cocaine and Ecstasy and hash. Bet they didn't tell you that."

D.I. McFarlane blinked several times in a row. "Would you like, in that case, to make a complaint against Mr. Watson and the others?"

"No," I said. "She'd never forgive me then."

I didn't sleep much that night. I read the itinerary for their American tour. I read it again and again until I knew every date, gig, and hotel without having to check the sheet.

In the morning I rang Fogarty.

"I want to speak to Staunton," I said.

"Staunton's away, Jo. . . . Her mother's had a stroke."

"Can't I talk to her, anyway? I want to wish her mother well."

"That's nice. I'll pass on the message."

I didn't know whether to believe him.

"I'm sure Bobby's still in some pub," I said. "Have you checked all the pubs?

"The pubs? You do realize there's probably a million pubs in Ireland?"

"You *have* to find him! I need to let him know something! My friends want me to go to California on tour with them, because they're in a band—"

"Well, you know, there are worse things you could do—"

"I can't! He'll come back and he'll go missing again because *I'll* be gone! And I'll be five thousand miles away in a different time zone and he'll have no phone, and my mobile won't work over there, and there will be no way to ring each other!"

"Ah, now . . ."

"*There will be no way to ring each other!*"

"Jo, listen to me now, listen, are you listening?"

"Yes."

"All right. If we find your father—if we find him, alive—"

"I'm not listening to this!" I stood up, ready to hang up.

"Okay, I'm sorry. Hear me out. . . ." He spoke slowly. "If we find Bobby, we will pass on the message. We'll tell him that you've gone to California, and that you'll be back in—how long?"

"I don't know . . . three weeks."

"Okay. And we'll tell him that you'll be ringing here every few days, how's that? Because Jo, if we find him, we'll be keeping a pretty close eye on him ourselves. You follow me, Jo?"

I sat down on the bed. "I can't go, Fogarty. I don't have a visa—"

"You don't need a visa for a three-week visit, Jo. Do you have a passport?"

"Yes, from when we used to tip in France."

"It's what he'd want for you. To be happy, to go to the beach, to play in the sunshine."

"I don't *care* about the sunshine."

He laughed. "You go and enjoy yourself now, will you? It's what he'd want. You hear me? You hear me, Jo?"

"Yes."

"Good girl."

After we'd rung off, I sat on the bed, letting the hard bounce of conversation drift away. The noises of the day began to trickle in. The Bengali children were calling to each other in the hallway. From outside, a drill was making a sound like *drrrrrrr*. I looked out the window. The glass was filthy but the sky was still a driving blue.

Go and enjoy yourself, now, Fogarty had said. It was a Bobby-type thing to say, though Bobby would say it more Northern. I could hear it now, exactly the way he would say it: *Go on, now, pet. Enjoy yourself.*

Part *III*

I'M BETTER OFF WITHOUT YOU

CHAPTER 23

I had never been on an airplane before.

On the Virgin VS007 to Los Angeles, I liked the twelve movies I could watch whenever I wanted to. I also liked the monitor showing where we were flying over, places with names like the Labrador Sea, Manitoba, Big Sandy, Harvey Basin. What I didn't like was being crammed in beside two other people, and having to annoy them every time I went to the toilet, which was often because of all the wine I was drinking. And I didn't like the way nothing was quite anything. It was never really day or night. The food left me bloated but wanting more. I couldn't sleep but I wasn't properly awake. I finally did fall sleep—for a minute, maybe more—until the red-sleeved arm of the air hostess snapped up the shade, letting in the new American light.

"It's beautiful," she said, as if telling me off for missing it.

We were flying over the Rocky Mountains. I imagined myself drifting down, a new powder-sugar me, sprinkling over the snow-peaks.

"We are beginning our descent into the Los Angeles area."

The engine whined and we dipped into the brown haze. The city gelled into boxy houses and ribbons of motorway with cars going the wrong way. I spotted the nine white letters, HOLLYWOOD tucked into its hilly bump.

"Do you have relatives in California?" asked the man sitting next to me. For eleven hours, we had been good at not speaking to each other. But now he was showing me his nice-old-man face, a face that cared if a girl had no relations in a strange city.

"Friends," I said.

We touched down. Some people clapped.

As we walked through passport control, a photograph of George W. Bush welcomed us to the United States of America, but the customs and immigration people didn't look so welcoming. They were big and impatient in their police uniforms and heavy belts. A large black woman checked my passport and a scowling Mexican one took my immigration form. Both told me to enjoy my vacation, but neither seemed to mean it.

The woman at Information spoke to me slowly, as if English wasn't my first language. She told me there were no trains to Bakersfield. I had to get a bus downtown and another bus from there. As I stood at the desk trying to figure it out, the older man from the plane walked past. A woman, plump and smiling, bounced up and down on his shoulder.

"Enjoy yourself, sweetheart," he said when he saw me. I was about to ask if I could get a lift into Los Angeles, but they were walking too fast and looked too happy to be stopped.

The bus smelled of sweat and hairspray and I was the only white person on it. We drove along the widest street I'd ever seen, the shops set way back from the road: Popeye's Fried Chicken, NIX Check Cashing, Lou's Fish Outlet ("You buy, we fry"). At a traffic light rap music boomed out of a Cadillac beside us, and a young black couple waited for the lights to change. The black man had chains around his neck and he wore a red tracksuit; his girlfriend had big hair and big tits and a sexy, pissed-off face. I'd seen couples like them in Dalston or Brixton, but these ones were the real thing, the sort our English black people tried to be like. The girl looked up at me a with a face that said, *What you looking at?* I looked away as quickly as I could. In America, I knew, black people had guns. They smoked crack and the girls had babies with six different fathers and the men shot each other and molested their own children.

Bobby didn't like it when I said these things. "People are people," he'd say. "It doesn't matter if they're from the slums of Los Angeles or County Armagh. They're all made of the same stuff."

But nobody here looked like anyone in County Armagh.

A woman, the biggest and blackest I'd seen so far, sat beside me. She dug into a Burger King bag and came up with a handful of onion rings that stank. I tried to pry open the window.

"Don't be opening no window," said the woman. "Ain't no telling what might come through it."

I wished I had a bag of my own, an empty one to breathe into. I had expanded since the plane. My feet were swollen in their shoes, my fingers greasy and too big for their rings. We drove onto the motorway—freeway, they called it here—a maze of underpasses and concrete bridges.

Suddenly I wanted to talk to the woman with the onion rings. I wanted to turn to her and say, "Nobody knows where I am," as if I was a lost five-year-old in the supermarket that she could return to Lost Property.

But then I saw the trucks.

Great beauties they were, eighteen-wheelers with chrome detail and long, chunky noses, not our usual flat fronts. A green Mack truck gained on our right, twice the size of the Scania. I tried to get a better look at it, but we were getting off the freeway.

We drove through an outdoor market, Mexicans selling handbags with Marilyn Monroe or James Dean on them. We passed a wall of orange and black graffiti in English and Spanish, big angry letters: DON'T FUCK WITH RAOUL!

"Is this the city center?" I asked the woman with the onion rings.

"What did you say?"

"Is this the center of town?"

"There ain't no 'center of town.'"

"But where do all the people live?"

"If it's rich people you're wanting, you better get your butt into the hills, out where there ain't no Mexicans or niggers like me, unless we're wiping some white baby's butt or cleaning out some swimming pool."

If Bobby was here, I knew she wouldn't be talking this way. He would be asking her, "Where are you from, yourself?" and she'd say something like "Me, I'm local to the area, how about you?" Everyone liked Bobby, even the biggest of old bags. I wasn't sure he knew it himself.

I had an hour to wait for the bus to Bakersfield. In the Greyhound station on Seventh Street and Alameda it looked as though some people had waited a lot longer than that. A whiskered white man, reeking of piss, lay across a bench. An old black man slept on another. A starved-looking girl in cut-off shorts sat reading *Us* magazine. Nobody really moved, apart from a homeless man outside the window, pushing a mountain of rubbish on a supermarket trolley through the slow, warm day.

Something gleamed behind the homeless man's load. I couldn't tell for sure but it looked like a truck. I picked up my suitcase and went outside. I wound through the parked buses, out through the barbed wire fence, and saw it.

It was a great big wine-and-silver truck, the American flag flying from its chunky nose. FREIGHTLINER, it said inside the little circle in front. The driver was cleaning out his cab with his back to me.

"Excuse me?"

I heard the dog before I saw it. The Alsatian jumped up only inches from my face. It barked and bared its teeth and made me fall back against the barbed wire fence.

"Dizzy!"

I kept my eyes shut.

"*Dizzy!* Come here!"

I opened my eyes.

The dog stopped jumping, but his teeth were still bared and he was growling. He sniffed my hand. I steeled myself for the bite, the crunch of my fingers in his mouth.

"*Dizzy . . . . !*"

Dizzy looked at his owner and looked at me. He looked at the owner again and slunk back to the truck. He licked the owner's fingers.

The owner—the driver—was about fifty, with a yellow mustache and pale blue eyes. He wore a baseball cap that said BATON ROUGE on it.

"Awful sorry about that. Can I help you, ma'am?"

I folded my arms in front of me, tried to still the shaking. "I was just looking at your truck."

"Nice rig, isn't it?"

"It's gorgeous."

The man scratched his ear. "You from England?"

"Yes. We drive a truck, too. We have a Scania 143."

"Is that a good make?"

"Scania is the king of the road."

His eyes crinkled. He looked at my suitcase. "Where you headed, young lady?"

"Bakersfield."

"Listen, I won't be going to Bakersfield. But I am going to Castaic. That's about eighty minutes closer to where you want to go. I could use the company."

I thought of Bobby. He would probably say it wasn't safe to take rides from strangers in Los Angeles. He wouldn't think be too happy about the Alsatian, either. But the truck! The truck was something he would like.

"Thank you," I said.

The trucker wouldn't let me lift my bag onto the cab. He took my coat and hung it on a wooden hanger in back. His name was Whitey, and he spoke with a Southern accent, like a man in a film.

"Is that your real name?" I asked.

"No, ma'am. I don't like to be reminded of my real name."

Whitey started the engine and we headed off. The truck made more noise than our lorry did; proud, lurching sounds. I felt odd being on the wrong side of the wheel on the wrong side of the road, but I liked being so high up, above the cars and the taco stands and the Greyhound buses I wouldn't be needing now.

"Do you own this truck?" I asked.

"I am my own owner-driver, yes ma'am. Brand-new rig, Caterpillar engine. Cost me a hundred twenty thousand to get that way, but it's the only way to go."

We drove onto a freeway, the 101. To myself I sang "101 Here I Come!" The American flag flew in the breeze.

"What's the engine size?"

"This is a twelve-point-seven-litre engine. Six miles to the gallon. Four hundred fifty horsepower, front and rear suspension."

"We have flat-fronted trucks in England."

"Yes, ma'am. We call them cabovers. Used to drive one myself."

We stopped to wash the truck.

"The water has been treated specially," he told me. "The other washes we call 'Streakin' Beacons,' on account of them leaving so many marks."

We watched as the truck was scrubbed and polished and made to shine. I felt as though I'd come all the way from England to help this Southern man wash his Freightliner. It had been hours since I'd even thought about Cosima.

"Do you know something?" I asked him when we were back on the road. "You can fit two of our motorways into this one."

"And there are bigger freeways than this one." We were quiet for a moment, thinking of better freeways.

I tried to imagine Whitey as a young man. He was skinny and his neck was wrinkled, but he had bright blue eyes that took in the whole of the road, like Bobby's.

"Where are you from?" I asked him.

"I'm from Baton Rouge, Louisiana. My grandparents were French and Irish. I have a great-great-grandfather who was Cherokee Indian."

"Do you have crocodiles where you're from?"

"No, ma'am. It's alligators we got. I do a little alligator hunting myself."

The freeway forked into two. Whitey went north on the 5. I looked at a long ditch, a trickle of black water running along the bottom.

"That's the L.A. River," said Whitey.

"That's not a river."

"Well, it ain't the Mississippi."

That the Mississippi River was a real thing, not just something from a song, made me feel like laughing. Three motorcycle sheriffs, wearing beige uniforms with mirrored sunglasses, waited at the side of the road.

Whitey picked up the CB. "Northbounders," he said, "White Castle here. Couple of bears waiting for you at the Van Nuys exit. On murdercycles."

"*Murdercycles,*" I laughed. "I heard that in a Charlene Sweeney song. Do you know that song?"

"I can't say I'm much for country music. I'm a jazz man, me."

"Oh."

"Chet. Basie. Dizzy. Bird. A little Coltrane, if I'm feeling abstract. None of them beer-drinkin', wife-beatin' songs for this old man. Sets me apart from the other guys, but I guess we're all apart anyway. We're all just in our own bubble of the road. Do you know what I mean?"

"I suppose so."

He looked at me. "Hey, Jo? You want to hear some Chet?" He sounded concerned, as if he was offering me medicine for an illness. I wasn't so impressed by what he'd said about country music, but I didn't want to ruin our mood, so I nodded. He switched on his CD player and a trumpet filled the cab. A man began to sing, his voice slurred as if he were drunk.

"Chet," said Whitey, loving the word. "Chet's about as good as it gets for this old veteran."

"Veteran?"

"Vietnam." He showed me his hand. "Still have an inch of shrapnel trapped in there."

"But what does jazz have to do with Vietnam?"

"Nothing, I guess. It's just that them jazz guys are so full of regret, it makes me feel better about my own regrets. About the things I could've done different."

We were coming into mountains. They were nothing like the Highlands or Snowdonia or the mountains of Mourne. These were rough mountains, brown and speckled as mongrel dogs. We passed a trailer park, children playing in an inflatable pool.

"Who lives here?" I asked.

"Poor fat people on welfare."

"Oh."

"The world is getting worse, Jo. Take this here job. Used to be, you had to train. Now we got guys up here from Mexico and Guatemala and El Salvador, and they're doing jobs on the cheap. I knew these guys from Guatemala, and they were in such a hurry to get their loads delivered, they were taking speed and speeding on the road, too. They didn't even stop to go to the bathroom, they cut a hole in the bottom of the truck. If you don't mind my language, ma'am, they defecated right through the bottom, the feces got in the engine, cost a small fortune to repair. It's all about money now and being in a hurry. Didn't used to be that way. Guys used to stop and talk to you. You used to have great conversations at truck stops, about the world and everything. Now half of them can't even speak English."

"The drivers in England say that, too," I said. "That nobody talks to each other anymore."

"*Nobody* talks to anybody these days." He pounded the wheel. Chet Baker was singing an even sadder song than the last one, with a tinkling in the background that sounded like an ice-cream truck at slow speed.

> *I'm happier without you*
> *I promise you it's true*
> *Except when the moon shines fat above me*
> *And I see you in the glow*
> *Until I realize it's just my own lonely shadow*
> *But I'm better off without you, I promise you it's so . . .*

We were coming up to a sign that said SIX FLAGS MAGIC MOUNTAIN. I could see a roller coaster from here, twice as high as any they had at Alton Towers. I watched as a carriage inched to the top. It was so tiny that it looked as though a bird could knock it off. I thought of the people up there as they teetered up to the highest point—slowly, slowly—with nothing they could do to stop it. In a moment they would fall, their stomachs staying in the air before their bodies flew out and splattered onto the ground. When the carriage finally dived, I thought I could hear the screams from here.

I wasn't so high anymore. My head hurt from being awake for so long. I yawned. Whitey looked at me.

"You must have that jet lag pretty bad. Why don't you have yourself a nap? You can sleep in the back."

I didn't know whether to go in back or not. If I went back and lay down, I could wake up in a stranger place than these dog-speckled mountains. I could wake up with him on top of me. But I could hardly hold my head up, so I climbed in back. Dizzy was waiting for me, panting. I stopped where I was.

"He won't hurt you, Jo. Pat his head."

I patted his head. He rolled over, showing me his stomach, but I was too tired to pet a big dog. I took the net off the bottom bunk. Beside Whitey's bed was a book: *My Stolen Horizon: The Journey of Thomas Fire Lake, a Native American.* I'd seen that book, but I couldn't think from where. I unbuttoned my shirt. I took my shoes off and I remembered. It was the rigid driver on the ferry who'd been reading it. Bobby was having his sauna that night. *Why aren't you in bed, Jo?* he'd asked when I finally found him.

I lay back, my head still full of the doggy mountains around me. Dizzy curled up at my feet.

I'm in bed now, Bobby.

I shut my eyes.

At first I thought we were at the truck stop at South Mimms, and that Bobby had come in with a box of KFC. I opened my eyes and the chicken smell was still there. I sat up, saw the tall sign through the window: GIANT TRUCKSTOP AT CASTAIC. Whitey was in the driver's seat holding a box of fried chicken; not Kentucky, but Popeye's. Dizzy sat beside him. Both of them were looking at me.

"I didn't know whether to wake you up or not."

Too dry to speak, I put my hand to my throat. He handed me a Coke and I took a long sip. He gave me a chicken breast. I tried not to stuff it in too fast.

"Hungry!" he said.

I was. I hadn't had this kind of food for a while. I'd been eating too much of that posh stuff that never filled me up properly. Jazz was playing from his stereo again, but it was a woman this time, one of those black ones from olden days, singing something about bourbon and bad men. Outside the evening air was stirring in its diesel blur.

"I got good news for you," said Whitey. "I got you a ride to Bakersfield, leaving in three hours time. Lady trucker called Lillian. Quiet lady, but she'll get you there safe."

"Okay." I tried to sound pleased.

"We'll meet her at Veronica's Bar. She likes exactly one game of pool before she hits the road again."

I showered in the truck stop. Whitey stood guard in the TV area because he said it was dangerous, though most of these American truckers looked more tired than dangerous. They dozed in chairs with towels around their necks, watching a rerun of *The Rockford Files* and waiting for the first free shower. Nearly all of them wore baseball caps; it seemed to be some kind of trucker rule in America.

Being clean made me feel better. Dressed and cleaned and freshly made up, I was looking forward to having a drink in Veronica's Bar. "Shower number three hundred thirty-four is ready," called the girl on the loudspeaker, and I wondered how she knew.

When I walked outside with Whitey the world had changed color. Lashings of orange and purple and yellow made a painting out of the sky, brighter even than the fake sunset in Cosima's club. And the trucks! Macks and Peterbilts and Freightliners and Kenworths and Internationals, preening themselves like movie stars, their bumpers rounded mirrors of the sunset.

"Look at these babies," said Whitey. "Getting their beauty sleep."

That was exactly right.

Veronica's Bar was really a shack with plastic where the windows should have been and half a swinging door to let us in. The floor was covered in sawdust, and a pool table took up most of it. A television with bad reception of Garth Brooks singing was fixed high up on the wall.

"There you go," said Whitey.

"That's not the stuff I like," I said.

Dollar bills plastered the walls. They had signatures on them from all of the truckers who drank here. I read some of the names: Kansas Bob, T.R. Troy, Kelvin of South Carolina.

"Do you have a dollar bill up here?" I asked Whitey.

"No, ma'am. I wouldn't like folks to think I'm a drinking man."

We stood at the bar. The funny thing about Veronica was that she looked English. She had knobbly wrists and orange hair and laugh lines that reminded me of women who worked in petrol stations. The most English thing about her was the way she didn't look pleased to meet me.

Her voice, however, was purely American.

"Any ID on you?"

"ID?"

"Proof of age?"

"I'm eighteen."

"Well, that's too bad. Because in the state of California, you have to be twenty-one to consume an alcoholic beverage. In fact, you have to be twenty-one even to be in this here establishment."

"She's doing you no harm," said Whitey. "This here young chicken probably doesn't even like the taste of liquor, do you, honey?"

"I do, actually."

"She's just off the plane from London, England," he said to her. "So the least you could do is give her a Coke and give me the same, and give us a family-size bag of those Lay's potato chips, too, please ma'am."

Veronica wasn't happy, but she did what he asked her to. "The kids drink in Europe, don't they, honey?" She asked as she gave us our Cokes and potato chips.

"Sorry? Of course they do."

"What I mean to say is, even little children drink in Europe, know what I'm saying? Everybody drinks. That's why they won't come and support us over there in Iraq. They're all too *drunk*."

Before I could answer a man sat on the stool next to me. He was short and stocky and he held a pool cue up between his legs. "You from England?"

"Yes." I didn't feel like talking yet. I was still trying to figure out a way to get some alcohol.

"Her daddy's a trucker, too," said Whitey.

"I was in the navy in England," said the man. "Stationed in Portsmouth. I met a girl there named Sandra. She was from, where's that place, damn, watchamacallit . . ." He snapped his fingers. "*Exit.* That's it. She was from Exit, Devon."

" 'Exit?' Do you mean Exeter?"

He snapped his fingers again. "That's it, Exeter. She was a marvelous girl."

"Your turn to shoot, Brody!"

He went back to the pool table. Whitey sipped his Coke and kept a watch over everybody. I looked at Whitey and he winked at me. It wasn't a flirty wink, more the way Bobby winked at me sometimes.

The pool man quickly missed his shot. He came back and sat down as if he'd never stopped talking to me. "I had a wife in Idaho and a boy at home. I loved my boy, but I was having problems with my wife, you know? *Communication* problems. I think you know what's coming here. I know you think I'm a terrible guy."

"No."

"Anyway, I met this girl from Exit, Devon, and she said, 'Well, Brody'—that's my name—she said, 'Well, Brody, just say the word'—she had that great accent, like yours—"

"If she was from Devon, her accent wouldn't be like mine."

"*Your turn, Brody!*"

When he went up again another man took his place. He had a red beard and a bandanna round his head and he looked like a Hell's Angel. "I hear you're from England?"

I agreed that I was.

"Are you from anywhere where that movie is, *The Full Monty?*"

"No, but I've been to Yorkshire. Many times."

"Her daddy's a trucker, too," Whitey said.

The Hell's Angel grasped my elbow and leaned closer, as though he wanted to tell me a secret. Whitey put a hand on his shoulder.

"Not too close, Big Toe. You can talk to her if she'll let you, but you keep your hands and your beer breath to yourself."

"It's my turn to talk to her, anyway." Brody was back. I thought Big Toe would object, but he gave Brody the stool, though he stayed hovering behind it.

"So me and Sandra," continued Brody, "we decide to run away together. We agree to meet at the train station at five forty-five. I wait for two hours, long after that train has gone. It isn't till late that night I learn there are two stations!"

A short man with a toupee came up to me. "My mother's English, you know," he said, as though I'd asked. "She looked like you when she was young. She was a beautiful girl. Like you. You're a doll."

Every man in the bar was waiting his turn to come and talk to me. It made me feel good, even though none of them was good-looking. With every new one that came up to me, Whitey smiled or winked.

But after a while I just wanted to talk to Whitey. We went outside and sat on the stoop with two new Cokes, ice cubes clinking in our glasses.

"Belle of the ball," he said.

I took a handful of Lay's. "In England we call these crisps."

"Well. That's cute."

It was only Americans who called me cute. I thought of that night when Cosima had said I was the cutest of her fans "intercontinentally."

"You haven't said too much about these friends you've come to see," said Whitey.

"They're in a band."

"One of them country bands?"

"Yeah."

He shook his head, and stared into the sky. It wasn't quite dark, but the sunset had folded into dark pink fans. It was nearly time to go.

"Can't I stay with you, Whitey? Just for one night?"

"Think what your daddy would say, Jo, spending the night with a strange man. I wouldn't like it if you were my daughter."

"He would like you. I know he would."

"Darlin', I can't. Got me a drop in Houston at the crack of dawn. Then I got to be getting home. My little one's in bed with the chicken pox."

He hadn't mentioned a family before. A "little one in bed with chicken pox" meant there were probably other kids as well, and a wife. I felt my energy draining away.

A woman was walking toward us. She wore a Stetson. She was so skinny that she seemed to be walking in profile.

"There's your ride," said Whitey.

She came closer. She was tanned and wrinkled. Everything about her was scrawny, from her nose to her thin, long hair.

"Evening, Lillian."

"How do, Whitey."

"This here's Jo."

"How do, Jo."

We watched as Lillian went into the bar for her one game of pool.

"Will you do something for me, Jo?" asked Whitey.

"What?"

"Will you take care of yourself? Take real good care of yourself?"

I took a sip of Coke and swallowed the wrong way. When I finished coughing, I looked away from him. I was embarrassed to have coughed so badly.

"You're gonna be all right," said Whitey. "You are a wonderful girl, you hear what I'm saying? Or really, I should say, a wonderful *young lady*."

My eyes were pricking. I kept my eyes on the darkening sky. Lillian came out of the bar with forty dollars in her hand.

"Won again, Lillian."

"Sure did."

We started walking, the three of us, to the truck stop.

"Hey, English!"

I turned around. Brody was in the doorway, his head sticking up from the missing half of the door.

"Yes?"

"Do you believe in fate? Do you believe that things happen for a reason?"

"I don't know."

"Do you think, for example, it was fate that I waited two hours at the wrong train station?"

"You could just have had a bad map."

"I'll never forget that girl," he said. "You hear me?"

"I hear you."

"I'll never forget her," he said again, sounding as though he would cry.

Lillian promised Whitey she'd take good care of me, and she didn't take bad care of me. But Lillian was so quiet that even her Peterbilt seemed lonely for conversation.

"Where are you from?" I asked her.

"Here and there."

I wondered if she and Whitey had ever got together. She wasn't pretty, and she didn't look like a jazz lover to me. As we rode the Interstate 5 north through Sawtooth Mountain, the truck heaved and complained like an old man talking to himself.

"This here's the Grapevine," said Lillian. "It's so steep they close it down sometimes because of the fog." She looked at me. "Don't suppose you'd care for a little country music?" She turned on the radio and the guitar twanged up at us.

"Fair play to you, Lillian," I said, but when the song began, it wasn't quite what I had in mind. It was about a girl who runs away from home and meets a black man with a Cadillac. She becomes a prostitute and a crack addict and the black man beats her up. Finally she calls her mother, but her mother is dead because one day the mother went looking for her and went through a red light and was killed. The girl realizes that it's all her fault and she gives up drugs and booze and hears the call of Jesus.

When the song was over, a man came on, loud enough to be sitting in the cab with us. "HOW DO YOU LIKE THAT! 'Jesus Loves a Sinner Who's Sorry!' So for any of you new listeners out there, welcome! To Gary's All-Night Call-In, and we've been having a real stimulating conversation about that Planned Parenthood Clinic up there in Fresno, the one that was bombed last week causing that nurse there to lose her left hand. We have a call right now from . . . Judith of Fresno?"

"Judy."

"Hello there, Judy. What have you got to say about all this?"

"Well, I first want to say that I do not personally condone violence of any kind. I am a peaceful Christian and I do not believe that we find our way by injuring another human being!"

"I feel a *but* coming on, Judy. . . ."

"But in my personal opinion I feel that anyone who promotes the idea of abortion, well, they are *definitely* going to rot down there in hell, so you don't need no bomb to make your point, they'll go up in flames anyway, you know what I'm saying?"

"I hear you, Judy."

"I mean it is a crying shame about that nurse, but she was a grown girl who could make her own choices. But what about the lives of those UN-BORN CHILDREN who have no choice in the matter, who are destroyed and yanked out of their mamas' bodies before they even see the LIGHT OF THE WORLD—"

I laughed. Lillian looked at me. Her eyes looked pointy and cross in the half-darkness, like black triangles.

"Everyone's got a right to what they believe," she said. "It is a free country, you know."

I wanted to say that England was a free country, too, but I knew my words would just drop to the floor like dead things. Suddenly I missed everybody in the world who wasn't Lillian. I even missed Brody and Big Toe and all the guys in Veronica's Bar.

Judy from Fresno was still shouting: "And not only that, Gary, but did you ever ask yourself what they do with them unborn babies?"

"Don't know that I have, Judy. . . ."

"Have you ever heard of a burger joint in Yucaipa, California, called MajorBurger? Did you know that the remains of an unborn baby were incinerated and mixed in with the meat there at MajorBurger, so that people were actually *eating* these unborn babies? Now this was scientifically proven, you know what I'm saying?"

The cab seemed to expand with the light of a passing truck and shrink as it was left in darkness again. I thought about what Whitey had said, about each of us being in a bubble in the middle of nothing.

The Grapevine leveled. We started going down. I imagined myself sliding out from under the truck, crushed into the road. I thought of Snowdonia, navy with nighttime, rolling us toward Holyhead with its smells of fish and oil. Of Bobby and me in our own little bubble; Bobby tucking me in while outside Welsh fishermen loaded bottles and water lapped against the dock at the exact point where the world finishes. And he had his own good smells on him: cigarettes, bananas. I was ashamed when he carried my sleeping body onto the boat. Too big, I thought I was. But I wasn't big at all then.

I had to ring Primrose. I hadn't rung her in case she tried to stop me going to America, but I would ring her now. Why hadn't I thought of it? Fogarty

didn't care anymore. Staunton had disappeared. But we would find him, Primrose and I. We'd visit every pub in Ireland if we had to.

"Lillian," I said, trying to keep the tremor out of my voice. "Do you have
a phone?"

"I don't go for cell phones. We're nearly there. You can call from the
motel."

Up ahead were a string of lights. We passed a billboard saying UNITED WE
STAND and then another: WELCOME HOME TROOPS.

We were in Bakersfield.

Lillian signaled, exited, and turned onto Buck Owens Boulevard. She
glanced at me. "Looks like what you need is a good night's sleep."

I didn't say anything, but the sudden niceness in her voice made me realize how sleepy I was. We pulled up in front of the Best Western Motel.

"You'll be okay now?" she asked.

"I will."

"You sure?"

"Yes. Thank you." I could hear how flat my voice was. There was no feeling in me now. I didn't want to phone anybody anymore, not tonight. I only
wanted to be in bed. I grabbed my bag and jumped out, leaving Lillian with
the engine running.

CHAPTER 24

*C*avala cavala, they seemed to be saying, *cavala cavala*. Their *cavalas* rippled
through the walls, into my bed and body as I slept. The Mexicans were fighting or talking loudly. Still half asleep, I opened the curtains to see if I could
find them, but there were no Mexicans out there, only a fat white couple by
the swimming pool, two Jack Russell puppies yapping in a playpen between
them.

It was 8:23 in the morning and already ninety-three degrees. I took a bath.
Afterward I spread a towel on the bed and lay on it, feeling the air go liquid on
my skin. I closed my eyes and nearly dropped off again, but the curtain

flapped against the open window. I knew I should go and close it, but I stayed the way I was, nearly daring someone to come along and see me lying naked against the itchy spinning-wheel bedspread. Finally I got up and dressed and went downstairs to reception.

"How are you today, Miss Pickering?" asked the man behind the desk.

"I'm fine. Has Cosima Stewart checked into this hotel yet?"

"I'm afraid we're not at liberty to disclose information about our guests."

"So she might have checked in?"

But he was checking in new arrivals, people who weren't her.

I went outside. The band would be playing here tonight, right next door at Buck Owens' Crystal Palace.

Buck Owens' was a pink, ranch-style mansion. Even at this time of day cowboys and frilly, long-skirted women drank and chatted on the balconies, as if they were at a saloon in an old Western. I wondered how they could bear to be dressed like that in this heat. I walked up to the building, but I still couldn't hear them. Then I realized they were mannequins.

The glare hurt my eyes and my skin was baking. From what little I'd seen of it so far, Bakersfield was a dry and bony place of motels and gas stations and earth scrubbed bare by the sun. A pickup truck clattered by with a bunch of Mexicans standing in the back, crammed together like squashed, dark fruit.

Two little girls with white-blond hair walked toward the Best Western. They carried plastic 7-Eleven cups which were nearly as big as their heads, the word *Slurpee* on each of them. The smaller one dropped her Slurpee. The drink spread into a big orange blister on the ground.

"You can't get another one," said the older girl. "Mommy will yell at you."

The younger child began to cry. I reached into my pocket. "How much are they?" I asked.

The girls stared at me as if I was the one saying *cavala, cavala*.

That was when I saw her, coming out of the Best Western. She wore a jogging suit and she was springing on the soles of her feet. She looked slightly different with her hair pulled away from her face, but her expression was pure Cosima. She had her morning, worried look, a look that meant she'd had too much to drink last night, and that everything she did today would be especially thoughtful and healthy. I followed her down the boulevard and left onto Riverside Drive.

She was still walking, quick and bouncy. I went faster to keep up with her. If I could catch her while she was on her own, I'd have a chance of getting through to her. We might go out for breakfast, eat hotcakes in one of those diners she'd talked about in the interview.

"I can't believe I only got here yesterday!" I'd tell her, and I'd tell her about everyone I'd met since then: Whitey and Lillian, the guys in Veronica's Bar. I would tell her about the religious radio station.

"People like that are the reason I left Texas," she would say, and she would laugh at those people, and I would wonder how it had ever frightened me, hurtling down the Grapevine and hearing that woman shriek about fetuses and burgers.

She was beginning to jog. I tried to keep up. Sweat poured into my right eyebrow. We passed a Baskin-Robbins, a Hertz car rental, a Dunkin' Donuts. We passed squat stucco houses, sparkling like Styrofoam in the sun. She crossed the road and ran toward the park. I tore over the road, in front of a female crossing guard herding children across the street.

"Crazy jerk! You should be arrested for that!"

I lost sight of her as she ran into the park. The signs at the park entrance were almost cheerful with things you couldn't do: NO DOGS, NO BICYCLES, NO ALCOHOLIC BEVERAGES. Following the path to a wooded patch, I was nearly knocked down by a whirl of legs, by jogging girls with the names of colleges across their chests: UCSD, UCLA, UCSC. I tried to jog myself but my breasts hurt when they bounced. My thighs rubbed together in the heat.

I went to the entrance and waited for her come back, but there must have been another way out because she never did. I went back to my room and lay down. I thought of yesterday afternoon, dozing in Whitey's sleeper, the ice-cream tinkle music and Chet Baker's voice like a cool palm on my forehead. I closed my eyes and the rest of the day swallowed me up.

It was six in the evening, two A.M. in the English and Irish morning. It had only been three days since I'd spoken to Fogarty, but the five thousand miles between us made it seem longer. The distance seemed a hopeful thing, an opening through which Bobby might come back. Compared to my five thousand miles, I thought of him traveling five hundred, back to Dublin and back to London, up the stairs at Shandy Street. I thought of him smiling at the BOBBY notes and shaking his head and saying, *What are you like, Jo!*

I didn't get through the first time. I had to find the international code and go through the motel operator. On the third try, I got through.

"Fogarty. It's Jo."

"Hello! How's the craic in the U.S.A?" He sounded cheerful.

"Have you found him?"

"I'm . . . I'm sorry, we haven't, Jo. We're doing our best."

I lay back on the bed.

Don't sink, I told myself. *Don't.*

Inside Buck Owens' Crystal Palace, three steps up from the dance floor, people sat at big tables eating big food: half-pound burgers, bricks of cornbread, jugs of beer. I went straight to the bar, where a real 1950s car stuck out of the wall as if it had crashed from the sky.

I was looking forward to my first drink since coming to America, but the girl behind the bar asked that same question:

"Can I have your ID, please?"

"I'm from England," I told her. "I've never even heard of an ID."

But she just turned to the next customer.

I had my hand stamped so I could come back in. I stepped outside. On the boulevard a rigid truck was parked and a police motorcycle was parked behind it, its siren lights swirling but no sound coming out. The driver and the sheriff stood in front of the rigid. The sheriff, a big guy with a mustache, was shaking his finger at the driver. The driver was at least a head smaller, a scrawny guy in cut-off shorts and a baseball cap.

The sheriff handed the driver a ticket. He got back on his motorcycle and tore away. The scrawny driver jerked his head to the right and then jerked it to the left.

I walked up to him. "Did he give you a ticket for speeding?"

"Son of a bitch! Redneck cocksucker!"

He had fierce gray eyes that reminded me of a husky. His face was pock-marked all over. I thought he might be good-looking without the pock-marks.

"Fucking *fuckheads!* Eight miles. *Eight fucking miles* over the limit! I mean, look at those greasy Mexicans, *under*-speeding, doing twelve miles an hour in their scum-mobiles, and you don't see them getting tickets for driving too slow, do you? With most of them not even legal here?"

I pointed to the back of his truck. "What's in your load?"

He narrowed his eyes at me, making slits out of them. "What's it to you?"

"Just wondering."

"You foreign?"

"English."

"So what are you doing talking to me? I ain't picking up no Eurotrash jail-bait hitchhikers."

"I was wondering," I said, "if you liked country music."

"If I like what? Country music? I might like it, as a matter of fact, I *might.* What are you going to do about it?"

"Well, it's just . . . I have an idea. I buy you a ticket for Cosima and Her Goodtime Guys, and you buy the drinks."

He pinched the tip of his baseball cap, pulled it down on his head. "Cor-rupting a minor. That's a federal offense. *No thank you, girly.* I've had enough trouble."

"But nobody knows me here. And they're a great band."

He looked down the boulevard as though expecting the sheriff to come back. "I don't agree. I think they're a faggot band. That drummer is an asshole-licking faggot."

"The keyboard player, you mean."

"Whatever. He's a queer fucking faggot."

But I could tell he was thinking about it.

Crystal Palace was filling up with men and women, most of them wearing cowboy hats and cowboy boots. Nearly all the women wore tight jeans with big belts and buckles, from the skinniest women to the fat ones, their big thighs and arses sealed in like denim pears. When we walked in, the warm-up band was on. Four rows of denim legs line-danced on the hardwood floor.

"Did you know that in London," I asked him, "Crystal Palace is the name of a place? And a football team?"

"Ask me if I care."

His name was Cleat, and Cleat didn't like to wait at the bar. He snuck a bottle of whiskey into my handbag. He pulled me toward a table where a couple was about to sit.

"That table has been reserved for us," Cleat told the couple.

"I don't see a 'Reserved' sign," said the man.

Cleat made a fist. "You need a better 'Reserved' sign than that?"

The guy put his hand on his girlfriend's back and guided her away.

"That isn't fair," I said to Cleat. "They were here before us."

"Just sit your butt down, little girl."

"My name is Jo."

He handed me the bottle under the table. I would rather have had Bacardi than whiskey, but it was great to be drinking anyway. Cleat kept fidgeting, tapping his hands on the table or jerking his head to look behind him. Finally, he said, "C'mon," and he pulled me up.

"We'll lose our table!"

"Leave your jacket. Nobody'll steal something that looks like that."

He dragged me to the handicapped toilet. I didn't want him to kiss me, not while I was still sober. I stiffened up, waiting for him to plaster me against the wall, but he didn't touch me. He took a tiny envelope out of his pocket and laid out white lines on top of a small square mirror.

"Oh, that," I said. "You have it here, too."

"Of course we 'have it here, too.'"

He rolled up a five-dollar bill, sniffed a line, and tapped the side of his mouth. "In fact, this here's from down the Interstate 5 near Palmdale, where a friend of mine has a little establishment."

He handed me the rolled note. I sniffed. The powder felt sharp and nasty as it went up my nose.

"This doesn't feel like the cocaine I had before," I said.

"That's because it's poor man's cocaine. Which is fine with me, because I'm a poor man, and not ashamed of it."

"What do you mean, 'poor man's cocaine'?"

"Crystal meth." He made a clicking sound with his mouth. "Speed."

"I don't feel speedy. I just feel numb."

"Is that a bad feeling?"

"No."

"Well, shut up then."

As we took our seats the announcer was saying, "Will you please give a warm Bakersfield welcome to Cosima and Her Goodtime Guys!" The crowd cheered. Rick came on. Sean came on. Cosima came on and the crowd whooped louder. She wore a white T-shirt and jeans and bright red cowboy boots I'd never seen. I wondered why I didn't feel more nervous, more excited. My feet and hands and teeth were jittering but inside, I felt dead and strange, as if I wasn't really here in California, or they weren't here; as if none of this was happening at all. The band kicked off with "Crash." When she sang "Crash! Go my dreams!" I sang along, just like everyone else did, but I still felt nothing.

"Okay, Miss Party Animal." Cleat leapt up and grabbed my hand. He pulled me toward the crowded dance floor.

"I can't dance," I said.

He dragged me down there, anyway. He put one hand on my hip and the other on my shoulder. He pulled me toward the stage. I tried to hold back, but he was strong for a skinny guy. I didn't want Cosima to see me until she was alone. I wondered what she would do if she looked down and saw me now, dancing with a pockmarked, husky-eyed bruiser like Cleat. It might be such a surprise that she wouldn't mind at all. Primrose Hill had gone, along with Mile End and black taxis and all of dingy old London. It had been blown away and replaced by this flat and boiling country.

I was dizzy, but I fought to get a look at her. Her face looked different up close. She wasn't smiling. Perhaps she'd seen me and hadn't been pleased after all. I was relieved when Cleat twirled me away from her again. Then he took me too far away. People danced between us, heads bobbing between her and me. The speed was making my teeth chatter all by themselves. Cleat stopped me mid-spin.

"You're right," he said. "You suck at this."

We spent the rest of the gig sitting down, sneaking shots of Cleat's whiskey into Coca-Cola.

Just before the encore Cosima said, "This next song is for Buck Owens himself. For giving us the best time we ever had and putting us up in his beautiful home!"

So she wasn't staying at the Best Western after all! I'd followed the wrong girl today. I'd never find her if she didn't stick to the itinerary! Before the encore ended I jumped up to look for the backstage door.

I tried to lose Cleat, but he stayed close behind me. The door said VIP ONLY and the area was clogged with people. I pushed my way to the front. A biker stood guard at the door with his big stomach and big beard. He wasn't a friendly-looking biker, not like Big Toe in Veronica's Bar.

"Your pass, please."

"I forgot to bring it. Can you give the band a message?"

"No way. I deliver no message."

"But I know them from England."

"I'm happy for you."

Cleat took my arm. "C'mon. We'll find them in back."

We went out to the parking lot. A group of guys came out with guitar cases, but they were only the warm-up band. Cleat lit a cigarette. I laced my fingers together, shifted my weight from foot to foot.

"What did you think of the band?" I asked.

"That blond guy is a faggot."

"Don't you have anything else to say about them?"

"Folk who play in a band ain't no different from anybody. They put their pants on one leg at a time, just like you and me."

I thought this was an incredibly stupid thing to say.

"And that other guy, with the ponytail," he went on. "I bet he's a faggot, too."

"No, he isn't."

"How do you know?"

I gave him a look that told him.

He let out a whistle. "No wonder they ain't putting you on no guest list."

We stayed there for three-quarters of an hour.

"C'mon, let's have another line in the truck," said Cleat. I wasn't sure if I liked this crystal meth, and yet when he suggested more of it, I was pleased, the way I was pleased when Bobby said it was time to stop for lunch. His truck stank of tobacco and diesel, much worse than ours. There were crushed beer cans on the floor, Zig-Zag rolling papers, empty Cheese Doodles packets. I picked up the Zig-Zags.

"We call these Rizla papers," I said.

"Let's get something straight right now. I don't care what you call things on some pitiful little island over fucking there. You're in America now, got it?"

"Fucking hell."

"Just say 'fuck.' *Speak our language.*"

The seat was covered in crumbs, so I put a magazine under my bum. Cleat pulled it out from under me and threw it in my lap.

"Don't sit on that. I *read* that."

On the cover was a picture of a man in army fatigues holding a gun. *History of the Uzi,* said the writing in the cover, and then below that, *Kalashnikov USA's AK-103.*

Cleat looked around for something to cut the lines on. "Hand me that *People.*"

"Why can't you use the *Small Arms Review?*"

"What did I just say to you? That magazine means a lot to me. *People* is just a bunch of stuck-up movie stars."

"Why do you read it?"

"I don't *read* it. That particular *People* has got some fine T&A, that's all, and that's 'tits and ass' if you're wondering. Try translating that into merry oldey fucking Robin Hood English."

He let me have the first line. I enjoyed the sensation of snorting. I tilted my head back to let it seep into my nose and throat. The lights from Buck Owens' Crystal Palace went down, leaving us in the dark. Cleat started the engine.

"They're still in there," I said.

"They've gone," said Cleat. "Probably out some door only fancy-schmancy people use. You'll see them tomorrow."

I sat up in my seat, ready to bolt out of a moving truck if he got weird. He drove us east, following the signs to Tehachapi. His fingers tapped out a rhythm on the steering wheel, a *ra-ta-ta* again and again. He kept looking in his rearview mirror. "That dude thinks he's busted me. He thinks I'm gonna pay a seven-hundred-dollar fine. I'll tell you, he ain't busted shit." He pulled his wallet out of his pocket, handed it to me. "Look in there. Don't steal anything. Just look."

I found a few rumpled dollars and a discount coupon for Spearmint-Rhino Gentleman's club in San Diego. I also found five driver's licenses, all with Cleat's face on them but each with a different name.

"But that cop can still trace you through the truck, can't he?"

"By the time he does that, me and this truck will be parting company. I've had enough of this old piece of crap."

Twenty-five minutes out of Bakersfield, Cleat killed the engine and left the high beams on.

"You can get down now," he said.

I stepped down and a tuft of earth pricked my ankle. The headlights made a long strip of light in the darkness. The sky was covered in stars. Cleat turned up the radio. It was a country station, at least.

"What is this place?"

"It used to be some Indian reservation, before they all started getting fat on casinos."

Cleat was making clanking noises in truck. I looked ahead to where the light fell off. Beyond that, it was total blackness. I turned toward the truck. I couldn't hear Cleat at all now.

"What are you doing?" I called.

He didn't answer.

"I want to go back," I said, my voice breaking. I thought of what he could be preparing there: crowbars, knives, rope. In ten minutes he could bind my arms and my legs. He could cut my tongue off, cut my breasts off.

"Just take me back to the motel, would you?" I thought of the man behind the desk at the Best Western Motel saying, "How are you today, Miss Pickering?" The fact that he knew my name seemed proof that I existed, that I would still exist tomorrow morning.

"You can look," said Cleat. "Over there."

"Where?"

I turned toward the blackness again. Cleat was wearing a Mickey Mouse mask that bounced and glowed in the dark. The mask was made of rubber, making his face as wobbly as jelly.

But his voice, when it came, was behind me.

"Stay in the headlights."

Two men! I felt arms encircling me from behind. I screamed.

"Shh." His body was warm. He pulled me into his groin. His arm moved against the side of my breast. He was gentle, comforting me for what he was about to do to me. I felt his hand going up in the shape of a gun.

"Bye-bye, Mickey."

He let out a click and a *bang!* that vibrated through my head. A flame lit up the night just in front of me. I screamed again. Mickey Mouse shattered, bright shards spraying the air. My heart was pounding so fast I was sure it would kill me before he did.

"What did you do?"

Cleat laughed.

"Who did you shoot?"

"It's a tree, doofus. Feel how warm my hand is."

But it wasn't his hand that grazed my arm. It was his gun. I could feel his breath against my neck. "Scare you?"

"No," I lied. "I don't like the smell."

He gathered me more tightly from behind. I lost my balance, falling back into him. He was soft for a skinny guy. He found my hand and slipped the gun into it.

"Go for it. Scrape the rest of that face off."

"No." I tried to give him back the gun, but he wouldn't take it.

"Raise it in the air." His voice was patient. "Keep your finger off the trigger guard."

I didn't even know where the trigger guard was. My hand was oily with sweat. The gun slid off my fingers, falling to the ground. He dropped down, caught the gun just before it hit.

"Don't worry," he said. "This is a safe revolver. A Ruger Vaquero. It probably won't go off if you drop it."

He was coming up from below now, grazing the gun along my calf, my thigh, under my skirt. He ran the gun against the crotch of my underwear. I stiffened, waiting for him to shoot my bits off. He stood up behind me, taking hold of my hair and clutching it like a rope. He molded my fingers around the gun again. He raised both of our hands toward the shattered Mickey, wrapped my finger over the trigger and pulled. The flame ripped through the air.

"Now try it by yourself."

I raised the gun and squeezed my eyes tight. I pulled the trigger, but it locked.

"Okay, okay. You're obviously too much of a *girl* for the revolver."

Cleat took the gun and went back to the truck. A minute later he pinned two new masks up: Minnie Mouse and Donald Duck. When he walked back to me, he had a different gun. It was black and plastic-looking, like a toy. He put the bullets in a box-type thing. He handed the case and the gun to me. "This here's called a magazine. Now shove that baby in."

"You do it," I said.

He kissed me on the lips. "You can do it. Just shove it up."

I shoved it up.

"Now, this is a beauty. A Glock 19, nine-millimeter, four-inch barrel length. Take it now."

I wouldn't take it. He rolled his eyes, aimed above the mask, and shot four times. The sound was terrible, but the shooting looked easy, rhythmic. When he handed it to me again, I took it. I pointed at the mask, and pulled the trigger. The flame reared up.

"Again!" He said. "Just shoot!"

I shot again. And again. The flame went so high I thought it would leap back and set me alight. I took my sixth shot, and Minnie Mouse shattered everywhere.

"Woooowwwwwwwsa!!" Cleat flew back to the truck, turned the radio up. He came up behind me again, this time with the whiskey. He poured a swig of it down my throat. A Charlene Sweeney song was playing on the radio:

> Get rid of him, just get rid of him
> You know that it's the right thing
> Live your life, ride in speeding cars
> And laugh and dance and drink in dangerous bars
> Smoke and weep and dye your hair.

Way ahead of us a strip of dawn was leaking into the night sky. I thought of Whitey driving under that sky, somewhere down in Louisiana. I thought of Bobby walking underneath it, along a potholed road in Mayo or Sligo. Same sky everywhere, though I had to admit it felt a lot bigger here.

"C'mon, darlin', don't let me down. Tell Donald he's a dead man."

I raised the gun and tried again. I fired, letting out a real superhero *bang*! Donald Duck shattered in the air. Cleat turned me around and kissed me, his tongue long and forceful in my mouth. With the gun still warm in my hand, we fell to the ground, not even making it to the truck.

CHAPTER 25

He looked like a sweaty pink eagle as he drove, eyeing the road as if it meant him harm. I didn't ask Cleat to take me to Victorville. He just did it. It made me think he wasn't a real trucker, going anywhere some girl asked him to. He didn't even have a CB. The only thing he had in common with Whitey was that he wore a baseball cap.

"If I wanted to find Whitey in Louisiana," I asked, "how would I do that?"

He flashed a look at me. "You ain't looking for no Whitey. The man you're looking for is the man you're looking *at*." He slammed his AC/DC into the stereo. The music was so loud it rocked the truck and made the windows rattle.

We picked up the Interstate 58 and headed toward Barstow. I opened the window, wanting to air out the part of me that he'd been inside of, but the hot air slapped me in the face rather than taking anything away.

Yet when I thought of his pistol grazing my leg or running along my panties, I wanted him inside me again, pounding me full of his hate and making me forget about everything else for a while, his face buried in my neck so I didn't have to look at it.

I flicked through his glove compartment. The Glock was still in there, along with warrants for his arrest. I read through them.

"What's a meth lab?" I asked.

"Speed laboratory. Or in this case, a trailer park down there in Pahrump, Nevada."

I went on to the next one. "You raped someone?"

"*Statutory* rape. She was willing. She just didn't happen to be eighteen like she said she was."

"*I'm* not eighteen."

"Then we better not be eating our waffles in no coffee shop where the pigs go. Anyway, the pigs don't give a shit about foreign pussy."

We stopped at the railway crossing. The gates were crossed and the red lights were flashing. The freight train came; no windows, no passengers. It was all brown-and-red containers and it must have been a mile long at least. Even after five minutes it was still going and I could see no end to it.

His hand was on my knee. It crept along my leg, moving up to my thigh until it brushed against the crotch of my panties. I kept my eyes on the train. My thighs tightened on his hand.

"Relax." His fingers slid into the edge of my panties, slowly pulling them off. I looked out at a cactus, twisted as though it was fighting for air. I leaned back, looking up at the telephone wires. I waited for him to go further, to prod inside, but his fingers just fluttered over me. He leaned over, put a beery kiss on my neck.

"That's all you get for now."

The train finally passed, giving its long American whistle.

In Victor Valley, Cleat's temperature gauge said 105 degrees.

"And that's Fahrenheit," I said. "How much is that in Centigrade?"

"How do I know? You think I care about the limey fucking interpretation of our weather?"

The Apple Ranch Motel wasn't really a ranch. It was a cluster of cabins just off Route 66. We parked and went into the cabin where it said MANAGER on the door. Inside, newspapers were piled high and the television was loud, showing a daytime soap. The manager was a big woman with long gray hair.

"I have only six cabins here," she said, "and they're all used up by musicians from the bluegrass festival, including three from London, England."

"They checked in already?" I thought of Cosima in one of these cabins now; showering, unpacking, putting on her new red boots. If she walked in this minute, she would see me with my hair like string and my face crusty from last night's makeup. She would see Cleat fanning his face with a flyer called *The Beautiful Sights of San Bernardino County*, his eyes darting around as if looking for something to steal.

"They haven't checked in yet," said the lady, and I was relieved. I would have to find a way of getting rid of Cleat before I could see her.

We parked under a tree set back from the driveway. I stayed on lookout while Cleat slept in the back. The heat was so strong I had to take deep breaths to remind myself that I still had breath inside of me. I was filthy from sleeping on the ground, and last night's speed grated like sand in my gums.

By four o'clock they still hadn't checked in. I was thinking we ought to go straight to the festival when a black Volkswagen convertible crackled along the drive into the small gravel lot. Rick and Sean got out, but Cosima wasn't with them. I heard Rick say, "Give it to her when we get there." Sean went to the cabin on his left, Rick to the one on the right. Five minutes later they both came out wearing different clothes, and Rick's hair was wet. They got into the convertible.

I shook Cleat. "C'mon. They're going."

Cleat lifted his head. He grabbed my neck and kissed me, forcing my mouth full of his bad smell.

At the West Coast Roots Festival, there were more people than I'd ever seen in one place, including any Truckfest. For hundreds of yards around the stage people sat on blankets or in fold-up chairs. I couldn't see the musicians who were playing, but I recognized the yodelly voice as soon as I heard it.

"It's the Del McCourys!" I said. "That was the first bluegrass band Bobby ever heard!"

"Who's Bobby? Some other guy you fucked?"

"Bobby's my *father*." I started to walk toward the grass but Cleat caught my hand and pulled me toward the food stands, which were selling pizza and barbecued meat and something called corn dogs. He bought us two corn dogs with my money. The corn dog looked weird, like a breaded sausage on a stick, but it tasted better than a sausage roll.

"I'm going to take a leak," Cleat said. "Don't go anywhere."

When he'd gone, I wandered toward the lake, where it was cooler. I could hear a banjo, nice and plucky, and then a girl singing in a nasal, old-fashioned voice like June Carter. I found them under a tree, three musicians, a family of button faces and dungarees and red-blond hair. I'd expected the girl to be older with a voice like that, but she didn't look much older than I was. The banjo player was around forty, her father probably. The fiddle player looked no older than fourteen. His hair was streaked with black and he had a nose ring, but he had freckles like the others and he played as sweetly as Vassar Clements. The girl sang "Over the Flame," a Charlene Sweeney song:

> Don't tell me that you know what's good for me
> Don't ask me if my mother might mind
> You didn't choose me for my morality
> It ain't the virtue in my eyes that makes me shine
> So take me as I am, boy, or leave me behind!

I sat in the shade to watch. A red squirrel scampered up the tree with a nut in its mouth. A few yards away, children sailed paper boats on the lake. I breathed in the music and the damp smells: a bark and wet-pencil smell. It smelled like the lake in Dundrum where Bobby used to fish, where he'd gone with his first love, Maire.

Cleat was suddenly upon me.

"Freckled faggots," he said, and dragged me toward the lake.

An announcement sounded over the park:

"Clog dancing will begin in Tent 1 in two minutes. Line dancing will begin in Tent 3 in four minutes. Cosima and Her Goodtime Guys will appear on the stage in thirteen minutes."

"Cosima's going to be on in a minute!"

He pulled me down onto a hard tuft of grass. He stuck his hand down my jeans.

"No, Cleat."

"You *like* it!"

It hurt but I did like it, sort of.

"Jesus, you're tight as a virgin. Are you a virgin today?" He stuck his hand in further. I clamped my legs tight.

"Fuck this." Cleat leapt to his feet. "I need a beer."

He bought a six-pack of beer for us to share. At the candied nuts kiosk a woman was giving free samples.

"Give us a taste of those vanilla pecans, lady," he ordered.

She gave one to each of us. It crackled on my tongue, sweet and delicious.

"And give me a try of those there caramel peanuts."

She gave us the peanuts. They were just as good.

"And let me try the Hawaiian style."

"Are you buying or are you sampling, young man?" asked the lady.

"Are you selling or are you giving me lip, lady?"

"I don't appreciate your tone, not one bit."

"Is that right? Well, I don't appreciate your *attitude*, Grandma."

The nut lady looked nice enough to me, a fiftyish lady with nice blond hair like Cosima's and a T-shirt that said BLUEGRASS IS GROWN IN THE DESERT.

"I'll buy the vanilla pecans," I said.

"No, you won't." Cleat took my wrist. "She don't deserve your money."

By the time I got Cleat to the grass, we had to sit at the back. I let him prop me on his lap to make me higher up. We were so far from the stage that I could barely see if there were people up there or not.

"Ladies and gentlemen, will you please put your hands together for—"

Before he could even say the name of the band, the crowd whooped and Rick's guitar sounded across the park. I bounced up and down in Cleat's lap. Though I couldn't see her, her voice as clear as ever:

I've been out of orbit for so long
That there's mold upon my heart
Got myself a slum on the wrong side of town
A life so perfectly apart
So the last thing I expected
Was to see you in these parts . . .

Everyone sang along: *And I never thought I'd see you in these parts!*

I thought of the Barbican, where Bobby and I had seen her play for the first time. That festival had been like a pretend version of this one. If Bobby could be where I was this minute! Even the idea of it would be enough to slice through whatever darkness he was having; Cosima and the Del McCourys and the Dale Mitchell Band all in one place, and the family who played "Over the Flame" with the young punk boy who played like Vassar Clements, under the tree with its Dundrum smells.

We were jostled from the front.

"Hey!"

Cleat pushed the back of the person who fell on us. I sat up to see what was going on. Line dancers were dancing near the stage. From this distance, they were tiny, tinier than the dancing cowboys on Sean's shelf.

A loudspeaker cut into the song:

"Would you please save your line dancing for the workshops. Would you please reserve line dancing for the allocated time and tent!"

There was a boo from the front. When Cosima finished the song, she laughed into her mike. "Hey, don't sweat it. You guys look great! We're not used to line dancers at our gigs."

She sounded like she was in a good mood. She had the same voice as when she dedicated "Crash" to me and my "truck-driving daddy." Sean came in then. His accent sounded incredibly Liverpool in this place. I wondered if the crowd would even understand him, these soft Yanks who spoke so slowly. "That's because we're an 'alternative' country band. Not the *real thing* like Garth!"

The audience let out a boo for Garth Brooks.

"Garth is gay!" shouted Cleat.

"*You're* gay!" shouted another guy.

I desperately didn't want Cleat to have a row with the guy in the crowd who said he was gay. But a new song started up, a slow one, and Cleat stayed quiet for once.

Jessie sits in her bungalow
Dreamin' of days so long ago

The sun was setting. Mosquitoes whipped the air. One mosquito landed on the head of a little boy and sat there, as if planning its route. After a while, it made a made a *W* in the air and settled on Cleat's knee. Cleat bashed it and killed it. He held his whiskey to my mouth and poured some into me.

I closed my eyes and listened to "Every Color of Love." I tried to think of Holyhead and the place where the world fell off, but the sun crept in behind my lids, sickly and yellow.

> *Every color of love is what she dreams of*
> *But Jessie never did have a lover*
> *None of those things really happened to her. . . .*

When I looked at the stage again, she had doubled: two tiny Cosima dolls in tiny red tops, as far away as a person had ever stood from me. Because there was nowhere else to rest, I let my head fall on Cleat's shoulder.

When I opened my eyes again, people were picking up blankets, dusting grass off their legs, gathering chairs and ice buckets. The stage looked even smaller now, surrounded by the littered grass.

Cleat stuck his face into mine, up close. His face was as cratered as the desert floor. "Show's over, little girl."

"But it's only just started," I said.

The smell of dying barbecue was strong, and the air was dancing with mosquitoes now. We got up and started walking, but I felt as though my head would roll off my neck. "I've had too much to drink."

Cleat sat us down on the grass. He took the tiny envelope from his pocket along with a tiny straw I hadn't seen before. He dipped the straw in the speed and stuck it into my nose.

"Sniff." He was always friendlier when he was giving me drugs.

After a few more snorts I got to my feet. As we walked, the trees seemed taller and the grass was greener. I wasn't tired or scared. I was ready to find her.

There was no backstage, just musicians milling around outside, behind the stage. The Del McCoury Band was standing with the Dale Mitchell Band, drinking beer from paper cups. An old drunk staggered up to us and handed me a marker. "Sign my shirt," he said. "I want your autograph."

"But I'm not famous."

"Sign it anyway."

I wrote *Josephine Pickering* on his shoulder. I wondered if he would go up to Cosima, too. I thought of her reading his shoulder and seeing my name.

The drunk turned to Cleat. "Sign my shirt."

"Fuck you," said Cleat.

"Hey, man," said one of the guys from the Dale Mitchell Band. "He's a human being, just like you or me. You don't need to talk that way to him."

A woman stood with her back to me. She had the same hair as Cosima and the same T-shirt. Slowly, I walked up to her. Hearing me, she turned around. Her face was old. Her T-shirt said BLUEGRASS IS GROWN IN THE DESERT. She was the nut lady.

"Have you seen Cosima Stewart?" I asked her.

"Not for about twenty minutes. Are you with the band?"

"I'm their friend. My name is Katie. Have they gone for the night?"

"I really don't know, honey."

"Tell her where they are, man." Cleat came up beside me. "She's come a long way."

"You two!" The biker charged up to us, the same one who'd stopped me in Bakersfield. "Okay, I'm going to ask you nicely, this is a backstage area—"

"I don't see no fucking backstage—"

"*This is a backstage area,* so will you please remove yourselves right now—"

"Don't be telling me what to do, scumbag—"

"Yeah? And why don't you crawl back into whatever cesspool meth lab you came from, tweaker?"

Cleat pushed him. The biker pushed Cleat. Cleat put his hands up, as if to surrender. The biker turned away, and Cleat leapt up on his back. The biker thrashed his arms around and bucked his back up and down, but Cleat was as clingy as a monkey. The Dale Mitchell Band ran up and tried to pull Cleat off, but they couldn't do it. His voice seemed to come out of his nose, one mad squeal: "*Tweaker? Did you say tweaker? You fucking look me in the eye when you're talking to me, man!*"

I edged behind a van, wanting to see what was happening while trying to stay out of sight.

A third man ran up to them. I couldn't see his face, just his hair swinging at his back. I leaned in to have a better look. It was Rick. He was tall and strong and fast and I felt myself swell up at the sight of him looking so good, like a real hero. He put his hands over Cleat's face, poked his fingers in his eyes. Cleat tumbled on the ground like a tick that's been flicked on its back. The biker picked up Cleat and twisted him into a headlock, forcing him to face Rick.

"Go on, Watson," said the biker. "Take your best shot.'

"I don't want to hit the guy," said Rick. "Just get him out of here."

Cleat forced his chin over the biker's hairy arm. "What's your problem, *dick!* Hit me, limey faggot! Hit me. Or are you too busy screwing little girls?"

Rick shook his head. He looked round at the others and gave a short laugh. "What's this guy *on?*"

Still keeping him in a headlock, the biker dragged Cleat toward the car park.

I backed off through the big RVs. I got to the car park just in time to see the biker hit Cleat in the stomach, hard. I wondered where I should go when I felt a hand on my own arm. The biker picked me up and swung me on the ground beside Cleat. I landed on my side.

"That goes for you, too, bitch. I see either of you again, it's gonna be a lot worse than a little tumble in the dirt, you understand?"

The biker jetted off, wiping his hands on his legs as if wiping himself free of us. Cleat was holding his stomach. I sat up and looked at my scraped calf. Some people walked by and shook their heads.

Back on the road, Cleat kept saying, "Fucking faggot, faggot limey scum!" It was only Rick he was swearing about, though Rick hadn't even hit him when he had the chance. I wondered if Rick had seen me after all. I didn't think he had, but one of the others could have told him that Cleat had been hanging around with an English girl.

"Why did you say that?" I asked. "That thing about little girls?"

"What, you think you're the only little girl he's fucked?"

"Yes I do, as a matter of fact!"

Cleat laughed his shrill, hyena laugh.

"I want you to drop me off," I said. "You drop me off at that Motel 8 back there. I don't want to stay with you anymore."

Cleat gave me a look, and I knew he wasn't dropping me anywhere. I hated him more than I had ever hated Rick. Yet the idea of being his prisoner excited me, down there in my privates. Until I saw where we were.

"It's too soon," I said. "They'll come back! I don't want them to see me with you!"

But he was pulling into the Apple Ranch Motel, right up to the cabins this time. He got his Glock out of the glove compartment and grabbed a towel from the back. He wrapped the gun in a towel, jumped down from the truck.

"Which one is it?" he called up to me.

"I don't know."

He opened my door, grabbed me by my neck, and pulled me down from the cab. "You hear me ask you a question? *Which one is it?*"

I nodded at the cabin with the yellow door. He bashed the toweled gun against the window, making the glass shatter with a dull sound. He climbed through the broken window. I backed off toward the truck, but he opened the door from the inside and pulled me in, slamming the door behind us. He threw me down on the bed, climbed on top of me, and pinned my wrists down. I scraped his face with my nail and he slapped me, not too hard. I wished I was as big as the biker so that I could put my fist through his stomach. Yet as I waited for him to pull down my jeans and fuck me, part of me wanted him to. He held my face in his hand, tight.

"How many times you fuck that faggot?"

"It's none of your business.'

"How many times did you fuck him?"

"All night long."

"All night long?"

"Only we didn't fuck. We made love."

Suddenly, Cleat did something strange. He eased off of me. He smiled. He smiled in the way a nice person smiles, showing his dimples. I sat up, wondering why he wasn't going to fuck me after all. The gun was still wrapped at the foot of the bed. He picked it up, took it out, began to polish it with the towel. I gasped, seized up. This could be the moment; he would shoot me and leave me dead on the bed for Rick and Cosima to find. But he put the gun down again. He looked around the room. He lifted Cosima's suitcase onto the bed.

"You know what I think?" He clicked open the latch.

I shook my head.

"I think you never fucked him. You want to know why I think that?"

"No," I said, though part of me did.

"Because a guy like that, one of those rock 'n' roll faggots like him, he doesn't fuck girls like you. He fucks skinny little bimbo groupies, you know what I'm saying?"

Cleat held up Cosima's electronic organizer. He clicked it on and a square of light lit up his face. He put it in his pocket.

"You're wrong," I said. "We made love. We made love all night."

Cleat picked up Cosima's camera and put the strap around his neck. "He didn't fuck you. If you were one of those bimbos who only open their mouths to drink champagne or suck little cocks like his, he might have fucked you. You got me? *He thinks he's too good for you.*"

He looked around again. Rick's guitar leaned against the wall beside Cosima's fiddle. Gently, he lifted it onto the bed and opened the case. "Fender," he whispered. "Beauty." He took the guitar out of its case.

"I can prove it," I said. "Before we made love, he sang to me on that very guitar. He sang me a love song."

Cleat held the guitar as if he was about to play. The idea of Cleat playing Rick's guitar made me bubble up with disgust. It was like rubbing shit or vomit all over it.

"Leave it alone,"

He strummed it.

"Leave it alone!" I yanked it from him, and with all the strength I had in my body, I brought it down on the floor. A crack ran through it, as loud as a gunshot itself.

Cleat went for me, as if to hit me. "Stupid bitch! I would've taken that!"

I lifted it up in the air, brought the neck down again. One of the strings flew out.

"If my girl did that to a guitar of mine," he said, "I'd fucking do that to her!"

"It's just as well I'm not your girl, then, isn't it?"

I waited for him to hit me. I wanted him to. I wanted to hear the sound of more things breaking; wood, bones.

But he held his hands up again in that gesture of surrender. He started going through her things. He held up the suede top and then the suede skirt.

"What do you think I could get for these? Cosima Stewart's glad rags?"

"Leave those! I love them. I have one just like it."

"I have one just like it." He made his voice high, with a fake English accent. He folded the clothing over his arm. He picked up Cosima's fiddle and stood it up on the bed against the wall. Carefully, as though he was dressing a shop window mannequin, he draped the top over her fiddle. He fixed the skirt on the bottom of the fiddle, gathering it in back so that it stayed up. When he was finished, the fiddle looked like a headless woman standing on the bed.

"Jo," he said, in his nice-man voice, "I'd like you to meet Cosima Stewart. Cosima loves you very much. She wants to be your girlfriend—your bestest, bestest girlfriend. That's why she's got you on all her guest lists! That's why she invites you backstage at the end of all her concerts!"

"She doesn't even know I'm here yet—"

"Yeah, and you don't *want* her to know you're here, either, because she thinks just the same as he thinks and you know it. That you're a little white-trash whore, a little white-trash slut not worth the sperm in his semen!"

"Shut up!"

"What's that, little girl?"

"I said shut up!"

"Why don't you make me?"

I picked the gun up from the bed. I shot the headless woman four times: in the lower stomach, the upper thigh, twice in the gut. The kickback made fire of the air. A piece of wood shot out of the fiddle and hit me in the shoulder. I didn't care. The shooting made me mad and happy, lit up with a million volts, full of crazy energy. Cleat sidled up behind me. He took my hair in his hand again, made a rope of it.

"One more time," he whispered.

I shot again and got her through the heart.

"You're getting good," he said, and pulled me down on the bed.

I awoke at dawn, my mouth as dry as the ground. I blinked, hard. My eyes were full of crust and it was hard to open them; the sun made me squint. All I could see was a telephone wire against the white sky. I didn't know where we were. I remembered driving. I remembered the night sky, busy with stars.

Cleat's arm made a strip of sweat around my hips but the rest of me was stiff and bare. His other arm moved in a funny way, eeling across my waist. I lifted my head.

At first I thought it was another one of his toys; a rubber snake, black and yellow, draped over us for a joke. When the snake started moving, my heart stopped beating. Seeing me, it stopped, its tongue stuck out, its face horrible and still. Then, slowly, it began to creep over us, its tail tickling my thighs. It stopped again, waiting for the right moment to bite me. My heart was beating now, loud enough to rattle the rattlesnake. The snake slid over me, its tail leaving my body but staying only a few inches away.

"Cleat . . ." I shook his shoulder. "Cleat!"

Without opening his eyes, he lifted himself on top of me and put himself inside me. I looked to the side and watched the snake slither into a bush. I looked up to the sky, which shook now with the groggy motion of fucking. Cleat's hand was at the side of my throat, cupping it. The pores in his skin were big and greasy. His breath was like old eggs. He came, finished, fell off. He began to snore, his bad-egg smell coming in short gusts upon my face.

It took some effort, but I pried myself out from under him. I didn't know how my clothes had become so scattered, but eventually I found all of them— my skirt on a bush, my top on a cactus, my shoes in the truck. The snake had gone, but I could still hear its distant rattle. I was dying for water, but there was no water in the truck. There were only Cheez Doodle bags and Pop-Tarts boxes and empty whiskey bottles. I sat in the driver's seat and opened the glove compartment. The Glock fell out, along with Cleat's arrest warrants.

The keys were in the ignition.

I looked at Cleat on the ground. He looked as though he was dying, spittle coming out of his mouth.

I looked at the keys again. I didn't do anything. I looked at Cleat again. I looked at the keys again.

Do it.

He would kill me. He would grab me and punch me and shoot me through the heart, just like I'd shot Cosima's fiddle.

Do it!

I locked the doors. I turned the keys to the right. The radio boomed on: DON'T TELL ME THAT YOU KNOW WHAT'S GOOD FOR ME!!

I let out a cry. I covered my mouth. Cleat was stirring. I fumbled with the button. I couldn't get it off, only down: *DON'T ASK ME IF my mother might mind!*

I fumbled for the gears on my left, found them on my right. I pressed the gas pedal.

I was hissing in my own head: *Right, dammit, right, keep to the right side of the road!*

The truck was off the road, parked uphill. I floored the pedal but the truck just dragged along the sliding sand. It juddered and stuck, its wheels rolling in place. I floored again. Heaving, the truck took the incline, whined, and made it to the road. I revved the engine. I crawled along. I kept flooring it. I picked up speed: 20, 30. 50. I drove. I turned the song up, the Charlene Sweeney

> *I'm not asking for silver, lace, or true-love vows*
> *I'm not asking you to give me your name*
> *But if it's fire you're wanting, I'm ready with a yes, right now!*
> *I am the harlot dancing over the flame!*

The fiddles came in, two of them, as if they were laughing.

CHAPTER 26

If I didn't find her now, I wouldn't find her until Wednesday. She had no gig tonight. All she had was a radio interview this morning. At the Esso station where I bought my water, I asked where KCVR Victorville was.

"Turn right. Keep on going."

It was easy. Even driving on the wrong side of the road was easy. It was so easy, it felt like a trick. I kept bracing myself for the smashing of my window, a hand grabbing my neck, a blow to my head. As I drove through the town, I kept thinking I saw Cleat: coming out of the Pink Dot convenience store, running down the street, drinking a can of Mountain Dew in the pickup truck beside me. I found the KCVR building and parked around the back. I put on Cleat's sunglasses and his hat. I tuned in to the station. The interview was just beginning.

"Must be nice to be spending so much time in the old U.S. of A. though, is it, Cosima?"

"Yes, it is, though it's kind of a crazy time to be here, with Iraq and every-thing—"

"And speaking of crazy, I hear you had a shock last night? A break-in, I hear?"

"It was pretty awful."

"A lot of bad people out there, Cosima."

"There are, but you know, at the end of the day, only things were dam-aged, not people. Things can be replaced."

"At least you guys have tonight to take it easy?"

"That's right. Sean's going to L.A. to chill with his partner, and Rick and I are staying with friends just outside of El Centro. Tomorrow we're going to Salvation Mountain, you know that place? This old boy called Leonard, this amazing character, he spent seventeen years painting this big hill—"

"It'll be hotter than hell down there, Cosima!"

"It will, but I love that landscape. It's almost aboriginal, you know what I mean? It's like you can feel the earth breathing."

"Let's hope it doesn't breathe too hard. Last time the earth started breath-ing it cost me eight thousand dollars to fix my roof!"

At the end of the interview, she sang "101 Here I Come," live. Suddenly her singing was loud, as if there were two of her. The black convertible had crept up beside me. Rick was at the wheel, his radio louder than mine. He killed the engine and just sat there, smoking. I lowered Cleat's hat and pressed my sunglasses against my face. I didn't let myself look at him, but I could feel the hardness in him today. He wasn't the Rick who sang about India or res-cued people from Cleat. He was the Rick who sent me off in trains and taxis, who'd sicced D.I. McFarlane on me.

The song ended. Two minutes later Cosima opened the door of the con-vertible. She was the closest she'd been to me since I'd come to California. I caught a whiff of her hair conditioner, Honeysuckle Blossom of Liberty. The smell brought the old Cosima back to me; her fingers on my face, her telling me to put blush toward the hairline, telling me to buy conditioner.

"What'd you think, Rick? Guy's a creep, isn't he?"

"I just caught the end. The insurance people rang. I had to take the call."

"Yes, I'm sure you did."

"What the fuck does that mean?"

"It means that every time I get asked to do an interview on my own, you conveniently—"

Rick started up the engine, drowning out the rest.

They backed out. I counted to five and backed out after them. I followed them through Victorville, past the Pink Dot and the bowling alley and onto the Interstate 15, headed south and sailing into the light. I felt like I was sailing into the light. Cleat would never find me now! I let myself glide closer to the convertible. They didn't look like they were fighting anymore. She was smiling and talking, and he had his hand on the back of her neck.

Cleat's clock read 11:25. A hundred and five degrees.

The road sign said: WELCOME TO SAN BERNARDINO COUNTY.

The freeway forked and we drove toward Palm Springs. To my right was a trucks-only route, eighteen-wheelers taking the incline. I thought of our lorry, alone in Primrose's yard. I knew it would seem so much smaller than it did before, now that I'd been in Whitey's Freightliner and Lillian's Peterbilt.

Just outside of Palm Springs spindly white windmills coated the hills, their arms reeling in the hot breeze. *Look at that, Jo,* Bobby would say, as if I wasn't already looking: *Look at that.* He could be a bit thick that way, telling me to look at what was so obviously there.

Cosima and Rick were doing ten miles over the speed limit, seventy-five miles per hour. I was doing seventy-two.

INDIO.

COACHELLA.

THERMAL.

MECCA.

The road narrowed to the 111. To our left fat thermal tanks pissed down water and steam jetted into the sky. The tanks made a sound like thunder, shaking the road beneath my wheels. I thought of what Cosima had said about the landscape: *It's like you can feel the earth breathing.*

Out of nowhere the sea came upon us. It was a moldy sea without waves, a silver fillet of water, birds coating it like breadcrumbs. Bent trees stood among the shallows. They looked as though they'd been begging forever and died standing up, branches outstretched for what they'd never got. Gulls squawked overhead.

SALTON SEA, 235 FEET BELOW SEA LEVEL.

I wondered how this sea could be *below* sea level. It was the kind of thing Bobby would know, the way he knew about the tectonic plates beneath the Giant's Causeway.

I had mosquito bites on my ankle, my elbow, and my arse. I scratched my ankle hard and made it bleed. I opened my windows to the sluggy air, but insects flew in so I shut it. Even with the windows shut, the smell was vile, like a vase of rank water after you'd left the flowers in it for too long. Rick and Cosima would have air-conditioning, for sure.

WELCOME TO BOMBAY BEACH.

Bombay Beach was a village on a swamp on the edge of this odd sea. A black man and his son waded through the muck, fishing for something that seemed bound to poison them. Rick feathered his brake lights, going slow as though he wanted to stop. There weren't any other cars now. I worried they'd notice that the same truck had been behind them since Victorville, but another car came between us. We drove past the worst houses I'd ever seen, falling-down shacks with engine parts in their yards and satellite dishes on their roofs that were twice the size of the houses themselves. A shirtless man drank out of a paper bag. He had tattoos from his elbows to his head, burnt into his skin from too much sun. Beside him, the fattest woman I'd ever seen read the National Enquirer, her legs sticking out from her yellow-and-green tent dress like stalks of squash. The brighter they all were, the poorer they looked, as if bad living had scraped them down to where there was nothing but cheap color.

"Not like you'd think of America, is it, Jo?" Bobby would say. "More like Africa, you'd imagine."

Except that most of the people were white. I thought of what Cleat had said about my being too white trash for Cosima and Rick. I wasn't even sure what white trash was, except I had an idea that the tent-dress lady and the tattooed man were it. This made me feel better. Rick would never make love to the tent-dress lady. Cosima would never tuck the tattooed man into her own bed.

WELCOME TO IMPERIAL COUNTY.

The road widened again. It was lined with billboards advertising beer and casinos in Spanish. Mexicans wearing cowboy hats and cowboy boots poured out of a gas station. They were oily, thick-haired men, like cowboys covered in shoe polish and fake mustaches.

WELCOME TO CALEXICO.

There were two cars between us now. One was a rigid truck just like this one.

KEEP RIGHT FOR MEXICO. And then: IT IS ILLEGAL TO BRING FIREARMS INTO MEXICO.

I couldn't see into Mexico, but I could see the cars creeping through the border control. Were we going to Mexico? We were moving closer to it. I spoke no Spanish. I *had* firearms! I would be held by the border patrol on that concrete island forever, or be holed up in a Mexican jail. The worst part was that Bobby wouldn't know.

The convertible signaled and turned left, staying on this side of the border. Following them through Calexico the traffic was so slow we barely moved. Sweat dripped down my neck and into my breasts. My thighs were crushed together and I could feel my heat rash getting red and angry again.

We headed east on the Interstate 8, following signs for Yuma, Arizona. As I let myself slide closer to the convertible, I had a feeling of slipping into them, as though we'd been set on opposite ends of a baking tray and were now sliding into the center, all waiting to be cooked together.

A hundred and seventeen degrees.

My eyes were heavy, my mouth salty. I tried to perk myself up with pictures of water: the lake at Dundrum, an English drizzle, the green in Chalcot Square. I was desperate for Coke, ice-cold the way it was here, but if I stopped, I would lose them. They owned me now and they could take me anywhere: east to Arizona, south to Mexico.

They signaled. I signaled. They exited. I exited. They turned north and so did I. The road narrowed. There were no houses nor people nor other cars. There was just scrub and cacti and earth the color of sawdust. I turned on the radio.

The Lucindas were singing "Turn to Rot." I couldn't tell which Lucinda it was, but her voice drugged and sleepy:

> I've been riding this dirty road so long
> My skin is dust, my teeth long gone
> I don't know why I keep going, I just know that I can't stop
> It's easier than waiting around for my brain to turn to rot.

I hadn't heard the Lucindas for a long time. Bobby and I used to listen to them a lot, before we discovered Charlene Sweeney. I wondered what Cosima would think of the Lucindas. I thought she'd probably like them, because they sounded a little like the Be-Good Tanyas and I knew she liked them. Soon, when we'd sorted things out, we would talk about the Lucindas and the Be-Good Tanyas and Charlene Sweeney, too, just like we had the first time she rode with us.

In fact, thinking about it now, it was a shame we hadn't kept talking about music. If we'd talked about it that night at Sean's flat, I wouldn't have gone into the bedroom with Sean, and she wouldn't have had her row with Rick and slammed the door, leaving Rick and me alone. Cosima and I would have spent the evening together. I would have been home before the dawn, still a virgin, and Bobby wouldn't have got as dark as he did and he wouldn't have left me alone on the Liverpool-to-Dublin ferry.

For as far as I could see the road wound like a long tongue through the scrubby hills. I ran over something, a rock or a dead animal. If my tire blew out, I would be stranded here. I'd get bitten by a tarantula or a snake. This was the sort of place where serial killers sliced you up with a carving knife. And, of course, Bobby wouldn't know.

We drove another fifty minutes. My tire didn't go flat. My eyes hurt. Another white rigid truck came between us; there seemed to be a lot of white rigids on these roads. I had to fight to stay awake, to keep my gaze fixed ahead of me. We crossed a railroad track and suddenly we were surrounded by sand dunes, creamy and vast on every side of us.

Like Egypt, is it not, Jo? You'd nearly be expecting to see camels!

Up ahead they must have thought the same. Rick pulled over. I stopped fifty yards or so behind the convertible. Cosima got out to take some photographs. Even from here, I could see the yellow plastic of her disposable camera, and I wondered why, until I realized. Cleat had taken her digital one. It was probably somewhere in this truck.

Soon we were all moving again. It was even strangely normal, now.

On the El Centro road, I saw the first foil box; it made square shadows on the sand. There was a sign, not like a road sign: THIS IS THE INSTALLATION OF SHERILYN KEITH, RESIDENT ARTIST OF IMPERIAL VALLEY, 2003. We passed another foil box and then another. The convertible was slowing down. It stopped in front of a house. A small, plump woman ran out to greet them. She was followed by a big man with shaggy brown hair, holding a little boy. I drove ahead and parked beyond a bend in the road. I got out of the truck. I kept myself hidden behind the bumper, my face sticking out just enough to see them all hugging each other. Rick ruffled the little boy's hair. They all went inside, and a chime sounded on the front door.

I was alone. I waited a while, but nothing happened. I walked to the middle of the road. A lizard stole across, making no sound at all. I had never heard such silence.

"Listen," I said.

Aye.

I stood there for as long as I could. Soon I would feel my skin begin to crack like a chicken on a spit. I got back in the truck and drove to El Centro.

The Happy Days Motel was an ugly stucco complex shaped around a pea-shaped swimming pool. My room was on the ground floor, just a few doors away from the Stage 7 Nightclub. The first thing I did, after using the toilet, was to phone Fogarty. I prepared myself for the voice, the cheery "How're ye" or "How's the craic," but I got his voice mail. I hung up.

I'd never enjoyed taking a shower so much, three days of grime sliding off my body, the sweat and the cretin's dried sperm between my legs and some blood, because I still bled slightly when I did it. I loved the smell of a cake of soap—how good even those words were—*a cake of soap!* Getting out of the shower, I allowed myself a moment of actual coldness before drying off. I opened my suitcase. Clothes were a problem. Everything I had was too dirty or too heavy for this place. I put on my jeans and T-shirt. I walked out and, with a map I'd taken from the room, walked toward Main Street.

Main Street was more of a path than a street. It smelled of hot tar and it was barely wide enough for a rigid truck. I walked past a thrift shop, a bail bonds shop, a soda shop. I passed the Church of the Nazarene, its handmade sign on an easel saying SINNERS WELCOME. Two old black men played checkers in front. "How you doing, beautiful," one of them called to me in a tired voice.

I kept walking until I found the only clothing shop on Main Street, Monica's Discount Wear. I went inside.

"*Hola,*" said a middle-aged Mexican woman with dyed orange hair. Mexican music was on the radio, all those moaning guitars and a singer dirging some *Cavala cavala*. A noisy fan whipped the air around.

"Can I help you?"

The rack was nearly falling over with dresses, all crushed together. They looked like dresses an old woman would wear, cheap and flowery, but because there was nothing else, I went through them. One of them wasn't too bad, a red-and-pink dress with spaghetti straps. I tried it on in the dressing room. It was a light cotton and cool on my skin. And it was only fifteen dollars, which was just as well because this place was too small to steal from, especially with that woman watching me. I came out and she whistled like a man.

"*Bonita.* Very nice." She walked up behind me in the mirror. She took a handful of my hair. "You do something with your hair, too? Jane's Hair Salon is just next door."

"There's nothing wrong with my hair." I brushed her off. I went into my handbag, expecting to feel my purse, but my fingers rubbed against the Glock nineteen. I shoved it down and dug out my money.

Back on Main Street I stood in front of Jane's Hair Salon. I looked at my reflection in the window. I had to admit my hair didn't look like much these days, just a brown pile around my head.

I was still wondering what to do when I felt a tug on my arm. A little girl with long black hair stood below me, putting a flyer into my hand. It was a painting of a mountain and a lake, several smiling sheep, a family playing with a baby lion, and the words *A Beautiful New World: Does It Await Us?* I turned the page and read:

> When you look at this idyllic scene, what do you feel? Does your heart yearn for the peace and serenity seen there? The Bible foretells that in God's new universe, there will be no poverty, no disease, no despair . . .

"I don't believe in God," I said.

She was so quiet I could barely hear her. "But you could go to a place like this which is really like a garden and there's lions there and the lions won't eat you—"

"Shoo! Go away!"

A young woman, also Mexican, charged toward us. The little girl ran off. The woman stood there with her hands on her hips, watching her go.

"I *hate* that," she said. "Those damned Indians."

"She was from India?"

"You joking me? India! No, they come down from El Capitan reservation, and some of them are Holy Rollers, you know what I'm saying? They put a

cute little girl out there while the parents hide in the soda shop seeing if she
can convert people. Anyway, why they gotta come down here now? They're
getting rich enough from their casinos."

"Are you Jane?"

"Sure am." She was skinny, with no bum or breasts, and she had short,
shiny black hair. Her eyes were rimmed with thick eyeliner. "You want me to do
something with your hair? Hold on—I think I can guess the answer to that."

This time I didn't argue. I followed her in.

Her salon was small and it smelled of wet hair and melting cheese. Jane
threw a heavy binder into my arms. "Look through that. Then tell me what
you want."

I sat down with the binder. I flicked through the models with different hair-
styles.

"Have you heard of Cosima Stewart?" I asked.

"Who?"

"She's a country singer. She's also a friend of mine. In fact, I'm here on
tour with her right now—"

"I don't listen to no country music."

"Well, I was hoping you could make my hair like hers. It's straight and
blond, about down to here." I put my hand to my shoulder to show her.

Jane shook her head. "And you're dark and frizzy. I don't know if I can
make that good for you."

"Can you try?"

She sighed. She sat me down and threw a sheet over me and started cutting.
I wondered if she could do a good job, cracking her gum and cutting so fast.

'You Australian?"

"English."

"Oh, yeah? She lifted her T-shirt to show me a tattoo on her waist. The
tattoo was in red and black, and it said: TO MY LOVE SID: RIP.

"We held a vigil for Sid Vicious when he died. I was only four, but I remember it good. My aunt Nina got me into them. You like the Sex Pistols?"

"I don't know them too well, actually." I'd never thought of my voice as
posh, but here in this place, it sounded "terribly terribly," as Bobby called it. I
didn't want to be white trash, but I didn't want to be "terribly terribly," either.

Jane shrugged. "That's okay, man. There's a lot of stuff I don't know, either. It doesn't make you a not-good person."

She put the bleach in, covered my head, and sat me under the dryer. The
bleach made my scalp sting and I tried to think of something to take away the
pain. A song came on the radio, MC Revel's "You Done Me Wrong, Mama."
The last time I'd heard this I'd been in a taxi going east down the Holloway
Road on the day that Rick sent me away from Cosima. I was about to sing
along in my head, but I got a surprise:

Tu me hiciste mal, Mamá . . .
Tu me haces sentir como mierda en un zapato . . .
Como un dolor en tu cabeza . . .
Y ahora te odio Mamá . .
Ojalá que estés muerta.

I laughed and turned to Jane, but she couldn't hear me over the dryer. I wasn't sure she'd find it funny anyway. Bobby would find it funny. Cosima would find it funny, definitely.

"This song reminds me of that awful day," I'd tell her.

"Yes," she'd say, "but that person singing it has probably never even heard of Holloway Road. He doesn't know anything about that day."

I imagined us going over the whole thing, right here in Jane's salon. She'd be having her highlights done ("Not too light," she'd say to Jane) and I would be having my hair bleached, just as I was now.

Finally Jane took the bleach out and rinsed me and blow-dried my hair. When she was done, my hair was two or three inches shorter than Cosima's. It was more of a yellow blond than a tawny blond, but the style was similar, and the color made my skin look creamy and my eyes bright. I wondered why I'd never thought of this before, why it had taken a bolshie, skinny punk girl from Mexico to make me more like Cosima.

Back in my room I took a bath, careful not to get my hair wet. I made up my face and put on my new dress and some new lipstick to match it. I thought of the makeover that Cosima had given me at Meg's Borderline three years ago, and how Bobby hadn't recognized me afterward. He would recognize me even less if he saw me like this. I'd walk into the pub, the pub where he was at this very minute.

"It's me!" I would say. "It's just me!"

Only this time, I would have turned into a beautiful blonde.

At eight P.M. I drove out to Sherilyn Keith's house. I parked at the bend and got out of the truck. I could hear them eating in the garden, Bob Dylan singing behind them. The shaggy husband was talking loudly.

"So I had to explain to the old bigot that Mehmet is an Afghan *plumber*, not a suicide bomber! Kids, I'm telling you, this is the single most terrifying time to be an American."

"It's always been this way," said Cosima. "You guys live in a rarefied world."

"Since when is El Centro a rarefied world?" asked Sherilyn Keith.

"Don't be coy with me, Sherilyn. This residency is a wacky detour thing for you, and when it's over you'll move back to the Bay Area. *I* was raised in a hotbed of conservatism with a capital C. I'm talking Christian Right, gun-toting morons, a place so trigger-happy you virtually get the death penalty for jaywalking. I'm talking *total xenophobia*."

"The British are as xenophobic as the Americans," said Rick.

"Maybe," said Cosima, "but you're a lot more apologetic about it. Jingoism with irony."

They laughed. They were in a good mood. I thought of going to them. I was blonder, calmer, prettier than I'd been the last time they'd seen me. I stepped forward, making a crunchy sound on the sand. I stopped myself. I'd done terrible things last night. Cleat had made me do them, but only Cosima would believe that, and she'd have to be on her own to believe it.

I got back in the truck.

It was ten o'clock when I got back to the motel. I phoned Fogarty but got his voice mail again. Music was blasting out of Stage 7 and into my room. I turned on the TV, but the music still vibrated through the floors and bed. I left the room. The sign above Stage 7 said TITO GONZALES BAND TONITE! I went in and paid five dollars. The nightclub had a long, empty dance floor dappled with silver from a mirrored ball hanging from the ceiling. On both sides of the floor Mexican men and women sat, some in groups and some on their own. As I walked through to the bar, I felt the eyes of the men on my bum and my legs, their eyes like hands. The girls just stared at me without smiling, their faces painted and round like unfriendly dolls. The Tito Gonzales Band played, but nobody danced.

I ordered a margarita. I waited for the barman to ask for my ID, but he just said, "You bet, *señorita*."

There was shouting from the dance floor, noise that could have been cheering or fighting. A man and a woman were dancing. The man was in black but the girl wore a blazing red dress. The man pushed her out, pulled her in, threw her over his knee. A crowd had gathered round them, calling out:

"*¡Yo, Mami!*"

"*¡Métele mano! Adelante!*"

A tall man in a green suit stormed up to the dancing couple. He went so fast that I thought he would hit the man in black, but he just grabbed the girl and danced with her. The crowd cheered louder. The dancing girl was faster than anything I'd seen. She seemed to have no weight or anything that glued her to the ground. Her hair swung like a whip.

A young man was sitting beside me. He was slim with thick black hair. His skin wasn't too dark and he didn't have a mustache. He motioned to the dance floor. "You dance?"

"I do not dance."

He smiled at me, showing good white teeth except for one chipped tooth in front.

"You're foreign." His own accent sounded mostly American, but there was something else in it.

"So are you," I said.

"I was born and raised in Calexico. I'm a Californian."

"You don't look it."

He made a gesture across the room. "Imperial County is eighty percent Hispanic."

"Really?"

"*Sí*. I'm Oscar."

"I'm Jo."

"Where are you from, Jo?"

When I thought about where I was from, all I saw was the motorway. Wherever Bobby was this very minute, that was where I was from.

"I wouldn't say no to another margarita," I said.

Oscar ordered a margarita and a beer for himself.

"Wherever you're from," he said, "do they all look like you? You look like a movie star."

The song changed to something faster. Oscar looked at the dance floor again. "C'mon, movie star, come and dance."

"I really don't know how."

"I'll show you how."

"*I* show you how." It was the man in the green suit. I thought Oscar would be angry, but he held his palms up to the other man. "Oh yes, he's good," said Oscar. "He's the best dancer here. You dance with him."

Green Suit was already guiding me to the dance floor.

"Look," I said, "I really don't know how to do this, I'll only—"

"Just feel what my feet are doing,"

I felt for his foot, but stepped on it.

"Relax."

The dancing couple swung by us, the girl whirling like a red flag.

"Look at me," said Green Suit. "Feel the pressure I put on your waist. No, don't hold onto my arm like that. Let go. *Let go.*"

I felt his hand on the small of my back. I braced myself for his hand to fall to my bum, but it didn't do that. He tried to lean me back against his knee. I stumbled, but he caught me.

"It's okay. I won't let you fall."

He tried again. With his arm around my waist, he put his knee behind my shin. He lowered me until I was upside down, looking at the silver ball and the dancing legs in the mirrored ceiling. He pulled me up.

"You take her now," he said, and before I knew what was happening, Oscar had me. He pulled me in, spun me around, lowered me back into the dip. I saw a flash of legs and cowboy boots, upside down. I felt a charge in my belly. He brought me up and my head rushed.

"Do that again. Dip me again!"

When I came back up a third time, I was laughing, hard. We danced another two dances. In between we drank four drinks.

"I'd never thought I'd have so much fun being thrown all over the place!" I said, and he laughed, too, and we shared a burrito, rice, and refried beans from the bar.

We danced one more dance, and then he suggested we go for a walk. We went walking along the tracks. The music drifted out to us from the club. We came to a freight train boarded up for the night.

"See these containers? Five of my cousins died in containers like these, trying to get across from Mexico. They suffocated with like forty-six other people because nobody opened the damn thing up."

"That's like that Cosima Stewart song, 'Where Is Home for a Girl Without a Country,'" I said.

"Like what?"

"Nothing. Your cousins must have wanted to see you pretty bad."

Oscar nodded. He looked sad. From the club, the song changed to something sad as well. He put his hands on either side of my face and kissed me. His breath was good, more like water than beer. He sang along:

> *Para mi amor*
> *No puedo dormir sin tí*
> *Tú eres mi amor*
> *Te has ido, y me dejaste llorando*

He brought his hand to my mouth. He traced my top lip and then my bottom lip. He kissed me again. He leaned me back against the container. He kissed my neck and throat. He kissed my breasts. His lips were soft on my breasts and the container was hard against my back. It would have been strange, I thought, if this was the very container his cousins had died in.

"What's your job?" I asked.

He came up to look at me again. "I work in my brother's tire store. You want to come work there with me?"

It didn't sound like the worst thing in the world, so long as the store was air-conditioned. Oscar could teach me Spanish during the day and salsa dancing at night. Of course, it would be too hot for Bobby. It would be too hot for both of us really, though I didn't mind the heat just now, the midnight air kissing my skin and Oscar kissing my breasts.

"Guess what?" I said. "I was nearly bit by a rattlesnake."

"No way."

"It's true."

"Was its head long or flat like a viper?"

"A viper, I think. I thought it would bite me but then it didn't."

"Then you're a lucky girl." He kissed me again, on the lips this time. The guitar kept on, sweet and lazy. I closed my eyes.

"¡SUCIA CHINGADA PUTA!"

I thought a bird had landed on me, an attack of shriek and claw, but it was a fingernail that hooked the edge of my eye. I put my hands up to protect myself, but the girl kept hitting my head and screaming. Behind her were lots of girls, all screaming their own *cavalas.*

"¡Gringa mendiga!"

"¡Chinga a tu puta madre!"

"Chocho!"

"Cunt!"

The girl's hand came down on my head, hard. "Whore! Cocksucking slut!" I lifted my knee, aiming for her groin. She saw it coming and stumbled back. I stuck my hand in my bag. I took out the Glock and pointed it at her.

"¡Ay Dios mío!" shouted another girl.

The girl put her hands up. The gun felt light in my hand—easy to hold, easy to shoot. I stepped forward and the girls scattered back. I saw now that they were all smaller than me, but the girl who'd been hitting me was the smallest.

She began to cry.

"I'm sorry." Her voice was hoarse and high. "I am Oscar's wife. *No me lastimas.* Don't hurt me! We have two children. He's done this before. It isn't your fault."

It was hard to believe she had two children. She looked no older than I was, in her pink tracksuit bottoms with her midriff showing, a white bandanna around her head.

I felt something wet on my cheek. I lifted my hand to touch it. "Am I bleeding?"

"A little." She put a hand on her own face to show me where. "I don't think they'll be no scar."

"Will you clean it off?"

She took the bandanna off her head and put some of her spit on it. She took a step toward me. She raised the bandanna to my face but stopped. Her hand was shaking. "Do you mind if I do this? It's what I do for my kids."

"No, I don't mind."

The fabric was coarse against my cheek. As she wiped me clean, I let the gun drop so that it aimed at the ground. All of the girls were staring at me. I counted eight of them. Most of them wore bandannas and heavy makeup around their eyes. One of them wore black lipstick, and she had on a Sex Pistols T-shirt.

"Is that . . . Jane?"

"Yes, it is. Yes." She gave a little laugh. "How you doing? It looks real good, your hair, you know? That blond, it makes you look like a movie star."

"That's what I said to her," said Oscar.

The others all said "Oh, yes," or "*Sí*," agreeing that I looked like a movie star, all except for Oscar's wife, who was still cleaning me off and crying.

"I have babies," she said. "Please don't do anything. Please don't do anything."

I noticed something on her neck. I moved her hand to look at the tattoo. "Xtina? Is that your name?"

"No . . . my name's Irene. I got that put on there because Christina Aguilera's got one just like it."

I looked at her face. She was extremely pretty. "Why are your eyes so green?" I asked. "Is that natural?"

She looked at Oscar, then back at me.

"Contact lenses."

From inside Stage 7 the song changed to something they'd played already. It was one of the mad *cavala* songs, too much brass and busyness, Bobby might say, but I was getting to like it.

"This is a good song," I said.

"It's very nice," said Oscar's wife.

Suddenly I wanted to talk to them all, the same way as I'd been wanting to talk to Cosima. I wanted to tell them about Bobby and Whitey and Cleat and everything that I had been through.

"It's been a while since I've had someone to talk to."

"Oh?" asked Oscar's wife.

"I did meet a man called Whitey. He was good to talk to. But since then I haven't had enough good conversations."

"We were having a conversation," said Oscar.

"Yes," I said. "We were beginning to."

Irene's bandana caught the cut and it stung me. Without meaning to, I jerked the gun up. The girls squealed. I looked at Oscar.

"Is this really your wife?" I asked.

He looked at her and back at me. "Yes."

"You can go with him though," said Irene, "if you want to."

She held the bandana an inch away from my face, as if she couldn't decide whether to keep cleaning me or not. Oscar nodded and smiled, his chipped tooth showing. Sweat was running down his face. I looked at the girls, their eyes like frightened baby eyes.

Suddenly all I wanted was my bed.

"Away you go," I said. It came out in Bobby's voice, and nobody understood. I tried again. "You can all go home now."

Back in my room, I looked at myself in the bathroom mirror. I had a cut below my eye shaped like the bottom half of another eye. I lay down on the bed but my head spun like the doggy mountains spinning away from the road. I pulled down the top of my dress to give myself some air. Oscar's cousins had had no air. I thought of being one of forty-seven, stuffed in that container like tuna in brine. My mouth filled with saliva. I sat up and swallowed a chunk of puke.

I dialed Fogarty and got his voice mail. "You're never fucking there," I said, and rang off.

Then, slowly, not even sure I remembered it right, I dialed another number. The phone rang three times before she answered.

"Hello!"

I didn't say anything.

"Hello?"

"Primrose."

"Guilty as charged." There was quiet on the line, and then: "Jo? That you?" I didn't answer.

"Jesus, Jo. I've been trying to get hold of you for days. I went to the flat, and them Bengali neighbors said they saw you leave with a suitcase, so I rang Fogarty, and he said you were in California!"

The music was still coming in from the club. Cradling the phone in my shoulder, I shut the windows, but it came in through the cracks, the floor, the bed.

"Are you there, Jo?"

"Is he back now, Primrose? Is he back?"

"Listen, my love, just tell me where you are. . . ."

The sirens came then, scaring out the music, an *eeeeEEEEEEEE* screeching round the corner.

"I've done some bad things." I started walking around the room. "I just need to talk to him!"

"We haven't found him, luv—"

My mouth flooded with saliva again. I hung up. I lay back on the bed. The sirens came back, *EEEEE*ing right to me. I went stiff until they *eeeed* off and gave way to the music:

Para mi amor . . . No puedo dormir sin tu

The sirens weren't for me. They were for the Mexicans, Pakis if you put saris on them. Bobby hated me using the word *Paki*, but Bobby wasn't always right. *Fucking lying yellow scum Oscar.* And now his Paki-spic music was coming in on me, coming and coming into my ears and mouth and every crack in the door and window. I was burning up so badly I was shivering. I pulled off my dress and lay down and covered myself with the itchy bedspread. *Tu es mi amor, me ha ido y déjame llorando . . .*

I closed my eyes and tried to find some blackness to melt into. A snake slithered across my hand and I threw it off, but it was just my own arm throw-

ing off my other arm. I shut my eyes again but the train came, so long there
was no end to it, its horn a blade through my brain, inches from my head! I
leapt up and heard it keep going, a real train, just behind these walls. I ran into
the bathroom and puked rice and burrito and refried beans in the bathtub. I
curled up on the floor, making the tiniest ball I could of myself. I tried to keep
my head from spinning: spinning like the doggy mountains, spinning like the
salsa girl, her hair swinging like a whip.

It's all right, baby. Her palm was cool against my forehead: *Everything's
going to be all right for you.*

I couldn't hear Cosima anymore. There was only the music and the train
and shouting in my head:

I'm going to die now, Bobby. This is the part where I die!

And those Tito Gonzales fuckers kept on and on.

When I opened my eyes, I thought I was in jail. I was curled up on the cold tile
floor and I was soaked in sweat. I unwrapped myself. My legs and back were stiff
and sore. I stood up and met my headache in the air. I turned on the shower,
washed away the mush of vomited burrito, and stepped into the spray. I dried
and dressed. My head still hurt but I felt as though something had snapped, like
the spiky desert breaking into creamy sand dunes.

I was ready to see her now.

At 9:15, I parked behind the bend near Sherilyn Keith's house. Rick was
putting water in the engine and the little boy was taking Cosima round the
garden. Everyone hugged, just like they had yesterday. Rick and Cosima got
into the car. Sherilyn Keith handed Cosima a paper bag.

"Papayas for the road," said Sherilyn Keith.

The convertible reversed down the drive. Cosima waved to her friends
and called out something I couldn't hear.

By 9:45, we were on the 111, following signs for the Chocolate Mountains.
Army helicopters flew above us. Gunfire boomed from somewhere. A sign said
DANGER: LIVE BOMBING AREA—KEEP OUT. We passed a trailer park, some starved-
looking dogs. It was 106 degrees.

After another mile or two the convertible slowed and stopped in front of a
painted hill. I couldn't think from where, but I knew I'd seen this hill with its
screaming words and colors, its flowers and circles and stripes. On the top of
the hill stood a cross, just above a pink-and-red GOD IS LOVE. Below that were the
words: JESUS I'M A SINNER COME UPON MY BODY AND INTO MY HEART. And then I remembered; it was where Cosima had done her interview for *Country UK*. In real
life, the hill looked even brighter and the paint still looked wet. The cross was
bigger than it had looked in the photo, as if a very big person was buried there.

I parked on the other side of a pickup truck, which was also painted in screaming colors and religious words, like the hill. I couldn't see Cosima and Rick, but I saw an old man shuffle toward them.

"It's a pleasure to see you again, Leonard," I heard Cosima say.

"Welcome," said the old man. "I came here eighteen years ago from Vermont when I heard the call of God—"

"We remember, mate," said Rick.

"Rick," said Cosima, "the camera's finished. Can you go to Niland and get another one?"

"Why don't we just leave it?"

"No way. Give me the keys, I'll go."

"*I'll* go."

I heard him crunching toward the convertible and opening the door. In my rearview mirror, I watched him drive away.

Cosima began to climb the hill. I'd hoped to find her alone today, but I hadn't expected it to be so soon. I took the Glock out of my bag and put it into my pocket. I got out of the truck. My heart was hammering and my body was stiff. She was moving fast, her legs quick and spindly against all that color. I started after her. About a third of the way up, she stopped to look out over the desert. I crouched down. I was wearing Cleat's hat and sunglasses, but I still didn't want her to see me yet, heaving and panting below her. When she continued walking, I kept my distance. The rash flamed between my legs. The next time I looked up I couldn't see her at all. With a heave, I made it to the top.

Cosima stood looking out, shielding her eyes from the sun. Beyond the hill the earth was flat and beige for as far as I could see. It was hard to believe that anything in the world existed apart from this place, like the Irish Sea or her Cake club or Shandy Street, E1.

She glanced at me, nodded. "Incredible, isn't it?"

"It is."

She gazed out over the view again. Then, so slowly that she hardly seemed to move at all, she looked back at me. I couldn't tell if she was looking at my eyes or her own reflection in my sunglasses.

I took my sunglasses off. "Cosima."

She took a step back. "Get away from me," she said. "Get away from me, you *sad fuck.*"

"*Cosima.*"

I reached into my pocket and pulled the gun out. It didn't feel as light as it had felt last night. It felt solid, a part of me, warmed by my body heat. I pointed it at her. I was quite steady. "Come back up to where I am."

She lifted her foot back up. I'd always thought she was taller than I was, but now she looked up at me. Her eyes were bigger than I'd ever seen them. She didn't breathe or blink.

"There's so much," I said, "that I've been wanting to say to you."

"Yes."

And yet now that I had her there, I didn't know what to say. The sun was so bright it seemed to bleach the thoughts right out of me.

"I'm sorry about the gun. I just need you to listen to me, do you understand?"

"I do."

"It wasn't my idea about the fiddle and the guitar. And your suede outfit. I always loved that."

The gulp went through her neck. "You've had a bad time, Jo."

Far away, the convertible was driving toward Niland. I looked at her again. "Do you think so?"

"Yes—I've been worried about you. You're looking . . . thin."

"Really?" This pleased me. "No black pasta out this way, you know."

"No." She cleared her throat. "This is strictly pork rind country."

"That's not what you ate last night, though, is it? You had fish and salad and wine?"

"Oh . . . yes! We did. The Keiths—they're nice people. Maybe one day you'll meet them." She took a step back.

"Stay there!" I went to her. I curled my hand around her arm and brought her back to where she'd stood a second before. Her arm was covered in goose pimples.

"Okay, Jo, I'm not going anywhere. Let's talk. Let's sit down."

"I'm not sitting down!"

"Okay. But I'd like to tell you something." Her forehead was beaded with sweat, and the hair around her face was wet, too. Still, she didn't seem to blink.

"I want you to know," she said, "that I know how you feel."

"No, you don't. You understand me in your songs, but in real life, you don't care anymore."

"Jo, I'm so sorry—it's true, I've been busy, but that doesn't mean I don't— I mean, I *do* understand you! I was like you—"

"When?"

"When I first came to London—I mean, I was a very sad girl, no job, no money, boyfriend just dumped me—living in a scummy flat in Dalston—" She stopped for air.

"You lived in Dalston? You never lived in Dalston!"

"I did. I'd moved to London to be in an Irish band, an Irish band actually—"

"You never told me you played in an Irish band!"

"Didn't I?"

"If we had talked more, more about your music, things wouldn't have gone so wrong that night. I wouldn't have got off with Rick. Bobby wouldn't have gone away. . . ."

"But I'm telling you now, Irish music was my first love!" Her voice was speeding up. "I mean, there's a lot of overlap between Irish music and country, a lot of overlap. I mean, your father must have told you—the roots of bluegrass are based in—"

"No! Forget the diddly-eye, that's not what I mean, I mean—I mean—Shit, *shit*, I forgot what I meant!"

I looked down the hill again. A car was crawling through the haze, but I couldn't see if it was a convertible or where it was going to.

"Tell me more," I said, "about when you lived in Dalston."

"I lived in a bedsit—it was horrible. I never slept. I was eating chocolate and vodka for dinner."

"What happened? Did you meet Rick then?"

"Rick? Yes, I met him in a folk club—the Old Maypole—open mike. Rick was doing a set on his guitar."

"And you fell for him? Right then and there?"

"No." She gave a little laugh. "I thought he was an asshole at first."

"He *is* an arsehole."

"But Jo, this isn't about Rick. I'm telling you that I *know* what it feels to be outside of everything. To feel that nobody wants you."

"But I only wanted to know *you*." My nose was running. I wiped it on my arm.

"I am your friend, Jo—"

"Shut up, let me talk!"

"I'm sorry."

"When you do that bit at the beginning of 'Let Me Touch You for Awhile,' just after the first verse, it's like—it's like—or when you were nice to me, when you gave me my new face or you tucked me into bed—we were just like—one person together—in the music together—"

"I understand."

"But then you stopped—and it was Rick who made you do it, but I was still walking around inside you, like my whole self is inside you, which is why I had to talk to you now. It's not like I want to hurt you—it's just—"

"I know—"

"You don't need me now, you have the tour and fame and everybody knowing you and Hell's Angels who don't let me see you and. . . . and . . ."

She nodded again, one long nod to show she was with me. Sweat was running down her cheeks like tears.

"Well, you're getting bigger and bigger and I'm getting smaller and smaller!"

Slowly, she lifted her hand, and wiped the sweat-tears off her face. Just as slowly, she held out her other hand. "Come down with me, Jo. Let's talk about it. We'll talk. I promise."

"You're only saying that because I have the gun."

"That's not true."

Just then, with the slightest jerk of her chin, she stole a glance down the hill. The convertible was down there, pulling up to the pickup truck. She looked back at me, quickly. I tightened my fingers on the gun. The gun didn't feel so solid now. It felt evil and greasy, like it might go off by itself.

"We're not going down there," I said.

"No?"

"Because once we get to the bottom, you'll never talk to me at all. It'll all be 'Cosima's not at home right now' and police to keep me away from you. You never talk to me. *You never talk to me!*"

"I'm talking now—"

"You're just doing it because you have to!"

"But Jo—"

"*What!*"

"Jo—Jo—what will you do?"

"What will I *do?*"

I hadn't thought about *doing*. Tomorrow I'd wake up and I'd be in a cell, a real one, and even if I got out, all I'd have would be another ditch to hide in or another tub to vomit in or a scrubby patch of earth to be fucked by some speed freak on, and the next time the snake would bite me. I'd always be going down into ditches and sewers and drains while Whitey would be climbing up in his Freightliner and Cosima would be high on her stage and lorries would fly into Chocolate Mountains saying "bears in the air" about choppers that flew not so far above them.

"There wasn't much to do at all."

I lifted the gun to my lips.

"*No,* Jo."

I screwed my eyes up tight. I put it inside my mouth, just slightly. It tasted of salt and metal.

"Josephine!" She was whimpering as if she loved me. "You can't do that!. . . . Let me look at you at least!"

I opened my eyes. Her eyes were so pale they were nearly white. I pulled the gun away, but kept it a few inches from my mouth.

"What do you see," I asked, "when you look at me?"

"I see . . . I see girl who's had such a hard time . . . I see a vulnerable young girl with a lovely face."

I thought of Meg's Borderline. Of Cosima saying to me in the mirror, *You have a lovely face, Jo.* In a moment I would blow my face to mince, and she would always see it that way instead. I pointed the gun at my heart. My eyes were streaming but they didn't feel like tears, just hot water flowing over me.

"*Think of Bobby!*" she said.

"You don't care what Bobby thinks."

"I do. And *you* do. Think of the moment when he learns what you have done. Think of *his* face."

I thought of Bobby's face. Of his eyes paled with confusion, his hair sticking up on his head. My finger stayed on the trigger but my wrist went slack.

"Come with me, Jo. Come with me, honey." She took a step toward me. I took a step back.

A fly landed on my hand. I swatted it away with the gun. I didn't mean to pull the trigger, but the gun went off and the air went alight. My vision went black and red. Cosima screamed. I opened my eyes. She was still standing, eyes wide and white, face dripping with sweat, unshot.

"I'm sorry," I stepped back. "I didn't mean to—"

My breath was stopped, my brain broken out of its skull, my arms locked behind me. *Cleat! Back to kill me!* And the menace of his words, "Easy does it, that's a good girl!" The gun slipped from my fingers. I fell back into Rick, his arms the only thing to keep me from tumbling like the gun down Salvation Mountain.

CHAPTER 27

I had never known how quiet mad people could be.

In the Imperial Valley Psychiatric Center, nobody screamed. Nobody tried to run away. There was one boy who pretended to run away. He was only nineteen but he was bald and bloated and looked twice that age. Big Ben, they called him, of the "morning shuffle." Just before breakfast he'd slide down the corridor in his slippers, making a swishing noise on the linoleum, giggling and looking over his shoulder. He'd be caught by two fast and quiet orderlies who brought him back to the dayroom and put him in front of the television. His morning shuffle was part of everyone's routine. After the third day I didn't even look up to see what the fuss was about.

The ward was both clean and dirty, with smudged walls and slippery floors and a smell of bleach and sometimes pee. I didn't mind the hospital food, the way it cushioned me on the inside: rice and potatoes and iceberg lettuce with gunky orange dressing. I could feel the food settling into my body, filling all the holes like glue.

I was given a drug called Risperdal that made it hard to go to the toilet. My eyesight blurred and my breasts swelled and dribbled out milk. I never knew what would come out of me next. When I told Patty, the meds nurse, she said, "That happens sometimes."

I shared a room with a girl called Melissa. She was only one month younger than I was but she had nothing to say to me. All she wanted to do was lie on her bed and listen to Pink on her Discman. When I asked her what was wrong with her, she said, "Abuse issues." In a way, I was glad. Even if she'd asked what was wrong with me, I wouldn't have known what to tell her.

The meds made my thoughts fuzz into each other. I didn't have stories in my head anymore, like this-happened-and-then-that-happened. When I tried to think of England, I mostly had shapes in my mind or motorways or the smell of pavement when it rained. When I tried to think of Cosima, there was nothing. In the big part of my brain where she used to live, now there was only fog and fur.

In the dayroom the TV was always loud. The shopping channel was on most of the time, selling things you had to send away for like tiny porcelain animals or airbeds. I liked the commercials for airbeds. People would take turns blowing them up and sitting on them and talking about the excellence of the airbeds and the number—*1-800-*AIR-BEDS—flashing over and over so you wouldn't forget it.

Dr. Pollack was nice. His brown hair was peppered with gray and he had a handsome, leathery face and a mustache like Whitey's. He looked like a country-and-western star, the aging corny kind we didn't much listen to. The window of his office looked over a golf course. On his desk he had a paperweight shaped like a human brain.

He asked why I thought I was here.

"Something went wrong." I said.

"Can you be more specific?"

"The police were disappointed with me."

"Disappointed?"

It was true. The police had been disappointed rather than mean. They all had mustaches too; worried mustache guys, the lot of them.

"I'm sorry, Constable," I'd said to one of them.

"You mean 'Officer,' don't you?" He thought it was cute, my calling him constable.

I was brought here on the 5150, which meant I was under observation for seventy-two hours at least, with a treatment team to work out whether I was "psychiatric" or just plain criminal. I wasn't sure how long I had been here, but I knew it was more than seventy-two hours, so I guessed they were still trying to work it out.

Dr. Pollack asked why I'd shot Cosima's fiddle and chopped up Rick's guitar. He didn't ask in an angry way.

"I did more than that," I said. "I stole a truck. I took speed with Cleat and I slept with him even though I am under the age of allowance, and I pointed a gun at the Mexican girl . . ."

Dr. Pollack did not want me to be quite this bad.

"You appreciate that it is wrong to steal and take drugs, but apart from the fact that Cleat Baker's truck was already stolen, *he* was the felon, sleeping with a minor—"

"Rick slept with me, too, you know—"

"Uh, that was England, you guys do things different over there, you might also bear in mind that he saved your life—but let's get back to why you're here."

I wasn't going to like the next part. I could hear it in his voice.

"I think we should discuss the suicide of your father."

My vision went again, the red spots in my eyes.

"This medication fucks up everything," I said.

"It is understandable, Jo, that with a shock like the one you've had—"

"And there's milk dripping out of my tits."

I'd made his mustache twitch.

"I'm sorry, Doctor."

"It's okay. It's okay."

And he made it okay. He wrote things on a notepad and frowned in a thoughtful way. He spread his words over me and made it better: *loss* and *shock* and *bereavement* and *delusion.*

"So you think I'm ill," I said. "I'm schizophrenic like Big Ben."

"I think you're suffering from what we call a brief reactive psychosis."

"But I *am* ill."

"Yes, for the time being, you are sick."

I liked being sick. I felt sick and mushy, mushy as the potato mash inside me, too mushy to be bad. I asked if he owned a gun.

"Sure do, Jo. I have a .357 magnum. Had it since I was in the Marines."

"You'll protect me then."

"What do you need protecting from?"

But it was time for occupational therapy, to press flowers into heavy books.

I couldn't feel my edges. I couldn't feel my skin or the tips of my hair. When I looked in the mirror (metal rather than glass, which made all of me slanted), my eyes were heavy, my hair a helmet of frizz. My nose and eyes were like putty, wanting to slip into the center of my face.

My key nurse, Brenda, was a big black woman who loved The Ricki Lake Show. When the women in the audience screamed at each other, she laughed and rubbed her hands together.

"You like it when they're bolshie," I said.

"What that's you say?"

"Bolshie."

"You ain't making no sense again, honey."

I didn't try to explain. Apart from when I was with Dr. Pollack, it was easier not to talk. My words didn't make sense to people here any more than Big Ben's morning shuffle did, or muttering Clifford, who was called that because he was always muttering about niggers or chinks but getting away with it because he was mad.

What I hated was when I didn't understand myself. Just before lunch one day, a smell hit my nose like steak and kidney pie, and suddenly I was in a transport caff in Bury St-Edmunds. I squinted to see the Scania through the window, but the window steamed and the lorry went as vague as a bruise in my brain. I shut my eyes and tried to get it back.

"What's the matter?" asked Brenda.

"I can't see it, I can't see the lorry."

"I hear you," she said, but I knew she didn't.

I began to wonder if there was ever a lorry. If even Bobby was a pretend father who'd lived only in my mind because there was nowhere else for a person as good as him to live. And then, like the CB when you couldn't hear the voice through the squelch, everything turned to static.

I couldn't believe it when they told me I'd been here thirteen days. I thought it had been a month at least. My mouth dried up. I was constipated. In the toilet, between trying to go, I fanned air into the creases of my body where the sweat gathered. My skin was still puffy from the sun (I had minor heatstroke, they said). I'd put on weight, but I felt less like a person than a fleshy, fatty, liquid thing.

"Please take me off the meds," I begged Patty.

"We can't force you to take them. But I would suggest you speak to the doctor first."

Dr. Pollack was away that week. I hated the idea that I could stop the meds and he would come back and, like all the other mustached men, be disappointed with me. I stayed on the meds.

Knowing that Dr. Pollack was away, I couldn't sleep. The one time I did sleep, I stopped breathing. I felt a pink thing inside me, Cleat's bad-egg breath mixing with the meds in my nose. I flapped my arms and feet, struggling to take in a gulp of air, just one! But my nostrils were clogged, my mouth full of wool, my panties stuffed up into me down there. I tried to scream but I couldn't. I bashed the bed and bashed the bed until I knew that I was dying or dead.

Then it stopped. Daylight poured through the bars.

"The thing about the meds," I said to Patty later, "is that they make me not myself."

"Of course you're yourself. That's your arm you're scratching now, isn't it?"

But it was the meds that made me itch. I was trying to scratch the poison out.

Later that day Brenda brought me to the visitor's room. Muttering Clifford was the only other patient, visiting with his mother. Apart from him, there was a family, but they didn't seem to be visiting anybody. They were religious people, all dressed in black and brown; I'd seen their sort in Stamford Hill or Golders Green. The man had a beard and glasses and he wore a tall hat. His young son also wore glasses, but instead of a hat, he had a black cap on the back of his head. The mother and daughter wore long brown dresses with long sleeves, even in this heat. The mother had thick chocolate-colored hair that looked like a wig.

"Fucking Jews," said Clifford.

The family stared at me as if I'd said it, but when I stared back, they looked away. The little boy dropped a penny on the table and the father said, "Quiet, Rafi."

When Dr. Pollack came in, I threw my arms around him and squeezed tight.

"Whoa! And good morning to you, Josephine!"

He didn't let me hug him for long. He stood back and held both of my hands in his.

"It was a terrible night, Dr. Pollack," I said. "I couldn't breathe at all!"

I waited for him to ask why, but he didn't. He kept looking at the family and back at me. The woman in the wig was standing up now, as though she, too, wanted to talk to him.

"Jo," said Dr. Pollack, "there's someone I want you to meet." He nodded toward the woman. The woman took a step toward me.

"She won't bite," said Dr. Pollack, and I couldn't tell which one of us he was saying that to.

The woman came closer. Dr. Pollack stood to the side of us, as though shielding us from the rest of the room.

"It's okay," he said to her. "Just tell her your name."

Up close, she looked even stranger. She had wide hips and a thin face as white as flour.

"Josephine," said the woman, "I'm Rosalie."

Part *IV*

HOME AWAY FROM HOME

CHAPTER 28

To Rosalie, early-morning phone calls meant one of two things—problems or in-laws. Her husband's parents, who lived in Philadelphia, liked to phone at this time.

"It's ten in the morning for *us*," they would say, as if everyone on the West Coast should observe the same time zone as they did. Seven A.M. was only half an hour before Rosalie awoke herself, yet it was early enough to seem like an injury to her. Despite the quality of her life now (and she did think of her life in terms of quality, like a fine loaf that had taken fifteen years to golden), in sleep she lapsed into her younger years, a wet, dark place where she lay in wait of some penalty.

And yet on this warm Friday in June, nothing much could be wrong. Joshua slept solidly at her side, avuncular in sleep as he was in life. The children slept in their rooms: Rafi with his half-finished essay on King Pharoah at the foot of his bed, Yael in her long T-shirt, the Coca-Cola logo in Hebrew across her chest. The ringing charged like an alarm through Rosalie's ears, pitching up crimes she'd been caught committing—drinking whiskey, smoking hashish, being caught in the son's bed by a livid Irish father, or simply, as her in-laws would have it, sleeping too late.

Without opening her eyes she picked it up.

"Hello?"

"Mrs. Chapkis?"

His voice wasn't any voice she knew. And nobody had ever called her *Mrs. Chapkis.* Still, he spoke with such authority that she nearly forgot her own name.

"Mrs. Brenner, now."

"I beg your pardon. This is Dr. Angus Pollack from the Imperial Valley Psychiatric Center."

"From where?"

"The Imperial Valley Psychiatric Center, just outside of El Centro."

She wasn't even sure where El Centro was. It was somewhere down *there,* near Mexico. It was the desert: beer, rednecks, cowboys, guns—nothing to do with her. Joshua coughed, cleared his throat, and smacked his lips together, readying himself to be awake for her.

"I do apologize for phoning at this hour, Mrs. Brenner. We've only just been given the correct information on how to locate you."

This was police language. She sat up. She was in trouble after all.

Joshua opened his eyes. "What's going on, Rosalie?"

She held up her hand to silence him.

"This may come as a shock to you," said Dr. Pollack, "but we think we have your daughter here."

"But I just saw her. At bedtime."

She thought of bedtime with her daughter, of Yael's grunted good night, the way she'd shut her door on Rosalie as she did these days, her insolent hair falling into her face. There *had* been trouble with Yael lately. She'd gotten a D on her book report on Isaac Bashevis Singer, said the F-word to her teacher at Hebrew school. Joshua worried about it, but Rosalie worried less. It was the age, she said. The girl was thirteen. But now she could imagine Yael running away in the night, catching a Greyhound bus or—God forbid—a *ride,* and ending up down there, in some psychiatric gentile hell.

"Rosalie?" Joshua would be silenced no longer. "What's going on?"

"They say they have Yael."

"What?" He leapt out of bed, his pajama tunic flapping as he opened the door and shouted into the hallway. "Yael!"

The doctor was trying to speak. "Mrs. Brenner—Mrs. Brenner—if I could just finish here—"

"Yael!" Joshua's shout drowned out the doctor. It was met with Rafi's tremulous reply. "What is it? What is it, Dad?"

"Get your sister."

"I think she just went to the bathroom."

"Knock on the door."

Rosalie heard Rafi's feet pattering down the hallway, his little fist on the bathroom door, and finally a reassuringly furious *"What?"* from Yael. "What is your *problem?*"

Dr. Pollack strained to be heard. "Mrs. Brenner! Are you there?"

"Yes," said Rosalie, but she was watching her husband. He continued to face the hallway, hands on his hips.

"I do apologize," said Dr. Pollack. "I should have said the young woman's name first. Her name is Josephine. Josephine Pickering, from England."

"Josephine Pickering?"

Joshua turned around to face her again.

"Is this a familiar name to you?" asked the doctor.

She was overcome by a shifting sensation, like wet sand sliding from one end of her brain to the other. She made a pyramid of herself under her nightgown.

"A familiar name?" she repeated, stalling for time.

The name could not have been more alien. She knew it, of course, but she had never spoken it, this grown-up name of a grown-up person. She tried to picture this person now in a hospital near the Mexican border. All she could see was a grotesque, infant creature, fighting for breath like a goldfish the kids once had, a fish that turned green, inflated, and died on its side. She hugged her knees as though to prevent another birth from coming out of her.

Joshua sat on the bed, just watching her now.

Joshua knew about the baby. He knew about the Irishman, the truck, the flight from Britain. It had only been two years later that Rosalie had met Joshua. In the early days he'd encouraged Rosalie to find her. "No matter how she's being raised now," he'd reminded her, "she is your daughter. A Jewish child of a Jewish mother is Jewish herself."

For once she hadn't obeyed him, and for once he hadn't pressed it, though every few years he said something. "One day," he'd say, "that girl is going to catch up with you."

Rosalie pressed the phone to her face now, shielding herself from her husband's rightness.

"Mrs. Brenner? Are you with me?"

"I don't know what you want me to do!"

"I was hoping you might come and meet her. I know what a shock this must be. But the girl has nobody."

She could believe this. There were no bodies down there, no bodies that were anything to do with her. If today were a normal Friday, Rosalie would iron. She would iron Yael's dress, Rafi's white shirt, Joshua's shirt and prayer shawl. After ironing she'd do the chicken. She'd stick a lemon inside it, with herbs and olive oil. She'd clothe their perfect bodies and feed their simple hunger. She'd have no one else's body to worry about.

"But it's the Sabbath today!" she cried.

Joshua took the phone from her. "I'm sorry, what's your name? Dr. Pollack? I'm Joshua Brenner. As you can imagine, this is very upsetting news for my wife. Can we call you right back?" Joshua wrote down a number. "Thank you."

He replaced the phone. He looked at Rosalie. "Looks like she's found you."

Rosalie began to cry.

"We don't have to go down there, do we? We'll call him on Monday. Let's just have a normal day, the way we normally do."

"Calm down, Ro."

"Let's have the kind of morning we would have if he hadn't called."

Joshua took Rosalie's hand. "But he *did* call. Rosalie, listen to me."

"It's just—"

"Are you listening?"

"I'm— Yes."

"This is what we're going to do. First of all you're going to calm down. Then we're going to call the doctor back. Then you will get dressed while I get the kids ready. Then we will go and see her."

"What about the kids?"

"We'll think of something."

"You want her to *stay?*"

"No, frankly, I do not 'want' her to stay. But if that is what the doctor thinks is best, then she stays."

"For how long?"

"We'll have to see."

"Tonight is Shabbat—"

"Rosalie! *Get dressed.*"

CHAPTER 29

But we'd hardly talked about Rosalie.

I remembered the few things Bobby had told me, mostly about what she looked like. I thought she might be pretty, like the Goths in Camden Town—long-legged girls in plastic boots with platform heels, dyed blond or black hair and spiky bracelets. I knew that forty-year-old women usually didn't dress this way, but I didn't think she'd be so the *opposite*, this frumpy woman in a long dress. Her nose was sharp and her eyes were small and she looked beaky, like a crow.

She was supposed to be helping me pack, but I didn't want her touching my things. She didn't seem to want to, either. She stood near the doorway of my room, her hands clasped in front of her. Melissa lay on the other bed with her headphones on, loudly ignoring us.

"I guess I'm not what you expected," said Rosalie.

My morning meds were kicking in and my head was fuzzy. I found it hard to get all my clothes in my suitcase. They took up too much space, as though they, like me, had expanded.

"I didn't expect anything."

"I should tell you, before we go—the kids—they think you're the daughter of an old friend from England. I said you're my old friend Louisa's girl."

"Is this my hotel, then?" I asked.

Rosalie gave a little laugh. "This is a place for people to rest, we told them. We said you needed a rest."

I found my Hardy's Haulage T-shirt and lifted it up to look at the lorry in the front. I placed it on top of the other clothes.

"You must be . . ." She tapered off.

"What?"

"Glad to leave."

Melissa turned up her Discman, and Pink's angry-bitch voice tore out. I didn't know if I was glad or not.

The *ummmm* of the freeway made it easy not to talk. I had to sit in the back between the two children. The girl crushed herself against the window, trying to get as far away from me as she could. The boy played his Game Boy, saying *"Yes"* when he went onto another level.

"Can Naomi come over for Shabbat?" asked the girl.

"I think we'll just stay as a family tonight, Yael," said Rosalie.

We were driving past a town called Fontana. I liked the sound of the word. It made me think of friendly things, like bananas and ice-cream cones and old-fashioned jukeboxes, things that were nothing to do with religious people. Ahead there was a sign for the Truck-town truck stop. Two trucks—one Kenworth, one International—exited and drove toward it. In a minute they would weave through the parking lot and slot themselves in beside the other trucks. The truckers would shower, eat fried chicken, feed their dogs, have a beer at the bar. Every trucker in that truck stop was luckier than I was right now.

I wanted to close my eyes, but it felt wrong to sleep in a car full of strangers. I kept myself awake by reading the road signs: ONTARIO. POMONA. WEST COVINA. EL MONTE. ALHAMBRA.

A cluster of buildings—a small, tall city—stuck up from the knot of freeways. The Interstate 10 merged into the 101. ("101 Here I Come," I thought, but this time the words just lay in my head, dead things after all.)

LOS ANGELES COUNTY.

"Can we go to Hannah's, Daddy?"

"It's nearly sundown, Rafi."

"It doesn't *feel* like nearly sundown."

He was right. It was light outside and hot in the car and my head was as mushy as rice pudding.

"I feel carsick," said the boy.

"Take the surface streets, Joshua," said Rosalie.

We got off the freeway and turned right on a street called Melrose. There were lots of cars but hardly any people. A few people, most of them Mexican or black, stood at a bus stop, but I didn't see many buses either.

"Where is everybody?" I asked.

"What do you mean?" asked Rosalie.

"I don't see any people."

"What are we?" asked the father. "Cats?"

"You know what she means, Josh." Rosalie turned to look at me. "L.A. is kind of a suburban sprawl. It's very different from London, isn't it?"

It seemed incredible that she'd ever been to London, that she'd met Bobby and married him and got pregnant with me, right there in Shandy Street.

"Why did you come?" I thought. Everyone looked at me as if they could hear my thought, even the little boy. His Game Boy gave out an electronic whine.

"What do you mean?"

I hadn't just thought it. I'd said it. It was the meds. They made me quiet most of the time and then say the one thing that I shouldn't.

"You didn't want to stay in that place, did you?" asked Joshua, the father. It made me worried to even think anymore, in case another wrong thing came out.

When I looked out again, Melrose had changed. It had turned into a parade of shops with saucy names. There were people now, girls mostly, going in and out of Nude, Princess, Lolita, Tattoo You, Agent Provocateur, Retail Slut. They swung their shopping bags, flipped their hair, pulled up in shiny little cars or got into shiny little cars and revved away. They had nose rings and naval rings and bare legs and suntans, even slicker versions of the girls I'd seen in Jenny K. Rosalie's daughter rolled down her window to get a better look. I also wanted to look but Joshua, the father, was talking to me.

"See, Josephine? This is the beginning of our neighborhood."

I hadn't thought they would live in an area like this. But as we turned right onto a street called Highland, the girls and the shops disappeared. There were only houses now, and palm trees. We took a second right onto Sycamore. Another Jewish family passed on foot, a bigger version of this family.

"The Gersteins are starting early," said Rosalie.

Joshua glanced at me in the rearview mirror. "Do you see, Jo? It's nearly Shabbat. That's why they're walking. You can't drive on the Sabbath. You can't work or use electrical objects either. Speaking of which," he looked at his son. "Turn off the game now, Rafi."

I expected the boy to argue but he didn't.

We parked in front of a small, peach-colored house. Yael, the girl, had ignored me all day, but when I got out of the car she looked me up and down. For the first time since before the hospital, I thought of what I was wearing: the baggy shorts that Brenda had got for me, and my tank top with GIANT TRUCK-STOP on it. I felt flabby and revolting with this gloomy, skinny girl looking at me. I couldn't tell if she was pretty. She looked pretty miserable really, though the possibility of prettiness was there. She had her father's droopy eyes but she had a full mouth. I thought she might look okay with a coat or two of lipstick.

"Come, Jo," Rosalie said. "You must be starving."

All I felt was bloated. Some Risperdal-tasting juice was sloshing around my stomach.

I knew that Jewish people didn't believe in Jesus, but in Rosalie's house there was no proof of any kind of God that I could see. The front room was plain and as brown as Rosalie's dress. There was a long table with a big candlestick on it. The shelves were stuffed with books, many with foreign-looking writing on their binders.

"Rafi, get your Game Boy off the table!" called Joshua. I'd only known him for a few hours, but he always seemed to be telling everyone what to do. Next, he turned to me.

"Josephine," he said, "in one hour we will go to synagogue, what we call shul. You might find it a little strange at first, a little unfamiliar."

"Oh."

Rosalie looked at him. "It's a lot for her to take in, Josh."

"I'll tell you what," he said. "Come with us tonight. If you don't like it, you don't have to come with us again in the morning."

This didn't sound like much of a deal to me, not having to go *twice*. All I wanted was to be back at the hospital, watching Ricky Lake with Brenda.

"Come, Josephine," said Rosalie. "I'll take you up to your room."

The room was small with a single bed, a dressing table with a mirror and a calendar with a picture of Israel above the month.

"You unpack, Jo. I'll be right back."

I sat down on the bed. The quilt was soft and cottony, not like the scratchy coverlets from the hospital. I was about to pull it back when she came back in. I stood up quickly. I thought it looked bad, my wanting to go to bed when I should have been unpacking.

"It's okay. Sit."

I sat. She handed me a plate with the biggest biscuit I'd ever seen, half of it white and half of it brown. She handed me a glass of milk.

"We don't usually eat in the bedrooms, but I'll make an exception today. Don't tell Josh or the kids."

I wasn't sure how to eat it. I broke it in two and bit off a piece of the brown section. It was more like a cake than a biscuit. My nausea slunk off and I was suddenly hungry.

"It's good," I said.

"It's called a black-and-white cookie. It's even better with the milk."

I didn't usually drink milk, but she was right; the milk washed it down a treat. I broke off another piece of the brown.

Rosalie sat down beside me. "You'll need to cover your arms and legs for shul. I'll loan you something."

"I'm not— I'm not feeling all that well."

She put her hand on my head. "You don't have a fever."

I felt strange with her hand on my head, as though she was my proper mother, but the black-and-white cookie made everything okay for so long as I was eating it. With her sitting beside me, her face was up close. There was nothing in her face that looked like anything in mine.

"It was nice of the band," she said, "not to press charges."

"Yeah."

In hospital I'd become good at not thinking about Cosima. I didn't want to talk about her now. I started on the white side of the cookie.

THE RHYTHM OF THE ROAD

Rosalie kept talking. "It was Cosima Stewart who put them in touch with Scotland Yard, and they contacted Primrose Hardy, and Primrose gave them my name. Actually, I don't know if you know this, but I met Primrose Hardy once—"

"Primrose? You met Primrose?" Though I'd never liked Primrose, the sound of her name woke me up now. "Did you see her lorries? Magnums, most of them?"

"Lorries—I saw some lorries, yes."

"Ours is a Scania, but it has the livery on it just like the others. Hardy's Haulage."

"Yes," she said. "I know about your lorry."

"Is it all right?"

"I'm sure it's fine." She stood. "Anyway, Jo . . . After the Sabbath we can talk some more."

She started to leave but she stopped at the doorway and looked at me.

"You must miss your father very much."

I didn't say anything.

"Bobby . . ." she said. "He was a very good person. He just—he always suffered from depression."

"He doesn't suffer. He just goes dark from time to time."

"Goes dark?"

"That's right."

She nodded and closed the door.

It was lovely to wash in a tub rather than one of those shower cubicles where Brenda waited on the other side of the curtain for me to finish. After my bath I put on some of Rosalie's body lotion and talcum powder. I put on her skirt and tights, though the skirt was too big in the waist and too small in the hips.

On our way to shul, Joshua and Rafi stayed in front, talking only to each other. Rosalie and I walked together. Yael lagged behind.

"I'm glad I don't have to wear a wig," I said to Rosalie.

"Only married women wear wigs."

"Why?"

"To keep us modest, for one thing. It shows we're not interested in attracting men apart from our husbands."

"But what if your wigs are more attractive than your real hair?"

She laughed. "That does happen sometimes."

As we turned onto Third Street I saw what Joshua meant by their "neighborhood." There were hundreds of Jews, the men with their tall hats and white shawls and some with little dreadlocks at the sides of their faces. The women wore long skirts and hats or wigs. I felt like I was in a foreign film with subtitles, those films that were always about wars and Jews. Bobby and I had seen a few of them in art-house cinemas when there was nothing at the Odeon. I could even imagine Bobby watching me now, from an art-house cinema somewhere in Ireland.

Rosalie and Joshua knew everyone in the temple. Everyone said, "Good Shabbos," to everyone else, though only the men shook hands.

We joined the women upstairs. We sat on an indoor balcony overlooking the big part below where the men prayed and sang. It looked flash down there, with gold and silver tapestries on the wall and all of these Jewish blokes rocking themselves and moving around in some sort of wandering dance. Again I thought of Bobby watching me in a film, trying to work out which language everyone was speaking. He would be eating popcorn, drinking Pepsi, wanting to smoke but not being allowed to because he was in the cinema.

Rosalie gave me a Bible and opened it. "That part is in English," she whispered. "Read from right to left."

I tried to read. I got as far as Judah and his daughter-in-law who pretended to be someone else so she could copulate with him and bear his son according to her destiny. I got confused at that part, though I pretended to keep reading. We mostly just sat there, doing our quiet version of what the men did below. I never knew when to stand or sit down or rock back and forth the way the other women did. Watching the men swaying down there, I felt myself sway on the inside. The cookie and milk sloshed against the walls of my stomach. I thought I would be sick right there in the synagogue. It wasn't until we were back on Sycamore Street with its smell of leaves and oranges that I felt better.

Back at the house the table was covered in a lacy tablecloth and set for dinner. There were chicken smells and a loaf of golden, plaited bread.

"Josephine? Come into the kitchen."

I followed her in. Rosalie opened the cupboards to show me their food, including an ordinary box of cornflakes.

"See the little *u* in the *O*?" she asked. "That's the *OU*. It means it's kosher."

"Is that right, Rosalie?"

She looked at me for a moment, and then she went on. "Kosher tells us what we can and cannot eat. We can't eat pork or shellfish, for example. But it's also what we eat with what. For instance, we can't have milk and meat at the same time—"

Someone was yelling in the next room. Rosalie ran in and I followed. Yael was yelling at her father, who sat in his armchair and looked worn out after all his praying.

"Dad, he's gross. He put a Tic-Tac up his nose and now he can't get it out."

"Tell him I want to talk to him."

"He's in his room. He pushed it *way up*."

"Rafi?" Joshua raised his voice. "Don't make me yell at you. Not on the Sabbath."

Rafi came slowly down the stairs, stopping on each step.

"What did you do, Rafi?" asked Joshua.

"Nothing."

"Yael said you put a Tic-Tac—"

"I got it out."

I thought there was going to be a row but that was the end of it. We sat at the table. Joshua poured red wine into cups, such a small amount that it seemed like a joke. Everyone took a sip while Joshua sang again in his funny language. The wine was sweet and watery.

"This is *Bir Kot h'mazon*," Rosalie whispered to me. "It's what we call 'doing the blessings.'"

Joshua sang over the golden bread and he put some salt on it. Then he cut the bread into slices and passed it around. "And we call this Kiddish," he said.

We had to queue up in the kitchen to wash our hands, though my hands were hardly dirty after a bit of yellow bread. Back at the table we ate some salad and something called gefilte fish. It was sweet and slimy in my mouth, sickening really, but I didn't want to be rude so I ate it.

After the first course Joshua seemed happier. "Okay, kids. Question for today. Since we have an English guest here with us, I will ask an English-related question. Who was the British subject who became the first president of Israel?"

Rafi came in before anyone else could. "Chaim Weizmann!"

"*You* knew the answer to that, Yael," said Rosalie.

Yael shrugged as if she didn't want to know.

"And did you know," Joshua said, "that because of his scientific work—he found a way to make acetone for explosives from chestnuts—the English government wanted to knight Weizmann? But instead of accepting the knighthood, he asked for British support for a Jewish homeland in Palestine. Did you know that, Josephine?"

"I didn't know that, no."

"The poor girl's tired," said Rosalie.

"What's knighthood?" asked Rafi.

"It's when you only do things at night," said Yael.

"*Yael,*" said Rosalie, but she was smiling.

I asked Joshua if I could have more wine. He frowned and then nodded at Rosalie. Rosalie left the room and came back with a different bottle.

"Because it's a special occasion," she said, pouring me out a little.

"Cheers," I said, lifting my cup.

"*Cheers?*" Joshua's face crinkled. "You mean, *L'chaim!*"

Everybody laughed, even Yael.

I went to bed after supper, though it was still light outside. As I lay down to sleep I saw my film ending, violins playing like the ones in *Fiddler on the Roof*. I saw Bobby watching the credits, waiting for my name to scroll down the screen before going next door to the pub to have a pint of Guinness and think about what he'd seen. He'd think about it so much that for a while, I didn't have to.

I slept for two days.

CHAPTER 30

Dear Mindy—
I'll tell you. Nothing could have prepared me for
the sight of her! I mean—

Rosalie deleted the sentence. She swiveled left on her desk chair, as the kids used to do when they were little. She swiveled right. She rewrote exactly what she'd deleted. She reconsidered. She deleted the words "I mean."

She wrote to Mindy nearly every day. Their e-mails were really conversations, paused but never finished. But this was a conversation she'd never had, not even with her cousin.

What could she say about Josephine? All she could think of was the way she looked—big and puffy, her skin a carroty color, her hair fried as if it had gone crazy, too. The doctor said the swelling was mostly from the medication, but as she sat in back of the Volvo while the children shrank away from her, it was hard to imagine her any other way. Yet it wasn't just this—the mental patient who had winched her way into her life—that startled Rosalie. It was the way her children looked beside her: Yael, petulant and petite at one window and Rafi at the other, his noodly fingers on the Game Boy. By comparison their faces were more exquisite than ever, faces that looked as if they'd been carefully thought out by God.

"She is my daughter," she said aloud. Her voice sounded stilted, as if she was auditioning—badly—for *Days of Our Lives*.

Joshua sat at the kitchen table with *The Jewish Review*. He had on his reading glasses but she knew he was waiting for her.

"Well?" He turned sidewise to look at her straight. For the first time in years she noticed the mild squint in his right eye. Strange how you could forget something like that about a person you knew so well.

"Well, what?" she said, but she knew that he wanted to talk about Josephine. To talk about her as they'd talked about his brother's new wife, the convert from Minnesota, the dyed redhead who spoke fluent Hebrew but made it sound Norwegian. Or the way they talked about Mindy's son, Harry, when he went through his glue-sniffing phase. Rosalie opened the fridge and took out the brisket from yesterday. She would make sandwiches out of that.

"She's very inquisitive," said Rosalie. "She asked lots of questions on our way to temple."

"She wasn't so inquisitive at the table."

"She's exhausted! And you sit there and expect her to know about Chaim Weizmann and his acetone explosives!"

"I don't expect her to know anything."

She looked over the foods she'd shown Josephine the night before. Josephine's eyes had been gluey, as if she wasn't listening, but when she'd said, "Is that right, Rosalie?" her eyes flashed silver.

Is that right, Rosalie? Are you at art school as well?

Joshua was still talking. "Have you spoken to her, Ro? About her father, I mean?"

"She insists he's alive."

She opened the drawer, took out a knife for the meat. Above her, stuck to the cupboard with curling scotch tape, was a drawing Rafi had made when he was five. It was a stick-figure family in purple crayon, all of them at Passover: Rosalie, Joshua, Yael, Rosalie's parents, and Joshua's parents who were in from Philly. In the corner was his lopsided signature: *Rafi Brenner, Tully Lieberman School.*

She jumped. Joshua was behind her, his hands on her shoulders. "It must be strange for you."

She patted his hand and left the kitchen. She walked upstairs. As she passed the guest room, the hallway smelled like a hospital ward; sweat and medicine and God knows what other kind of poison leaking out of there.

CHAPTER 31

In sleep I felt as though I was in a fish tank, drowning in my own syrupy self. A few times I opened my eyes, expecting the green-glow of the hospital at night, or the footsteps of the night nurse on the ward. I heard voices from downstairs: something about an essay, something about a dentist. I heard Rafi saying, "Is she going to sleep forever?" and Rosalie saying, "Keep your voice down, Rafi."

When I tried to lift my head, it was huge and heavy. All I wanted was silence. Any silence would have done: the fish-tank glow of sleep, a lizard stealing across the road, or the best silence, Bobby and me like cats in our own pools of sunshine.

It was the music that woke me up properly. I couldn't figure it out; rap or hip-hop music, angry black voices, in this place! I put on the dressing gown Rosalie had left for me (a robe, she called it) and walked, wobbly on my feet, into the hallway.

The door to Rafi's room was open. Rafi sat on his bed, playing his Game Boy, his upper body dancing to the rap music. I tried to hear what the rapper was saying, but the words weren't in English.

"What are you listening to?" I asked.

Rafi was just a little boy, and a four-eyed one at that, but I felt nervous standing in his doorway, as if I could get in trouble just for being there. He didn't look up from his game. "They're called Getting Chai. They're a little like N. Sync, except they sing in Hebrew."

"I didn't know Jewish people could play this kind of music."

"They're everybody's favorite."

"Are they your favorite?"

He shrugged. "They're just everybody's."

I took a step into his room. His shelves were stacked with board games like Risk and Monopoly, all with that foreign writing on them.

"How old are you, Rafi?"

"Nine and three-quarters. Yael's thirteen."

"I've seen people like you in London."

"Yeah. I have a cousin in a place called Golden Green."

"Do you mean Golders Green?"

"I guess so. My great-great-grandparents were from Poland and Russia. They were chased out by the pogroms." He sounded proud of this.

"What are pogroms?"

"It's where Russian people chase you."

Bobby and I knew a Russian driver called Vlad. He drove for a tampon company called Simply Sanitary and he seemed tired all the time. I couldn't imagine him chasing anybody.

"What do you mean, 'chase you'?"

Rafi sighed like an old man and put down his game. He climbed up on his desk and, stumbling under its weight, pulled down an atlas from the top shelf. He eased it onto the desk and opened it. "You can come and look if you want to."

I went to look.

"This is Lithuania," he said. "That's where my dad's people were from. They were chased to this place here—that's Warsaw now—and then they were chased to America. Dad says our name wasn't Brenner originally. They were just given that at Ellis Island."

"What was your name originally then?"

"We're not sure. Bratowski or something."

Rafi pointed to another place on the map. "And that's Lodz, that's Poland now, that's where the Chapkises came from, that's Mom's side."

"Nobody ever told me that Rosalie was Polish."

"Only sort of. They went to New York like a hundred years ago. Then they went to Encino."

"Where's Encino?"

"It's where Grandma and PopPop live. They're on vacation in Barbados now."

"Are they nice?" I'd never even thought about my grandparents, apart from Josephine Pickering and Bobby's father ("the auld bastard," Bobby called him), whom I'd never met.

"They're really nice."

"Can I have a look at that, Rafi?"

I went through the atlas until I found what I was looking for. My heart puffed up at the sight of it, the jagged pear shape. "That's Britain. That's where I'm from."

"The whole country?"

"In a way. We drive up and down in our truck."

"You drive a truck?"

"We have our own Scania. That's a bit like a Freightliner here."

"Do you know Rabbi Oliansky? He gets to check all of these trucks, the food they carry, you know, check it to see if it's kosher."

"Raf? Are you doing your essay?" Joshua stood in the doorway, blocking the light from the hall. "I don't see even a *trace* of paper or a pen—"

"It's there." Rafi pointed to a pile on the bed.

"It's 'there.' I see." Joshua gestured to the CD player. "It must be feeling very lonely, forsaken for a computer game and a rock group."

"It's a rap group."

"A rap group! I do apologize!"

"I was just showing him where I live," I said.

"She drives a truck, Dad—"

"Yes, I know." Joshua looked at me, but not quite. One of his eyes seemed to look past me. "Rosalie will take you shopping, Josephine. After you've put some clothes on."

As I walked out and down the hallway, I heard Joshua saying, "Right, Rafi. Egypt."

Rosalie drove me to a place called Fairfax Avenue, where all the restaurants and shops had that foreign writing—Hebrew writing, Rosalie said it was called. There was even a Chinese restaurant with Hebrew writing on it.

"We need a chicken," Rosalie said in the car, as if I'd asked. "And we need whitefish and chopped liver. And I have to have my dress altered for my nephew's Bar Mitzvah."

Nearly all of the people who worked in the shops were women. Most of them had accents of some kind.

"Hello, Rosalie. How ees Joshua and little ones?" asked the lady butcher.

"They're fine, thank you."

"And this person, it is?"

"This is Josephine. She's a friend from England."

"Josephine?" The lady butcher looked at me. "A big girl."

Rosalie told me that a lot of the people who worked in the shops were Russian. I wondered why Rosalie would want to be friends with the kind of people who had chased her great-grandparents away. I supposed those people could have been chased away themselves, but why had it taken them so long to leave? I was about to ask her, but we were at the tailor's, which was small and cluttered, with barely room for the two of us. I went outside to wait. I bought a corn dog from the hot dog place next door. Standing in the sunshine and eating the second corn dog I'd ever eaten, I didn't feel too bad. The corn dog was delicious, better than any sausage roll. I was happy not to be with Cleat, who had bought me my first corn dog. Mostly I was happy not to be thinking about Cosima anymore. I could feel another film begin to roll, and this time Bobby was in it. Because of the war in Iraq, a nuclear bomb had fallen over Britain and everyone was evacuated. The men had gone to one place, the women to the other. Bobby had been sent to Ireland, and I was sent to live with an oppressed people who had been chased away by Russians—

My corn dog was yanked away from me.

"This is something we do not eat!" There were sharp lines in the middle of Rosalie's forehead, making her look angry and old.

"I'm sorry," I said.

She just looked at me. She looked at my hair, my arms, my legs.

"I forgot," I said.

"I know," she said. "It's not your fault."

But it was too late; my little bit of happiness had gone.

"Come on, Jo. Let's go to Hannah's for a treat."

"Hannah's" was Hannah's bakery, and Hannah herself didn't look so religious to me. She was fat with big breasts and tight white jeans that showed off every bump and lump, and gold chains that dripped into her tits. Her face was as dark as a gypsy's.

"So tall, your new young friend is, Rosalie. She could never be mistook for one of yours, no?"

I was already getting sick of their questions, which never seemed to be asked to me, even when they were about me. I was more interested in what was under the glass: the nutty rolled-up cakes, crescents half-dipped in chocolate, yellow biscuits with sprinkles on them. There were black-and-white cookies as well.

Rosalie watched as I tried to choose. "You can't decide, can you?"

I shook my head.

"Hannah," she said, "can you give me a black-and-white cookie to eat here, and maybe three plain butter cookies and, well, okay, give us a rugala too, and a marzipan strawberry. And just a black coffee for me."

"And a glass of milk, please," I said.

We sat at a table near the window. I took a bite of the rolled-up nutty thing. I couldn't decide what I thought of it. I took another bite and decided it was good. I swallowed. It was great, really.

"Why aren't you having some?" I asked.

"I'm on a diet."

"I didn't think you'd be on a diet. It doesn't sound very religious."

"A Jewish woman should keep herself attractive. She should keep herself beautiful for herself *and* her husband."

"Oh."

"On second thought, maybe you're right." She put one of the rugalas on her own plate. I took a bite of the marzipan strawberry.

"See this marzipan?" I said. "Usually we just eat this as icing on top of a

Christmas cake. But this is better. I love the way it looks like a real strawberry
and then isn't."

"Uh-huh." She nodded. "I never liked your English Christmas cake, all of
that caramelized fruit. You know, to be honest with you, I was never crazy
about English desserts period."

"Cosima feels the same way. Except sticky toffee pudding, she likes that."

"Sticky toffee pudding?"

"You'd like it. It hasn't got any fruit in it."

I was smiling, too much. My face hurt. I let go of my smile, but my face
went rubbery.

"Have you got any photographs?" I asked. "Of you and Bobby?"

"I might, somewhere. I'll have to look." Rosalie glanced up at Hannah,
and then leaned into me. "I always wondered how Bobby would explain it all
to you. It's hard for a little girl to understand."

"He just said you weren't the family kind." A crumb of marzipan stuck in
my throat. I took a sip of milk to force it down. "Except you sort of look like
the family kind now."

"Rosalie!" Hannah called out, "You know who was in here today? Linda
Oliansky, the rabbi's girl. What a looker she's turning into!"

"She's very pretty, yes." Rosalie looked confused, as if she didn't know
what to do next. After a minute she started gathering up the food. "Let's walk
a little," she said. "We can take these with us."

We walked along Fairfax.

"When I was young," she said, "I was like you. I was wild. Not many people know this, but after I left England, I even sold my body for drugs a few
times."

It was hard to imagine, her body being something she would get money for.

"I ended up in rehab. Then I relapsed. My parents sent me to Israel, to
work on a kibbutz with my cousin, Mindy Rabinowitz. We're best friends
now, though she lives in Chicago."

"Is that where you met Joshua? Israel?"

"Yes. He was a young scholar at the yeshiva."

"And you fell in love with him straightaway?" I thought of when Cosima
had met Rick for the first time. I wondered if Rosalie had thought Joshua was
an asshole too, at first.

"I don't know if it was so instant. I was used to men who, you know,
swept me off my feet but made me feel bad—I mean, not *bad* exactly, but un-
fulfilled. I remember the day Joshua took me to the Wailing Wall. I remember
how it felt, with the heat and the sun streaming into me. He showed me that
a life without God is like a cup with a hole in the bottom. It doesn't matter
how much you fill the cup, the nourishment goes right through it."

I understood that thing about the hole, but I didn't know what to say about it. We just walked for a few minutes.

"Why don't you have pictures in your house?" I asked. "Of God I mean, or of angels, or something like that?"

"God is in everyone. He shouldn't be objectified on a mug or a painting or a key chain you can buy at the drugstore."

"Oh."

"Though between us"—Rosalie kept her voice low, as if someone was eavesdropping—"I think we missed the boat with that one. It means the gentiles got the most beautiful art, because they were quite happy to paint *their* Jesuses and Marys!"

I thought about Bobby's aunties, Niamh and Mary in Newtonards, and their plastic Jesus and Mary statues from the gift shop at Knock airport. It was true that they didn't mind showing off their God, or at least his mother and son.

"The point is," said Rosalie, "that God is everywhere. God is within you." She pointed to my chest.

"There's nothing like that in there."

"So what is in there?"

I thought about it. "Music. I have music in me a lot of the time. Or I did, before they put me on those drugs."

"And what makes you think music isn't inspired by God?"

"If God is in the music, then all he's done is push me away from it."

"The trick, Jo, is to find your own music."

"How do I do that?"

Suddenly, there was music, "Sunrise, Sunset" trilling from her handbag. I didn't even know she had a mobile phone, but she took it out now, as small and shiny as mine.

"Hi, Josh! Yes, just a few more errands . . . What? Oh, no! . . . Okay. I'm coming home now."

She put the phone back in her bag. The line in her forehead was back. "Yael missed her dentist appointment. We've got to go home."

"Right now?"

"I'm so sorry. I promise I'll talk to you about this later."

But she didn't look as though she would.

I wasn't on the Risperdal anymore. I was on Prozac, which didn't feel like anything because it took three or four weeks to come on. Now that my head was no longer so furry, Cosima came back into it, but I didn't want her to. I thought of the last thing she'd said before she'd seen the gun: *Get away from me, you sad fuck!* I saw myself as she had, sweating and snotty on top of Salvation

Mountain, sticking Cleat's greasy Glock in my mouth. I tried to be in the film again, but I couldn't imagine my sweaty, snotty self starring in a movie.

Rosalie and Joshua and Yael spent the afternoon at Rabbi Oliansky's house. At dinner I waited for Joshua to offer me wine, but there was no alcohol tonight, not even religious alcohol. Yael's eyes were bloodshot. She stared at her food and hardly ate it. Joshua and Rosalie kept looking at her and Rafi kept looking at Joshua and nobody looked at me. The room was full of chewing sounds.

"So, Josephine," said Joshua, breaking the silence, "what do you think of California so far?"

I'd nearly forgotten that I was in California. I tried to think what it meant to me now: AC/DC blaring from Cleat's truck, Freightliners and freeways and trains with UNION PACIFIC on the side, Oscar's cousins dying in a container with forty-seven other Mexicans, a burrito, rice and beans puked up in a bathtub of the Happy Days Motel.

"It's nice," I said.

"You must find it very different from England."

"It's warmer."

"Do you think the people are very different?"

"They sound different."

"We sure do. Who was it that said that we are two countries divided by a common language? Was it Winston Churchill who said that?"

"I don't know." I felt stupid not having an answer to any of his questions.

Joshua turned to his son. "Now, Rafi," he said. "Egypt."

That night Rosalie and Joshua argued in their room. I couldn't hear what they were saying, apart from once when Rosalie said, "She's very young." I couldn't tell if they were talking about Yael or me. I went to my room and found two books that Rosalie had left for me on the bed. The first was called *Being at Home with the Torah* and the second was called *It's Fun to Be Jewish*. I opened *It's Fun to Be Jewish*. On the first page there was a picture of a young girl with her head cocked to the side. Three balloons hung over her head, a different question in each one:

"Who am I?"

"What is my reason for being here?"

"What does it mean to be Jewish?"

I thought of the little Indian girl in El Centro and the flyer about the Garden of Eden and the lions who wouldn't eat you. This Jewish stuff looked more complicated. The book was thick, with writing in English and Hebrew. I turned to the inside cover where it said, in big, careful writing: *This book belongs to Yael Brenner, who is now in the Third Grade.*

Suddenly I heard creaking from downstairs. I went to the landing overlooking the stairwell and the front door. Yael was sneaking out of the house.

Her hair wasn't tied back from her face but loose, and she was wearing jeans. She let herself out, so quietly I barely heard the door shut behind her. It was ten-thirty at night.

I wondered if I should tell Rosalie and Joshua. They might think I was being a responsible adult if I did that, but then Yael, who didn't seem to like me much anyway, would really hate me. I went back to my room and tried to read *It's Fun to Be Jewish*. It was hard to concentrate. I was excited that someone else might get in trouble apart from me, but the next morning Yael was back in her bed just like she normally was.

Rosalie took me to Jewish Families in Need, the charity store where she did her volunteer work.

"Everybody in the house should do something productive," she said. "I think you'll feel better about yourself if you help a little."

I didn't see how tagging dresses would help me to feel better about myself, but hardly anyone came into the store so at least we had time on our own. Rosalie gave me some items to organize into a gift box for poor Jewish families. I set out the items as carefully as I could: matzoh bread, matzoh ball soup mix, grape juice, six candles, a bunch of bananas, apples, sugar cookies, half a dozen bagels. I kept the breadstuff separate from the fruit, and I tried to place the apples so they wouldn't roll around when the carton was picked up.

"Look," I said to her. "Look how I've arranged everything."

"That's great, Josephine."

She was putting a dress on a hanger. It was a plain maroon dress with a long skirt.

"We just got this in. It's hardly been worn."

"Are you going to try it on?"

"It's too long." She held it up to me. "Why don't you try it?"

I didn't tell her that I didn't like it, that it didn't look something I'd even consider stealing.

"Try it," she said again. "What have you got to lose?"

It wasn't just that I didn't like it. I didn't want to admit that I might be too big for it. I took it into the fitting room and tried it on. It seemed to fit, but the bulb in the cubicle was out so I couldn't see. When I stepped out, Rosalie was waiting. She backed up to look at me.

"Ooh," she said.

"Is it horrible?"

"Turn around."

I did a slow spin for her. When I turned to her again, her face was tilted to the side and some of her real hair was sticking out of her wig.

"What?" I said.

"You look so . . . elegant."

"Elegant." It wasn't a word I'd ever heard before, not about me. She was staring so hard at me that I looked away. I tried to put my hands in my pockets, but there weren't any pockets.

"Jo?"

"What?"

She handed me the photo. The girl in the photo was closer to how I'd expected Rosalie to look. She had dyed black hair, black lips, piercings in her ears. She was sitting by a pool, somewhere bright and sunny, but she didn't wear a swimming costume and there was nothing sunny about her.

"I was looking for the one of Bobby and me on our wedding day and I found this instead. I thought you might like to see it, anyway."

I sat in the armchair, the one chair in the shop. Rosalie sat on the arm. I kept looking back and forth between the girl in the photo and Rosalie now.

"You look good," I said. "You look so . . . pissed off."

"You could say that again. Always sulking about something! I remember the day that was taken. Our maid had brought her daughters to the pool that day. Two pretty Guatemalan girls, twelve and fourteen. Like stunning little fishes they were."

"Did you swim with them?"

"You're kidding. I went upstairs and ate. That's what I did most days after school. I was always eating."

"You weren't fat."

"I felt fat."

"I've *always* felt fat."

"Feeling fat is every girl's prerogative. Her actual size has nothing to do with it."

I didn't know what *prerogative* meant, but it made her sound wise, the way a mother should sound.

"Actually," said Rosalie, "I was the loneliest girl in the world."

I looked up at her, trying to see if I could find any leftover loneliness.

"Were you the loneliest girl in the world when you met Bobby?"

"I sure was."

"And he made you feel better?"

She thought about it. "In a way, he did."

"But it got bad again? When I came along?"

"It wasn't like that."

"What was it like?"

The door burst open and Carol, the manager, came in with a heavy carton. "Look what the rebbetzin gave us!" She held it up to show us.

"How nice, Carol," said Rosalie, but she stayed where she was.

"How can you see from there? Come look!"

Slowly Rosalie went up to look.

"Brand-new candlesticks," said Carol. "Excellent silver."

"What do you think, Jo?" asked Rosalie.

"Nice," I said, but I hardly glanced at the stuff.

I had to admit the dress was slimming. Back in my room, I put it on again. *Elegant*, Rosalie had said. And I did feel elegant, walking around the room, not showing any flesh: taller, slimmer, simpler. I felt like I was in a movie again. I was getting ready to meet a young man for supper, a Jewish man. We would go to the kosher Chinese restaurant, maybe.

I sat down and opened my eyeshadow palette, trying to find a match for the dress.

Someone was behind me. I turned, expecting to see Joshua in the doorway. But it was Yael who stood there staring at me.

"Hello," I said.

"Hi." She looked annoyed, as if I'd gone to her room instead of it being the other way around.

"See the dress that Rosalie bought me?" I stood up to show her.

"That looks like a dress that Mom would like."

"Is that bad?"

She shrugged. "It's flattering on you, I guess."

I sat down again. I started on my eyeliner, but Yael stayed where she was. I could feel her watching me.

"How do you keep it so even?" she asked.

"Practice," I looked up at her. "Would you like me to show you?"

"I'm not allowed to wear makeup. Just a little lip gloss on special occasions."

"You can wipe it off afterward."

She looked into the hall, and then closed the door.

"Just a little, I guess," she said.

"Sit down there."

Slowly, as if she didn't really want to, she sat in my place. I'd never put makeup on another person before, and I was nervous I would poke her in the eye. I crouched beside her and dipped my finger into some brown shadow.

"This color is called Autumn Damask," I said. "Close your eyes."

I rubbed it over one of her lids, and then the other. I picked up the eye pencil.

"Open your eyes now, and look up at the ceiling."

"Ooh, that tickles."

"You get used to it."

The mascara was hardest. I tried to dab lightly on her lashes, but she blinked and gave out a small cry. I'd left a smudge below her left eye, jagged like a black toothmark.

"Sorry." I wet my finger and wiped the smudge away. "Now the blusher. See what I'm doing? I'm brushing it up toward the hairline, to emphasize your cheekbones."

The lips were last. I outlined them with pencil and filled them in with crimson lipstick. I stood back so that we could look at her in the mirror. Her eyes didn't look hangdog anymore but smoky and wide. Her cheekbones were high and her lips were moist and red.

"What do you think?" I asked.

She looked at herself for so long that I wasn't sure she liked it.

"I *so* don't look thirteen anymore."

"You so don't. Sixteen, maybe even."

"Really?"

"You look like a model, Yael."

"Really?"

I nodded.

"I want to show you something." She jumped up and ran out of the room. A moment later she came back with a shopping bag that said BANANA REPUBLIC on it. She was giggling. "Shut the door, shut the door!" She pulled off her school skirt. She leaned back on my bed and pulled on the skirt from Banana Republic and then stood up to show me. The skirt was plastic and she looked as though she'd poured herself into it. It was exactly like the skirt I'd wanted at Jenny K two years ago, the one Bobby said I didn't have the build for. He'd annoyed me when he said that. Seeing Yael with her skinny legs— seeing that she *did* have the build for it—I realized I was still annoyed. In a way, it felt good to be annoyed with Bobby. I could imagine him right now, eating his all-day breakfast and waiting for me to finish with all this dressing-up stuff.

"There's one problem," I said. "You can't wear your school shirt with the skirt."

"I know, but I don't have anything else to wear with it."

I dragged my suitcase out from the closet. Yael watched as I went through my clothing and dug out the red tube top. It was a top that I'd stolen but wouldn't wear, because it showed my midriff and my midriff was especially flabby at the moment. I handed it to Yael.

"Are you sure?" she asked.

"Why not?"

She turned her back to me to change. I'd always thought Yael was flat-chested, but from the side, I saw the beginnings of breasts, just the faintest swelling. Soon Rosalie would buy her her first bra. I thought of the day I'd bought my first bra. I'd had to ask the lady at Marks & Spencers what size I was.

Yael faced me again. In my tube top her stomach looked so flat that I could see her muscles move when she moved. In the middle of all her flatness, something twinkled.

"Is that a rhinestone in your belly button, Yael?"

She grinned. "Uh-huh."

"Where did you get that done?"

"Melrose. I go there all the time without them knowing."

"Where did you get the money?"

"Grandma Chapkis. She doesn't know what I use it for, but she wouldn't mind. She isn't religious. She's a Communist. Though Dad says she's very rich for a Communist."

Just then the door opened. I stiffened myself for Joshua, but it was Rosalie who stood there. Her eyes went between the two Yaels, the real one and the one in the mirror. Before she could say anything, Joshua was behind her.

"Yael." He spoke slowly. "What have you done to your stomach?"

"Nothing."

"When did you start mutilating yourself? And where did you get that top? Does that top belong to Josephine?"

"No." Her voice was tiny.

"Don't lie to me."

"It doesn't!"

Even Rosalie was on his side. "Jo," she said, "Yael is not supposed to wear makeup."

"We were just fooling around," said Yael.

"Go put something decent on, Yael," said Joshua. "And wipe that dirt off your face, and take that thing out of your stomach, and then you will come down and talk to us."

"But Dad—"

"DO AS YOU ARE TOLD!"

Yael ran out.

For the rest of the day I stayed in my room. I tried to get back into the film, but I couldn't. Strangely, when I thought of England, *that* was the movie—Shandy Street in black and white, a sixties version of our neighborhood, poor pregnant girls hanging the washing from balconies, men drinking cans of lager at the dole office, cockneys singing "Roll Out the Barrel" down at the Shandy Arms.

From downstairs I heard Rabbi Olianksy, and this time he brought his wife.

Rosalie and Joshua rowed all evening. I stood outside their bedroom door again. I heard my name more than once. I also heard the words *disturbed* and *troubled* and *boundary*.

Rafi saw me in the hallway.

"Do you like my new glasses?" he asked. "We went to Dr. Levinson's to get them and then Mom took me to Hannah's Bakery for a treat."

"When did she take you to Hannah's Bakery?"

"This morning. Before they got mad at Yael."

I thought I was the only person that Rosalie had taken to Hannah's Bakery in the last few days. It didn't seem so special now that Rafi had been as well.

The voices rose on the other side of the door. Rafi started to walk away.

"They want to send me home," I called after him. He stopped and looked back at me, his eyes big and stupid-looking in his new glasses.

"Back to your own mother?"

"They can't send me back to my own mother."

"Why not?"

"Why don't you ask them that?"

Suddenly I wanted him to know the truth. I even thought of telling him, but he walked away, as if he knew there was something he didn't want to know. He shut his door and a minute later, his Getting Chai music pounded out, his fake Hebrew rap.

I went downstairs. I went outside, not bothering to shut the door behind me. I walked down third street and turned left on Fairfax. I bought two corn dogs, eating pork on purpose. I hadn't smoked since the hospital, but now I bought a pack of Marlboros and smoked five fags on my way to Rosalie's.

As I walked back along Sycamore Street, Rosalie was in the window. She threw open the door before I even got there.

"Where have you been for the last hour, Jo? We were about to call the police!"

"Can't I go for a walk?"

Joshua was behind her again. I knew that Joshua had talked Rosalie out of me by now, just like Rick had talked Cosima out of me.

"If you're going for a walk," he said, "you can tell us first! And you *stink* of tobacco. Did you think we wouldn't smell it?"

"I don't care if you smell it or not!"

"Josephine," said Rosalie, "we promised Dr. Pollack we'd take care of you."

"So it isn't that you're really worried. You just don't want to get in trouble with Dr. Pollack!" I pushed past both of them. I ran upstairs and shut the door, wishing I had music of my own to drown them out.

It was two A.M., and my head was jagged with worry. I hadn't phoned Fogarty in weeks. I'd let myself be soaked up by this life, this little house of strangers who worried so much about themselves.

We weren't supposed to go into the den without asking, so that was exactly where I went. Joshua's liquor cabinet was in there. I took out the Glen-fiddich, the only non-Jewish thing in the whole place, and poured some into a glass. The whiskey felt rough going down, rough and good. I poured another.

I did not phone Fogarty. I paced around the room, running my hands over the backs of books on the shelves. The bottom shelf was filled with photo albums, all labeled with things like *Our Wedding, 1990,* or *Joshua's Bar Mitzvah, 1971,* or *Philadelphia, Summer 1994.*

Rosalie's computer was humming on the desk. I touched the keyboard and the screen lit up. A list of e-mails came up, including six which said "Re: Josephine." I clicked on one:

Dear Mindy—
What a difference a couple of days sleep has made! It wasn't a mental patient who walked into the kitchen this morning. It was a tall and ruddy shiksa: big bosom, big hips, hair clean and combed, face no longer so puffy. First time I saw her, I had a terrible thought: *That face could be beautiful if it belonged to someone else.* Her eyes are still a little glazed, probably from the medication. Her voice is weird. (And as if that wasn't enough, later I look out of the tailor's and there she is, this buxom bottle blonde nearly hanging out of her top, eating a corn dog! And since when do they sell corn dogs on the corner of Fairfax and Beverly?) Oh, I must run now Mindy, more later. . . . XR

Dear Mindy—
She isn't stupid, not stupid at all. She wants to know why there are no pictures of God in the house, and why we cover our heads.
    I tell her about my early life, how wild I was when I met you in Israel. Even though we seem so different, there are ways we're quite alike. And now that we're having this trouble with Yael . . .

The rest was about Yael, so I scrolled down until I found the one from yesterday:

Mindy—
Food disappears overnight; cookies, bread, those almond cakes that Rafi likes. Like a raccoon, Joshua says, but I'm not sure that she's the thief. It could be Yael. (Yael's so skinny, but who knows? Eating disorder, maybe? What's next!)

I found Yael in Jo's room. Yael was wearing this teeny miniskirt and a tank top that probably belonged to Jo, her stomach bared to the world (and a rhinestone in her belly button!!) and I'll tell you, she looked like a little hooker, like a miniversion of Jo the other day. And here was Jo, teaching her how to do it. She'd smeared this reddish powder over my little girl and it was like she'd smeared blood over her eyes. I wondered if I would have been so mad if Joshua hadn't been there. Okay, Josephine was defiling my beautiful child, but on the other hand she was also giving her little sister (yes, sister) a makeover. Surely even a good Jewish mother can show a little tolerance? It's not as if I didn't test a few boundaries myself at that age!

5:00
It's only a few hours later but my thinking is very different on this. We have spent the afternoon with the rabbi and the rebbetzin.
    I have been fooling myself by trying to put Josephine, Yael, and myself on the same plane. Swearing at your Hebrew school teacher or missing a dentist appointment isn't stalking. It isn't holding people at gunpoint or stealing trucks or taking speed. It isn't (and sorry for my crudeness) opening your legs for any old felon, white or Mexican, or ending up in an insane asylum in the desert out with the *goyim*. Mindy, coming to terms with our Jewish identities gave us an anchor. It gave us the lives we have today. But what will "getting back to her roots" mean to her? What are HER roots? An itinerant life on the highway? Sleeping around? Fast food and ignorance? God forgive me—I look at her sometimes and it seems impossible that she could have come out of my own body.
XO R

There were other e-mails but I didn't read them. I lit a cigarette, using the bin as an ashtray. There was no hole in the bottom of my stomach now. It was like concrete down there.

I pulled the first photo album off the shelf, the one marked *Kids, the Early Years*. I started to go through it, slowly at first and then quicker, barely stopping to read the captions: *Yael at eight minutes old. Yael at twelve minutes old. Cousin Eli on his first bicycle. The Rabinowitz kids. Rafi at nursery school. The Oliansky kids. Cousin Nate, two months*. Babies and toddlers, toddlers and babies, bicycles and paddling pools and babies. Every baby in the world was in there, just about.

CHAPTER 32

W ake up, Rosalie."

He shook her shoulder.

"Rosalie. You have to come and see."

She didn't want to come and see.

"Ro, you need to deal with this!"

She sat up. He was holding her robe for her. She grabbed it and put it on. She followed him down to the den. He threw open the door and gestured to the destruction.

The floor was a crazy gallery of faces: kids, grandparents and great-grandparents, cousins, aunts and uncles, vacations in Baltimore and Pennsylvania and Israel, the Leibowitzes, the Porters, the Olianksys, babies and Bar Mitzvahs and weddings, Rosalie and Joshua under a canopy of their own. It was all here—every person, every fragment that made up the whole of their lives, served up in a mess of broken binders, loose photos, plastic casings.

There were cigarette burns in the desk, fat ones that looked like angry bugs. There were three stubs in the garbage and two stubbed out in the carpet. The Glenfiddich bottle stood on the desk beside a glass of whiskey.

Joshua lingered in the doorway. She avoided looking at him but she could see him anyway: the pursing of his lips, the sympathetic tension of his features.

"Go to work, please, Josh."

"I have the day off today, Ro."

There were footsteps on the stairs. Yael was rarely awake this early, but here she was now, padding up to her father, her eyes crusty with sleep. She let out a gasp when she saw the carnage.

"What *happened?*"

"Nothing happened."

"But Mom—who did this?"

"Josh," said Rosalie, ignoring her, "the kids haven't seen my folks since they got back. Will you wake up Rafi, get him ready? Will you take them to Encino, please?"

Joshua put his hand on his daughter's back, as if protecting her from Rosalie's dismissal.

"And Josephine?" he asked.

She thought of Josephine, passed out on her bed from all that whiskey. She was not ready for Josephine to be awake.

"Let her sleep. You three get ready to go."

Joshua and Yael didn't move.

"Go!!"

Rosalie was rarely the yeller in this family, but now a wave of tension broke over her body and yelling felt good. She wasn't even sure whom she was mad at—Josephine for trashing her den, or Yael and Josh for just staring at her, wanting an answer she couldn't give.

When the others had gone, she stayed in the den. She walked slowly to the desk, her feet squeaking against the plastic casings. She knew she should salvage the photographs, retrieve each one and give it a loving inspection before returning it to its home. Instead, she sat at the computer and met her own words on the screen:

```
 . . . opening her legs for any old felon, white or
Mexican, or ending up in an insane asylum in the
desert out with the goyim . . .
```

Just a few hours ago, Jo had stood where she was standing now, reading these words. She probably hadn't understood them all.

"What's *goyim?*" Rosalie could imagine her asking, her voice going up and Irish at the end, the way his had. Jo asked a lot of questions—more than Yael and Rafi ever had.

But she wouldn't be asking about *goyim* now. Hurt would have driven the questions right out of her.

"I'm sorry, Jo," she said aloud.

Rosalie's neck was aching. She turned her head in a slow circle. She heard a crick in her neck and said "Ow" though it didn't really hurt.

A photograph jammed into her foot. She picked it up. It was black and white, sepia-tinted. It was of her grandfather—her *PopPop*—as a young man, slim in his white shirt and suspenders, his hair center-parted, his face pale and soulful. He leaned against the stoop of an old brownstone, one hand on his hip. In tiny pen at the bottom it said *Flatbush 1939*.

"Flatbush?" That was when he'd had the sewing store. He still talked about it more than three decades later, when Rosalie was small.

"We didn't sell any of these cheap things you see now," he'd tell her. "Wooden buttons only, brass, Bakelite, ivory, too, when I could get it. And those wooden specialty buttons? I carved those myself. Every single one." Even as an old man he made buttons, though not to sell. He made them for Rosalie. Her favorites were the yellow-and-blue boats. For her sixth birthday he'd taken the buttons off one of her new dresses and replaced them with the little boats.

PopPop was handsome as a young man, but something seemed to be wrong with his ear. She touched the brown spot on the photograph. It was a cigarette burn. It still smelled of Jo's cigarette.

She gathered her robe around her, tied the sash in a double knot.

"What the *fuck* does she think she's doing?" Rosalie said, using the F-word for the first time in fifteen years. She charged upstairs, making noise on each step. She was dying to knock, to feel the strike of her hand against the door. She wouldn't even wait for Jo to say, "Come in." She would yell from the foot of the bed, towering over the toxic lump that lay there.

"You think you're the only person in the world? You think you're the only person who has ever suffered?"

She stood at Josephine's door, ready to do it, dying to do it. *Josephine's door.* Of course, it wasn't Josephine's door; it was the door of the guest room. Josephine was a *guest* here. A guest who had been treated well, as well as her own— Rosalie stopped herself, arresting her hand just before it struck.

As well as her own.

The energy drained out of her. For a minute or more she stood doing nothing. Finally, as quietly as she could, she turned the knob and went in. The room was dark and Josephine was asleep, breathing heavily. There was a book on the bedside table: *It's Fun to Be Jewish*. Sticking up from the book to mark the place where she'd stopped reading, Jo had put the photo of Rosalie by the swimming pool, the one Rosalie had found by accident. Rosalie had promised to look for the one of herself and Bobby, but she hadn't done it. She backed out of the room and closed the door behind her.

Nothing was easy to find in the hallway closet. She had to wrestle through coats and duffel bags, shopping bags and hats, rolls of gift wrap and old toys, wig boxes and umbrellas. Finally, in the very back, she found the suitcase with a baggage tag on it: BRITISH AIRWAYS, 1986." She took it down to the den and opened it. She had never even unpacked it! She took out a Nikon camera and six (undeveloped) rolls of film. She took out Crazy Color hair dye, three black dresses from Kensington Market, a leather bracelet with spikes, seven pairs of fishnet tights, and a copy of *Culture and the Urban Myth*. She took out the Implications cassette. Stuck to its bottom was the snapshot.

Rosalie and Bobby stood on the steps of the registry office. He was smooth and clean-shaven. His hair was brushed. He didn't look dark at all; he looked simply young, a blue-eyed Irish groom. She stared at herself, looking for her youth in her younger face. Behind the spiky hair and the eye makeup, she couldn't even find her own eyes.

They stood beside the Armenians, their new, brief friends. What were their names? Lisa and Brad? Lisa and Burt?

"Excuse me? We were wondering where youse lot were from? Greek, are you?"

"Ask them about the thing first, Bobby!"

She was, she realized, smiling. She looked down at Jo's glass. Rosalie never drank these days, apart from the occasional Manischevitz. She picked up the whiskey and smelled it. She took a little sip. It tasted of the walkway to Kenneth Estate, a broken bottle dancing at her feet. It tasted of Bobby in bed, his strong, hairy legs parting her soft ones. She took a bigger sip.

Rosalie always bathed in the upstairs bathroom, but now she ran a bath in the downstairs one. She brought in the whiskey and the old portable tape player, shaking the dust from it. She didn't turn on the light. The window was frosted, casting the bathroom in shadow and making it feel dirty. Outside it could have been any place and any season; it could have been the East End of London in February. She inserted the cassette, pressed PLAY. The sound was skewed to begin with, wounded from nearly two decades of disuse. It cleared and gave way to a synthesizer, slow and dreamy and slightly discordant. Conor Morrow's falsetto, foreign and familiar at once, mingled with the steam. She let her robe drop to the floor. She eased herself into the bath.

> *The last time I saw you, Julie*
> *You were standing in Sugar Lane . . .*

She felt the clutch of an old waiting in her loins; of hearing footsteps in the corridor that weren't his, of looking out the window and watching other men walk down Shandy Street. Of the very first time she'd waited, holed up in her student room, burning and freezing from the shame of being cast away by him. She'd lit candles and sat in that other, swiftly cooling bath.

He did come, finally; stood there at midnight with a bottle of his own. She was so afraid he'd go away again that she didn't get dressed. She clutched the towel around her body, hoping it wouldn't slip.

He talked about the day his mother had died. About the ambulance and the Orange March and the cups of tea that had got him lost in the hospital. Of the father who'd said, *Typical of our Bobby to be late for his own mother's death.*

"Since she died," he'd said, "I don't look at myself. It's as though she took my face with her."

"A shame," said Rosalie. "A face like yours."

All she had to do was touch him. He'd held her so tight he nearly cut off her breath. She held herself up for as long as she could before finally allowing herself to be pulled down, thinking:

Go on, okay, drown me.

She lay back now, drenching the back of her head in suds. She lay back further until her face hovered below the surface of the water.

She came up, her lips sputtering.

And yet, no matter how dark he was, however plagued by his dead mother and his cruel father and the Terrible Beauty and God only knows else, there was one thing she couldn't deny about Bobby Pickering:

He was the sweetest boy she'd ever met.

She climbed out of the bath. She stood before the mirror, looking at her naked self. She'd never liked her body. She'd hated it, really. Being religious was handy this way; she could dress to hide herself, even from herself. But now she wanted to look at her body, to meet it like an old friend.

She wrapped herself in a towel, a nice fluffy one.

Josephine didn't like her own body either. That new dress was lovely on her, so lovely that even Jo looked proud, not wanting to admit a dress like that could make her proud. Come to think of it, she'd been wearing it when she gave Yael her makeover. While Yael had been baring her stomach in a trashy tank top, Josephine had stood back in her long dress, arms and legs covered, as demure as any good Jewish girl.

They would go to Hannah's Bakery. Not today—Rosalie couldn't face it today—but soon, maybe tomorrow. She would shut off her cell phone, and they would talk. And eat. Jo loved those black-and-white cookies! She had her own way of eating them. She broke the cookie evenly, along the line. She ate a bite of the brown side, took a sip of milk, ate a bite of the white side, took a sip of milk. Exactly like Rafi used to, except Rafi always started with the white side and Jo began with the brown.

Rosalie ran a towel through her hair. She put her robe on. She went down to the den and slowly, she began to clean.

CHAPTER 33

As soon as I opened my eyes, my bones were crunchy with fear. I knew they would send me back to hospital, and this time, I would stay there. I lay in bed, waiting for the footsteps in the hall, the knock on the door. I waited fifteen minutes. I waited twenty more. Finally I got up and dressed. The house was quieter than I'd ever heard it. Even Rafi wasn't listening to Getting Chai.

I went downstairs, tensing as I passed the shut door of the den. In the kitchen Yael was eating cornflakes and reading *Seventeen* magazine. She jumped and started to hide the magazine, but seeing that it was me, she didn't bother.

"What time is it?" I asked her.

With her chin, she motioned to the clock. She had no interest in me anymore, not since I'd gotten her in trouble.

"Two o'clock! Where's Rosalie?"

"She's at Grandma's."

I went back to my room and stayed there for the rest of the day. Later, nobody called me down for dinner. When I heard Joshua and Rafi singing downstairs, I nearly wished I were with them, saying blessings and doing Kiddish. I tried to read from *It's Fun to Be Jewish*. I wanted to memorize some of it to recite back to Rosalie, but I couldn't concentrate.

When the knock finally came, I leapt up to answer it, ready for any part of her she wanted to give me; ready, even, for her crinkled forehead and her words about how much I'd disappointed her.

But it was Joshua who stood there with a plate of food.

"Why didn't Rosalie bring it?" I asked.

"Rosalie is still at her mother's. I think she needs a little time alone."

He put the tray on my desk, and backed into the doorway again.

"Is it my fault?" I asked. "About her needing time alone?"

As soon as I asked that, I wished I hadn't. I didn't want to give him another reason to be cross with me. He didn't move. He gave it some thought.

Finally, he looked into my face. It was odd, because he'd never really done that. His eyes, now that I saw them, were a pale brown. One of them was slanted, only slightly, but the other one was wide open. He didn't look so know-it-all, facing me like that.

"You've had a hard time. She knows that." He cleared his throat. "Josephine—Jo—if you want to know the truth—we both know it."

I couldn't think of what to say. I wanted to tell him that I was sorry about the den. The words were right there at the front of my mind. But I thought that if I tried to speak, I would cry, so I did nothing.

"Well," he said, and he nodded at me and walked out, gently closing the door behind him.

At nine o'clock the next morning there was another knock on the door. This time it was Yael who stood there, twisting her fingers and standing as far away from me as she could.

"You have a visitor," she said. "I think it's a man."

"Is it Dr. Pollack?"

"I think he's from England."

She started to leave but I caught her arm.

"Yael? What do you mean, 'from England'?"

"I didn't really see him. Mom's downstairs talking to him."

I ran into the bathroom. I scrubbed my face. There was no time for real makeup, but I dashed on lipstick as quickly as I could. I tried not to run downstairs. When I heard Rosalie talking to someone, I did run. At the bottom of the stairs, I saw his jacket, slung over the banister: HARDY'S HAULAGE! I kept running. I slipped going through the hallway, but I didn't fall. I'd have to try hard not to run into him, not to squeeze the breath right out of him.

Rosalie was in the living room, her face long and white with all of her serious words.

He sat with his back to me. He was still, the way he was when he listened. I slowed down to take him in. I inhaled, breathing in our life together—the way it had been, and would be soon—the air in the cab warmed by our words. I let out a sound. He turned to look at me.

His face and body had puffed out. His hair was cut close to his head. It was a turtle of a person who sat there, face tilted up from a big back, eyes like blue marbles, right on mine. It wasn't him, not even a changed him.

Primrose.

Everything went sharp: the potato kugel smell from the kitchen, the floor beneath my bare feet, the sad circles of Primrose's eyes, the fat little ball of her head. Joshua stood on the other side of the room, one arm around Rafi, the other around Yael. They were all staring at me.

"You've found him?" I said.

"Yes, my love."

"And he's waiting for me now?"

She shook her head.

"I asked you—he's waiting for me now?"

"Jo—I'm so sorry."

I held onto the doorjamb to keep from falling. I couldn't swallow. The red spots came into my eyes. My throat was clogged with gunge and my heart went *wawer wawer* like the siren. Still, I couldn't swallow. The hole at the bottom opened wide and every part of me was spilling out of me. I began to fall.

Rosalie took hold of me, her hands on my shoulders.

"Breathe." She put her face close to mine. "Breathe!"

I couldn't.

She took a deep breath herself, to show me. She put her hand on my lower stomach. "From here."

I forced the words through the throat, the gunge.

"I let him die."

"No."

"*I killed him.*"

"You were the reason he lived so long."

"*I'll die!*"

"No. You'll live."

They said I could have whatever I wanted that day. I could eat as many cookies as I wanted. I could go to the movies, or drink Glenfiddich, or go to bed.

"There is no one thing that will make it better," said Rosalie. "Not yet. So just choose the little thing that will give you some pleasure, even for an hour."

I decided to go to the truck stop in Castaic. I thought I might find Whitey up there. Rosalie asked if I wanted her or Primrose to come with me and I said I wanted both of them to come. The three of us drove up in the late afternoon.

We went walking through rows and rows of parked trucks. I stopped at every Freightliner, even the ones that weren't his color. Two were wine with silver fittings. Some had dogs, Alsatians even, panting from the passenger seat, but none of the trucks belonged to him. Rosalie and Primrose followed close behind me. They were so close that sometimes, when I backed up, I backed into one of them.

"I think you've looked at every truck, luv," said Primrose finally. "Must be two hundred trucks you looked at."

I stood facing the trucks with their big backs to me. I thought of Whitey driving through Memphis or Baton Rouge, his Chet Baker playing. Whitey was a tall man with a big truck and a big dog. Whitey was alive and I still couldn't find him. I began to cry.

"Oh, honey," said Rosalie.

One of the trucks revved its engine and flashed its rear lights at us. Quickly Primrose guided me back to the gasoline pumps. I was crying in a stupid way now, like a three-year-old. Rosalie put her arm around me. "Do you have a number for him?"

I shook my head.

"Do you remember his registration?" asked Primrose.

I shook my head again. My nose was running.

"I'll get a tissue," said Rosalie.

"No! Don't go. *Don't go away from me!*"

"Okay, I won't. I'm here, Jo."

They stood and waited for me to stop. Then I had the hiccups. Primrose giggled.

"Don't laugh at me," I said.

"I'm sorry, ducks," said Primrose. She went into the shop and came out a minute later with a napkin and a can of Dr. Pepper, a straw sticking out of it. She wiped my face with the napkin, then she held the Dr. Pepper up to me and I drank some.

"I've never had this before." I said.

"Do you like it?" asked Rosalie.

"It tastes of cherries."

They watched as I took another sip.

"Can we stay here for a while?" I asked. "Just to see if he comes?"

"Sure," said Rosalie.

We stayed another hour. Every time a truck gasped and lurched into the parking lot we jerked our heads up to look, but it was never him. After a while we stopped looking for him at all. We just watched the trucks driving in and out. It was nice and cool at least. Rosalie said we were getting a breeze from the northern lakes.

"Look at that one," Primrose pointed to a tanker. Most of the trucks flew American flags, but on this one the flag was embossed in its great square nose, stars and stripes woven into the metal.

Rosalie put her glasses on to look at it. Primrose just stood there with her hands on her hips, shaking her head. Like me, she'd never seen anything like it.

The tanker stopped with a lurching noise. The driver sprang down from the cab. He grinned at us. "I'd like to think it's my good looks you're looking at," he said, "but I know the girls only like me for my truck."

"It's a beauty," said Primrose. "You the owner-operator?"

"Sure am. And it's not just the tractor I own, but the whole rig. It's brand new, too, a sapphire-drawn convexing elongated stainless mirror."

"Crikey," said Primrose.

We waited as he fueled, went inside to pay and came back out.

"You girls drive?" he asked, climbing back into his cab.

Primrose put her hand on my shoulder. "We girls do."

He reversed, made a circle and exited, saluting us through the window. His rig threw the sky back at us, a metallic belly of blue. It cruised past Veronica's Bar, did a U-turn and headed onto the Interstate 5, the most stunning silver animal I'd ever seen.

"What would Bobby say?" asked Rosalie.

I didn't even have to think about it.

"He'd say 'Jesus, Jo, you don't see the likes of that on the M4.'"

Rosalie laughed. "That's exactly right! You sound just like him!"

For the next few minutes no more trucks at all came in. The sky was marbled with pink and white, not so spectacular as it had been with Whitey and me, but nice enough.

"Josephine," said Rosalie. "You can stay with us, you know. For as long as you like."

I looked at Primrose. She nodded as if to say "Up to you."

I looked from the pink rim of the horizon toward the east, where it paled to white.

"I think it's time," I said, "I was getting home."

CHAPTER 34

When I said *home*, I didn't mean Shandy Street. I only went back to Shandy Street once. Primrose came with me. When we opened the door, the BOBBY notes shuddered from the walls and floor. Some of them hung cockeyed from the cabinets. Primrose put her hand to her heart.

"I don't know what I was thinking," I said, "writing all of these."

"You wanted to give him a warm welcome."

"Shandy Street was never a warm welcome."

She didn't argue. We moved my things to her place.

They found Bobby near the Glens of Antrim. Fogarty said that bodies often got swept up to the north of Ireland or maybe even the Isle of Man, but it surprised me anyway, Bobby pitching up so close to where he was born. I wanted to look at him, but they told me he was too disfigured after nearly six weeks in the sea. When I heard this, I let them keep the coffin closed.

We buried him in Drum. Father Donnelly gave a sermon. He talked about what a "kind and sensitive soul Bobby was" and " 'twas a pity we never knew how better to assist him in his painful journey."

Good Guy Mike spoke after him.

"I didn't know our Bobby all that well," he said, "but there was one thing he did that we can see in front of us right at the minute, which was to raise a lovely girl. First time I saw them together, she was just a wean, and jeez, you ought to have seen the way he looked at her, and here she is now with them lovely eyes she got from him, and wouldn't she be enough to make any man proud?"

But I wasn't enough, I thought, to keep him alive.

After his speech, Good Guy Mike played the flute. He was good at it. He held his flute like he loved it. If he'd known I'd bashed up Rick Watson's guitar and shot Cosima's fiddle to bits, I didn't think he'd have made a speech like that. Primrose squeezed my hand when he played. I didn't look at her because I already felt the tickle in my nose, and I didn't want to cry in front of relations I didn't know that well.

I didn't make a speech of my own. I had no words that were enough for what I wanted to say. I sang. I sang "Eileen McMahon," and though my singing wasn't great, there were tears in the eyes of Aunties Norah and Adele.

Fogarty came, with Staunton. I hadn't spoken to Staunton since Dublin, since we'd eaten Madeira cake and watched the armless Iraqi boy on *Newsnight* and Staunton had said, "What a state the world is in." She and Fogarty looked smart in their navy Garda uniforms, slim and able next to all the big old aunties and uncles.

Bobby's father wasn't there. Aunt Anne told me he died seven years ago. I didn't care. He'd never even wanted to meet me, ever.

Everyone came up to me at the wake, neighbours and relations and people I'd never met came up to say how well-behaved Bobby was as a boy and how devoted he was to his mother. Father Donnelly told me he was the most beautifully behaved altar boy he'd ever seen, and the quietest.

"He wasn't quiet just to be nice," I told him. "He was quiet because he had so much to work out in his own head."

"Aye, right enough."

But this sort of thing didn't interest him.

"Pardon me there, Father." Primrose came through with a plate of food for me, sausage rolls and ham sandwiches and minipizzas. She looked awkward holding one of Auntie Niamh's cream-and-gold plates. She must have thought so, too, because she was so holding it so tight that she looked as though she'd squeeze it to bits rather than drop it.

"Have you far to travel tomorrow?" Father Donnelly asked me.

"Yes," answered Primrose.

"Will you be taking the ferry from Larne?"

"Belfast Harbour," said Primrose. "Look, Jo's a little tired, aren't you, luv?"

I was. I let her lead me to a table.

"Where's your food?" I asked her. "I want you to eat with me."

"I've been stuffing my face all day, but all right," She plucked a sausage roll off my plate. Staunton and Fogarty came to sit with us. Staunton had a Madeira cake for me, made by her mother.

"So she isn't ill?" I asked.

"My mother will be making Madeira cakes on her deathbed, so."

Primrose got a knife to cut it.

Later, the wake moved on to Mullen's in Bushmills. Mullen's was an old pub, with no pop music or karaoke. It was just musicians, young and old ones, sitting in a circle and giving it "the auld diddly-eye." Good Guy Mike led them all with his flute. The music went from happy to sad, happy to sad.

Staunton sat next to me but all of a sudden, she stopped herself in the middle of a sentence and said "Oh, 'The Floating Crowbar'! I love this tune!" She ran up to the session, picked up a spare tin whistle and shoved in next to the musicians. I was amazed at how she just knew how to play the tune, and when they changed to another tune, she knew that, too. She looked happy playing there, as if she finally felt better about the state the world was in.

A farmer in a tweed cap sat in her place beside me. I'd seen a lot of old people today, but he was easily the oldest; he might have been ninety.

"I'm Ricky," he said. "You won't remember me."

He was right.

"But I remember you, so I do. Your father took you in here about sixteen years ago, it would have been. The craic was ninety that night—a great session that night."

"But Bobby never liked Irish music."

"He liked it that night. The two of youse listened to it together."

"I was just a baby."

"I'd say you were a good listener, though."

"She *is* a good listener," said Primrose, coming up with a pint for herself and a Bacardi and Coke for me. "This girl hears everything."

I'd never thought about it before, but it didn't sound wrong.

Back at Aunt Anne's, as I was getting ready for bed, there was a knock on my door.

"Come in." I expected to see Aunt Anne with a clean towel or an extra blanket, but it was Good Guy Mike. He had a guitar with him.

"What's that?" I asked, though I knew what it was.

"I think you should take this away with you."

"I can't play it."

"You could learn a few chords. I'll teach you tomorrow."

"We have an early ferry tomorrow."

"Ach, anyone could teach you a few chords. You could teach yourself, or learn it off the Internet." He laid it across my arms. I didn't know what to do with it.

"Lift it up," he said. "You don't want to let it hang like that." He positioned my right arm across it and my left hand on the frets. "There you go. It's a fine instrument. Lovely cut of wood, that is."

He looked sad, as though he was giving away his favorite pet.

"Are you sure you want to give it to me?"

"I am. So long as you don't go smashing this one up."

So he did know.

"I was only messing," he said when he saw my face.

"No, you weren't."

"Ah, well." He put his hands in his pockets.

"Why are you giving me your guitar?"

"I have another one."

"That's not the real reason."

"I don't know, sweetheart. It'll keep you out of trouble."

CHAPTER 35

2004

I haven't learned to play it yet. Every now and again I take it out of its case and hold it the way Mike taught me to. Or I mime along to whatever music is playing. But then I put it back. I always keep it with me, though. I keep it in the back of the truck.

Today—and I don't mind admitting it—I drive a rigid. It's a small rigid, too, barely a seven-tonner. Since I got my Class 3 license, Primrose started me off with one of her little Ivecos. She bought the Scania off me, gave me a good price for it. I've a good bit of cash put away now, but I may not go for a Scania when I get my HGV. You never know what new models will turn up by the time I'm twenty-one. I could buy a MAN or even a Mercedes. I could paint it like the Grand Ole Opry, winning at Truckfest for murals and paint-work, because there's no point in driving if they don't look at you once in a while.

Sometimes I think I'll wait on the artic. I'll go to Baton Rouge and find Whitey, ride with him in his Freightliner, listen to Chet as much as he likes. Or I'll save up for one of those chemical tankers, a sapphire-drawn convexing elongated stainless mirror, turn myself into a silver bullet shooting along the highway. Or I'll lease a straight truck (an American rigid), deliver for Rosalie and Joshua, cart their kosher food around. And maybe then I'll pick up that guitar, learn to play as well as Rick or better, make the boys want to follow me.

But for now, I don't mind driving a rigid as much as I thought I would. It's better to drive a rigid legally than an artic illegally. I keep my rearview mirrors free of the cops, and likewise, I don't turn up in other people's mirrors anymore. I don't use the CB much, either. I've had enough of squelch and static.

Rosalie e-mailed me on my eighteenth birthday, which was the same day I got my Class 3 license. It was a clever e-mail, more like a card. She and Joshua found a photo on the Internet of an Iveco exactly like mine, the same model and color and everything. They downloaded it and printed the word CONGRAT-ULATIONS in fancy lettering at the top. I have it taped to my dashboard.

Rafi sent me a few e-mails as well. He had a lot of questions about the truck, like how heavy a load does it carry, how many wheels has it got, how many gears. I e-mailed back and he e-mailed again with more questions. Lately he hasn't e-mailed me so much. Rosalie says he has a girlfriend.

Sometimes Rosalie asks if I ever think about coming back to see them. I say that one day I will, but for now I want to be home. I have a bedsit of my own down the road from Primrose's house, but by "home" I don't just mean that. Home is mostly here, on the British and Irish roads.

I still listen to country music—Charlene, Hank, Dolly, Johnny, Alison—all the ones who were safe because we never knew them. Last month I discovered another great band, Dale Watson and His Lonestars. (I wish Bobby could have heard them; Dale's voice is deeper than a wishing well, and he sounds like he's joking and crying at the same time.) I still buy *Country UK*. I read things about Cosima and Her Goodtime Guys, though part of me doesn't want to. Two months ago they brought out a new record called *When*. The review in *Country UK* said:

> With the highly produced When, *Cosima Stewart and Her Goodtime Guys are exploring a largely uncharted oeuvre, a super-slick world of jazz-country fusion. The music can't be faulted technically, but the lack of their earlier grit does create, at times, a soulless impression.*

I haven't bought *When*. It's nothing to do with the music, which I know I would like no matter what "oeuvre" it is. It's because I don't want to think of how I was then, of how I poisoned their lives with my vomit and sweat and snot and tears. Of the stain I was on all of their shine.

One day I do see Cosima. I see her in Aldershot. She looks thin and lonely on a big stage. She wears a clean white shirt and blue jeans with a big buckle. She doesn't sound too "jazz-country fusion" to me. She sounds sweet and clear, her best self. She isn't live. She's singing on the television:

> *Where are you going, stranger?*
> *Wherever it is, won't you take me along?*
> *Never thought a stranger*
> *Could touch the part of me that was as hard as stone*
> *Won't you hold me in the darkness?*
> *Be my home away from home.*

I'm in the Teapot Truckstop Bar with a half-pint of lager in front of me, only half, because I have to drive.

The camera pulls back and Sean is on the keyboards, his hair dyed back to his natural brown which makes him look calmer somehow. And Rick has had a haircut; no more ponytail. A new bloke is playing with them, on saxophone. They are all together but they look separate, each alone in their own version of the song.

There are three televisions in this place. On the one above the bar David Beckham is playing for Real Madrid. The sound is low with just the odd cheer furring out of it. Barcelona is in the lead.

"Oy! Toby, you cheating cunt!" A fat driver leans over the pool table, the crack of his arse showing. He wears a T-shirt that says LICK MY AXLE. On the telly above the pool table David Blunket talks to the camera. The sound is off, but words roll across the bottom of the screen: *U.K. citizens may be forced to carry an identity card by 2013 . . .*

> *I'm the kind of girl you never wanted to meet*
> *I was raised a million miles from your glittering city streets*
> *You're a shooting star in the cold, dark sky*
> *And I am just the dark . . .*
> *But, darling, just for today, before the magic fades*
> *Be my home away from home.*

If Cosima were here in person, and if I'd never met her before, I would talk to her now. I would tell her that she wipes the floor with the rest of them—even Charlene, even Alison. She'd be nice the way she was before she got to know me. She might even join me for a drink, and we could start all over again, with just us two women drinking, and maybe keeping in touch. E-mails. Texts. Nothing funny, just *How's the tour?* and *How is Rick?* and *How's the new rigid coming along?* That kind of thing.

Cosima is humming now, her eyes closed. The sax comes in with one long note. Rick trills behind him.

"Pint of bitter and a bag of scampi fries, my lovely!" The fat driver is beside me now, yelling his order to the barmaid.

It's time to go. If I'm honest, even if she were here—and if I were allowed to talk to her—I might still be going. I could never be her normal friend. I'd always want to be something else. I'd always want to climb inside the song and stay there.

And now I even go before the song ends. I go as she's still humming. I've six tons of tinned corn needing a home in Fraserburgh.

Next summer, Primrose tells me, she'll send me to Brittany with metal sheetings. Or, if I prefer, the south of Spain with microwaves. Between drops, I'll wander round Malaga or Jerez eating tapas, drinking sangria. Maybe I'll even play a chord or two on Mike's guitar by then, give it a bit of the old flamenco.

I climb into my lorry. I'm not so high up, not so top-of-the-world. But there are things to look forward to. I look forward to starting on the M25 south and ending up in Andalusia, where the land is baked and dried up as Bombay Beach. I look forward to Brittany. I've never been there, but I imagine trees huddled close together like broccoli.

But today I'm on my way to Fraserbugh with six tons of tinned corn in a rigid Iveco.

I still talk out loud to him. He listens to me from the passenger seat. He isn't in darkness and he doesn't make me drive because I'm already driving. We'll pass a MAN with *Bladerunner* all over it, or a fillet of Salton Sea coated in its bird-crumbs, or a tanker making its silver strip through the desert, or just a deer gazing at us from the side of the road, down from the mountains of Mourne, and he'll say, *Jesus, slow down, will you, will you look at the sight of it, Jo, will you have a look at that.*